To: Shar

I hope you will enjoy this story of a family over 150 years.

Blessings to you,
Denise Bell

CARAMELLE

there's no place like home

~~*~~

STEPHANIE RENÉE BELL

~*~

Caramelle
Stephanie Renée Bell

Copyright ©2012 by William and Denise Bell
Published by William and Denise Bell
Printed and bound in the United States of America

Scripture quotations:

The Holy Bible, New International Version®, NIV. Copyright ©1984 of the Holy Scriptures Zondervan. All rights reserved.

NCV Scripture taken from the New Century Version® of the Holy Scriptures Copyright ©2005 by Thomas Nelson, Inc. All rights reserved.

NKJV Scripture taken from the New King James Version® of The Holy Scriptures Copyright ©1982 by Thomas Nelson, Inc. All rights reserved.

King James Version of the Holy Scriptures

Cover Design: Stephanie Renée Bell
Stock photos

Page Design: Stephanie Renée Bell

Notice of rights

All rights reserved. No part of this book may be reproduced or transmitted in any form or by any means, electronic, mechanical, photocopying, recording, or otherwise, without the prior written permission of the publisher

Trademarks

In this book trademarked names are used. Rather than put a trademark symbol in every occurrence of a trademarked name, we state we are using the names only in an editorial fashion and to the benefit of the trademark owner, without any intention of infringement of the trademark

ISBN-13 978-1475264388
ISBN 10:1475264380
Library of Congress Control Number: 2012914349

Dedicated to
STEPHANIE RENÉE BELL,
For the courage she displayed, shining her light in dark places

Prologue

"All the ends of the earth
*will remember and turn to the L*ORD*,*
and all the families of the nations
will bow down before him,
*for dominion belongs to the L*ORD
and He rules over the nations.
All the rich of the earth will feast and worship;
all who go down to the dust will kneel before Him—
those who cannot keep themselves alive.
Posterity will serve Him;
*Future generations will be told about the L*ORD*.*
They will proclaim His righteousness
to a people yet unborn—
for He has done it."

Psalm 22:27-31
NIV

†

It was another warm, sunny day of 1851 in Birmingham, Alabama; a region well-known for its muggy, summer climate. The hospitable natives were more than accustomed to Alabama's atmospheric conditions, and found the good points of that particular time of year in which to take pride. Vivid flowers graced the earth in full bloom, crops prospered, and the famous rolling hills of the Old

South carried tall trees tinted with a rich forest green. Despite the at-times-unpleasant heat, the Southerners took advantage of summertime to hold grand parties and get-togethers in majestic mansions, where gentleman dressed in coats and tails while ladies sported fashionable hoop dresses and large, feathered hats of all sorts of colors and designs. Children would laugh and play tag outside as their fathers and mothers socialized in the shade with freshly-squeezed lemonade, and the youth would behave much as they do today—young men looking for a young lady to court, and the young ladies giddy at the thought of having their first beaux.

This particular day, a luncheon was being held at the home of the prestigious and esteemed Taylor family, where games of croquet, dancing, music and of course, extra Southern hospitality by way of cooking inhabited the list of features.

Nathaniel Taylor III happened to be the most respected man in all of Birmingham. He was rich, owning the most land of anyone in the state of Alabama, being the head of a large cotton production and manufacturing company, and possessing over one hundred slaves to work the fields, with fifty more to tend to the buildings and property. There wasn't a man who didn't respect Mr. Taylor, and if anyone dared not to, he would be hung no sooner than he had made up his mind.

Behind every successful man is a strong woman, and Mrs. Taylor was just that. Lucinda Preston Taylor was the only daughter of a general in the French and Indian War. Her father received a Purple Heart along with other accolades, in recognition of his many achievements, and his goal for his daughter was to marry a rich man without a drop of French blood in his body. Known for his tendency to be biased, General Preston had always harbored a hatred for the French, thus giving him more than good reason to take part in the war. His plan for his daughter succeeded when he met Nathaniel on a business trip. He knew right away that this was the man Lucinda was to marry; therefore they were wed in the late summer of 1831, with Lucinda only being sixteen at the time. Nathaniel was twenty-two, and already had his heart set on beginning a cotton corporation, seeing from the success of his two older brothers—who had already jump-started their corporations— just how much money one could make in the cotton business. With the help of his new father-in-law, his dream became a prosperous reality.

A year later, Lucinda bore a son, Nathaniel Jr., and the following year, on Christmas Day, a girl was born into the Taylor family. They named her Noëlle Joy, her name referring to Christmas carols. Three other children were born not long after Nathaniel Jr. and Noëlle, two more girls and a boy: Wilhelmina, Daniel, and Anna.

Noëlle was by far the family's pride and joy next to Nathaniel Jr., as each family had one—whether they switched from child to child over the years or remained stuck on one.

Noëlle had every physical and personality aspect with which to attract admiration from all whose acquaintance she graced. Her flawless skin was a fair ivory just as her mother's. She had long, silky, raven hair and a slim figure that every girl envied—her stunning blue eyes could pierce any young man's heart. She wasn't overly shy, but just coy enough to be charming, and was confident about everything upon which she set her heart.

A time during which her parents worried the most was her teen years, when they knew young men would undoubtedly be setting up notions and accumulating the audacity to ask to court her. As for a pre-arranged marriage, Mr. Taylor had already attempted this seemingly old-fashioned yet secure design. He would have stuck to it as well, had it not been for the fact that by the time Noëlle and the groom-to-be reached fifteen, the young man had set his sights on another young lady and had eloped with her to the North. The abortive attempt at marriage didn't break Noëlle's heart, as she never liked him in the first place and knew he only broke their engagement because of the other girl's money—as she had a rich father on his deathbed and was the only successor to the inheritance. So at the present time, the Taylors decided to watch and see what would happen, prayerfully hoping that a decent, affluent young man with business acumen would soon fall as a blessing on their humble doorstep.

Noëlle sat quietly on a bench in the shade of an oak tree, watching her younger siblings playing tag in a nearby field and a group of adults gathered around her father, who was skillfully conveying accounts concerning the history of the business. A handful of young men—those too old for tag yet too young for adult conversations with the intimidating Mr. Taylor—were bunched near a fountain adjacent to the back porch of the house, a few feet away from the adults, engaged in a hushed and seemingly-serious discussion.

Their scheming was far from abstruse to the keen Noëlle. She knew a lucky party of her multifarious admirers was working up the large amount of necessary courage to stride up and murmur a predictable, meager "hello" to her, as, at seventeen years of age she had long since learned to decode the actions, whims, and rituals of males her age. At the present, one of the young men was standing inside of the circle, his solemn, gray eyes riveted on the ingratiating Noëlle while his peers seemed to be daring him to make a move.

She sighed and looked away from him—feigning her lack of regard, but not before taking notice of how handsome he was. His name was Robert Collier, and he was the handsomest and most popular boy in the area. The Collier family owned almost as much land as the Taylors, and their plantation began less than a mile from the Eastern wing of the Taylor property. Noëlle would never forget sneaking out at night after supper when she was little to meet

Robert on the property border to gaze at the stars and catch fireflies.

As one might expect, that was before the metamorphosis occurred. She had been educated with grammar, etiquette, and piano lessons, thus transformed into a lady. Before then, she used to take part in a myriad of lurid things, such as playing in the mud, romping around the house with dirt all over her shoes or licking the jelly off her breakfast plate when Mrs. Taylor wasn't looking. How she remained the family favorite despite all of her earlier mishaps, no one knew. They were too busy marveling at what a lady she had become. She was to be sent off to a boarding school in Boston when she turned eighteen, and was the most prized and praised by her elders.

It should come as a surprise to no one that the appealing young lady attracted as much attention as she did. Though she possessed natural beauty, attire might be second to blame. Being the daughter of a rich cotton manufacturer, her long, elegant dress was made of only the finest materials. The article was an off-the-shoulders strap with a wide hoop, and sky blue with navy-and-white trim. Large, white bows and ribbons lined the scalloped hoop, and a satin ribbon daintily wrapped around the waist. Noëlle's hair was swept up into a classic bun, with dark curls dangling in back and another ribbon tied around the top. Pearls circled her graceful neck, and her shoes were composed of stylish, black leather heels. Other accessories included a blue-lace fan, which hung around her wrist and a blue-satin parasol with which to shield her from the bright sun.

As Noëlle sat reminiscing about her past while watching the children run and laugh, she suddenly heard a particularly persistent bird amidst the chorus of "chirps" coming from the woods not far behind where she was seated. She ignored it at first, until it became even more unremitting. It was then that she realized who it was.

Noëlle bit her lip, looked to see if any of the adults were watching. Seeing that none were, she abandoned her parasol and quietly slipped out from under the tree into the cool forest—leaving Robert and his friends watching her curiously. She made her way down a dirt path, quickening her pace slightly until she reached a clearing.

"James? Is that you makin' that awful chirpin' noise?" Noëlle whispered into the silent forest, her eyes scanning the vast area. "James?"

"Lookin' mighty fine there, Miz' Taylah!" came a deep voice from behind her.

She heard a thud and turned around to see James, one of the field workers, standing with a wide grin on his face.

He made a mock bow, taking off his tattered gray hat and holding it to his stomach.

Noëlle sighed.

"Don't call me that—you know how I hate that. It makes me feel like my momma, 'specially comin' from you."

James smiled again as he rose, showing off perfect white teeth. They only complimented his already-attractive chocolate skin even more, Noëlle thought to herself.

"I mustn't be thinkin' these things—Momma and Daddy would whupp me good if they heard me," she thought.

But it wasn't a lie to say that he was handsome. James was only seventeen, yet looked as though he were twenty. He was tall, with a muscular frame from long hours at work in the field and had large, twinkling dark eyes shining beneath his handsome forehead, along with perfect cheekbones.

Noëlle had known James her whole life. Her father bought him and his pregnant mother from another plantation in Georgia for her to work in the house and James to learn the trade of the field. A year after they arrived, the mother died of complications while giving birth—the child perishing as well. James was left to be raised by the many other slaves available, and grew up to be bright, strong, and one of the most useful in the fields. Noëlle oftentimes would sit and watch them work, particularly James. When he had time off they would secretly play in the woods and build "fortresses" out of spare materials James brought from the fields and cabins while Noëlle would sneak in slices of apple pie and sausages.

They had always been as inseparable as a slave and daughter of a slave owner could be, and had managed to keep their friendship mostly a secret. Mr. and Mrs. Taylor didn't mind very much when Noëlle and James were younger, though, when the only existent feelings were harmless, childish relationships based upon fun and games.

"I wanna show you somethin'—if you ain't too busy with your party," he stated before picking a flower from a nearby patch and handing it to her.

Noëlle smiled as she accepted it, tucking it into her hair.

"What could you possibly want to show me right now? Aren't you busy?"

James pretended to look thoughtful.

"I'm supposed to be . . ."

Noëlle sighed again.

"James, don't make it hard for yourself again. You know what happened the last time you didn't work—Daddy hired that new man to oversee y'all down there and you got yourself whupped so bad you came runnin' to me for some of Momma's medical cream."

James scowled.

"'Ella, when will you quit worryin' 'bout me? Those scars are what makes me a man—accordin' to ol' Thomas."

"Scars don't make a man, James. 'Sides, Thomas never was and never will be right about anything. I think you ought not take his advice."

"Do you wanna see it or not?" James persisted, ignoring her lecture.

"See what, James?" Noëlle asked in vexation.

"What I said I wanna show ya,'" he returned while throwing his hands up in the air.

Noëlle glanced nervously back down the trail she had taken.

"I don't know . . ."

James laughed at her anxiety.

"You just a worry-wart. C'mon," he stated as he grabbed her hand and led her along through the forest. "Good grief, girl, you act like I'm 'bout to take you to get whupped by somebody's mammy—quit draggin' ya' feet."

Noëlle frowned.

"I might as well be if my daddy found out about th—"

She stopped in mid-sentence when they reached another clearing and her eyes fell on a wooden structure on the ground.

A small rowboat large enough to hold two persons, skillfully painted in a sky blue with navy trim and the words "S.S. Noëlle" on the side sat in the middle of the clearing, with two matching oars leaning against it.

"James," Noëlle whispered as she slowly walked over to the craft.

"I finished it last night, but knew you'd wanna rest up for that party, so I 'cided to wait 'til today to show it to ya.'"

Noëlle ran her fingers along the smooth, sanded surface of the outside of the boat, marveling at the handiwork.

"So, do ya' like it?" James asked after he noticed she hadn't yet commented on her gift.

"Like it?" she repeated as she turned around. "I love it, James! It's beautiful," Noëlle cried as she hugged him.

He chuckled slightly when they drew away.

"I'm still sweaty from work, 'Ella—you gon' get ya' dress all dirty."

"I don't care," she stated as she hugged him again.

"When are you takin' me out on it?"

James shrugged as he scratched the back of his neck and looked up at the sky, squinting in the sunlight streaming through the trees.

"Well, I haven't given it much thought yet. I figured it'd be a mighty dangerous trip, don'tcha' think?"

Noëlle's face fell. "I s'pose you're right."

James bit his lip and gently placed his hand on her chin. "I'll think of somethin,' though."

Late that night, after all the guests had left and everyone had turned in for bed, Noëlle was awakened by a tap on her window. She got up to see James standing on the lawn, beckoning her to come down. She motioned for him to wait, and then left to change out of her nightgown into a simple dress, wash her face and straighten her hair up. After sneaking out of the house, she hurried out the back door to where the same oak tree she sat under the other day concealed James.

"What is it?" Noëlle asked in a slight whisper when she reached the tree, unable to hide the excitement in her voice.

James scanned the premises nervously before replying.

"We gon' take that boat ride you begged me to take ya' on," he answered.

Noëlle's blue eyes lit up and a smile filled her face.

"Oh James, I knew you would!" she exclaimed as she wrapped her arms around his neck.

"Now you can't be thankin' me all loud like that right now," he said quietly as he took her hands in his. "Those watchmen are out tonight, Noëlle," James added solemnly, lowering his voice to a whisper.

Noëlle's smile immediately faded, and she searched his eyes as he cast another apprehensive glance about him.

"Why? What's happened now?" she asked, anxiety lacing her tone. He sighed as he turned back to Noëlle.

"It's not like they after you, 'Ella. It's that new boy your daddy bought last month—he's more rebellious than a chicken with its head cut off—leasin' that's what he 'bout to become he keep up his bad temper."

Noëlle swallowed.

"You mean Thomas's brother—Peter?"

James nodded, and then frowned when he noticed the uneasy look on her face.

"What is it?"

Noëlle shook her head as she looked away from him.

That new slave had been nothing but trouble since the day he arrived. At twenty years of age he was abusive in his ways and far from mature, and every chance he got he would stare at her in a way that made her feel uncomfortable. James didn't know that Noëlle had witnessed one of his "fits" at work. One night while getting a drink of water from the kitchen, she heard crying and commotion coming from the well outside. She hurried out to see what was going on, and was shocked to see Peter repeatedly beating one of the kitchen hands—a slave girl of only fifteen years of age whom Noëlle knew to be sickly.

Noëlle hurried over and pulled Peter off of the girl as best she could, only to be hit with the same leather strap he was using on his primary victim. He told her that if she were to report to anyone what she had witnessed, he would be sure to pour gasoline over their entire house and property and light a match. With that, Peter walked off angrily, and Noëlle sent the girl back to her cabin with some ice and bandages.

Peter's outward appearance seemed to match his character, as he had deep-set, piercing ebony eyes, a long scar on his neck, and despite his wiry frame was tall and strong enough to snap a man in

"I don't care," she stated as she hugged him again.

"When are you takin' me out on it?"

James shrugged as he scratched the back of his neck and looked up at the sky, squinting in the sunlight streaming through the trees.

"Well, I haven't given it much thought yet. I figured it'd be a mighty dangerous trip, don'tcha' think?"

Noëlle's face fell. "I s'pose you're right."

James bit his lip and gently placed his hand on her chin. "I'll think of somethin,' though."

Late that night, after all the guests had left and everyone had turned in for bed, Noëlle was awakened by a tap on her window. She got up to see James standing on the lawn, beckoning her to come down. She motioned for him to wait, and then left to change out of her nightgown into a simple dress, wash her face and straighten her hair up. After sneaking out of the house, she hurried out the back door to where the same oak tree she sat under the other day concealed James.

"What is it?" Noëlle asked in a slight whisper when she reached the tree, unable to hide the excitement in her voice.

James scanned the premises nervously before replying.

"We gon' take that boat ride you begged me to take ya' on," he answered.

Noëlle's blue eyes lit up and a smile filled her face.

"Oh James, I knew you would!" she exclaimed as she wrapped her arms around his neck.

"Now you can't be thankin' me all loud like that right now," he said quietly as he took her hands in his. "Those watchmen are out tonight, Noëlle," James added solemnly, lowering his voice to a whisper.

Noëlle's smile immediately faded, and she searched his eyes as he cast another apprehensive glance about him.

"Why? What's happened now?" she asked, anxiety lacing her tone.

He sighed as he turned back to Noëlle.

"It's not like they after you, 'Ella. It's that new boy your daddy bought last month—he's more rebellious than a chicken with its head cut off—leasin' that's what he 'bout to become he keep up his bad temper."

Noëlle swallowed.

"You mean Thomas's brother—Peter?"

James nodded, and then frowned when he noticed the uneasy look on her face.

"What is it?"

Noëlle shook her head as she looked away from him.

That new slave had been nothing but trouble since the day he arrived. At twenty years of age he was abusive in his ways and far from mature, and every chance he got he would stare at her in a way that made her feel uncomfortable. James didn't know that Noëlle had witnessed one of his "fits" at work. One night while getting a drink of water from the kitchen, she heard crying and commotion coming from the well outside. She hurried out to see what was going on, and was shocked to see Peter repeatedly beating one of the kitchen hands—a slave girl of only fifteen years of age whom Noëlle knew to be sickly.

Noëlle hurried over and pulled Peter off of the girl as best she could, only to be hit with the same leather strap he was using on his primary victim. He told her that if she were to report to anyone what she had witnessed, he would be sure to pour gasoline over their entire house and property and light a match. With that, Peter walked off angrily, and Noëlle sent the girl back to her cabin with some ice and bandages.

Peter's outward appearance seemed to match his character, as he had deep-set, piercing ebony eyes, a long scar on his neck, and despite his wiry frame was tall and strong enough to snap a man in

"Don't hug me, now—the boat'll tip for sho,'" he stated with a laugh.

About an hour later, James brought the boat to the opposite bank (opposite of where the cabins resided, so that they were unseen), and after helping Noëlle out, they began to stroll along a willow-tree-shaded area on the water's edge.

James chuckled after they had continued on in silence for a while.

"You never did put it on. You was too busy lookin' at it," he said while looking straight ahead, though holding a twinkle in his eyes.

"You know I'm bad with clasps, James."

He rolled his eyes.

"If you would only ask for help," he pretended to complain as she turned her back to him and handed him the necklace.

James brought it around her neck and closed the clasp, then turned her around to face him.

"There. Now you're servin' it its purpose," he stated as he carefully placed her hair over the chain.

"Stop makin' fun of me and tell me how I look, silly," Noëlle demanded with a smile, her blue eyes shining.

James became serious as he caressed her cheek with his hand.

"Beautiful—even without the necklace."

The moon peeked momentarily from behind the thick, navy clouds, bathing the earth in its haunting glow as slave boy and daughter of slave owner shared a kiss.

After parting, they stood holding each other, not wanting to break the moment.

" 'Ella," James began slowly. "Do you want to—"

"James," Noëlle interrupted as she drew away from him slightly. "I don't think that would be a good idea."

"Well what other ideas do you have, Noëlle? It ain't like we can get married or nothin.' This is the South, 'Ella, and people are gettin' ready to fight and die for what we're doin' right now."

Noëlle didn't reply, but instead remained silent. She had an uneasy feeling in her stomach, and suddenly felt as though they were being watched; though somehow not by a human.

"'Ella," James said, softening his tone as he raised her chin up with his hand to look into her eyes. "I love you—ain't that enough?"

Noëlle hesitated before answering him. How could she possibly resist when he put it that way?

"I would die for you any day, James, but I don't want you to die for me . . .

"James, I just don't want you to go gettin' yourself hurt . . ."

During her sentence, the distance between them decreased, and they soon shared another kiss.

James had begun to hold Noëlle more tightly when she suddenly drew away and covered her mouth with her hand to stifle a scream. Her eyes were riveted on the ground. A snake was slithering near her feet, and she quickly stepped to the side.

James cursed under his breath and raised his foot to step on the creature. Noëlle covered her eyes, but when she opened them was surprised to see that even though she heard the thud of James's foot, the snake remained where it was—alive and exposing its forked tongue.

"Did you step on it?" she asked anxiously.

James suddenly looked nervous.

"Yes . . ." he said quietly, his voice laced slightly with fear.

"Then why isn't it dead?"

He shook his head slowly as he watched the reptile.

"I don't know," he replied in a hushed tone as their eyes met.

Noëlle swallowed hard.

"I'm scared, James."

"No need to be—let's just get outta' here!" he said quickly as he grabbed her hand and they hurried off into the night, in the direction of the empty slave cabins—those that hadn't been used in years.

Despite Noëlle's warning and uneasy feeling, they slept together that night.

The next morning, around four o'clock, Noëlle woke to find James gone, and a note reading that he had to work. He was one of the few slaves that knew how to read and write, and she had always been proud of him for it.

Noëlle sat on the edge of the bed in the empty cabin, realizing she would have to hurry to get home in time before her family woke up to find her gone.

So she set out on the half-mile trip across the property to the house, and only when she made it to her room with the knowledge that everyone else was still asleep did she breathe a sigh of relief.

A bit of uneasiness remained in the back of her mind as she recalled the strange occurrence with the snake. What could it possibly mean?

Pushing the thoughts out of her mind, Noëlle clutched her locket and began to wash her face.

Three weeks had passed since that night, and Noëlle and James continued on with their lives, not seeing each other as much as before upon James's suggestion to lie low for a while. He would still nod and greet her as "Miz' Taylah" out of respect were he to see her in the presence of her parents. Noëlle would acknowledge him with a nod, feeling nervous every time such a situation came up. This was the only secret she was keeping from her parents at the time, and if she thought before that night things were rocky, they were even more difficult now.

Noëlle was tormented by nightmares just about every night, and always dreamed of the snake. Adding to her troubles, she was beginning to feel very strange lately—dizzy oftentimes and even fainted once. Her appetite was no longer in existence, and she ate solely because her mother told her to do so.

It was when she was out walking along the lake one afternoon that she collapsed under the summer heat and poor physical condition from which she was suffering. One of the field hands saw this—an older man that was much like a father to the slaves and a longtime friend of the family—and came rushing over.

"Miz' Taylah, are you alright?" he asked as he helped her back to her feet.

Noëlle looked around to see Grandpa—as they called him—standing at her side.

"I'm alright, Grandpa," she replied, though she was struggling to stand.

"I know how much you love this lake, child, but you can't be out in this heat."

Noëlle held her head as she felt a wave of pain shoot through her entire body.

"One of y'all boys come and carry Miz' Taylah into the house!" Grandpa yelled to the field, where several other boys were picking cotton.

That's when James looked up to see the commotion. He was the first one over, with Peter and Thomas not far behind.

"What's wrong?" he asked, trying to hide the worry in his tone.

"Can't you see Miz' Taylah here ain't feelin' well? Carry her into the house!" Grandpa ordered.

"I will," Peter quipped, but James cast him a hostile glare before gently picking Noëlle up himself.

Grandpa walked beside James to the house, and soon commanded Thomas and Peter to return to their work when they began to follow.

"I'm alright, James," Noëlle whispered as she closed her eyes and rested her head on his shoulder.

"No you ain't, Miz' Taylah. We gettin' you home now," Grandpa stated while James remained silent.

When Mr. and Mrs. Taylor, who were enjoying lemonade and small talk with some guests on the porch, saw the two slaves and a limp Noëlle coming from the field, they immediately rushed out to meet them.

"What happened?" Mr. Taylor asked anxiously.

"Lord have mercy, she's unconscious!" Mrs. Taylor cried.

"She collapsed while walkin' along the banks of the lake, Massa' Taylah," Grandpa replied.

"Quick, get her in the house!" Mrs. Taylor exclaimed.

James handed Noëlle over to her father, and Mr. Taylor hurried toward the mansion, Mrs. Taylor and Grandpa at his heels.

"Get the doctor James, quickly!" Mr. Taylor called over his shoulder, and James sprinted for the stables.

After hopping onto one of the fastest horses Mr. Taylor owned, he raced to Dr. Lawrence's plantation, which was approximately two miles away from the Taylor plantation.

As he urged the horse on and bolted down the dirt road, James prayed he would make it in time.

Back at the mansion, Noëlle's parents laid her on her bed, and proceeded to place cloths soaked in cold water on her forehead and arms to cool her off.

Grandpa and Mr. Taylor stood fanning the unconscious Noëlle with more cool cloths, while Mrs. Taylor helped several kitchen hands fill the bathtub with ice from the icehouse.

A half hour later, the doctor finally arrived.

Mr. Taylor paced the floor of the sitting room outside of the closed door where Noëlle, Mrs. Taylor and Dr. Lawrence were, and Grandpa played his harmonica while sitting in a chair—watching the nervous father.

"I don't understand how this could have happened, Grandpa," he stated nervously while turning on his heel to pace in the other direction. "She's always seemed immune to the heat."

"We don't really know what's happened yet, sir," Grandpa replied while rubbing fingerprint marks off his harmonica with his shirt. "I'm sho' Miz' Taylah will be jus' fine."

No sooner had the words left his mouth than did the door open.

Mr. Taylor looked up expectantly to see Dr. Lawrence standing in the doorway, a slightly anxious look on his face.

Dr. Lawrence was an elderly man that had birthed each one of the Taylor children, as well as a good friend of the family.

"Well, Eldridge?" Mr. Taylor asked.

Dr. Lawrence sighed before replying, "Nathaniel, has your Noëlle been seein' a young man lately?"

Mr. Taylor frowned.

"You mean 'courtin?' "

"I s'pose."

"Not exactly . . .Lucy and I haven't found anyone for her just yet. Why do you ask?"

"Well, accordin' to your daughter's symptoms and a few tests I ran, she's with child."

The rest of the day and well into the night, Noëlle ran a high fever and became delirious not long after. While their daughter suffered, Mr. and Mrs. Taylor contemplated the cause of the sudden dilemma. She wasn't courting anyone, and the only time she was around other boys was at church socials or parties. There was only one possibility left, yet neither parent wanted to believe it to be true. However, soon enough they realized that they didn't have a choice, and it would be better to have the culprit dead before any more trouble arose.

That night, Mr. Taylor called for a messenger to notify the white farm hands to meet him at the oak tree on the Taylor property.

There was now a lynching scheduled for that night.

James bit his lip as he nervously paced the floor of his cabin that night. He was worried about Noëlle, and hadn't yet heard any word from the house. What could possibly be wrong with her? James knew that Noëlle was as immune to the heat as were the slaves.

Thomas lay on his bed, whittling by candlelight while whistling a tune.

Suddenly, the door burst open, and a sweaty and out-of-breath Peter rushed in, closing it hard behind him and placing the board over the knob to lock it.

"What's wrong with you, boy?" James asked him in annoyance.

Peter bent over, his hands on his knees, and panted before answering.

"They's gon' be—they's gon' be a lynchin' t'night," he finally wheezed out. "Massa' Taylah done gathered up a whole bunch o' white men and they's gon' hunt e'ry cabin down 'til they find him."

Thomas stopped whistling, watching Peter with a look of unease on his face.

"Why they after somebody?" James asked.

Peter looked at James as if he was born yesterday.

"Ain't you heard 'bout Miz' Taylah? Ol' Doc' Lawrence done said she with child." Here Peter laughed. "I figured they s'pose it's some ol' nigga's baby—and they gon' hunt the boy-"

"Miz' Taylah's with child?!" Thomas interrupted from his corner, then chuckled. "Oh my, what nigga' couldn't control himself now?"

James, who had remained silent upon hearing the news, suddenly became angry.

"Why don't you shut up, Thomas? They need to be after you. You and yo' thick-headed brother here."

Thomas dropped his whittling and sat up, a sinister look on his scarred face.

Peter grabbed James's shoulder and roughly turned him around, his dark eyes laughing acrimoniously.

"You sho' is gettin' defensive, James. Is that yo' baby over there, or somethin? Huh? You been a suga' daddy to a white girl?"

The anger boiling up in James to the point he could barely see straight, he threw a punch at Peter, who ducked.

Peter then kicked him in the leg and punched him in the face.

James fell back for a second, but soon recovered and charged toward Peter.

Before he could reach him, strong arms clasped tightly around his armpits, and he found himself in a virtually unbreakable hold.

Peter smiled crookedly before punching James in the stomach repeatedly.

"We can't have no nigga' actin' like he good enough for a white lady 'round us, now, can we Thomas?"

Thomas laughed as James yelled in pain.

"No sir, we sho' can't!"

"As a matter o' fact, why don't we feed him to that ol' search party—turn him over to 'em?"

Peter was about to finish James off, when he suddenly cursed loudly and grabbed his foot, collapsing to the ground.

A large, black-and-red snake lay hissing on the dirt floor of the cabin.

Immediately, Thomas grabbed a shotgun from underneath his bed and fired at the animal. The gun smoke cleared to reveal the snake, still alive.

"C'mon Peter, we gettin' outta' here!" Thomas shouted as he grabbed the howling Peter and dragged him out the door, leaving James alone with the reptile.

James fell to one knee, holding his throbbing stomach, watching the snake closely.

He suddenly felt afraid—a strong sense of anxiety had come over him since the snake appeared. Even though the creature had chased his attackers away, he still felt as though the animal wasn't on his side.

All fears were confirmed when it lashed out at the injured James.

He was backed up to a corner, closed in by the poisonous animal.

It was then that he heard horses racing toward the cabin, and the shouts of angry men. The snake almost seemed to snicker at James's growing fear.

Seconds before the door to the cabin was kicked open it swiftly slithered off.

"This must be him!" one man shouted, carrying a torch and shotgun.

But Mr. Taylor quickly stepped inside and looked at James closely.

When he saw that James was injured, he took pity on him.

"He didn't do it—this is the one I trust most," Mr. Taylor called over his shoulder, then lowered his voice. "Do you know who did it, son?"

James swallowed nervously and took a deep breath, as the air inside the small cabin was becoming tenser with each passing second.

He opened his mouth to speak, but before he could say anything, the men standing in the doorway suddenly directed their attention outside, where a slave boy came sprinting over.

"Massa' Taylah, Massa' Taylah!" he called while pushing his way inside the cabin.

"What is it, Solomon?" Mr. Taylor asked the winded child.

"It's Peter—he up to no good again. Him and his brother, Thomas, came runnin' to my momma's cabin claimin' they was gon' set all the property on fire—even yo' house, sir!"

Mr. Taylor stood up straight and clenched his jaw.

"I knew that boy was no good!" came a cry from the crowd at the door.

"He's probably the one that's behind all of this! Let's not waste our time here—we've got ourselves a slave to lynch!" another man shouted, and the huddle hurried out of the cabin, Mr. Taylor following behind.

James shuddered as his thought process attempted to figure out what the past train of events was supposed to symbolize.

He never did reach a conclusion, but knew this marked the beginning of something big.

Peter wasn't caught, but Thomas was apprehended that night and executed. There wasn't a trace of evidence to suggest where the other slave had run off to, and despite a thorough search of each plantation in the surrounding area, he wasn't found.

James, meanwhile, counted his blessings from then on. He still wondered just how he had lived through the past ordeal, but moved on nonetheless. Besides, Noëlle's fever had finally passed, and she was slowly recovering. He hadn't seen her since the day of the manhunt, but each day received good news from the house regarding her condition.

Noëlle, on the other hand, was worried—for the child and James. Her parents still hadn't yet told her what was to be done with the infant after it was born, and she wondered just how long she and James would manage to keep the secret.

One warm, sunny afternoon when Noëlle was beginning to feel better, she and her parents shared a long conversation. It began with the question of how things had gotten to the way they were, and despite the fact that she had been telling enough lies as it was, Noëlle lied again by saying she was raped by someone wearing a bag over his head. Her parents, of course, believed the story, and explained all that had happened while she was ill—concluding with the disappearance of Peter. Noëlle wasn't surprised that he was their prime suspect, as she knew his character all too well, yet marveled at just how much they were overlooking James.

Mr. and Mrs. Taylor ended the conversation with their plans for the child. If he came out dark, he would be sent straight to the slave cabins to be raised and brought up much like James was—an "orphan"; as they would keep Noëlle's identity a secret to avoid further embarrassment. If, on the other hand, the child came out to be lighter, he would be raised in the household and would pass off as "white"—with the excuse for his father being that the man died shortly after marrying Noëlle.

In the meantime, Noëlle was kept upstairs during parties, and never allowed to see guests—as her "predicament," as they had called it, was beginning to become more and more manifest as time inched by.

It was a warm, stormy, spring afternoon of 1852 when little Solomon came running from the mansion to the fields with the news that Ms. Taylor was in labor.

It was all James could do to hide his excitement and anxiousness, and he had to leave the field—claiming he was getting a drink of water—in order to laugh and celebrate. However, celebration turned to apprehension and hard prayer when Solomon returned later that night to announce that Noëlle was struggling, and the labor was far from easy. She was running another fever, and even Dr. Lawrence was worried for both her and the child. She had been in labor now for six hours.

Whenever sickness or great misfortune hit the Taylor house, all the slaves would gather in each other's cabins and sing spirituals and pray together. This was their way of supporting the family, because for a slave to work on the Taylor plantation was a great honor, as they were the kindest of all families in Alabama.

For James, this time was especially hard, despite whether or not any of his friends knew it. He left the crowded cabin he was staying in to go sit outside, and to be alone. He hadn't even spoken to Noëlle since that night, and had only seen her from afar. She only came outside to get fresh air, as the pregnancy often left her weak and no longer able to run along the banks of the lake or walk through the fields.

It was then James actually realized just how much had changed because of their actions. He didn't think so much change could come from what they had done.

The rain finally died away to reveal a beautiful sunrise, and Solomon's tiny frame could be seen hurrying through the fields toward the cabins.

He was bearing good news; Noëlle had finally given birth to a girl, and though the mother was still running a slight fever and exhausted, the doctor suspected they would both be alright. She named the child Hazel Roxanna, as her eyes were a warm hazel, and Roxanna meaning "dawn of day," as she was born at dawn.

No one denied that the infant was beautiful, and though during the first day her skin appeared to be a light pink, it soon began to darken to a light milky chocolate, which seemed to be just barely too dark for her to pass off as white, yet just barely too light for her to grow up around darker people and feel a sense of belonging. Her hair proved to be halfway as well, too curly for one side of her heritage, yet too straight for the other.

The plan had already been set, and after staying with her mother for as long as she was to be nursed, Hazel was taken away from the mansion to the slave quarters to someday be brought up to learn cooking, cleaning, and caring for children.

During their short time together, Noëlle placed the locket James had given her around Hazel's neck, as since the day she received it had planned on giving it to her daughter—were she to have one—someday.

Noëlle tried as best she could to hide her great disapproval of sending her daughter away, yet fell into depression not long after the transaction.

Hazel wouldn't be far in body, but rather in spirit, and Noëlle knew she was destined to be ridiculed by her peers because of the way she looked. Noëlle didn't care that her own social status had been marred; a part of her had been torn away from her, and this weighed more heavily on her mind.

One year turned into two, and two into five. Hazel grew into a healthy child that was much like her mother in many ways, but mostly in the sense that she enjoyed the outdoors. She would oftentimes forsake her duties at the well to fetch water or churn butter in order to chase a butterfly or catch a frog. This exasperated the other kitchen hands, who ended up chasing her around various oak trees and later giving her a whipping with the strap. But there was something different about Hazel, as no matter how many times you put her to the strap or paddle, she would always go back to her old ways. Eventually the women decided to let her grow out of it, knowing someday she would.

One evening, when Mr. Taylor was throwing a dinner for the recent employment of the vice-president of his company, Hazel was put in charge of preparing the banana pudding. At just seven years old and being quite adamant and the type to not listen to instruction, she completely forgot to peel the bananas before putting them into the pudding. When dessert was served, the guests and Mr. and Mrs. Taylor were at first surprised at the strange texture of the pudding, but Mr. Taylor soon started a chain of light-hearted laughter to ease the tension in the air.

From then on, Hazel was put in charge of cleaning, and only allowed to cook when she turned thirteen. Until then, she was to be taught by the other kitchen hands, and could only assist them with small tasks such as handing them an egg or measuring the flour.

Although as Hazel grew older she could often be a burden to those looking after her, she was still thought of as the sweetest, most unique slave girl the Taylors owned. The auspicious Hazel was always laughing, sharing jokes she heard from one of Mr. Taylor's party conversations with the other kitchen hands, and spreading a sense of joy about the plantation that had never really existed there before she was born.

As much as she was mischievous she was beautiful, with hair as dark as her mother's and wavy—somewhat like her father's. To match her name, Hazel's eyes were a light shade of hazel, and her skin color remained a half-and half, milk-chocolate color. And just as Noëlle suspected, Hazel was often ridiculed by the other slaves her age, and was given such names as "Milky," "Syrup-eyes," or the favorite, "In-between." At first it would bother Hazel, and she often ran all the way from the kitchen to the field to cry to James, who would tell her to pay them no mind and send her back. But as she began to get older, she became more and more used to the nicknames, and soon shrugged them off.

Shortly after Hazel was born, Noëlle was sent off to the boarding school she had originally planned on attending, and stayed for four years. During this time she would often think about James and Hazel, and wondered how they were doing. She wrote home every month, and her parents always began each letter with "everyone here is fine" to almost vaguely inform Noëlle that Hazel was doing alright.

Still, it wasn't easy for her to be sent off to a new place to live by herself, and to be torn away from her family for so long. Nonetheless, Noëlle eventually got as used to her new life as best she could. She did, at least, get the chance to visit each year for Christmas time—however, then she would only catch glimpses of Hazel and James—sometimes not seeing James at all, as he was often busy at work.

When the time finally came for Noëlle to return home for good, she came back with the news that she was engaged to a college professor she had met while at school. Albert Hawthorne was an older, wealthy man that could support Noëlle, and when he arrived at the Taylor plantation with her, Mr. and Mrs. Taylor were very impressed with him. Professor Hawthorne was quiet, very reserved and would usually only speak when first spoken to. He taught English, surprisingly, at a University near the school Noëlle had attended. They often enjoyed lunch together at a local café, and eventually began to court.

As Noëlle walked along the bank of the lake one autumn afternoon soon after arriving home, she realized that she didn't want to see James again. She knew in her heart that she didn't love Professor Hawthorne, but on that day only a year back when he proposed to her she didn't have much of a choice but to say yes. She was sure her parents would approve of him, and more important than this factor he was rich, and keeping money in the family was more important than whether or not you're in love.

But then, there was James. Noëlle also knew that she still loved him, and her heart broke at the mere thought of seeing him again. She couldn't stand the fact that there was nothing she could do about the situation at hand. All she could do and all she could hold onto was Hazel, the single glint of hope that had survived the rough storms over the past four years. Noëlle prayed that at least Hazel's life would be better than her own, and counted on the fact that a part of she and James would carry on.

When Noëlle got closer to the fields where James was sure to be working, she turned around and began to walk the other way, accepting the fact that she wasn't as strong as she thought she was. Out of habit she had begun to make her way towards him, and she now cursed herself for acting like a foolish seventeen-year-old as she headed back home with a heavy heart and tears streaming down her cheeks.

That summer, Noëlle and Professor Hawthorne were wed. While their house was being built, they stayed with the Taylors for a few years. The wedding was a big event, and family as well as friends filled the Taylor mansion for the reception afterwards. Noëlle enjoyed socializing with her loved ones, but still felt an emptiness inside of her that had existed for years.

One chilly, autumn night several years after Noëlle's return, Hazel sat on the floor of her and James' cabin, watching him whittle and smoke his pipe by candlelight.

"Papa?" Hazel finally asked.

"Hmm?" James replied quietly, briefly looking up from his work.

"That ol' Jimmy was at the back door of the kitchen today again, askin' for some apples to sneak back to his cabin. But this ain't his plantation—why he always comin' over here like that?"

James frowned thoughtfully.

"I reckon it's 'cause he ain't gettin' disciplined enough over on that Collier plantation."

"Oh," Hazel stated while twisting the chain on her locket. "How old is he?"

"Eight or nine, I s'pose—'bout your age."

"Oh. He sho' don't talk like he eight or nine—you shoulda' heard him today, Papa. He was talkin' real bad 'bout those spirituals we be singin' while we work. Jimmy says they ain't no such thing as God. Ain't he wrong, Daddy?"

"He sho' is—God's got to be the only thing us slaves can hold onto," James replied firmly.

Hazel remained silent for a few seconds as she continued to watch her father whittle.

"Papa?"

"Hmm?"

"Toby said Jesus was black; is that true?"

James chuckled slightly.

"No, baby, Jesus was Hebrew."

"Oh. What's 'Hebrew?' "

James briefly set his whittling down in his lap to rub his chin thoughtfully.

"Well, 'cordin' to the Good Book, Hebrew people come from another land far away from here."

"How far?" Hazel persisted.

James sighed.

"In another country, 'cross the ocean."

Hazel's brown eyes widened.

"'Cross the ocean!? How they get over there?"

"They was born there, I s'pose."

"Oh. What they look like, Papa?"

"Well I heard tell they look a little darker than white folk, but ain't quite Negro either."

"Does that mean I'm Hebrew?"

James smiled at his daughter's naiveté.

"No, Hazel."

"Oh. Can I wish I was, though?"

He shook his head.

"Nope. You've gotta be you."

Hazel sat contemplating her father's last words for a moment, then spoke up again as a thought came to her mind.

"Was Momma Hebrew, then?"

James stopped whittling and looked intently at her.

"Your momma was a slave that died when you was born—I already told you that," he lied, using the same lie he had used since Hazel was old enough to speak.

"You always say that, Papa. But if Momma was black too, why do I look so different?"

James returned to his whittling and puffed his pipe a few times before replying.

"Momma was a lighter slave, Hazel. Now why don't you stop jabberin' off at the mouth and bring us some more kindlin' from that pile outside the door?"

Hazel sighed and got up to do as she was told.

"Alright, Papa. But I still say Momma must've been Hebrew, or somethin.'"

James shook his head slightly as he smiled once she left the cabin.

Though his race-oriented conversations with his daughter could oftentimes be lighthearted and made him laugh, he still wondered what she would do were she to be sold off the property—out of his watchful care. James could always think up an excuse to visit his daughter at the kitchen, whether it be to deliver firewood for the stove or grain from the fields. They were never far from each other, and he had always had a sense of slight over protectiveness over Hazel for a myriad of reasons, one of which being that she was different. She could pretend to be strong on the outside and claim she ignored the insults and name-calling, but James could see at the end of the day when she returned to the cabin from the kitchen that she was being hurt by and tired of her tormentors.

That wasn't the only concern on James's mind, though—there were plenty of older slave boys, around the age he himself was when Hazel was conceived, that thought they were men and able to have their way with the slave girls. It was even more dangerous for Hazel, as despite their daily hurled insults toward the girl, James knew they had their eyes on her, and were undoubtedly waiting for her to grow up. For this reason he would walk her from the kitchen to the cabin when her work was through, as when the days got shorter the older slave boys could often be found climbing several of the various oak trees lining the dirt path from the house to the fields and cabins.

James realized that he couldn't protect her always, and wondered what Hazel would do were he to have to join the war, perish suddenly, or if she was sold. It was foolish for a slave to count on sticking together with other family members, as so many families were broken up from auctions, lynchings, or unsuccessful escapes for freedom, where oftentimes half of a family might escape safely, while the other might not, or they would end up separated.

If none of those events took place where James would be separated from Hazel, there was talk going around about consequences of the war if the Union were to win. Stories about slaves being freed spread quickly about the South, and as nice as it seemed to sound for James's people, there were dangers as well. If Union soldiers were to raid the Taylor property, James and his daughter would be separated for sure. Or how would he support her if they were suddenly independent? James knew finding a job in order to feed and clothe his daughter wouldn't be easy. He and the rest of the slaves received no pay for their duties, but were fed and clothed nonetheless.

Though he couldn't see the future, he worried often, and prayed that he could be around long enough to protect her from the harsh realities of society in that day and age.

A few more years passed, and soon Hazel was thirteen years old. In the past decade, great change had overtaken the Taylor property, one instance being that Noëlle had given birth to three children, each one a boy. James and Noëlle never got the chance to carry on a conversation, and were only able to speak to each other when their paths crossed, with mere courteous greetings.

Every time Noëlle and Professor Hawthorne came to visit from their now completed house on holidays, Noëlle marveled to see how much Hazel would grow each year, and looked forward to her annual visits with her family.

One summer evening, Hazel made her way alone down the long, dirt path leading to the cabins, as her father wasn't able to walk with her that day on account of work. When she received word from Solomon—who remained the fastest runner and designated messenger (along with Hazel's best friend)—earlier that day that her father wouldn't be able to walk her home, she had Solomon tell him that she would be fine and would make the trek herself . . .

"You sho' that's such a good idea, Hazel?" Solomon had asked while watching Hazel churn butter on the back kitchen porch.

"Of course I'm sho.' I ain't no little girl—I'm almost fourteen years old."

Solomon laughed.

"You may think you old, Hazel, but you still that same ol' awkward kitchen girl that puts unpeeled bananas in her puddin.'"

Hazel grabbed a nearby rag to playfully whip her friend for bringing up embarrassing memories, but he was too quick and dodged it before taking off down the field to deliver another message.

Hazel shook her head as she watched him, chuckling slightly as she went on with her churning.

As she now walked down the dirt path home, she clutched a tin bucket filled with cornbread and fried chicken—her father's supper—in one hand and her blue shawl around her shoulders. Hazel had spent two months of sprinting ahead of a smiling James to the cabin when they would walk home together, in order to get time in to add to her shawl before she had to go to bed. James had requested scraps of yarn from the women's knitting station to give to his daughter as a thirteenth birthday present, and ever since, she had worked religiously on her shawl and worn it at night or during wintertime upon finishing it.

Hazel smiled as she recalled a proposal Solomon had made earlier. He told her he would meet her halfway down the path to walk her home, as he couldn't walk her the whole way due to work.

He had always been different from the other boys towards Hazel. If he were to call her a name, it would be out of genuine affection, and they knew each other well enough to know when the other was joking. Though they differed in age by nearly five years, Hazel and Solomon had always been good friends, and she had viewed him as an older brother for as long as she could remember.

Solomon wasn't quite thin, but wasn't exactly as strong as his peers either. He was somewhere in between, and it had been a joke between he and Hazel to reverse the intentions of her nickname "In-between" by using it on each other—as they both had a slightly similar predicament. Solomon wasn't the most popular of the boys his age, but he was still credited for his speed, sense of humor, and wit.

Hazel's smile vanished suddenly when she heard a sound from one of the oak trees to her right. It was a calm night, without any breeze, so she knew she was being watched. Beginning to pick up her pace, Hazel began to wish Solomon would show up soon. Being as familiar as she was with the path, she knew she hadn't yet reached the halfway point and wouldn't meet Solomon until a few more minutes had passed.

The bright, full moon swiftly hid behind a dark cloud, casting an eerie, turquoise shadow on the surface of the earth. Hazel stopped walking when she heard the noise again: grass rustling beneath footsteps. Silence surrounded her for a full minute before she started up again, this time nearly jogging. As soon as she did so, she caught a shadow dodging in and out of the tree trunks and bushes from where the sounds came.

Once again, Hazel stopped dead in her tracks. She wasn't known to be a coward, and was always thought of as being as brave as the boys, but this didn't mean she was deaf to the stories told over the kitchen table while kneading bread or in the cabins while knitting with the other women. Hazel had always thought they were mere tales that the women made up, but it was slightly over four years ago that something made her change her mind.

Bursting through the door of the cabin where Hazel and the women were knitting came a slave girl in her teens with bruises on her face, neck and arms, along with tears running down her cheeks. Hazel was whisked home to her own cabin with her knitting before she could hear what had happened, and as soon as she went inside, her father was already setting out with Solomon, his shotgun over one shoulder. Hazel asked where they were going and if she could come along, but James grabbed her arm firmly and made her promise him she wouldn't leave the cabin until he came back and wouldn't open the door to anyone. Hazel had never seen her father that angry before, as he was usually laughing and joking, so she did as she was told and asked no more questions.

James's anger also aroused questions in Hazel's young mind, but she never received her answers until a year earlier, when she was thirteen. Hazel, not having the guts to ask her father about that eventful night, instead turned to Solomon. He had found some way or another to dodge answering her questions for three years, but eventually ended up telling her. The girl had set out from the cabins to the kitchen to retrieve her shawl, which she had forgotten earlier. On the way back, a group of boys were waiting in one of the oak trees. The girl was able to escape, but not without getting bruised emotionally and physically.

Ever since Hazel found out the truth about the slave girl, she no longer deemed the women's stories as "tales," and harbored a secret fear of the same thing happening to her.

Hazel now listened as closely as she could, watching the area she had once seen the moving shadow in the trees and bushes. She felt her mouth go dry when silence reverberated around her. There had to have been someone there, she couldn't have only imagined it.

Hazel stood in place for a few more seconds, then finally began to walk again, the palms of her hands beginning to sweat. She had only taken about four steps when there came a thud from behind her, and the path was shadowed in front of her.

Hazel swallowed hard and dared herself to turn around. When she did so, she looked up into two piercing, dark eyes deeply set in an ebony, scarred face.

Before screaming, she assessed the situation. He was tall, but didn't look strong. Hazel figured she could outrun him if she ran for her life.

But her assumptions were far from confirmed when the man grabbed her arm in a grip that made her fingertips go numb. She screamed as loudly as she could; out of fear but mostly pain. Hazel was soon brought to her knees as hot tears streamed down her cheeks. She knew her arm would soon break if he didn't let go.

The man continued to grip her arm, watching her suffer before picking up her abandoned lunch tin. Still holding on tightly, he fished through the bucket with his other hand, then savagely stuffed a piece of cornbread into his mouth.

Hazel desperately clawed at the man's rough hand, which was now causing her own to turn blue. No matter how hard she scratched and pried, he wouldn't let go, though. She buried her face in the dirt, sobbing uncontrollably now.

The man tossed the other half of the cornbread, then knelt down to grab Hazel's jaw to roughly tilt her face up towards him.

"Is you the little mongrel James and Noëlle Taylah had?" he demanded in a hoarse voice.

The question went clear over Hazel's head and she continued to sob.

This only angered the man more, and he gripped her arm more tightly.

Hazel's shriek drowned out the cracking sound of bone separating from bone, and the man repeated his question.

"Is ya'? Is you that little half-nigga'?" he spat as his eyes flashed violently.

In her current state, Hazel couldn't possibly answer him, so instead she cried harder.

Obviously being fed up, the man finally let go and got to his feet, towering menacingly over the wailing girl.

"I know who you are, girl. Ain't no other slaves look like you 'round here. Yo' nigga' lovin' white mama and yo' nigga' daddy gon' pay the same way you's 'bout to."

Hazel's bloodshot, teary eyes looked up in horror to see the man untie a leather strap from around his waist and lash it out to the side, swiftly snapping a branch off of a nearby bush.

"Where you headed to in such a hurry, boy?" James asked a rushing Solomon as he prepared to open the door of his cabin—having just got off from work.

"I promised Hazel I'd walk her home t'night, sir," he replied as he walked backwards down the path leading to the mansion and kitchen.

"That's right—you meetin' her halfway. How 'bout I come with you?" James asked as he took his hand off the doorknob.

"Sure, sir," Solomon replied, and the two set off.

Roughly five minutes later, they began to hear commotion up ahead.

Immediately James knew something was wrong, and he and Solomon bolted down the path.

A minute later they reached the scene, where Hazel was receiving the beating of her life from the heavy leather strap the man brandished.

Anger bubbling up inside James to the point he could kill, he tackled the man in an instant.

As they struggled, Solomon looked from the disheveled Hazel to the scuffle—not knowing what to do. But when he saw just how bad a state Hazel was in, he was at his friend's side in no time.

Solomon clenched his jaw tightly when he saw that her face was badly bruised and bloody, her arm bleeding and in a strange position.

James and Peter wrestled a few minutes more, and after finally knocking him out, James hurried over to Solomon and Hazel.

"Get her home to Miz' Esther—she'll know what to do. Go, now!" James ordered firmly between breaths.

Solomon frowned.

"What about you, sir?"

"Go, boy!" he yelled before an arm wrapped around his neck and threw him down.

Solomon watched as the fight continued, and was about to carry Hazel to the cabins, when she clasped her hand around his wrist.

"He gon' set fire to the house—tell my papa," she whispered.

"I gotta get you home, Hazel," Solomon replied, not comprehending her words.

That's when it happened.

A loud explosion erupted from the direction of where the Taylor mansion resided and a cloud of smoke and flames shot up into the air.

"I told you I'd get back at y'all for killin' my brother!" Peter yelled as he abruptly pushed the stunned James off of him and took off down the road towards the mansion.

James turned to the shocked Solomon and Hazel, made a gesture to the cabins, then bolted off after Peter.

"Get help, boy!" he called over his shoulder, and soon darkness and smoke enveloped his frame.

"C'mon, Hazel, I'm gettin' you to Miz' Esther," Solomon said as he picked her up and hurried in the opposite direction down the path.

Hazel was beginning to lose consciousness, but soon saw a sight over Solomon's shoulder that caused her blood to freeze.

Soldiers and costumed figures on horses were galloping around the fields—their presence ubiquitous. Gunshots reverberated through the once silent night; the property was being raided by the Union, and the Southerners were protesting.

Before Hazel could warn her friend, he suddenly stopped running, and she turned to see a costumed figure standing in front of them, blocking the path.

"Where do ya' think y'all goin' t'night?" he asked before drawing out a large shotgun.

Fear engulfed Hazel, and she drew in her breath.

"Please don't shoot the girl, sir—she's already hurt," Solomon begged the man, fearing for his friend's life.

The man smirked behind his hood.

"Alright—I reckon' I'll shoot you, then."

And that's just what he did.

Solomon's knees buckled suddenly, and both he and Hazel fell to the ground.

Hazel watched in terror as he held his side, then eventually lay still.

The moon was hidden behind smoke and clouds—the night was dark.

"Hey, you ain't one of them, are ya'?" the man asked as he took a step closer to look at Hazel.

Her heart was in her throat and she couldn't speak. She just sat there, watching him with a mixture of shock and fear on her bruised face.

Before the man could take another step closer, he looked up and behind Hazel suddenly, as another explosion could be heard.

"Them Yankees gon' pay for this!" he yelled angrily as he raced down the path to the mansion, leaving Hazel and the fallen Solomon alone.

Despite the shock overtaking her, Hazel knew her friend was dead. Terror lacing her thoughts, she began to crawl up the path to the mansion—where her father was.

She stopped suddenly when she heard a hissing noise coming from behind her, from where Solomon's motionless figure lay.

Hazel slowly turned around to see a black-and-red snake curled around Solomon's leg, looking at her with a laugh in its narrow eyes. They glowed a bright red suddenly, and she sat mesmerized. The creature remained where it was a few seconds more, then it finally slithered off—as if its task had been completed.

Hazel held her stomach when she suddenly felt it lurch. She had to get to her father. Fear causing her entire bruised body to tremble, Hazel continued to crawl down the path, her mind beginning to drift.

She saw figures—ghosts—dancing around her, throwing rocks at her and laughing maniacally. They began to chase her off the path and into the field, calling her names as they did so. Hazel scrambled as best she could away from them, but they never left. Soon she was on the outskirts of the back lawn of the mansion. Lacerated bodies of black slaves and white soldiers scattered the landscape, and Hazel felt she couldn't breathe. Gunshots echoed throughout the dense air, and smoke rose from the plantation-turned-battlefield. The flame-engulfed mansion was slowly deteriorating, and every piece of property smoldering. The lifeless smell of death mixed with the smoke permeating the air. Men on horses dashed by, and chaos and destruction lingered everywhere Hazel turned.

She watched in horror at what looked to be Mrs. Taylor running from a soldier on a horse abruptly shot down. Next came a kitchen hand being shot several times.

Hazel felt as though she were going to faint as the ghosts continued to torment her. She covered her ears and buried her face in the bloody grass, trying to wish it all away.

That was when she heard a shrill shriek coming from the back porch and looked up.

She spotted her father, fighting a soldier away from whom she perceived to be Mrs. Hawthorne. Feeling empowered by the fact that she needed to be with him, Hazel began to inch forward—having an insane notion in her mind that she could help him and prevent him from getting killed.

But soon a round of gunshots fired, and her father's limp body collapsed onto the bloodstained porch. Hazel heard herself scream, but felt as though she were watching life's occurrences from the clouds, as if she herself had died with him.

Noëlle screamed James's name at the top of her lungs, but before she could get to him was pushed down the steps of the porch—seconds before another explosion erupted from the already demolished building.

The final blast caused even more smoke to fill the air, and Hazel began to cough and choke as her eyes burned while the world went gray and black.

She was close to unconsciousness and most likely death when a hand suddenly clasped around her wrist. She couldn't see who was dragging her away from the danger, nor perceive what exactly was going on, nonetheless she staggered along with her rescuer as best she could — tripping over cadavers and feeling nauseous from the intoxicating smell of blood.

Another hand grabbed Hazel's other wrist, and soon she was picked up and carried. Consciousness finally fled, and she was forced into submission to the darkness.

"They's been talkin' 'bout them Yankees makin' a raid for a long time now, Miz' Hawthorne. We sho' is lucky. James did fight bravely and Hazel's gon' be jus' fine."

Noëlle put her face in her hands as more tears streamed down her cheeks.

Esther, one of the kitchen hands and a mother figure to the slaves, sat beside the sobbing Noëlle, consoling her as best she could.

Noëlle, who had managed to escape the final explosion after being pushed down the steps, had hurried into the field, only to find Hazel cowering in the grass. Knowing that if she were to flee the property it would only be with Hazel—now her sole living relative—she grasped her wrist and was soon joined by Esther. They reached the old abandoned cabins on the other side of the woods to hide out and seek shelter. From there, Hazel was bandaged up and now resting in bed.

They dared not return to the battlefield to retrieve the bodies for proper burial until they were sure all danger had passed.

Dawn had finally arrived, but it was a smoky, dark and dreary one, with rain draining from heavy clouds. The weather seemed to be mourning as much as Noëlle was; for nearly her entire family had been killed, as well as the man she loved all along.

Noëlle and Esther simply couldn't believe such ruin could overtake the Taylor family in the course of an hour. It was almost as if a dark force was working against them, wiping out every living being on its malicious agenda.

With this conclusion in mind, Noëlle's thoughts raced to the encounter with the snake she had so long ago. Could it possibly have anything to do with the past train of events? Was there more to the animal's appearance than what there seemed? If none of these questions could yet be answered, it was obvious that the animal had certainly left a profound mark in Noëlle's mind.

Before she could put together any other significant notions, Hazel began to stir, and Esther quickly took a seat on the edge of the bed to change the cloth on her forehead.

Noëlle watched quietly, reasoning restoring her senses. Once again hardship had hit her family, and yet once again Hazel remained a glint of hope. The past was filled with lies, struggles, trials and now death. If ever Noëlle felt a sense of fear, it was then. Everyone she looked up to, every being she turned to for comfort, advice, or simply love—whether she reciprocated it or not—was gone. It was now her turn to be the comforter, assistant, and main source of tangible affection—for the remainder of her posterity. She didn't know what lay ahead, but prayed that brighter days lined her daughter's path.

~ Chapter I ~

†

"There is a time for everything,

and a season for every activity under heaven:

a time to be born and a time to die,

a time to plant and a time to uproot,

a time to kill and a time to heal,

a time to tear down and a time to build,

a time to weep and a time to laugh,

a time to mourn and a time to dance,

a time to scatter stones and a time to gather them,

a time to embrace and a time to refrain,

a time to search and a time to give up,

a time to keep and a time to throw away,

a time to tear and a time to mend,

a time to be silent and a time to speak,

a time to love and a time to hate,

a time for war and a time for peace."

Ecclesiastes 3:1-8
NIV

†
1980s

Chicago, Illinois—the city with the highest crime rate in all of America. Under towering skyscrapers filled with successful businesses lie the streets, where at night gangs of abject teenagers roam about in search of a fight, drugs, sex, or money. This was the only thing they could truly hold onto and count on: their gangs. This was basically all they had, as family was a forgotten concept. You become one with the streets because you have to. You learn how to fight in order to survive. You may pick up a few friends; a few people to "assist" you through life. You may even find a substance with which to help you reach that place where the world fades away as your brain cells decrease. Most did just about anything—unthinkable things—for the sole purposes of receiving money and/or so-called "love," and the sad part of the story is that this was life for them. This was all they knew; this was their reality.

Having just barely turned fifteen years old, Lorena Gabrielle Selenez was one of the most notorious of the female gang-bangers where she lived. She was second in command, or "vice-chief," of *Chiquitas Poderosas* ("powerful girls"), a rising *Latina* gang found on the West Side of Chicago. Because she resided in Cabrini-Green, the nation's most impoverished high-rise, this should come as no surprise. Lorena had dwelled in housing projects her whole life, and had lived virtually face-to-face with everything a parent shields their children from since she was born. She lived with her grandmother, as both her parents were in prison. Her mother was black, with some Caucasian in her blood, and according to her grandmother their family came from a long line of unfortunate mishaps when it came to relationships.

Lorena was given a silver locket by her mother when she turned thirteen, and two pictures to place inside of it. The pictures were said to have once belonged to an ancestor of hers, from Alabama—though Lorena never could understand their significance or which of the photographs was of her ancestor. One picture was of a woman of about thirty, or so, dressed in an elegant, 1800s style, high-collar dress. The other was of a younger woman, seemingly in her late teens and dressed similarly, though this picture didn't look quite as old as the first—giving Lorena reason to believe that the latter was taken at a later date. The factors the two women had in common were mostly their eyes, as they both held a distant, melancholy gleam. The other similarity was a single, silver, heart-shaped locket both were wearing in the pictures. Lorena suspected it must have been the same piece of jewelry, rather than duplicates. This idea gave the story a particularly interesting twist of which any other version would be void.

As for Lorena's father, he was a gang-banger (as was her mother) who was born in Puerto Rico and immigrated to America with his family when he was very young. The Selenez family was larger than average, with eight children, and lived in the Bronx of New York for a while, until the parents divorced and half of the children lived with their mother, who moved to Chicago.

Lorena, not surprisingly, had never met her father, but her grandmother on his side had taken care of her when her son ducked out and left Lorena's mother to care for the child by herself. Lorena's Hispanic grandmother took care of her until she turned seven, or so, when the woman died of a heart attack. From there, Lorena was shipped through various orphanages and oftentimes abusive foster homes. This cycle continued until her grandmother on her mother's side moved from Alabama to Chicago. The woman made the decision upon hearing that the daughter she herself was forced to give up was in prison and had long since given birth to a child.

Lorena's mother was young, having had her child at just fifteen, and though attaining a change of heart regarding her streetwise ways upon conceiving her, she was blackmailed by the gang she was in to remain true to her "first priority," as they had called it. Elsa Jordan would visit from time to time when her daughter was under the care of her boyfriend's mother, but soon enough her gang persuaded her to make an abortive move that landed her in prison for five years.

Lorena never understood her mother's actions, that is, until she herself was forced to become the vice-chief of *Chiquitas Poderosas*.

Life for Lorena was a daily habitual sequence, consisting predominantly of fights, boys, money and school, respectively. Though *Chiquitas Poderosas* was much respected at school and on the streets, there still remained the few that thought they could challenge the growing *Latina* gang, and Lorena had the battle scars to prove it. She knew everything there was to know about guns, knives, and other lethal weapons— had even stabbed various people several times. She was one of the best female fighters on the streets.

Because most successful gangs were built around having many connections and hardcore members, it was unorthodox that *Chiquitas Poderosas* took on such a rise. After all, though, they had mostly their vice-chief to thank; Lorena wasn't ignorant about how to run an organization. She was skilled in her field and almost always succeeded in overthrowing opposition. Surprisingly, though, things weren't always this way. Lorena at first had only tagged along with the once small *Latina* gang as a "Wanna-be"—a member over ten years of age, usually pre-teens, that gangs gave tasks such as stealing and collecting money until they became "hardcore" (members that were in it for life). Wanna-be's weren't usually initiated until they had proven themselves, and it didn't take Lorena long to do so.

Initiation—known as being V'd in—was usually accomplished with a test of endurance. The potential member was given ten minutes during which to withstand blows from various selected gang members, and weren't allowed to defend themselves. If they survived, they were in.

Lorena's gang acumen led to her being V'd in at age fourteen, and not many of the other members considered the chance of her becoming vice-chief. But when their current chief, Marisol Carvajal—a longtime friend of Lorena's—deemed her to be vice-chief, the other members soon witnessed that Lorena was in fact able to handle her new position. The only existent problem was that Lorena wasn't given a choice on whether or not to accept it. Being in a gang limited one's choices, and living with the consequences wasn't easy.

"How was school?" asked her grandmother upon her entering the room.

Lorena shrugged, not feeling like sharing the happenings of her day.

She had just walked through the door of their apartment on the sixth floor of the housing project, and her grandmother, Elena Jordan, was standing in the tiny cubicle known as the kitchen, preparing a meal on a testy stove.

Their apartment wasn't much of a living quarter at all. It was made up of three rooms; four counting the bathroom. The living room and foyer were one and the same, and the crevice of a kitchen resided on the far left wall—thus it couldn't exactly be referred to as a "room." The furnishings were very plain, with an old, beaten-up couch near the window of the living room, a few hard-backed chairs, a meager card table with two more broken-down chairs for meals, and a lamp that looked as though it dated back to the days of Albert Einstein that sat on the floor—without a shade. The refrigerator was scheduled to meet its life's end at any given time and the stove only held two burners that at times refused to work. The pantry was composed of a small, cardboard box against the wall, and the pots and pans sat in a solitary cabinet that hadn't yet been devoured by termites. The dull, gray carpeting of the apartment was shabby from being tread on for years, stained from liquor spills caused by former tenants, and not especially pleasant to gaze upon. Lorena's room was slightly smaller than her grandmother's (which could hardly be considered "big") and held a vintage metal bed with a tattered mattress, another box for Lorena to keep her clothes in, and a Rubbermaid container for her things. The bathroom contained a rust-and-grime-stained washbasin with a leaky faucet and ornery knobs, a very poor bathtub, and a toilet that overflowed seemingly every other day.

Though Ms. Jordan did her best to keep the apartment clean, it was no easy task with the small amount of money they possessed. The government provided some financial aid for the small family, but other than that Lorena's grandmother still had to work to help them get by. Being just under fifty, working wasn't difficult for her, but the thing that worried her more than bills and taxes was her granddaughter.

Lately Lorena had been quiet—anxious—and despite the already existent lack of food, had a very small appetite. Once Ms. Jordan found a bruise on her arm, but when she questioned her about it, Lorena merely claimed she had hit it on a doorway. The grandmother didn't want to be guilty of a crime many parents and guardians commit, "over-protectiveness," yet didn't want to be impartial when it came to deciphering when to hold on and when to let go.

She now watched Lorena walk over to the couch, plop down, and grab the old-fashioned, rotary-dial phone to make a call.

The girl cursed under her breath when no dial tone met her ears, and she placed it back onto the receiver.

"The phone's out again, Gram," she said as she rubbed her eyes, her voice holding a trace of an Hispanic accent.

After doing so, Lorena caught a glimpse of her hands and frowned when she saw black, sooty residue staining her fingertips. Her mascara was getting too old to use. . . again.

"I know," Ms. Jordan replied wearily as she turned back to the pot of canned green beans she was preparing. "I've got to work on the taxes once I get a bite to eat, so I was hoping you'd stop by the office to pay the bill."

Lorena raised an eyebrow and smirked.

"With what?" she asked as she played with the chain on her locket.

"The money's on the table. There should be some extra cash for you to bring back a few groceries—there's the list as well."

Lorena sighed and finally got up.

"Alright," she voiced, heading to her room to retrieve something. She quickly grabbed a knife from behind her clothes box, then hurried back to the living room—swiftly sliding the weapon into her pocket before her grandmother could pick up on her actions.

"I'll be back soon," she said as she stuffed the money and list into her jeans pocket, then walked out the door.

The trek to the telephone company's office was about a mile from Cabrini-Green, but Lorena was well accustomed to it.

It would be dark by the time she would make it back to the apartment, causing it to be reasonable for the teen to carry her knife in her pocket as well. It was a good, sturdy weapon—one of Lorena's most prized possessions next to her locket; she received the knife as an initiation gift from the gang.

As Lorena made her way down the semi-crowded sidewalk, she was well aware (to the point of oblivion, if possible) of the many male faces staring at her as she passed, and had learned to simply ignore a random hoot or whistle. Most of the guys were harmless, but there were still the few she passed after sunset that had to be dealt with by drawing the knife and/or resorting to sticking them—a method of stabbing without killing the victim. At some point in time, however, they usually backed off upon seeing her attire up close. A gang member's attire revolves around their rank, and because Lorena was vice-chief she dressed to match so. Around her left wrist was a bracelet made with leather and multicolored beads, symbolizing her status of vice-chief. Along with this and her evident scars, the guys often chose not to start any trouble.

Even though her lifestyle wasn't exactly that of your "average" girl (not living in the 'hood) Lorena's outward appearance wouldn't suggest so. Her hair—which she often thought of as "unruly" (much to the disapproval of her envious peers)—was slightly below shoulder length with a natural hazel tint and slight curl. Her almond eyes were a golden brown, and she held a light, yet slightly bronze, milk-chocolate complexion. She wasn't quite thin and couldn't be considered as heavy, but rather was trim and athletic—due to the exercise she received from fighting.

That day Lorena was wearing denim capris over white sneakers and a light pink tank with the word "oxymoron" in bright blue, block letters across the chest. Her hair was pulled into a ponytail with a solitary strand hanging loosely in her face, and below her hairline was her favorite neon pink headband (which matched her pink wristbands and leg warmers). Lastly, Lorena wore her silver hoop earrings to compliment all of her other ear piercings, her locket—as always—and lastly a few silver bangles and rings.

On route to the phone bill office was a barbeque shop where a friend of Lorena's worked. After consulting her watch to see that there was plenty of time to run her errands and have a chat, she decided to enter the shop.

Lorena opened the door of the relatively small building and walked inside. The strong but sweet, hickory-smoked smell of barbeque met her nose as she walked up to the counter, where various types of pulled pork and other meats sat on display. The blue-and-white-tiled floor far from matched the walls, which were paneled in unfinished wood. The somewhat low ceiling was composed of yellowing grocery-store-type panels, with dull, orange, gigantic track lights which cast a dim, yellow glow about the place.

Seeing no one behind the counter, Lorena rang the bell to hear a voice call from the back room, "Just a second!"

The storefront was empty with the exception of an employee sweeping around tables and chairs.

Tony was his name. He was about fifteen—Lorena's age—and attended the same high school as her. He was from the Italian community, and was known around the area as the "church boy." It was a well-known fact that Tony was a strong believer, and attended one of the popular churches on the South Side of Chicago. His Bible went with him almost everywhere, and it'd be a wonder to catch him without it. Though Tony wasn't the type to bash it over your head, his impeccable faith remained quite manifest; even if just by looking at his face. It wasn't that he was always happy, but rather always content. If he ever swore no one caught it, if he ever argued no one witnessed it, and if he had ever said an ill word regarding women, no one heard it. Tony was quiet, and usually only spoke when spoken to.

The fact that the young man was so sickeningly Godly, in Lorena's eyes, was his only idiosyncrasy—and the solitary reason she steered clear of the non-existent chance she had with him. The girl knew he was quite far from bad looking, and what pained her most was that he dressed much like the boys on the street. The only difference was that he kept himself clean, wore no gang symbols and stood up straight—all of this being accomplished while still looking good—if not better than all of the gang bangers. As for his physical build, Tony had dark, slightly-curly, medium-length hair, olive-tinted skin, and large, dark eyes that seemed to reflect whatever they focused on. He was tall, smart and practically perfect—giving Lorena one more reason to curse the reality that she hadn't any chance with him.

That afternoon Tony was dressed in black jeans over white Converse All-Stars, a white t-shirt and of course, his silver cross around his neck.

Lorena hadn't realized she was staring at him while waiting on her friend to appear, until he looked up suddenly from his sweeping.

¿*"Como estas, 'Tonio?"* Lorena asked with a smile, calling him by the nickname she had given him.

"Sono bello, lo ringrazia," Tony replied while returning the smile, speaking in his native tongue.

One of the only reasons he and Lorena ever conversed was to joke around by talking in their native languages, Italian and Spanish; which are similar, but not quite the same.

Tony returned to his sweeping and Lorena pressed the bell again.

"Hey, Candy! ¡*Ven aqui, chica!*" she called impatiently, telling her friend to come out.

Finally the swing door opened and out walked a teenage girl carrying a slab of raw meat, which she soon set in the display case.

"Don't slip me any skin with cow blood on your hands," Lorena stated playfully as she watched her friend briefly wash her hands in a sink near the counter.

Candy laughed, her green eyes twinkling.

"You sure, Lorena?"

Candy was Caucasian with naturally-brown, shoulder-length hair that was currently dyed black—giving her a classy grunge look. Her eyes were an emerald green, and she had a few freckles that complimented her slightly-tanned skin. Her full name was Candice, but she hated it so much that she forced all of her friends to call her "Candy" instead.

"Did it hurt?" Lorena asked suddenly as Candy sat down in a chair at a table along a wall.

Candy frowned as she straightened her red, leather mini-skirt (which matched her red, leather jacket that she wore over a green-and-black-striped tube-top).

"Did what hurt?"

Lorena rolled her eyes as she sat down opposite her.

"Your tongue, girl."

Candy smiled as she reached into her pocket and withdrew a stick of bubble gum.

"Oh, I was hoping you'd notice."

A silver stud sat in the middle of her tongue, with two smaller ones embedded on its left and right. This formation was one of the *Chiquitas Poderosas* symbols.

"Power, unity, money," Lorena mused. "I told you I was *working* on getting you in, *chica*—not that you actually are in."

Candy sighed.

"I know, but I just wanted to do something wild to get on Carvajal's good side," she stated before blowing a bubble.

Lorena smirked.

"It'll take more than getting on her good side to pull this off."

Candy rose and walked behind the counter, where she poured 7UP from the soda machine into cups.

"Thirsty, Tony?" she asked.

Tony glanced up from where he was sweeping in a corner, and shook his head.

Candy shrugged and proceeded to place lids over the two cups.

While she did so, Lorena took it upon herself to watch sweeping by the oblivious Tony, whose presence she had almost forgotten. His silence was mysterious; too mysterious for her own good.

Lorena often stared at him, partially for the purpose of checking him out, but mostly trying to figure him out. He was a walking mystery, she concluded.

There is no way a guy that hot can be so—

¿"Estas occupada, chica?" Candy's voice broke into her thoughts.

Abruptly Lorena turned back around in her chair.

"What?"

Candy looked from Tony to Lorena—twice—as she set the cups down and resumed her seat.

"Don't bite off more than you can chew," she finally stated quietly before taking a sip of her soda.

Lorena blushed and smoothed her ponytail.

"I haven't bitten at all," she replied, lowering her voice as well.

"You sure are acting like you want to."

Lorena chewed on her straw for a few seconds, realizing her friend was right. There was no denying her evident affinity for the youth; not aloud, at least.

"He doesn't have any chance with me . . ."

"And why not?" asked Candy, a mischievous smile creeping onto her face.

Lorena rolled her eyes.

"Please shut up. He's a church kid, and why would I have feelings for one of them?"

Candy chuckled.

"Talk too loud and he just might hear you," she stated as she looked over Lorena's shoulder, watching Tony continue to sweep as though he were the only being in the building. "But you gotta admit—"

"Admit what?" Lorena said in a tone much louder (and with more astonishment) than she had intended.

Candy's eyes widened and Lorena bit her lip while taking a quick glance behind her to see that he was making his way to the back storage room.

"Admit that he's sexy . . .what did you think?" Candy finished while raising a pierced eyebrow.

"Whatever, girl."

"Whatever?! A blind chick could see that I'm right," Candy leaned back in her chair and crossed one leg over the other, running her fingers through her spiked hair. "Besides, you know that he wants you, right?"

Again, Lorena felt the blood rushing to her face, and gritted her teeth.

"Why am I supposed to care? He ain't the only hot guy around, and sure isn't the last guy on the planet." Lorena looked to the back of the store to make sure Tony was out of earshot, then continued, "Everyone says he's sweet, but all guys put up a front."

Candy shook her head and smiled.

"Okay, okay. I'm just messin' with ya,' anyway—you know the only guy for you is Michael Jackson, girl."

Lorena finally laughed.

"Exactly."

A bell rang suddenly, signaling that the front door had opened, and Tony emerged from the storeroom to take his place behind the counter, then waited on the customer.

"But anyway—about the gang—" Candy began, changing subject.

"I said I'm workin' on it."

"Is she leaning towards yes, no . . .?"

Lorena sighed.

"We're the *Chiquitas Poderosas*."

"Yeah, but not *'Latinas Poderosas.'*"

Lorena smiled.

"You've got a point there. I just wish Marisa would understand."

"Keep working on it—she will."

Lorena was in the process of convincing Marisol Carvajal, the chief, that the gang should be open to all nationalities of females, rather than just *Latinas*. It wasn't an easy task, but she was determined to have her friend in it with her.

"What time is it?" Lorena asked suddenly.

Candy looked at her watch.

"About five thirty—"

"I've gotta go pay the phone bill. My gram's gonna kill me for sure," Lorena stated as she rose and finished her drink.

"I'll come with you," Candy said, then turned to the counter. "I'll be back soon, Tony."

Tony nodded from where he was helping customers, and the two girls left the store.

"That'll be $101.91."

Lorena reached into her pocket and brought out the necessary currency, then handed them to the clerk behind the counter.

The phone company's office was as drab as could be with its yellowing walls, filthy brown carpeting, sagging ceiling, and a disgustingly-overpowering cloud of cheap cologne and cigarette smoke which permeated the atmosphere.

Candy had meandered off to a gumball machine while her friend took care of the bill.

After finishing her business, Lorena headed for the door, informing her companion that she was done.

Now headed for a market, they made their way down the half-crowded sidewalk, chatting about school and local gossip. It had now reached nightfall, and most of the remaining people on the street were gang bangers.

"So who's cuter—Greg Smith or André West?" Candy asked.

The two were in a deep discussion regarding boys at school, and were now trying to decide which was the cuter between the two cutest.

Lorena laughed.

"Neither, *chica*. I'm thinkin' Cobra's the hottest of them all."

Candy raised an eyebrow in amusement.

"I forgot about him. You got a little somethin' goin' on, Lorena?"

Lorena smirked.

"He's nineteen and still in the eleventh grade—my man's gotta have some intellect."

"Well, he's got enough 'intellect' regarding the streets, though. He's just about to be elected chief, you know."

Lorena sighed.

"Yeah, but still—I just can't see—"

She stopped in mid-sentence and both paused when they came to an alleyway.

About fifteen guys, dressed in gang attire, were huddled in a circle, hooting and cheering.

"Hey, let's see what's up!" Candy said as she grabbed Lorena's arm.

Lorena frowned as she fished through her jeans pocket for a stick of chewing gum.

"Wait a minute—you don't just join any old crowd."

"You do if Cobra's the one doing the fighting the crowd's watching."

"And how do we know he's the one fighting?"

"That's his gang, ain't it?"

The two girls made their way to the outskirts of the circle, but when they found that they couldn't see very well moved to a wall to stand on crates.

Inside of the circle, two black teens were engaged in a fight, their knives drawn. One lunged, and the other dodged.

"I told you it was Cobra!" Candy exclaimed excitedly.

Lorena remained silent as she watched the two continue, chewing her gum to ease the sudden tension in her stomach.

Cobra, apparently the stronger of the two, was moving about with finesse and dexterity. It was more than obvious he was waiting for the right opportunity to make his move.

And it came soon enough.

The challenger, looking winded and defeated, didn't seem to see the knife before it punctured his side. The victorious Cobra watched his victim fall to his knees, a smile on his face as he slyly wiped the blood off of his knife onto the ex-opponent's shirt.

Cheers erupted from the crowd, and the few allies belonging to the loser helped him to his feet. After reciting a few hostile words, the victim's gang departed with their fallen member, leaving Cobra to be congratulated by the crowd.

"I knew he'd win it!" Candy stated triumphantly as she alighted from the crate, Lorena following behind.

Gazing outside of the crowd surrounding him, Cobra became aware of the presence of his extended audience.

"He's looking this way—now's your chance," Candy stated exuberantly with a smile on her face.

Lorena frowned.

"My chance for what?"

Candy rolled her eyes.

"Your chance to get his attention even more by playing hard to get—what else? Now c'mon, start walking off as though you're not interested—that gets 'em every time."

Candy's resolution was successful, as before the two had gone a block, jogging footsteps could be heard on their trail.

"Wait up, ladies!" Cobra called and they stopped walking.

"I told you so," Candy muttered seconds before his arrival.

"What's happenin,' Cobra?" she asked aloud.

He shrugged and smiled as he leaned up against a nearby light post.

If one were to meet the young man on the streets, they should be very much afraid of him. Cobra was among the most intimidating of the gang bangers around the area, with his many battle scars and tattoos. Adding to this was his physique, which to most girls more than made up for his usual lack of respect for just about anyone. He was muscular, with a dark complexion, not quite tall or short, with his dark hair in cornrows. At first glance one might not think his face to be handsome, what with its many scars, though the feature about him that most seemed to lure others in were his eyes, which were an unusual shade of blue; almost a gray, if you looked closely enough. People of his color usually have dark eyes; Cobra was an exception to the rule.

Of his family history, no one knew—only that he was raised in an orphanage, most likely the child of an unwed mother forced to put her child up for adoption. This was the story of many of the teenagers living on the streets.

"Just whuppin' some GFL butt," he replied carelessly with a wave of his tattooed hand, referring to an infamous gang.

"I noticed. I wonder how they figured they'd beat you," Candy stated with a laugh.

"Yeah. I know that I don't have a clue as to what those niggas want with the NGBs," Cobra said, this time referring to his own gang, "Notorious Gangster Ballers," one of the most dangerous male gangs around.

"So what've you been up to, Madam Vice-President?" he asked, changing subject while addressing the silent Lorena.

She had been quiet since he had come up to them, listening to the conversation only half-heartedly. Lorena always attained an uneasy feeling when around her recent crush . . . a sense of fear; despite the many people technically more threatening than he with which she had dealt with in her past.

"Nothin' much," she replied coolly, keeping her eyes on the pavement—where they had remained since the beginning of the encounter.

A peculiar silence lingered, and Candy watched the other two. The oblivious and almost suddenly-shy Lorena was standing with one hand stuffed into her pocket, the other fiddling with the clasp on her necklace. Cobra, on the other hand, had taken it upon himself to watch her closely, his piercing eyes seeming as though they had recently found a bird upon which to prey; an invalid to take advantage of. . . but then, they were only mere teens suffering from something known as a crush. That is, at least one of them was. The other emotion is commonly referred to as something else… something less harmless and even destructive.

"I've gotta get back to the store. I'll see you tomorrow, Lorena," Candy quipped suddenly, hurrying off down the sidewalk, leaving her friend looking after her despairingly.

Lorena and Cobra had never carried on a conversation on their own; any words they exchanged were with the aid of the gregarious Candy. Now that she was gone, Lorena vowed to call her later to "express her disapproval."

"So what are you doin' out here this late tonight?" Cobra asked, bringing Lorena out of her hard glare after her friend.

"I have to pick up some groceries," she answered shortly, still keeping her eyes away from him as she began to head down the sidewalk in the direction of the nearest market.

Immediately Cobra followed; he wasn't known for being brushed off.

"How 'bout I help you out?"

Lorena didn't reply, as she knew him well enough to know that his offers were often to be received as commands.

She allowed him to walk alongside her, not really knowing what else to do. Besides, some extra hands to carry the bags would be helpful.

"So . . .is Carvajal givin' you a hard time?" he asked, slightly smiling sideways at her.

"It depends on what a hard time is."

"Well, you beat me to the punch—I'm still workin' on gettin' that spot myself."

Lorena was about to say something else, when they suddenly passed a black teen around Cobra's age, who hurled an insult.

Cobra flicked him off and spat a curse, then resumed walking with Lorena.

As they strode through the door of the small, dimly-lit, smoke-filled market, he shook his head in annoyance.

"All these niggas think they bad when they don't even know a gun from a knife. Don't that make you mad, Lorena?"

She sighed as she withdrew her list and they headed over to the dairy coolers.

"I guess so, but it's when they start a fight that I get mad," she said as she picked up a half-gallon of milk.

Cobra smirked as he looked over her shoulder to see the list, then he himself picked up a half-gallon.

"I hear ya' on that one. Especially if they some bony wannabe wantin' some beef."

Lorena couldn't help but smile as she picked up another half-gallon.

"Or if you get into the fight they think the first and only punch they land on you means they've won the battle," she added.

Cobra laughed.

"Or become a member."

"Or vice-chief!"

Here they laughed, until both reached for yet another half-gallon and Lorena dropped the handful she was carrying.

"My fault," Cobra said as they both knelt down to pick them up.

After retrieving all of the fallen items (and attracting glares of annoyance from surrounding customers), they began to return the extra cartons to the shelf.

"I don't know how we ended up with all this milk—the list only says one," Cobra stated.

Lorena smiled as she placed the last one she was holding back on the shelf, then turned to her companion for another one.

He handed her the carton and she looked directly up into his eyes for the first time that evening.

Before she could prevent it, her heart skipped a beat.

Cobra looked as though he might move in closer, but was forced to postpone his actions when a nearby voice interjected, "Did any spill?"

"Uh, not that I know of," Cobra answered the elderly employee. "Do you see any, Lorena?"

Lorena bit her lip.

"Um, no."

The employee left, and the two continued their shopping.

"What would your grandma have to say about a gang banger walkin' you home?" Cobra asked once they reached the housing-project floor Lorena lived on.

She smiled as she walked up to her door, Cobra following close behind.

"She doesn't know you, so she doesn't know your status."

He took hold of her arm and turned her back to the door and around to face him, all in one swift but gentle maneuver.

"I wanna get to know you," he said quietly as he set the grocery bags down, looking into her eyes.

Lorena swallowed as he bent his head down closer to hers.

Seconds before a kiss could occur, she turned away.

"I'm sorry," she whispered as she closed her eyes.

Lorena couldn't understand why she was so nervous—he wouldn't be the first guy she had kissed.

Cobra took her chin in his hand and turned her face back to his.

"Don't be," he said quietly as his eyes burned into hers and their lips inched closer together.

If Lorena thought she was strong enough to resist him the first time, she was right. But come the second, she failed.

~ Chapter II ~

"You should know that your body is a temple for the Holy Spirit who is in you. You have received the Holy Spirit from God. So you do not belong to yourselves, because you were bought by God for a price. So honor God with your bodies."

I Corinthians 6:19-20
NCV

☦

"Lorena, Lorena, Lorena. I think you've been avoiding me all day long, *chica*."

Lorena turned from her locker to see Marisol Carvajal standing there, an expectant look on her face.

Marisol was seventeen, two years older than Lorena, and one of the most intimidating girls at school. Disagreeing with her was unwise, arguing pointless, and fighting unthinkable. Marisol's physique was that of your average tough girl—matching her chief status. Each day she was decked out in the most dominant of gangster apparel, thus her role was manifest. With tattoos to spare and a slightly muscular build, it would be thought of as keen to forsake provoking her. Other than that, Marisol's cornrowed hair was dyed blonde, her eyes were brown and skin olive.

Lorena replaced her math book, closed her locker and sighed.

"I've been dealin' with mess all morning."

"What kind?" Marisol asked as they made their way down the crowded hall towards the cafeteria.

Lorena patted her stomach as her reply.

"Oh. I thought you said you were gonna see a doctor about that..." She smirked.

"Please—the last thing I need is some quack tellin' me about my body."

Marisol laughed as they squeezed through the crowd of students.

"Well, maybe it's your grandma's cookin.'"

Lorena glared at her sideways as she stopped to get a drink of water from a fountain.

"Don't talk about my grandma."

Marisol raised her eyebrows in amusement as she leaned against the wall.

"Girl, you are upset this morning. Maybe it's not just a stomach pain."

"What are you talkin' about?" Lorena asked as she paused before taking another sip.

"Oh, I don't know . . . except that Candy chick's been spreadin' a rumor about you and Cobra spendin' some 'quality' time together last night."

Lorena stopped drinking and looked up at her.

"Maybe your problem ain't food poisoning," Marisol continued, a mischievous gleam in her eye.

Lorena frowned.

"Shut up—all he did was help me shop at the market."

"Well, whatever you two did has got you upset."

Lorena knew her friend was right—she wasn't acting herself that morning.

Though something was bothering her, it couldn't have been Cobra . . .or at least she didn't think it was. The night before, she had been with him for about five minutes, and after that he left and Lorena went on with her usual routine. She made out with guys all the time, and had even gone farther than that before. She couldn't understand why she was handling this particular acquaintance so differently than the others.

Before they had gone a yard down the hall, a voice sounded behind them, "What's up Carvajal—Selenez?"

Marisol and Lorena turned to see Cobra, along with his crew, walking up to them.

"The usual mess," Marisol replied as they slipped each other skin.

"Vice pres., *qué pasa?*" he asked Lorena with a smile.

She merely shrugged again, the usual uneasy feeling she had when around him returning.

"Lorena here's feelin' bad—stomach pain," Marisol spoke up for her friend's silence.

Cobra frowned.

"That's too bad," he stated, then changed the subject. "There's this party happenin' tonight at Dwayne's place. They say it's gonna be bananas. You two bringin' the gang?"

Marisol shrugged.

"I guess so. We've gotta cancel somethin' else to do it, but we'll be there."

Cobra smiled.

"A'ight then, I'll see you there," he replied smoothly as he started off with his crew following, but not before caressing Lorena's face with his hand and placing a gentle kiss on her lips. "Get well soon, baby girl."

When they were out of hearing distance, Marisol punched Lorena's arm and smirked.

"Sure is gettin' hot in here!"

Lorena smiled, but not before playfully shoving her friend. "Shut up, please!"

That night, as Lorena stood applying eye shadow in front of the bathroom mirror, the sound of the front door opening signaled that her grandmother had just returned from work. She would undoubtedly want to know why Lorena was fixing herself up.

A minute later there came a knock on the bathroom door.

"Come in—I'm just doin' my makeup."

The door opened and Ms. Jordan appeared, leaning against the doorway.

"Hey, Gram. How was work?" Lorena greeted her grandmother cheerily.

"Where are you off to tonight?" the woman grilled.

Lorena sighed as she opened the cabinet to retrieve her mascara. "Just a get-together with friends—nothin' to worry about."

"And exactly what 'friends' will be participating?" Ms. Jordan asked, skepticism lining her voice.

"Candy—I mean Candice, and the rest of the girls," the teen half-lied.

This time Ms. Jordan sighed, then walked off to the living room.

"You're not upset, are you, Gram?" Lorena called before closing the cabinet and taking one final glance at herself in the mirror.

After receiving no response, she rolled her eyes and exited the bathroom into the living room, where Ms. Jordan was sitting on the couch, a newspaper open in front of her.

After standing in front of the silent woman for close to a minute, Lorena sighed once again and sat at her grandmother's feet.

"Gram?" she pleaded, resting her arms on her lap.

Ms. Jordan finally set the newspaper over on the opposite cushion, then looked down at her granddaughter (who was attempting the puppy-dog-eyes maneuver).

"'Rena . . .I don't even know your friends—" she began slowly, only to be cut off by the pleading teenager.

"But Gram, they're nice . . ." Lorena's voice faded as she contemplated the lack of truth behind her statement. ". . .to me," she added skillfully, possibly sparing herself unwanted trouble.

"I'm not trying to judge, but—"

"But you are judging. I promise I won't get into trouble. Please let me go and have some fun."

Ms. Jordan sighed, noting the anxious look in Lorena's eyes. She often worried about her, and having witnessed (and even experienced herself somewhat) the fate of her own daughter, didn't want to see the same or even similar fate happen to her granddaughter.

"You haven't even sat down to talk with me in a while. I've got news for you, you know."

Lorena seemed inquisitive.

"Oh?"

Ms. Jordan nodded.

"Guess who called me at work today."

"Who?"

"Your mother—apparently they're letting her out a month earlier than when they originally planned. She'll be arriving here tomorrow night."

Lorena half-frowned and blinked several times, allowing the words to register.

"Why?" she asked finally.

Ms. Jordan shrugged and chuckled slightly at the girl's peculiar inquiry.

"I don't know—you can ask her that when you see her." Here she shook her head. "It's been nearly five years since we last saw her, you know."

Lorena ran her tongue along her teeth and twisted the chain of her locket.

"I guess."

"But anyway," Ms. Jordan stated, changing the subject. "As for this 'get-together'—I suppose you can go. Just don't party too hard."

Lorena's mind was still on the news of her mother's upcoming return, and it took a few seconds for her to realize she had just gotten off the hook.

"Thanks, Gram," she replied as she smiled and hugged her. "I won't be out too late."

"Good—be careful," Ms. Jordan said as she watched Lorena grab her purse off of a nearby chair and hurry out the door.

"There she is—Lorena, get over here, *chica*!"

Lorena's sprinting frame could be seen approaching down the smoggy alleyway, and her welcome party breathed a sigh of relief.

Marisol sighed and crossed her arms over her chest before shrugging to the rest of the group of *Latinas*, then when Lorena was within reaching distance, grabbed her arm.

"Look at the time—you're running late!" stated Marisol, annoyance inhabiting her tone.

"The party started over a half hour ago!" one girl—Anita—exclaimed while snapping her gum, clad in heavy eye shadow and a tight mini-skirt and tank.

A chorus of "yeahs" echoed from the rest of the group, and Lorena sighed.

"Look, I'm sorry—my *abuela* wasn't too excited about this."

"It doesn't matter now—let's go," Marisol stated while smoothing a rebellious lock of hair, and the gang made their way to the end of the alley, where three cars lined the curb.

"What happened to 'fashionably late'?" Lorena asked as she slid into the passenger seat of Marisol's red Mustang, while three other girls entered the back.

"What are you doin'?" asked Marisol in a rather acrid tone, ignoring the question as she stood at the passenger door, hands on her hips.

"What do you think I'm doin'?" Lorena returned equally as acrimoniously.

"I think she wants you to drive, *chica*," Isabella, one of the other passengers, stated from the back seat.

"I think we need to get over to that party, Lorena—*vamanos!*" added Paulina, the girl sitting directly behind her.

Lorena glared at her, then alighted from the vehicle and made her way to the driver's seat.

Inside of the warehouse when the CPs entered, was loud music, blaring disco balls, enough smoke to out-fog a casino, and of course, people. The dance floor was crowded with couples moving to the music of the latest pop song blaring through the speakers, while there remained the few that stood against the wall—making out, drinking or smoking. A few fights were taking place, the kinds that broke out over a stolen girlfriend or unreturned borrowed money (those to which no one paid particular notice).

The warehouse had been vacant for years, and it wasn't very often that the police bothered to patrol the area in which it resided, so the partygoers were virtually safe from harm; that is, the law's harm.

"Circulate *chicas*—make the CPs look good," Marisol stated as she straightened her leather miniskirt.

"I'm gonna go get some water—" Lorena said as she began to walk off for the refreshment table, but was soon arrested when Marisol grabbed her arm.

"Not so fast—what's this I hear about that Candy girl wantin' to talk with me?"

"How did you know about that?"

Before Marisol could reply, Paulina quickly brushed by, but not before Lorena could stop her.

"Paulina, I thought I told you to keep that a secret!" she exclaimed.

"You told me not to tell anyone—not that I wasn't supposed to tell Maris,'" Paulina defended herself as she brushed Lorena's arm off her shoulder.

Lorena rolled her eyes.

"That girl couldn't keep any secret at any time, 'Rena. You oughta know that by now," Marisol stated with a laugh.

"Muchas gracias, Carvajal," Paulina replied sarcastically with a glare, then directed her attention to a seating area in a corner, where a crowd of guys were talking and laughing. "Hey, look—it's André. I'd better go—"

"I don't think so!" Marisol interjected, looking at her adherent as though she had lost her mind. "That boy is mine, *chica*."

"Every boy is yours . . ." Lorena muttered.

"What was that, Selenez?" asked Marisol as she raised her eyebrow expectantly.

"*Nada*, Madam President," Lorena replied with a mock bow and Barbie smile.

"That's what I thought," Marisol stated with satisfaction, then turned to Paulina—who was still drooling after André. "I suppose you can have him for tonight. There's always the rest of the NGBs to choose from."

"*Gracias*, Marisa! I'll see you two later—much later! *¡Hasta luego!*" Paulina replied exuberantly as she hurried off to her destination.

"The rest of the NGBs, eh?" asked Lorena as Marisol brought out her compact and began applying more blush.

¿"Sí, sí—y qué es tu problema?" she returned, frowning in confusion. "So what's the deal with Candy?"

Lorena sighed.

"She wants to know if she could possibly . . ." Lorena's voice faded off as she noticed a particular person staring at her from across the room. It wasn't hard to see where Cobra's electric eyes were directed, even from afar.

Lorena felt her heart board its roller coaster, and shivered.

"If she could possibly what?" Marisol's persistent voice attempted to break her trance.

Lorena saw him grin, make a gesture to a group of guys behind him, then begin to stride confidently in her direction.

"Uh, hello? Anybody home?" Marisol asked in annoyance as she replaced her compact and glared at the distant Lorena.

"Look," she replied as she cocked her head towards Cobra.

Marisol smiled when she saw who her friend was staring at.

"Ah—look who's comin' for his second helping."

Lorena rolled her eyes.

"Shut up, Carvajal."

Marisol raised an eyebrow.

"What? I'm just commenting on the game."

"Well just stop—okay? What am I s'posed to do?"

"What do you think you're s'posed to do?!" Marisol stated with a mixture of surprise and exasperation. "Girl, you're givin' the CPs a bad name—that's nearly two counts in one night! First there's the famous 'I can't come to the party on time 'cause *mi abuelita* doesn't like my friends,' and now our favorite, 'I see a sexy-to-the-bone guy walkin' over and I start to panic!' "

"I was just askin' you a simple question. You'd think a girl could get some advice these days . . ."

Marisol crossed her arms over her chest.

"What is your problem? Ever since this Cobra guy got into the picture you've been actin' real shady on me, *chica*."

Lorena shook her head and sighed.

"I don't know—he just ain't my type."

Marisol's jaw dropped to the floor.

"If he ain't your type, you don't have a type!"

Lorena sighed and nervously ran her fingers through her hair.

"He's almost here—I've gotta get some water anyway," she stated as she walked off, shaking her arm free of Marisol's death grip.

"Lorena? Lorena!" Marisol called after her friend. "Come back he—hey there, Cobra. What's happenin'?"

Cobra smiled, then frowned when he noticed that someone was missing.

"Nothin' much—where's Lorena? I thought I just saw her over here a second ago."

Marisol donned a phony smile.

"Oh, you know how she is—she's gotta have water every five minutes."

Cobra began to scan the area, his eyes skillfully roaming the premises.

"Yeah—that means she's at the refreshment table. I'll catch ya' later, Marisa."

Before Marisol could prevent losing another companion, Cobra was off, dodging in and out of random people, on his way to the refreshment table.

Marisol sighed, then headed toward where the NGBs were huddled together, dragging a few CP members with her along the way.

Lorena filled her paper cup with yet another helping of water, then quickly downed it—keeping her eyes on the crowd.

"He wouldn't follow me . . .would he?"

"What's happenin,' sexy?" came the drawl of a nearby drunk teen.

Lorena glowered at him in disgust.

"Get away from me."

"Yeah—get away from her," added Cobra, who had strode up behind Lorena, placing his arm around her waist.

The kid nodded and staggered off with his bottle of liquor, obviously choosing to take Cobra's word for it.

"These stupid niggas are gettin' on my last nerve, here," Cobra stated as he watched him go.

"I thought you were talkin' with Marisol," Lorena replied, focusing on controlling the quiver in her voice.

"I asked her where you were at—so here I am."

Lorena nodded and swallowed.

"Oh," she said as she began to pour herself another drink of water.

"Hey," Cobra interjected as he tilted the jug back and set it down. "Ain't you had enough of that? Watch out—you might end up like that lil' nigga by drinkin' too much."

Lorena smiled slightly.

"It's just water," she replied before taking a drink.

"A'ight, a'ight—that's enough of that," he said as set the cup back down on the table and turned her around to face him. "There's somethin' I wanna show you."

"Really. What is it?"

Cobra managed to take his eyes off of her in order to cast a quick glance around the room.

"You'll see—c'mon," he replied with a lopsided grin as he took her hand in his and led her across the room to a back alleyway exit.

Cobra held the door for her and Lorena walked out into the fresh, night air.

Closing the door behind him, he headed over to a fire escape—Lorena following close behind.

"We're going up there?" she asked as she raised an eyebrow.

Cobra smiled.

"After you."

Together, they ascended the fire escape and when they reached the roof, Cobra instructed Lorena to look up.

The mostly clear night sky was filled with a kingdom of glowing stars painted on a navy canvas, and the bright, full moon illuminated a handful of lavender, wispy clouds. The Sears Tower, standing tall over its younger siblings of skyscrapers, seemed to reach to the heavens as its narrow silhouette completed the painting. A gentle breeze soared mildly from Lake Michigan, which sat peacefully adjacent to the city.

"Wow—this is . . .gorgeous."

Cobra smiled and followed Lorena's mesmerized gaze at the vast wonder of starry eternity and urban life below, then shifted his eyes onto his hypnotized companion.

Lorena slowly began to walk forward, pausing when she reached the three-foot, concrete wall lining the roof's edge.

Cobra—not surprisingly—soon followed and placed his hands either side of her on the low wall, thus closing her in.

"Tell me, Lorena, what's Spanish for 'beautiful?'"

Lorena drew in her breath before biting her lip.

"Bonita," she replied quietly as she watched Cobra's hands cover her own.

"Bonita . . ." he repeated before lowering his head down to her neck, there placing a tender kiss. "And how about, 'I want you so much?'"

A chill ran up Lorena's spine as Cobra's arms wrapped around her waist.

"*Yo te quiero mucho,*" she managed to reply in a near whisper.

Once again, he turned her around to face him, and looked directly into her eyes.

"*Yo te quiero . . .mucho,*" he stated softly, yet firmly.

Lorena swallowed and felt her heart stop beating as momentum began to push the two closer together. As their lips locked passionately, she suddenly attained a sense of defeat, as if she had just been sucked into a black hole and there wasn't any turning back. She felt as though she had reached the point of no return, and suddenly . . .her fear vanished.

~ Chapter III ~

"The kingdom of heaven is like a treasure hidden in a field. One day a man found the treasure, and then he hid it in the field again. He was so happy that he went and sold everything he owned to buy that field. Also, the kingdom of heaven is like a man looking for fine pearls. When he found a very valuable pearl, he went and sold everything he had and bought it."

Matthew 13:44-46
NCV

✝

If ever there were a time for a girl to fear her own grandmother, it was that time for Lorena. Don't think her fear was due to forgetting to clean her room, take out the trash or wash the dishes—no, this time the fear was genuine, as the cause for its existence was far more severe. There were four-letter words Elena Jordan attempted to ban from the interior of their home, but at the moment it was in Lorena's hands as to whether or not to bring the ever prohibited three-letter word into her grandmother's presence. You see, Lorena was now a walking, breathing and living example of the effects of this word; that is, if the expected side effects appeared.

Lorena now stood outside the door of her apartment, contemplating whether to enter or run away to another country. The latter notion existed solely because of the previous night's occurrences. As one might expect, Lorena's sudden lack of fear led to her sleeping with her "crush." Now though she was a virgin only in some senses, she hadn't yet gone quite as far as she did that particular night. Not only had she broken her promise to "not be out too late," but she had also broken an even bigger, unspoken yet unbreakable promise to not have "it" too early. Lorena, having the friends, personality and views of life and morals that she did, didn't herself necessarily see a problem with having sex whenever she so pleased. But unfortunately, the oh-so-Godly Elena Jordan had other views in mind, and thus made it clear to her granddaughter that they were to be respected.

It was almost three o'clock in the morning. Church would start in less than seven hours, and of all senses to hit her during the current period of peril, Lorena was hungry. There was no way she would turn around, walk back down the dark, muggy, maniac-and-druggie-infested stairwell (due to a broken elevator) in order to flee to another country on an empty stomach. Besides, there was someone far more formidable than her grandmother that accompanied the option of escape: "Marisol Carvajal."

Seeing it futile to attempt rescuing herself by way of running for her life as she knew it, Lorena took a deep breath, placed her key into the keyhole and slowly opened the door.

The first thing she perceived was that the lamp was on in the living room, and next she saw her grandmother sitting on the couch, talking on the phone.

"Oh, no—it must be the cops," she thought.

The phone was immediately hung up when the girl was spotted, and the first of a long string of words Elena Jordan recited were, "Lorena Gabrielle Selenez!"

From there, speech was performed predominantly by the elder of the two, as the teen had long since learned to stay as silent as possible in order to get the lightest devisable punishment.

When asked where she had been for the five hours past her designated curfew, Lorena did the only thing she had the courage to do: lie. She claimed that she and her friends got held up by a gang on their way back, that she barely escaped without punishment. It would have been ridiculous to call the police to report the imaginary gang, so instead Lorena was sent straight to bed, and was told they would discuss things further after church.

Coincidentally, that morning's sermon was on the topic of lying. During the whole service, Lorena sat as stiff as a board, and gained a sense of paranoia as her grandmother chatted with other members afterwards. She felt as though everyone knew what she had done, and was sure they were glaring at her when she wasn't looking. Feeling as though she might suffocate, Lorena decided to wait for her grandmother elsewhere and quickly asked to be excused as she made her way to the vacant bus-stop bench outside of the small Baptist church.

Smoothing a seam on her "holy"—as she called it—meeting-the-knees skirt, Lorena suddenly began to shiver as a breeze met her skin, and she rubbed the goose bumps from her arms. It wasn't necessarily a hot day, but it wasn't quite cold either. The lake usually provided the city a gentle breeze, and that particular day Lorena felt very sensitive to it.

She had begun to twist the chain on her locket as she stared down at the pavement, when she noticed a shadow approaching and eventually blocking the warm sun.

When Lorena looked up to see who was standing in front of her, she felt her stomach lurch and a chill run up her spine.

"Olà, Lorena."

"Of all people to talk to me now—the 'holy-kid' himself," she thought.

"Hola, Tonio," Lorena replied as politely as she could.

Tony's church was only a block down from hers, and every Sunday after service Lorena would watch him cross the intersection separating the two churches, then take his seat at the bus stop. He always boarded the bus by himself, though, and Lorena wondered why his family never seemed to accompany him.

"What's happenin'—you look kinda' drained," he stated with a slight frown.

Though his affability was usually comforting, his presence was only making her situation worse, and her stomach moved faster.

Lorena merely shrugged and looked away from his questioning eyes.

"Is it alright if I sit here?" he asked.

She smiled lightly.

"Don't let me stop you—you always do."

Tony smiled and blushed slightly as he sat down beside her.

"How did you know?"

"I see you from the steps of the church every Sunday, 'Tonio."

"Oh—I see you sitting on those steps, too. But . . ."

Lorena frowned as his voice faded off.

"But what?"

Tony shrugged and smiled a little, revealing his dimples, as he looked down at his hands.

"I never really thought you actually noticed me."

For the first time that morning, a full smile entered Lorena's face.

"How could I not, 'Tonio— you're 'Mr. Mysterious,' and mystery always catches my attention."

" 'Mr. Mysterious,' eh?" he asked as he looked at her and shook his head, still smiling. "I don't think I've heard that one, Lorena."

She chuckled.

"That's because it's new."

Tony looked thoughtful for a moment.

"So . . .no more ' 'Tonio'?—what if I liked ' 'Tonio'? "

Lorena shook her head.

"'Tonio stays—he's not going anywhere."

"That's good. So where did 'Mr. Mysterious' come from?"

"I don't know—you tell me."

Tony raised his eyebrows.

"You're sly enough, aren't you? What do you wanna know?"

Lorena smiled.

"Too much for you to tell me right now—it would take at least a thousand years."

"And I don't think we have that much time. So enough about me, what's been goin' on with Lorena lately?"

Lorena sighed and tucked a stray stand of hair behind her ear, now focusing across the street.

"Stuff," she replied shortly.

"Ah, I see. What kind, and why do you keep gettin' quiet when I ask that question?"

Lorena shrugged slightly.

"I don't know. I guess I'm just . . .surprised that you asked me that question . . .or maybe not surprised," she stated quietly.

"Any particular reason why—that you feel like tellin' me?" Tony asked softly. "Remember, I'm Mr. Mysterious—spilling other people's secrets isn't my specialty," he added with a smile.

Lorena shook her head and chuckled.

"I guess it's not . . .but . . ." Her voice faded as she frowned and bit her lip, looking down at the pavement. "Have you ever met someone that you can't figure out how you could be real with because they're different from you?" she finally asked in one breath.

"Actually, yeah—I have," came Tony's response as he looked at her.

Lorena soon turned to meet his gaze, then bit her lip again.

"If you haven't already noticed, I'm not that good at making sense."

Tony smiled.

"You're making plenty of sense, Lorena—stop worryin' so much. If you don't wanna tell me somethin,' it's cool."

Lorena smirked and sighed.

"I only make sense at the wrong times—I didn't mean it that way, 'Tonio."

"Listen, I'm not upset about it—aren't there things I haven't told you about myself?"

"I guess so . . ."

"Well then, don't sweat over it."

A silence followed, and the sun concealed itself behind a tall cloud.

" 'Tonio?" Lorena finally spoke up.

"Yeah?"

"Do you get along with your parents?"

Tony rested his head back on the glass structure behind the bench, and placed his hands on the back of his head.

"Most of the time—but sometimes they can get to me. Why do you ask?"

"Incoming relative."

"Who?"

"My mom—fresh from prison. I know I shouldn't be upset about it . . .but, I mean, I'm just not too fond of people who abandon me for other people."

"Hmm . . .lemme guess—her gang?"

Lorena smirked.

"You got it. I know I can't really talk, but at least I don't have a ki—"

Here her she stopped in mid-sentence, realizing the potential lack of truth behind her statement.

Tony, sensing it best not to ask her to finish her sentence, changed subject within a subject.

"So . . .basically you're not gonna give her another chance," he stated before yawning.

Lorena sighed.

"I didn't say that . . . I just . . . I just get sick thinkin' about it all. I never really liked gettin' pity or sympathy from other people. And I guess the same goes for reincarnated affection. I guess it just seems like a phony joke to me."

"What does—grace?"

"I don't know," she replied quietly. "I don't really know how to act in a situation like this. Besides, I've got other things on my mind right now."

As Lorena finished her sentence, a bus could be seen coming up the lane, and soon it came to a halt in front of the stop.

"Well, things will work out," Tony stated as he rose to his feet. "If you need to talk you know where I am."

Lorena put on a smile for the sake of being thankful.

"*Gracias por todo*—everything."

Tony returned the smile.

"*Prego, mi amica,*" he replied, then jogged to the bus door.

Before boarding, Tony turned around suddenly.

"Be joyful always, Lorena," he called over the roaring engine, then finally entered the bus.

As the vehicle pulled off, Lorena's thoughts hung over his last words.

It was around noon when Lorena and her grandmother returned home from church. The first thing Lorena wanted to do when she walked through the door was collapse onto her bed and sleep the day away—which was, not surprisingly, part of her usual Sunday afternoon ritual.

As she made her way down the hall to her bedroom, she was stopped by her grandmother's voice calling from the kitchen, "'Rena, I'm going to need you to stop by the market and pick up a few things for tonight's dinner."

"Unbelievable," Lorena muttered, her voice void of alacrity, then sighed. "Am I shoplifting today, Gram?" she asked aloud, sarcasm lining her tone.

"Of course not—the church took up a special offering for us this morning after the sermon—when I told the reverend about your mother's return—remember?"

Lorena raised an eyebrow and yawned as she closed her eyes, leaning her head back on the wall.

"I must've missed that part," she stated through her yawn. "So how much did the old hypocri—I mean, 'brothers and sisters in Jesus' give us, Gram?"

Ms. Jordan sternly frowned her disapproval as she retrieved her wallet from her purse.

"Twenty dollars—make it work," she replied as she handed the girl the bills and change.

Lorena raised both eyebrows as she looked from her palm to her grandmother.

"Twenty bucks? That's all we're worth to them?"

Ms. Jordan sighed.

"Lorena, it's a blessing from the Lord—be a little gracious, now."

"Or maybe that's all they think my mom is worth," Lorena added sarcastically under her breath, and thankfully, Ms. Jordan seemed not to hear.

"Here's the list—be sure not to forget anything—you've been very prone to forgetfulness lately."

Lorena nodded and sighed as she accepted the piece of paper and stuffed both it and the money into her purse.

"I swear—"

"Lorena," Ms. Jordan warned.

The teen rolled her eyes.

"I declare, then, Gram," she began while correcting herself, "someday I'm gonna make it so that you won't ever have to worry over bills, buy cheap food, or take unwanted 'pity' offerings from a bunch of hypocrites—and yes, I said it, 'hypocrites.' Everyone and their momma knows when the reverend claims he's out tending to the sick and elderly he's really 'tending' to the 'sister' in need next door."

"Lorena Gabrielle Selenez!" Ms. Jordan gasped at her granddaughter's blatant speech. "I should have whupped you hours ago and now I'm starting to change my mind . . ."

"Maybe so, but you'd never actually do it, Gram," Lorena stated as she smiled innocently and placed a kiss on her grandmother's cheek, then headed for the door.

"What am I gonna do with you?"

Lorena placed her hands over her chest in a dramatic pose.

"The only thing left to do: tie me up and throw me into the lake."

Ms. Jordan shook her head and eventually smiled.

"Go on to the market before I ground you for a year, girl."

Lorena laughed as she exited the apartment, and Ms. Jordan stood in the doorway as she watched her go.

"I'll be back soon!"

It was a chilly, dull and cloudy Sunday afternoon as Lorena made her way down the familiar sidewalk to the market. She passed the barbeque shop and kept on walking, not at all feeling like talking with Candy—as she would undoubtedly end up spilling the beans concerning the night before.

It still weighed heavily on the girl's mind, but it suddenly seemed less realistic—as if she had only dreamed it. Lorena was well aware of the possible consequences of her actions, and had heard the "say yes to abstinence" speech well over one thousand times, but her spirits had lifted almost as soon as she concluded her conversation with Tony. Perhaps it was due to escaping breathing the same tense, dry air as the judgmental church congregation. Or maybe it was the fact that she and her grandmother were on good terms. Whatever it was, Lorena didn't care—all she knew was that life looked good enough to eat at the present, and tomorrow could worry about itself. Besides, no consequences had shown up...yet.

After purchasing the designated groceries and stuffing them into a cart she found in an alley, Lorena strolled down the almost-empty sidewalk, pushing her cart with a light spring in her step.

It was when a voice sounded from behind that her bubble burst.

¡*"Buenas tardes, Selenez!"*

Lorena halted dead in her tracks and sighed.

A few seconds later, Marisol came walking up, carrying—of all things—an infant.

"Hey, Marisa," Lorena greeted accordingly. "Who's that you got there?"

Marisol smiled and played with the baby's cheeks, and he giggled.

"My little cousin—Juan. *Mi tia* made me take him out for some air. Wanna hold him?"

Lorena felt her stomach churn, turn, and state its disapproval loudly.

"Uh, no—I-I'm good."

"Whatever. Boy, have you got lots to tell me! I heard all about it, *chica*. Congratulations!" Marisol stated exuberantly as she punched her friend's arm.

Lorena felt the ground move beneath her feet, and took a deep breath.

"Gee, thanks."

Marisol frowned when she noticed the one-sided enthusiasm.

"Hey, you're lookin' kinda green," she stated with slight concern, then laughed. "Oh, it's just nerves and after effects—you'll get used to 'em come the third or fourth time around."

Lorena swallowed hard and scratched the back of her neck.

"I need to be goin,'" she stated as she prepared to walk off, then decided against it when an idea came to mind. "Wait a minute... Marisa?"

¿"Sí?"

"I'm short a few bucks—could you hook me up?"

Marisol raised an eyebrow in curiosity as she wiped little Juan's mouth with a towel draped over her shoulder.

"Why—what are you buyin'? Ain't that enough groceries right there?"

Lorena sighed.

"Please, Marisa—it's important."

"How important?"

"Real important—my grandma needs some aspirin for her heart. I forgot about it at the market," Lorena lied.

"Okay, okay—if it's that serious," Marisol replied as she frowned and fished through her purse for her wallet.

After finding it, she attempted to get a few bills out with one hand.

"Here, hold Juanito for me," she finally said as she handed Lorena the baby.

Marisol counted out five dollars, then handed them to Lorena as she handed Juan back over.

After counting the money, Lorena frowned.

"Five bucks? I thought you and *mi abuela* were cool, Marisa."

Marisol paused and looked up at Lorena from where she was attempting to place her wallet back into her purse.

"How sick is your grandmother, girl?! Ain't five enough?"

"C'mon, Carvajal—just gimme about five more."

Marisol sighed and muttered some curses under her breath as she, once again, handed Juan over to Lorena.

"Alright, here it is—five more bucks. That gives you ten total. Anything else?" Marisol asked sarcastically.

"Nope—this will do just fine," Lorena replied as she returned Juan to his cousin for the last time.

"Good. How much aspirin does the woman need? God knows what you're really buyin'—you're gettin' awful shady, Selenez."

Lorena shook her head and smiled, then headed down the sidewalk with her cart for the market.

"Muchas gracias, Marisa."

As soon as she got home, Lorena set the groceries on the card table, then hurried to her room with a smaller sack in hand.

"Do you plan on helping me put these up, Lorena?" asked her grandmother sarcastically after the girl disappeared.

"I'm coming!" Lorena called into the living room as she took the contents out of the bag.

After placing three pregnancy test kits on the bed, she nodded with satisfaction and quickly stuffed them back into the bag when her grandmother began to call her again.

"Lorena, any day now!"

"Coming, Gram!"

Once Lorena had swiftly shoved the bag under a pile of clothes, she exited her room to the living room.

"What do you need me to do, again, Gram?"

Ms. Jordan sighed as she placed a can of spinach on the counter. "What do you think, Lorena—give me a hand!"

For two hours, Lorena and her grandmother prepared a succulent meal of spinach, macaroni and cheese, baked ham and rolls. Almost as soon as the meat came out of the oven, it had reached the hour when the third party was scheduled to arrive, and already Lorena was nervous. She was about to meet someone she hadn't seen in almost five years, and this someone just happened to be her own mother.

As the complete meal sat covered in foil on the card table (which had been dressed up with a tablecloth), Ms. Jordan told Lorena she could now get the rest she had been wanting all day—at least while they waited for her mother.

Lorena graciously accepted and announced she was going to nap for a while. But as the girl lay on her bed in the dark room, staring up at the ceiling, she realized that sleeping was the last activity she wanted to take part in. Her nerves had ruined her appetite for rest, so she decided to give her grandmother some company instead.

When Lorena silently entered the doorway of the living room, her grandmother took no notice of her appearance, as she was engrossed in a large book: an album, sitting on her lap as she slowly flipped through the pages.

"What are you up to, Gram?" Lorena finally asked.

Ms. Jordan looked up and smiled, then patted the sofa cushion beside her.

"Come see."

Lorena walked over and took a seat, then studied the photographs inside the album.

Most of the pictures were in black and white—dating back to the early sixties—and taken of a young girl of about five or six. Some were of the girl by herself, eating a lollipop or riding in a wagon, and others were of her with a young woman and young man.

"Who are they?" Lorena inquired when no recognition took place.

Ms. Jordan smiled.

"The two adults are your great-auntie and uncle. The little girl is your mother."

Lorena raised her eyebrows and cocked her head to the side.

"That's my mom? Where did you get these pictures from, Gram, if she wasn't living with you then?"

Ms. Jordan ran her finger along a picture before replying, a distant look in her eye.

"Well, you already know most of the story: I gave your mother up when I was eighteen, or so, and my older sister and her new husband offered to raise her. Your great-auntie Catt sent me pictures and letters about your mom all the time; I suppose she wanted me to catch a glimpse of her growing up as best I could.

"But I wasn't planning on getting pregnant—my boyfriend at the time and I were young, careless and easygoing. We never really considered what to do if a child entered the picture. And then, your mother was born." The woman paused and sighed, then turned to her granddaughter. "Don't get me wrong, Lorena, I loved your mother very much . . . but, I was pressured into doing a lot of things, and I didn't have the money or resources to take care of a baby, let alone make sure she was clothed and fed until she was grown.

"I just . . . didn't have any other choice. And despite the blessing amidst hard times your mother was, having a baby during that time in my life wasn't a good decision . . . and I suppose that's why I try to shelter you as much as I do. You see, there's lots of candy in life—out in the open and very easy to access. But eating sweets before dinner will spoil your appetite for the actual meal; do you see what I mean, Lorena?"

Lorena blinked several times, then turned away from her grandmother's gaze.

"Sure, Gram," she replied quietly, straining to hide the anxiety in her voice.

Ms. Jordan sighed lightly and smiled, giving her granddaughter a hug and placing a kiss on her cheek before rising from the sofa.

"Anyway, you can flip through it some more yourself," she stated as she handed Lorena the album. "I'm going to go wash up for dinner. You'd probably best do the same after you get through with that."

Lorena nodded as her grandmother exited the room.

Not long after closing the photo album, returning it to its shelf and changing her attire for dinner, Lorena heard a knock on the front door.

She remained where she was seated on her bed, and watched through the open doorway her grandmother hurrying down the hall to answer it.

Lorena could hear the reunion from her room, and knew she would be asked to join soon enough.

". . .she's here somewhere—Lorena, come out here!" called her grandmother's voice cheerily.

The teen sighed, pried herself off the bed, then headed out the door and into the living room, where her grandmother stood with her arm around someone else, a woman of thirty. The latter was of medium height, slightly taller than Lorena and looked nearly half-starved, giving her a delicate frame. She had long, dark hair pulled neatly back into a ponytail, a brown complexion with a hint of copper, and dark, almond-shaped eyes. The only factor giving away the woman's age was the darkness under her eyes, but without it she could have easily passed off as a college-age being. Despite the weariness of her countenance, her eyes held a serene glow which captivated one's attention.

Lorena hadn't seen her mother in nearly half a decade, and the solitary significant aspect she remembered of her was a hopeless aura she possessed—due to the many negative angles of her life. But as she looked upon her mother now, Lorena realized that the familiar haze of hopelessness that had once clouded her existence was now replaced with something else; something. . .different. It wasn't exactly that she was exuberant with happiness, but rather satisfied. . .with life. Strangely enough, Lorena had seen this aura before, in someone else.

When Elsa Jordan's eyes fell on her daughter, who had aged a good five years since the last time she had seen her, she beamed with joy and her eyes overflowed with tears.

Lorena, who had remained silent, suddenly felt extremely uncomfortable, as she never liked to watch people cry—whatever be the reason behind the tears.

"Let me look at you, 'Rena," Elsa finally managed to whisper, and Lorena obediently stepped forward.

After placing her hand on her daughter's cheek, Elsa eventually enveloped her in a warm hug, and Lorena finally smiled.

Elena Jordan looked on at the much-awaited reunion, tearing up quite a bit herself.

"Why don't we dig into this food before we drown this place in tears?" the grandmother proposed, and they soon sat down to dinner.

The remainder of the evening was spent in the living room, chatting about Lorena's school at one time, but eventually conversation turned to Elsa, and how life was treating her at the moment including while she was away.

She went on to explain some of her schedule at the prison, and a few of the hardships she endured.

Just when Lorena was beginning to think she had only dreamed of seeing the "new-and-improved" aura her mother possessed, Elsa's tone and countenance changed as she began another aspect of her story on a different note.

"As you know," the woman began, "there are people who come to visit prisons and correctional facilities, bringing messages of hope and peace—whether be it church groups, gospel singers, or choirs. Well, it was about four years ago—nearly a year since I arrived—that one of these groups came to speak to us.

"This group consisted of four people in their late twenties—two men and two women. Each one shared their personal testimony with us before singing a song—Christian music that sounded a lot like normal contemporary music only with different lyrics. And each person's story began with the fact that they were gang bangers—all of them." Here Elsa paused, rubbing her forehead with one hand. "Their stories were so . . .gripping. I mean, there I was, this gan banger, tough girl who had ended up in prison, and then here were these people who claimed to be a lot like me one day, but something had changed them.

"They had all grown up in Christian homes, but none of them really believed until later on in their lives—not until something drastic had taken place. Each person encountered a near-death experience, and afterwards believed that life wasn't in their hands and that they couldn't always get away with everything." Elsa's voice softened. "I guess that's what happened with me a few days after they spoke. You see, Mom, Lorena . . .I'm born again."

During the climax of the ex-gang member's speech, her eyes had brightened and her tone almost sounded completely different than the other two remembered it to sound—there was a peaceful edge; a burning excitement that sent shivers down Lorena's spine. At the present, the girl was sure there was something different about her mother, and that she hadn't only thought she had seen the change in her. Though to her grandmother (who went on to burst into tears) this was a good thing, Lorena felt almost afraid, and even more betrayed than she ever had before. Someone she couldn't even see or feel had stolen her mother away from her . . .again.

~ Chapter IV ~

"Do not withhold good from those to whom it is due, when it is in the power of your hand to do so. Do not say to your neighbor, 'Go, and come back, and tomorrow I will give it,' when you have it with you."

Proverbs 3:27-28
NCV

☦

The next day, Monday, arrived responsibly—taking its place as the least-appreciated day of the week. Wise students reluctantly rolled out of bed, while the irresponsible few were forced to be aroused by an oftentimes-annoyed parent. Office workers chugged their first of a long string of mugs of coffee, and persuaded themselves to slide into the car or bus for the dull, dreary commute to the job. Garbage attendants climbed into their tall, uninviting trucks, and prepared themselves for the dirty job of babysitting Chicago's waste. And lastly there were the teens—those who fit into none of these categories—who roamed the streets, meandering aimlessly with their friends or strutting dutifully to the footstep below death's threshold.

That particular day, Monday's preference for cynical sunshine wavered and eventually faded shortly after dawn, and instead a mass of formidable, oppressive clouds blanketed the sky. It was a day where a sense of oblivion and the temptation to soar into daydreamland permeated the air—and many took advantage of it. The dark, rolling and floating empires of ice crystals held another desire: to fall as hard and fast onto the earth as possible. This was their threat, and they held the gun loaded, poised and ready.

With her hair styled, makeup applied and attire of jeans, halter-top and leather jacket donned, the vice-chief gang leader exited the crowded stairwell into the parking lot, and then onto the sidewalk—her backpack slung rebelliously over one drooping shoulder.

It was almost five thirty, an hour Lorena could seldom be found headed to school. But she had a sane motive: getting out of her apartment before her mother and grandmother awoke. The former's speech the night before had half-scared the teen out of her senses, and the only thing she wanted was to avoid remembering the look in her mother's eyes when she told her story. For this reason, Lorena had gone to great lengths to wake up at half past four, setting her alarm clock and forcing herself to down a whole mug of her grandmother's off-brand coffee—and black, as they were out of both milk and sugar . . .again.

Feeling her stomach lurch, Lorena now stopped to take a seat at the nearest bus stop. At the present, the area was empty (as was the rest of the sidewalk) and the girl felt free to sigh heavily and place her head in her hands.

Lorena's head was now throbbing from the caffeine rush she was functioning on, and her early-morning allergies were taking their toll. Her eyes were burning as were her ears—something that only chanced to happen were she to run a fever—but the girl brushed it off, thinking her body was simply stating its disapproval for receiving only two hours of sleep. Two hours, because while the rest of the apartment's occupants slept soundly, Lorena was wide awake, her mind refusing to dwell on the task of falling asleep, but rather on her mother's conversion.

Now she had to suffer, and suffer she did. She couldn't remember ever feeling so terrible in all her life. Lorena felt as though she had been hit by a truck, and the driver was currently backing the vehicle up and accelerating over her defenseless body—repeating this action over and over.

But the world continued to turn, and Lorena coaxed herself to get up and walk to school.

The school day went by as one of the worst in history for the ailing teen. She spent much of her time throwing up, and twice she couldn't make it to the girl's room in time before vomiting in front of the whole tenth grade. After being found unconscious (by a concerned Candy) on the bathroom floor, Lorena was finally taken to the nurse, whose thermometer proved that she was running a high fever.

After suggesting that the girl be sent home immediately (and if things worsened, to the ER) the nurse placed a call to Lorena's grandmother, who said she would be right over.

Lorena, whose mind was wandering, feared her mother would be the one to pick her up. Seeing this as a most avoidable event, she made up her mind that she would leave before anyone could arrive to take her home. From there, she would find Marisol and instead have her friend take her over to her place—as Marisol was the only person she could trust at the present.

As Lorena lay on a small bed in a side room of the nurse's office, dealing with a sense of the room spinning, nausea and a splitting headache, she waited for the right moment to escape. After five minutes had passed, she realized that the nurse wasn't about to leave the office any time soon, and came up with an idea.

"Mrs. Fuentes?" Lorena called weakly through the open door separating the examining room and side room.

An elderly Hispanic woman soon appeared, dressed in a white nurse's uniform and strict, cat-eye glasses.

"Yes, Lorena?" she asked in a soft tone that was far from matching her rough exterior.

"I was wondering if I might please have a soda—for my stomach."

Mrs. Fuentes sighed as she glanced over her shoulder into the other room.

"I think I'm out of those right now."

Lorena pretended to look even wearier than she actually was.

"Oh . . .well, that's okay. I'll be alright," she replied quietly, feigning her desperate (though cleverly-disguised) need for a soda.

Mrs. Fuentes, being a God-fearing woman who would rather sell her right arm than watch a child suffer, relented in retrieving a soda from a machine in one of the hallways.

"I'll go get you one from a machine. Will you be alright by yourself for a few minutes?"

Lorena smiled gratefully.

"I'll be okay—thank you."

Mrs. Fuentes returned the smile, mechanically, then exited the office for the nearest drink machine (which Lorena knew for a fact was on the other side of the school—they were much too poor to afford more machines).

Lorena waited until the persistent "squish" of the orthopedic shoes was far away and eventually muted, then moved herself to a sitting position as fast as possible. This only caused her more pain and light-headedness, and she was forced to take a moment to recover.

After the world was almost right side up again, Lorena stood up and made her way to the nurse's front office. After checking to see that the hallway was empty, she made a left turn out of the office—intentionally opposite of Mrs. Fuentes's route. Once in the hallway, Lorena inched along toward the nearest exit, hoping she wouldn't meet a teacher or janitor along the way.

Finally, the teen reached an exit and cautiously stepped out into the unseasonably warm, city air. As her head began to throb harder, Lorena searched for the window of the twelfth grade history classroom. She moved along the school perimeter as quickly as her head and stomach permitted, then dropped gingerly to her knees—into a bed of soil—upon spotting the window.

Realizing that her next task was to get Marisol's attention, Lorena removed one of her silver thumb rings and—while keeping her body crouched below the window—began to tap a signature *Chiquitas Poderosas* distress code. Through the relatively-thin glass, the girl could hear the teacher's sleepy drone upgrade to a tone of curiosity and annoyance, and she immediately ceased tapping—hoping her friend had gotten the message.

Deciding to wait, Lorena slowly shifted her back to the brick, exterior wall of the school, leaning against it and taking slow deep breaths. A low rumble of thunder sounded in the distance, and she hoped she would be able to reach shelter before the rain was unleashed.

As soon as Lorena's patience had dissipated and she had made up her mind to give the signal once more, the sound of rustling gravel met her ears.

Before she could turn to see who was approaching, a sharp pain shot from her torso to her head, and Lorena dropped to one elbow—wrapping one arm around her stomach and the other around her head.

"Hey, *chica*, take it easy," Marisol stated as she knelt by her friend's side and placed her arm around her shoulders, careful to avoid the window. "Paulina told me you weren't feelin' well."

Lorena, whose mind was beginning to wander even more, looked around in slight confusion.

"Help me—help me to your car," she voiced quietly.

Marisol frowned.

"Let's get you to the nurse, okay, Lorena?" she replied as gently as possible as she started to help Lorena up.

"No," Lorena protested, remaining on the ground. "Please, help me to your car."

"Lorena," Marisol sighed, "I'm gonna take you to the nurse—"

¡"*Oyé, Marisa!*" interjected Lorena firmly. "I've already been there—she called my mother and she's coming to take me back home. But I don't want to go—I need you to take me to your place. You can go back to school once I get there—just don't make me go back home...not right—" Here she was interrupted by a sudden fit of violent coughing, and Marisol's concern grew. "Not right now," Lorena barely finished.

"Lorena—" Marisol began in a soft, out-of-character tone.

"Please, Marisa—*a tu hermana de CP*...I need your help."

Marisol seemed skeptical as she bit her lip for a moment, then finally sighed in defeat.

"Alright, *vamos*."

After helping the half-unconscious teen out of her car, Marisol assisted Lorena (who was now coughing again) up the steep, iron staircase leading to her top story apartment in one of the worst slums of the city.

They made their way down a dim, rotting hallway and Marisol finally withdrew a key from her purse to unlock a door. She soon opened it to reveal a room no bigger than a "fortunate" teenager's bedroom, with murky-green, peeling walls, pitifully gray, worn-to-threads carpeting with patches of concrete here and there (which made Lorena's home look fit for royalty), and a solitary, cigarette-smoke-clouded, dusty window across from the door—which itself was crumbling to pieces and ready to pop off the hinges. A very tattered and tiny cardboard box filled with Hamburger Helper and various other food substitutes sat in the far left corner, adjacent to a hotplate which was plugged into the wall. A rather unsightly, rust-ridden wash basin acted as the apartment's only existing sink, and the extra-mini refrigerator was similar to that of a hotel, only twice as archaic. Other than a sack of cutlery, plastic cups and plates, along with two beds holding dirty, raggedy, moth-eaten blanket-covered mattresses, the one-room apartment possessed yet another door; this one in worse condition than the first and slightly ajar to reveal the sardine-case-like bathroom—which held only the bare necessities: a termite-eaten, wooden toilet and a smoke-stained mirror.

Marisol lived by herself—with the exception of a roommate and boyfriend (who oftentimes visited for extended periods of time)—and had lived so since she was fifteen. She and her great-aunt far from got along, so the girl was kicked out to survive on her own; which didn't come as too much of a challenge for the gang leader.

Lorena, who had visited the apartment countless times in the past, was as used to the quarters as its occupants, and each time she walked through the door she felt as though her own apartment was a palace.

"I would have cleaned the place up a little had I known you were coming," Marisol stated as she kicked a stray sock from the middle of the floor. "You already know Angelina can be a real mess when she's sober—but don't worry, she probably won't get back in 'til sometime tomorrow morning—roarin' drunk and out of it."

Lorena didn't reply, but allowed herself to be aided to one of the beds, where she gratefully laid down.

"Do you want some water or somethin,' Lorena?" asked Marisol as she opened the refrigerator.

But Lorena merely shook her head, then began to shiver as she closed her eyes.

Marisol walked over and sat on the edge of the bed, then placed the back of her hand on Lorena's forehead and frowned.

"You're runnin' one heck of a fever, there, 'Rena—you sure you don't want me to get you to a doc,' or somethin'?"

Marisol's inquiry was met with silence.

Lorena had fallen fast asleep; her breathing slow and shallow.

"May I help you?"

"Yes, please. I received a call from here saying that my granddaughter had been rushed in for treatment—they wouldn't tell me what was wrong, though, and I—"

Elena Jordan's voice was suddenly stifled as she was unable to finish her sentence, due to the tears trailing down her cheeks and the lump in her throat.

"It's alright, Momma." Elsa comforted her mother quietly as she placed her arm around her trembling shoulders, then took a deep breath—attempting to control her own fears. "Her name is Lorena Selenez and we would like to see her."

The stern, middle-aged ER receptionist glanced up from a computer, her fingers hovering over the keyboard—ready to type.

"What is your relation to Ms. Selenez, please?" she asked calmly.

Elsa sighed impatiently.

"I'm her mother—Elsa Jordan—and this is her grandmother—Elena Jordan. Can we please see her or at least get some information on her condition?"

"One moment, please, ma'am," replied the clerk as she tapped rapidly onto the keyboard.

Elena dabbed at her eyes with a handkerchief, then sighed as the receptionist continued to type.

"The school nurse only said she had a fever—she didn't say anything about sending her to the hospital," the grandmother voiced quietly as she began to get a hold of herself.

"We'll get to the bottom of this—don't worry," Elsa consoled.

"Alright," the receptionist finally spoke up. "Ms. Selenez was brought in with a high fever. They held her in the ward to stabilize her breathing—which was very shallow—and she's currently on the fourth floor; patient's holding."

"Shallow breathing? Oh, Lord have mercy!" Elena cried before burying her face in her hands.

"Come on, Mom—I'm sure she's fine now," she stated comfortingly as she began to lead her mother away to the elevators. "Thank you for your help."

When Lorena awoke, she was enveloped in hugs and covered in kisses, amidst the hum of hospital machinery, "beep" of the EKG, and the one hundred recitations of "my poor baby" cried by her grandmother.

After greetings had been exchanged, explanations came next. Lorena, whose temperature had dropped to a degree which went more easily on her mind, lied in saying she had wandered out of the nurse's office and blacked out. Elena Jordan, who had it in her mind to march down to the school immediately and demand to speak with the woman running the nurse's office, was far from happy about the turn of events. And Elsa, who had recently proven herself able to keep a level head in times of peril, stated that it was probably "just a mistake"—though secretly she wanted to do the same as her mother.

Over the course of twenty-four hours, Lorena's temperature continued to drop, until the thermometers reached a healthier, more normal reading.

Elena wanted nothing more than to have her granddaughter home where she belonged, and waited impatiently for the doctor's release.

That night, while Lorena was still running a slight fever, Elsa had insisted her mother return to the apartment while she stayed with the girl—knowing the woman was tired and Lorena was obviously recovering. After a lot of coaxing, the grandmother was finally persuaded, and she left around ten o'clock that night.

While Lorena lay sleeping soundly, Elsa sat in a chair beside the bed, watching a game show on the muted television set.

Though the show was interesting and comical, Elsa's mind was thousands of miles away.

The receptionist's account of Lorena's arrival at the ER was lacking one crucial element—who had brought her there in the first place? She doubted it was the school's doing, as they would have tried to reach the apartment again or at least notify the hospital staff to inform a relative should they arrive with this question in mind. Not surprisingly, this led her to question her daughter's explanation. If she really had blacked out on the school grounds, surely someone would have found her and called 911—but apparently, this wasn't the case.

Elsa sighed when she realized the show's credits were now rolling by, and switched the set off with a remote.

After sitting in silence while staring at the far wall, she now turned to Lorena, who remained dozing.

Gently, so as not to wake her, Elsa removed a few stray strands of hair from her daughter's forehead. Being in a hospital room reminded her of the day Lorena was born—the last time either of them had been in one. She remembered the fear she felt when on her way to the hospital and her joy after she was born. She could see it in her mind as clearly as though it had occurred only yesterday, especially her daughter's face peering curiously up into hers for the first time—her eyes filled with the trust of a helpless being having reached safety.

Those days had long since passed, and despite her knowledge of the infamous crime it was to millions of teens, she wanted them back; or at least, she wanted the ambience they shared at that sacred moment in time. She had missed too much for time to make up, and each day she spent imprisoned by both man and God's judgment was torture, as each day her thoughts were spent on Lorena. She couldn't return to the past in order to change her decisions, but instead was forced to make all upcoming decisions twice as wise as those of a saint.

Before the impatiently-raging tears could be unbridled, Elsa cleared her throat and swallowed, shifting her thoughts to the locket around Lorena's neck. Upon seeing it, she smiled, a sense of gladness greeting her as she realized that the teen held it in high esteem.

Elsa had taken Lorena's hand into hers when she noticed another bracelet—beside the hospital band—around her wrist. This one was made of a suede and leather string with multi-colored beads lining a section—an article of jewelry far from unfamiliar to the ex-gang member. Elsa knew it should come as no surprise that her daughter was involved in a gang, but it was the fact that her status, manifested through the bracelet, was vice-chief that caused her great worry. Elsa herself had only reached third-in-command, and knew that her own former status was dangerous in and of itself.

As soon as she had made up her mind to speak to Lorena about it, there came a light knock on the door and it opened. A middle-aged man with graying hair at the temples—wearing large, black glasses and a white coat—stood in the doorway, holding a paper-filled clipboard in one hand.

"Ms. Jordan?"

"Yes?" replied Elsa.

"I'm Dr. French," the doctor said quietly in a professional tone while walking forward and extending his hand.

"Nice to meet you," Elsa stated as she rose and accepted the handshake.

"Likewise. I've been your daughter's physician during her stay here—including her visit to the ER, and I thought I might brief you on some discoveries we made through various test results."

Elsa swallowed and nodded stiffly, then sighed somewhat shakily.

"Perhaps we'd best discuss this outside," Dr. French suggested, then led the woman outside into the quiet hallway, leaving the door slightly ajar.

"Doctor, I would appreciate if you told me quickly if something is wrong," stated Elsa slowly while rubbing the back of her neck.

"I would, Ms. Jordan, if it were a matter of there being a problem. But rather we're faced with, well, an occurrence. After running the appropriate tests on your daughter as part of the necessary procedure matching her symptoms, it turns out that she is, in fact, pregnant."

Before Elsa knew it, she had drawn in her breath, though she had been holding it, and swallowed at the same time.

"Dear God . . ." she mumbled while closing her eyes and rubbing her forehead. "I never really . . .I mean, it's just not going to be . . ."

"I know that this news must be a little hard to take—though a new life is always to be welcomed should the instance arise."

"How many—how many—"

"Only a few days," the doctor answered the incomplete, yet predictable question. "The primary symptoms showed up a little early in her case. I'm also not going to be very quick to doubt slight exhaustion, dehydration and a little malnutrition."

Elsa sighed as the doctor continued.

"Ms. Jordan, is there any chance your daughter is involved in a gang—perhaps an abusive relationship? The tests results showed virtually no signs of drug use, though."

"I guess that's the one thing she wouldn't lower herself to," Elsa replied quietly while shaking her head slowly, the sudden news still taking its time to register. "I'm pretty sure she's involved with a gang—as for the relationship, I honestly don't know whether or not it's abusive, though obviously there is one." Here she paused, and Dr. French remained silent. "Doctor, you have to understand that a baby right now would . . .would make things harder. I myself had Lorena at the same age—fifteen—and it wasn't easy for me, as I was involved in a gang as well. It just makes things difficult, adding to all of the other obstacles confronting teenagers."

Dr. French sighed.

"It's not the first case of its kind and certainly not the last. It almost seems as though I see them more often these days." He shrugged his shoulders slightly in conclusion—almost sympathetically. "I hope things go well for both you and your daughter."

It was a couple of days after Lorena's release from the hospital that she walked down the sidewalk with her mother, on her way to the nearest children's used-clothing store. Elena, who had recently received a slight—yet temporary—pay raise, had insisted part of the money go to the funding needed for clothes, bottles, and other necessities for the baby. She had sent the two shopping as soon as possible, as the woman knew for a fact that times were going to get much harder during the upcoming months and the supplies needed for the baby would have to be bought soon—her company's department was sure to lose money in the future, and the boss had foretold an expected drop in income.

The skies were mostly cloudy, the air muggy, and ambience tense. It was Wednesday, and Lorena had been allowed to miss school that day—due to a remaining sense of weakness.

As soon as the girl saw her grandmother again, she was first greeted with a lecture—which escalated into a screaming match—scolded some more, then very awkwardly prayed over, wept about, hugged and kissed upon, and finally given an earlier curfew of nine o'clock and sent to her room.

Lorena—who upon herself hearing of the turn of events wasn't as surprised as her mother and grandmother—was twice as scared.

It was as if the news was old, though; as if she was already aware. The turn in the road was either coming or it wasn't, and Lorena gained a strong sense of the knowledge that it was—long before anyone else. As a matter of fact, she could almost see it coming before even meeting Cobra. As vice-chief, the pressure to be like "everyone else" was even stronger on the girl, as she was now being watched and even imitated. Lorena had known that someday she would meet a guy and the pressure would suffocate her into surrender, or if not that, he himself would. Some girls pretended to be tough and live oblivious to the possibilities, while others simply pretended not to care about whatever was done to them, and whether or not it happened. Though each girl could pretend as much as she pleased, the shadows continued to lurk. To Lorena, it was a curse from which she didn't see any escape. And to each pretender, whether it existed in their subconscious or conscious mind, it was simply a bitter fate.

As these thoughts traveled through Lorena's mind, she suddenly was reminded of the presence of her mother, when a question was thrown to her.

"Is this the place you told me about?" Elsa asked as they stopped outside of a run-down, barred-up, brick building on a strip mall next to a liquor store.

Lorena nodded silently, and was about to follow through the open door after her mother when a particular face on the opposite sidewalk caught her attention.

Elsa, pausing when she caught her daughter's averted stare, sighed.

"You coming, Lorena?"

Feeling a sudden burst of anger rising inside of her, Lorena grimaced and clenched her fists.

There stood the one aspect she hadn't yet considered; the reason why she couldn't have hid the truth a little longer . . .

"In a minute—you go on in." With that—before Elsa could stop her—the girl had crossed the street.

Marisol Carvajal, standing with a tall, handsome Hispanic guy—covered in battle scars—(her boyfriend) was suddenly roughly turned around to face an angry Lorena Selenez.

"What's the idea of leavin' me hangin' like that, eh, Carvajal?" stated Lorena swiftly.

Marisol, taken slightly off guard, frowned in confusion more than annoyance.

"What are you talkin' about, Selenez—and why are you stressin' me?"

"That hospital joint you tried on me the other day—I thought I told you to leave me at your place. I guess you didn't think that takin' me to a doctor would bring my family into this!" Lorena spat, shoving the other while the boyfriend backed off from the catfight.

"What?! I saved your butt, Selenez!" Marisol shoved right back, before rattling half of her next sentence off in Spanish. "Right about now you should be thankin' me that your sick tail wasn't left to die in the dirt outside of school!"

"Hey, if you wanna start somethin' we can continue this later," Lorena challenged heatedly.

"Yeah, I do! Clancy's lot, knives—"

"Fists—straight up ol'-fashioned, jitterbug style!"

"Alright then. When and what time?"

Lorena briefly pondered over this aspect, then frowned—trying to think of a night when both her grandmother and mother would be out. After remembering the church prayer meeting scheduled for that night, Lorena decided she would fake feeling sick in order to make the appointment.

"Tonight—six o'clock sharp."

"I'll be there," replied Marisol coldly.

Rather reluctantly, the two quickly shook on it, then turned to go their separate ways—Lorena with a bad attitude and Marisol the same, along with a confused and high boyfriend.

The crowd, which had gathered due to the popularity of the two leaders, soon dispersed and continued on with their activities.

Elsa, who had witnessed the whole thing from the storefront doorway—yet hadn't comprehended any of the inaudible words—knew that she had just laid eyes on one of the gang members, and judging by the interaction and body language, undoubtedly the chief.

"Lorena," she stated directly as she grabbed the girl's arm upon her reaching the other sidewalk, "what was that all about?"

"Just a discussion with someone who got on my nerves," Lorena replied shortly, beginning to regain her composure as they entered the store.

Elsa smirked.

"Well, it was a discussion like that which led to a fight which later led to my getting thrown into jail." She paused and sighed. "I would have come over to break it up had those cars not decided to drag across the street."

"Well, jail's not my living preference right now. Hey, look at these little shoes—aren't they cute?"

Later that evening, after the shopping had been completed, Elsa and Lorena returned home to find Elena sitting at the table, sorting through a pile of business papers—her reading glasses propped on her nose.

Elena, who was known never to remain angry at anyone for long, greeted daughter and granddaughter with a warm hug, then asked Lorena if she was hungry—completely in her "grandmotherly" way.

Lorena, who politely refused (despite the rumbling of her stomach), instead announced she was going to take a nap and left for her room, closing the door behind her.

Beginning to put some dinner on, Elsa soon struck up a conversation with her mother.

As Lorena lay quietly on her bed in the darkness of the room, while distantly staring out the window into the clouded sunset, her ears naturally began to tune in to the voices humming softly from the living room.

"...I just hope she's going to be able to adjust to this change. It won't be easy from now on," sounded her mother's calm, slow murmur. "And somehow I feel as though I could have prevented..."

"Don't blame yourself, Elsa," interjected Elena's slightly-deeper and obviously-aged, though almost matching, tone. "These things happen and I'm afraid we can't dwell on the 'what ifs' and 'why didn'ts.' Right now the girl needs stability."

"Which reminds me," began Elsa, "of something that happened today—while we were shopping."

Lorena's ears immediately opened and her senses instinctively sharpened.

"We were about to step inside a clothing store, when Lorena suddenly stopped and..."

Lorena frowned in disappointment when her mother's voice suddenly faded, almost uncertainly.

"Go on—she was exhausted. I'm sure she's asleep by now," reassured her grandmother with certainty.

Through a wall and door, Lorena could feel her mother's smile of relief.

"Well," Elsa continued, "she stopped when she saw someone across the street, then left to head over there. The next thing I know she's arguing with a tough girl that looked to be in her early twenties—and obviously not the kind of person she should be hanging around," she concluded, deciding not to inform her mother of her suspicion of the girl's identity being a gang chief—Lorena's gang chief.

It was official: Lorena owed Marisol an apology. . . someday.

At this point, she had begun to feel sick with contempt. Her mother's words couldn't have spawned a greater feeling of defiance and a distinct want—no, need—to adhere to defensiveness and basically never allow herself to trust the being who bore her ever again . . .if she had ever even dared to try doing so in the past.

Barely half an hour later (after the conversation changed to other subjects and eventually ended), Lorena emerged from her room, pretending to look as though she had gotten some sleep, and asked if she might go sit on the old Jacob's roof—a vacant apartment about a block away which provided a particularly extravagant view of the sunset (as well as being one of Lorena's favorite spots).

After receiving consent, Lorena set off, wanting nothing more than to be alone.

Elena, before letting the girl go, had informed her that she didn't have to attend the prayer meeting that night if she didn't want to, but she should expect both her and her mother gone when she returned.

Lorena, of course, declined, and left the apartment with the thought of the scheduled duel fresh in her mind. She didn't really want to battle her long-time friend—not because she was afraid to, but simply because she didn't want to—and had begun to feel a sense of regret for her actions and words committed and stated earlier. Marisol had always been there for her, and had always understood each family crisis and dilemma Lorena encountered; each time in a way no one else did. And Lorena knew that her friend was only trying to help when she had taken her to the hospital.

Feeling as though she existed to be the scum of the world, Lorena sluggishly took her seat on an old air duct sitting on the roof of the slightly rundown building.

Lately she felt as though she had been harboring dual personalities; leading a double life—and it was beginning to take its toll. She hadn't once given thought to a child arriving, and as the realization occurred that she was soon to be a mother, Lorena felt the world spin and her heart leap. She didn't honestly know whether or not she felt ready, but was certain that she felt afraid. There weren't many things that could actually scare the teen, but this realistic and crucial element had obviously joined the short list.

She hadn't yet formally socialized with anyone outside of her family, and wondered what her friends would think about the child; what Marisol and Cobra would think. Lorena was almost certain they would want her to abort it, and even though it was wise to them, she knew she couldn't and wouldn't bring herself to actually do it. Even adoption was out of the picture for the teen.

There was something that had been tugging at Lorena's morals for as long as she could remember, and it was a feeling of wanting to prove something to her mother; to show her that if she wanted to abort her child, she would, and if she didn't, she wouldn't. Lorena wanted her mother to witness her independence and ability to make her own decisions, almost as a way to silently escape the actions made against her in her past. The case stood that Lorena didn't want to leave her child, simply because she herself had been abandoned in a sense. If she had to endure the worse torture from friends she wouldn't slip and fall. Lorena was a natural-born fighter, in many more ways than one.

Just as she was beginning to let her thoughts wander and eyes actually focus on the cloudy sunset, footsteps on the iron ladder came as an interruption.

Soon her mother appeared, looking slightly winded from the climb, and joined her on the air duct.

"Your grandmother gave me directions to this place, but I couldn't miss your lonely frame huddled not far from the apartment."

Lorena shrugged her reply, wanting to do anything but start a conversation.

"This view is nice—you have good taste," Elsa complimented, but the recipient's eyes remained focused straight ahead and face unmoved.

The woman sighed, then patted her knees while looking around.

"I've noticed you still wear your locket. You really like it, don't you?"

Lorena ran her tongue along her teeth before shortly replying, "Yes." She paused to smooth a seam on her jeans. "As much as anyone would an item given them by a stranger."

"Lorena—"

"I don't wanna talk about it."

This time, Elsa shrugged.

"Alright then," she stated in conclusion, swiftly changing subject. "Let's talk about that encounter you had earlier—"

"Mom," Lorena began, the title sounding unfamiliar and strange coming out of her own mouth, "I really don't want to talk right now," she repeated quietly, but firmly before clenching her jaw.

"She was your gang chief, wasn't she?" Elsa pressed, ignoring the disguised plea.

Lorena rolled her eyes and sighed.

"Maybe."

"Those kinds of people aren't always the best influences to have, 'Rena."

Lorena, now certain of the fact that Marisol was the only living, breathing, sane person she knew, took back each and every ill word she had voiced about her.

"Do you actually expect me to take advice from you? 'Older women teach the younger women'—I've heard your people's teachings. I just don't apply them like Christians do—or don't, I should say. There are too many hypocrites around to argue the truth in your religion."

"That's the problem, Lorena—it's not a religion."

"Then what is it? Some sort of imaginary force that can cause normal people to join a cult? A voice, maybe, that can speak to your heart and make you drop that cigarette. Or perhaps it's a warm, gentle breeze that makes a certain teenage girl we all know decide not to have a freakin' baby because she knows good and well that she didn't want to take care of me!"

A long, tense silence followed Lorena's passionate speech.

Immediately she felt sick to her stomach again, cursing herself for placing a revealing image before a blind person without a heart with the desire to see.

"Is that what you want, Lorena? You wish you had never been born?" asked her mother softly, the pain in her voice manifested by a slight cracking.

Lorena looked away, not feeling the droplet traveling down her cheek until it had fallen and splashed onto her arm.

"Gram told me once that having a baby before you're ready is a bad decision—therefore making the baby cursed," she replied quietly.

"I'm sure she didn't mean it that way—"

"Then what did she mean? I'm obviously not a blessing," Lorena stated hopelessly, swallowing and holding her head up high, her intense eyes focusing on the distant, sunset-illuminated city skyline. "If I were, you wouldn't have had any reason to have betrayed me."

The clouds looming overhead, which had slyly matured into dark thunderclouds, suddenly began to pour heavy rain onto the earth below.

"We can finish this back at home—let's go," Elsa stated over the pounding rain as she rose.

But Lorena remained seated on the rooftop, hugging her knees to her chest and still gazing out at the city. Her face was motionless and expressionless as stone; her eyes cold as ice.

"I'm staying here."

"Lorena—"

The woman was cut off by her daughter's frigid glare.

Seeing that she wasn't about to budge, Elsa headed to the fire escape, then exited the roof, leaving Lorena sitting alone in the rain.

~ Chapter V ~

Pilate said, "I have Barabbas and Jesus. Which do you want me to set free for you?"
The people answered, "Barabbas."
Pilate asked, "So what should I do with Jesus, the one called the Christ?"
They all answered, "Crucify him!"
Pilate asked, "Why? What wrong has he done?"
But they shouted louder, "Crucify him!"
When Pilate saw that he could do nothing about this and that a riot was starting, he took some water and washed his hands in front of the crowd. Then he said, "I am not guilty of this man's death."
All the people answered, "We and our children will be responsible for his death."

Matthew 27:21-25
NCV

†

Lorena didn't have her duel with Marisol that night, and from that day forward her relationship with her mother dissipated into a pile of dust. As school let out upon summer's arrival, Lorena began to have less and less to do with the CPs, and didn't care that she hadn't breathed a word to Marisol since the afternoon encounter.

She was often struck with morning sickness, and was almost always found laid up in bed—feeling weakened and ill.

It was upon hearing of the recent death of a distant brother that Elena announced she would have to leave for a few days to attend the funeral—which was to be held in Alabama. Having only enough emergency funds to purchase one plane ticket, she left by herself a few weeks before the fourth of July. Thus, Lorena was left alone to live with her mother, and to her this was no bed of roses. When they seldom spoke it was short and to the point. Other times, if one aggravated the other, an argument broke out.

During the week since her return from the hospital, many of Lorena's friends had stopped by to visit, their reactions to the news usually being that of excitement; that is, the reactions of those not involved in the gang. Several of the members had paid their vice-chief a social call, and during it strongly advised that she aborted the child, in order that she may be able to stick with the gang. Lorena had ignored them, simply telling them that she had heard too many bad things about abortions, including the procedure and physical and emotional pain involved. Also, there was money to consider—though Lorena hadn't yet spoken with him since before her hospital visit, she knew Cobra probably wouldn't want a child, yet wouldn't want to pay for an abortion either. Therefore matters were confusing at the present and were only scheduled to get worse.

Lorena, who was now about another a week into the pregnancy, lay in bed one evening, dealing with a strong headache.

Elsa was in the living room, reading (of all things) her Bible along with a spiritual book given her by Elena.

The apartment was silent and dull, until the atmosphere was suddenly interrupted by a knock on the door.

Lorena, listening only half-heartedly as her mother got up to answer it, reversed sides of the cold, wet cloth lying on her forehead. Her sinuses were beginning to bother her and she had started sniffling when her bedroom door slowly opened. Inside, it was dark, as Lorena couldn't put up with much light, and she had to squint in order to identify her visitor.

¿"Qué pasa?"

"Marisa!" Lorena voiced with more excitement than she had originally intended, and reached over to turn her lamp on to the dimmest setting.

In the doorway, after Marisol walked over and pulled up a chair to the bed, Lorena noticed her mother's silhouette leaving for the living room while closing the door slightly.

"What are you doin' here?" she asked as she propped herself up on a pillow, directing her attention to her friend.

"Usual stuff—you know I had to come see you. Isabelle's been spreadin' the rumor that you're laid up in bed with a kid and sick, so here I am."

"That's just like her to get it around town as fast as possible," Lorena replied conversationally.

"So how do you feel?" Marisol asked after a brief silence.

By light of the dim lamp's yellow tint, Lorena thought she could see a dark, black bruise formation around Marisol's left eye—the one not facing the light—and two, swollen mosquito-bite-looking bumps residing on her left arm.

"I'm alright," she replied, changing her mind at the last second to forsake verbalizing the truth. "You?"

Marisol shrugged.

"The usual."

Lorena nodded, focusing on a ball of lint on the blanket.

"I'm sorry," the two stated in unison.

They both laughed.

"What are you apologizing for?" asked Lorena.

"Stuff...that I said—you know."

"Why? I'm the one who got mad at you for savin' my butt."

Marisol chuckled.

"It's all good, 'Rena. I headed over to Clancy's lot that night, you know, and when you didn't show up I figured you probably weren't feelin' well."

"In a way," Lorena replied slowly.

"I was only gonna apologize when you came, anyway."

"You know I didn't wanna fight you, Marisa. I was just bein' a class-A jerk."

The two laughed, then moved on to a different subject.

"I know this is slowin' you down and all, so don't worry about makin' the meetings for now," Marisol offered.

Lorena smiled.

"*Gracias*, but not for good. I'll be right back in the action before you know it."

Marisol shook her head and grinned.

"Don't rush, *chica*. We don't need our vice-chief gettin' sick on us again."

They both laughed, and another silence fell.

"So . . .I'm guessin' you're not plannin' on keepin' it, eh?" asked Marisol.

Lorena sighed.

"Marisa, I don't have the money for—"

"So put it up for adoption," Marisol replied with a shrug. "Besides, there ain't no way Cobra would want another baby momma on his tail. The gang needs you, *chica*; who would you rather stick with—a kid or a group of friends you've known your whole life?"

Lorena rubbed the back of her neck and looked away, unable to answer her friend's inquiry.

The next morning, as Lorena got up to fix herself some toast, she found her mother sitting at the card table, reading the newspaper.

They shared merely a quick glance, and Lorena proceeded to prepare her toast.

As she waited for the slice of bread to pop up, she realized that Marisol didn't have to have seen her the previous night, and it was basically all thanks to her mother that she had. Lorena knew her mother wasn't fond of her friend, and wondered slightly as to why she had let her visit. She did owe her mother a thank you, and if there was one good thing the CPs taught her it was to give credit where credit was due.

"Um," Lorena began uncertainly, picking at the peeling countertop, "thanks...for—you know—um, letting my friend see me."

Elsa turned a page before replying a quiet and conclusive, "You're welcome."

Lorena, her self-inflicted, scum-of-the-world sense returning, sighed and rubbed the back of her neck.

A few seconds later, the toast popped up, giving the girl a start, and she quickly grabbed it and placed it onto a plate (un-buttered, as her stomach had turned on her completely).

After awkwardly walking past her stone-silent mother to the doorway of her bedroom, Lorena paused and turned, watching her read the paper.

"Um...I'm gonna go eat my toast...," she stated with a slight frown in confusion, "...in my room," she concluded skillfully (not quite).

Elsa looked up with a glance so deprived of expression that Lorena nearly shivered, then finally entered her room.

Once inside, she closed the door and threw the plate of toast onto the bed, kicking the bedpost while cursing under her breath.

Life was hard...too hard.

The next day, there came another visitor at the door, this time a girl not looking quite as "tough" as the first had (according to Elsa), and Lorena was allowed to leave for a bite of lunch at the local diner with Candy.

Elsa, who was reading a particularly interesting newspaper article concerning the rise in mission trips to foreign countries and the great need for evangelists, was soon interrupted by a sudden knock on the door.

Realizing that just barely half an hour had passed since Lorena left, she wondered who it could possibly be.

Through the peephole, Elsa saw an older teenager—a black guy, with an athletic, husky build—wearing blue jeans and a white t-shirt, and holding a bouquet of flowers, which, to Elsa, seemed to stick out like a rose amongst thorns.

Elsa, guessing (yet hoping against hope) he was an acquaintance of Lorena's, reluctantly and cautiously opened the door.

"Yes?"

He looked up suddenly from where he was kicking at a rock on the ground and instinctively stood up straighter.

"Is-is Lorena home?" he inquired as politely as possible.

Elsa shook her head, then glanced at the bouquet. Somehow she couldn't help but wonder if she was speaking to the baby's father. It wouldn't have been sane to doubt it.

"No, she left with a friend about a half hour ago," she stated shortly. "Would you like me to give her a message—maybe take those off your hands?"

The guy suddenly remembered the flowers he was carrying, and awkwardly held them out, feeling strangely inferior to the woman to whom he was speaking. Despite the difference in skin and hair color, he couldn't help but notice her obvious likeness to Lorena— mostly in the level, composed tone of voice; the pressing stare.

"Yeah, thank you," he replied in a tone much unlike his usual, then quickly strode off.

Elsa watched him go, and clasped the cross around her neck. Though he seemed polite and was clean cut, the impression she received from him wasn't a good one.

"Guess who's been asking about you."
"Who?"
"Guess!"

Lorena rolled her eyes, then frowned as she dipped a tater tot in a pile of ketchup on her plate.

Candy and Lorena's meals had just been served and they were now discussing school and other light subjects in a booth at the diner.

"I don't know, girl, tell me."

"Tony," Candy replied with as straight a face as she could manage, but soon enough began to snicker.

Lorena smiled slightly and shook her head. She hadn't given much thought to Tony, and now wondered how he had been doing lately.

"That's not even funny, Candice."

Candy's laughing ceased, and she playfully tossed her paper straw wrapper at Lorena.

"Hey, don't call me that—and what are you talkin' about? It is funny—but cute."

"Whatever," Lorena replied as she tossed it back. "What's he been up to these days?"

"You mean besides droolin' over you?"

Lorena rolled her eyes again and cast a casual glance behind her shoulder to hide her blushing.

"Just the usual: church, school, work, church, family, church—and did I mention 'church?'"

Lorena chuckled.

"You can't say he's not dedicated."

Candy smirked and took a sip of her soft drink.

"More like 'crazy.'"

Lorena frowned as she dug into her hamburger.

"Leave him alone, he's probably some kind of secret agent, or somethin.' I bet he could whupp us any day."

"Dream on, sista,'" Candy retorted. "But anyway, he sure is nice to look at," she added with a mischievous gleam in her eye.

Lorena didn't comment, but instead ate in silence, refusing to let her mind dwell on Tony any longer.

"So . . .I guess you're nervous," Candy stated after a pause.

Lorena adjusted her necklace and frowned.

"About what?"

"You know . . .the whole abortion thing. My mom had one recently, you know, and she said it was torture." Candy placed a stray strand of hair behind her ear. "You might wanna have Tony say a little prayer for ya' before you go through with it," she added with a laugh.

But Lorena wasn't laughing.

"Who said I was gettin' an abortion?"

"Everyone—Marisol more than anyone . . .and maybe Cobra, though I'm not sure about what he thinks—have you talked to him yet?"

"No, I haven't."

"Well you should." Candy looked thoughtful for a moment. "You know what? I was thinkin,' Cobra's not quite as hot as Tony."

Immediately Lorena stopped eating and sighed.

"Would you please stop talkin' about him?! Good Lord, sometimes I think you've got a thing for him."

"Lorena, I could have a thing for any guy that cute."

After exiting the diner where they had eaten lunch, Lorena and Candy slowly made their way down the sidewalk, discussing light subjects.

As they stopped to wait to cross the street, footsteps sounded behind them and one of the waiters from the diner approached. His name was Javier and was around eighteen, or so, and was a friend of theirs from school.

"Lorena, Cobra wants to see you," Javier stated.

Candy raised an eyebrow in amusement.

"Are you gonna talk to him?" she asked her friend.

Lorena shrugged slightly. She hadn't yet considered how to approach him regarding the situation at hand.

"I don't know . . .I guess so."

"He's waiting at the entrance when you're ready," Javier said, then glanced down at his watch. "I gotta get back to work. See ya,'" he added as he jogged off to the diner.

"Thanks, Javier," Lorena called, then sighed and made her way over there herself, leaving Candy standing in front of a magazine shop—pretending to look interested in the window selection.

When Lorena crossed the intersection leading to the diner, she found Cobra standing where Javier said he would be, with his hands stuffed into his pockets.

"Hey," he stated as he greeted her with a hug and kiss.

"Hey," replied Lorena with a smile.

"You and Candy already got somethin' to eat, right?"

Lorena nodded.

"She beat me to the punch," he said with a laugh. "You wanna go for a walk, then?"

"Uh," Lorena glanced in Candy's direction, signaling a question as to whether or not she could head out with Cobra. Candy smiled and shooed them off.

"Let's go," Lorena said with another smile, and the two strode slowly down the sidewalk, hand in hand.

After about a minute of walking in silence, Lorena decided to bring up the subject that both minds were focused on.

"So . . .um, I guess you already know . . ."

"Yeah—everyone does," Cobra replied shortly, his usual easygoing tone absent.

Lorena nodded slightly.

"How do you feel about it?" she asked slowly.

"Well, I understand you ain't been feelin' well and all, Lorena, but the kid's gotta go."

Lorena frowned in disappointment. She had expected his reaction to be this way, but wasn't as prepared for it as she thought she was.

"What?"

"I've got about five other kids—Lord knows how many more. I ain't gonna deal with another.

"That don't mean I can deal with an abortion."

"Heh, neither can I," Cobra smirked. "A brotha's gotta keep his hustle up for money, and I sure don't feel like jackin' God knows how much money for the procedure," he sighed. "Lorena, I've got over fifteen other babes who did take my advice to give a kid up—"

"Hold up," Lorena stated as she immediately stopped walking and grabbed Cobra's arm. "What did you just call me?"

"Yo what you talkin' 'bout, 'Rena?" he defended himself, swiftly brushing her arm away. "I didn't call you nothin.'"

"That's a lie—'fifteen other babes'—I know you ain't gonna stand up here, tell me how to deal with my own child and call me a babe!"

"What?! That little mongrel is as much mine as it is yours!"

"Oh, so now you wanna make some claims?!"

"That's right—I always have made claims. And you wanna know why, Lorena?" he asked, lowering his voice while he roughly took hold of her arm, his eyes burning angrily down into Lorena's. "It's because I own you."

Lorena gritted her teeth and attempted to free herself from his iron grip.

"Let go of me!"

"You better listen to me! You can fight, keep the kid, and even play like you strong enough to hustle these streets—but I'll always have a hold on you, Lorena, always."

With that, Cobra shoved her just hard enough for her to nearly lose her balance, then with one final acrid glare, calmly walked off down the sidewalk.

"Go on then—get outta' here!" Lorena screamed after him, then tore off in the opposite direction as hot tears flooded down her cheeks.

Summer continued, and because her side effects were beginning to bear down even harder as time passed by, Lorena spent most of the season at home. When school did return, she often missed days due to feeling under the weather, but was able to take her work home and dutifully accomplished it there. A principle of Lorena's was to stick to school as much as possible, and a dream of hers to attend college. She knew it was far-fetched—growing up in the ghetto without much money—and despite the upcoming busy days after the baby arrived, she still held a piece of that dream in her heart. Her dreams and aspirations were instilled in her by her grandmother, who fervently hoped that Lorena would be the first female in the family to reach the higher education college provided. Lorena had always been smart, and took quickly to learning, but somewhere around the pre-teen years she began to straddle the fence of education and peers. Her grades held up, and with more effort than would have been necessary (thanks to the gang), she somehow managed to remain at the top of her class.

It was now late February of 1984, a month where the world seemed to stand still as time moved more slowly. It wasn't the beginning of the school year or the end, and humankind felt a sense of boredom—despite the rush of their busy lives. While everyone else moved automatically, Lorena simply moved, though not very quickly. The baby was due in a month—a boy, as the doctors had discovered—and so many plans, doctor appointments, and visits from church members were being made that Lorena felt as though life was spinning while she did her best to maintain her grip. Being only a few months under sixteen, Lorena was still a young teenager, but with a baby due so soon she was forced to have to grow up a little faster; or at least pretend to do so as best she could. And for nine months and beyond, that's what she did.

In the late evening hours of the fifteenth of March, Lorena was rushed to the hospital, where two hours later, Nathan Antonio Selenez was born. Nathan, meaning "gift," was a name decided upon by Lorena, and as for the middle name, she had long since made up her mind that her son would have "Antonio" in his name, somewhere.

A few days later, Lorena and little Nathan were released from the hospital, and once again the tiny apartment was constantly filled with friends, distant relatives, and church members. After the post-pregnancy, "assist-the-mother" rituals had passed, Lorena began to feel the weight of caring for a child almost virtually on her own. Her grandmother's work hours changed to a less flexible time, her mother had recently gotten a full-time job at the local diner, and Cobra had somehow suddenly "disappeared" off the face of the planet.

Because dropping out of school was the last thing Lorena would do, every school day from seven o'clock to three thirty, Nathan was bussed off with his great-grandmother one day (in the secretary's office) and spent the next being entertained by Elsa and her fellow waitress friends during the lunch hours. This caused extra tension to arise between Lorena, her mother and grandmother, because Elena and Elsa didn't feel that this was the ideal way for a child to be brought up. Lorena, on the other hand, refused to drop out or put her son up for adoption, and when her mind was set, it was set.

Along with these obstacles, Lorena had altogether forsaken the gang, and it was usually one of the furthest things from her mind. When she got home from school, she had to feed Nathan, change his diaper, give him a bath and finally put him to bed. After that came homework, and Lorena always found herself doing it alone. Her love for her son was deep enough to cause her to drop the "average" teenager's life, thus she made the decision to inform Marisol of her resignation from the gang.

It was an unusually cool, late spring evening when Lorena made her way down the sidewalk to her friend's apartment, a sleeping three-month-old Nathan in her arms and baby-supply bag over one shoulder. Her mother and grandmother both had to work the night shift that evening, so Lorena was forced to take Nathan with her.

Deciding to take the inside stairwell, Lorena walked through the entrance to the lowly building, then climbed the staircase to the top floor. After heading down the dim, muggy hallway, she knocked on the farthest door on the left.

Inside she could hear a mumbled curse, then a muffled voice call in Spanish, "Come in!"

Slowly, Lorena opened the door, and the first thing she saw was drug paraphernalia. A few girls from the gang and a couple of guys were sitting on the floor, leaning up against the wall. Each teen's eyes were glazed, and smirks rested hysterically on their shining faces. Each pair of eyes shifted with languid gracefulness in her direction. None of them seemed to be actually looking at her, but rather into a dream world only an influenced mind could fathom.

Lorena, being so hypnotized by the deranged image of happiness in the eyes of her audience, failed to notice Marisol striding over to the bed holding the kits.

"Marisa . . .this is some tea party . . ." Lorena stated slowly in an awkward tone, deeply regretting bringing Nathan along with her, yet glad at the same time that he was asleep.

"Right on," Marisol replied shortly without casting a glance in her direction. She began to start the process when Lorena interjected, "Just a second," as she grabbed her hand, much to Marisol's disapproval.

"Get away from me!" Marisol shouted in annoyance, desperately shaking her hand free.

"Marisol, would you listen to me? You can't afford to get wasted like this! Maybe-maybe you don't have to do this—maybe this can hurt you."

"Yeah? That's just like you, Selenez—you always were afraid of H and anything else like it. Well guess what, this is the real—this is my god. You know where you and your religious *abuelita* and mamma can go!"

With that, Marisol took her trip to "paradise."

"Marisa!" Lorena yelled in frustration as the baby began to cry. "I-I don't need this anymore—I don't have to take this anymore!" she concluded as tears rolled down her cheeks and the bracelet around her wrist was torn off and thrown onto the floor.

Lorena rushed to the door and down the hall, but could still hear her former friend's voice calling after her—trembling and laughing hysterically from the drug, "The CPs don't need you either! Your god can't save you or any one of us!"

~ Chapter VI ~

"For we are to God the aroma of Christ among those who are being saved and those who are perishing. To the one we are the smell of death; to the other the fragrance of life . . ."

II Corinthians 2:15-16
NIV

†

Lorena hurried down the semi-crowded sidewalk with a very unhappy Nathan in her arms while pushing her way through idle bodies and relentless rain pouring from gray clouds overhead. Her emotions were all colliding inside of her, and she couldn't feel anything but confusion and agony. The confusion was due to her lack of understanding why Marisol's last statement seemed to cause her to hurt so much, and agony because of the realization that a chapter of her life was slowly closing, despite how hard she tried to keep it open. Something meaningful was taking place that she couldn't yet grasp; two forces were at war, and a battle was reaching its peak.

Blinded by rain, tears, and anguish, Lorena soon found herself standing in front of a diner.

Gripped by panic and desperation, Lorena for the first time felt an uncontrollable need to be with her mother. She couldn't fathom just what had gotten into her, but heeded her instincts nonetheless.

Knowing Elsa would be on the job inside of the diner, Lorena opened the door and stepped inside.

It didn't take the many faces staring her way for her to realize that she looked a complete wreck. Her hair hung lifelessly in her face, her mascara melted down her red cheeks, and her clothes were so soaked that they adhered to her violently trembling body.

Little Nathan's cries soon filled the building, and Lorena felt herself soaring into a state of overpowering shock.

Before she could get a hold of the moment, she was suddenly surrounded by people—her mother's fellow employees—people with whom she was familiar.

Nathan was quickly whisked away by a middle-aged woman wearing one of the signature striped uniforms, and as a loud clap of thunder sounded another employee led Lorena to an empty booth distanced from other curious customers.

"I-is my m-mom—" Lorena tried to ask through chattering teeth as someone came forward with a blanket to wrap around her shoulders.

"She's in back—I'll go get her," replied a young waitress, and Lorena was soon left alone.

The woman who had earlier taken Nathan was now pacing up and down the floor on the opposite side of the room, bouncing him up and down while trying to console him.

It was after a bright strike of lightning and another reverberation of thunder that the lights went out. Customers began to show unease as they shifted in their seats, and cooks along with waitresses instructed everyone to remain calm.

The eerie, blue tint of the outside world dimly lit the diner, and Lorena continued to shiver and wait for her mother.

A few seconds later, Elsa emerged from the back room, looked to where a waitress was pointing in Lorena's direction, then rushed over that way.

"Lorena, baby, what's wrong?" she asked worriedly as she knelt in front of her, taking Lorena's quivering hands in one of hers and placing the other on her cheek. "Your hands—they're as cold as ice!" she added, frowning in deep concern.

"I'm al-r-right," Lorena stuttered out a lie as her mother asked one of the waitresses to bring a cup of tea over.

"Let's sit over there instead. The wind is picking up," Elsa stated as she guided Lorena from the booth to a bench on a far wall.

Once they had relocated, Lorena wiped at her eyes as tears began to slide down her cheeks again.

"Tell me what's wrong, Lorena," Elsa repeated softly with concern as she gently removed the damp, stray strands of hair from her daughter's face.

Lorena swallowed, keeping her eyes focused in front of her.

"I . . .I'm lost . . ." she began slowly and quietly, her petrified lungs not providing much wind with which to voice her feelings. "I want to—I want to . . .come back, but . . ." Her voice caught as her throat swelled and tears cascaded down her cheeks. "I don't know how," she finished as she buried her face in her hands and began to sob.

Elsa took a deep breath as she held Lorena close, tears of sadness mixed with joy filling her eyes as well.

"You can learn how, you don't have to stay in that place. God doesn't want you to." She swallowed, then sighed. "I don't want you to, Lorena," she added quietly, and more prayerfully and hopefully than any statement she had ever voiced.

"But I'm afraid," Lorena voiced as she almost reluctantly pulled away from her mother—somehow as though she later recalled actually feeling a real and tangibly strong force giving her a tug that she failed to resist.

Elsa swallowed once again, feeling overwhelmed with the desire to be able to pull her daughter from darkness to light.

"You don't have to be, though, Lorena. Where you are right now is causing you to think that way—it's not from God."

Lorena's breaths came quickly and her pulse quickened at the mere mention of His name.

"Lorena—" Elsa began as she took Lorena's face in her hands, but was cut off when the teen shook her head and pushed her hands away.

"I don't want to get hurt!" Lorena heard herself shout as she stood up, and she suddenly found herself trembling even harder than before. "I don't want to get hurt!" she repeated louder, and the customers began to gasp and point.

Suddenly feeling possessed by a powerfully unyielding force, Lorena threw down the blanket and bolted for the kitchen, her eyes scanning the area for a knife (she no longer carried her own).

Before anyone could stop her, she had swiped a chef's knife from one of the counters, then rushed out the door into the hammering storm.

"Lorena!!" Elsa screamed as terror engulfed her and she tore after her daughter.

Chicago's usually-pleasant, breezy atmosphere had transformed into a whirlwind of cans, newspapers, beer bottles and other urban debris which soared through the air in upward, rotating motions. The sheets of rain shot horizontally against Elsa as she attempted to reach Lorena, who had disappeared some ten feet ahead. Visibility was no more than your hand stretched out in front of you, but Elsa continued on in desperation, until something hard hit the back of her head and blackness overcame.

Lorena was lost in a world not only of white sheets of rainwater and the boisterous howl of the wind, but also loud voices echoing harshly inside of her head.

"Use it, use it!" they shouted louder and louder, and soon Lorena could actually see dark figures surrounding her in a circle.

A black-and-red-striped snake slithered at her feet, and she soon collapsed under the pressure, the knife still gripped tightly in her hand.

"USE IT!" they shrieked in ethereal voices laced with the burning, unquenchable desire to drink of the wayward teen's blood and devour her flesh.

Holding her head so hard that she felt it might explode, Lorena gritted her teeth as her eyes rolled into the back of her head.

Finally with a scream of surrender, defeat and agony, she followed orders and thrust the knife into her chest.

"Elena, if there's any way we can help you or your family, just let us know."

"Thank you, Diana. I'll do that."

"See you on Wednesday."

Elena waved goodbye to her friend, Diana McCullough (the reverend's wife), then made her way down the front steps of the church with a sigh, taking her time, as she was weary.

She had spent the past five days literally at her daughter and granddaughter's bedsides in the hospital, staying with Lorena longer, as Elsa was released earlier. A piece of debris had knocked her out, and a few of her fellow employees from the diner had rescued her from the storm to call for an ambulance. Fortunately she had only received a minor concussion, therefore the doctors kept her overnight. As for Lorena, her condition was much worse. She was found unconscious and bleeding in the middle of the street shortly after stabbing herself, and was rushed to the emergency room. The doctors weren't expecting what they found, though. Lorena's wound proved to be that which one would think would prove to be fatal, yet when the doctors removed the knife and commenced operating with the notion that she wouldn't survive surgery, they were amazed to see that she made it through and even showed signs of improvement despite her great loss of blood. But what baffled and surprised the doctors most was the fact that the knife had stabbed relatively close to the girl's heart—had it been any closer than a centimeter she would have died instantly.

Though things were looking up for a short period, soon afterwards Lorena came down with pneumonia due to being wet for so long and exposed to surgery afterwards. The doctors informed Elena that they expected her granddaughter to pull through due to her youth and strength, but were also certain she would have permanent respiratory problems because of where the knife had punctured and the degree of the pneumonia.

Even without this aspect to weigh on the grandmother's mind, there was still the way Lorena had been stabbed. The doctors had told her it was attempted suicide, and then there was Elsa's painful side of the story to back it up. Elena knew the girl was depressed, but still wouldn't bring herself to think she would resort to this. The doctors suggested counseling, and more importantly that Lorena see a psychiatrist regularly from then on. It was even taken into consideration that if things worsened she should be sent off to a crisis home for troubled teens to stay for some time. But what the doctors and relatives didn't know was that things would, in fact, get worse before getting better.

Elena now slowly made her way to the bus stop, gathering her fare together to get to the hospital to visit Lorena.

A handsome young man, dressed in a dark suit and tie, was coming up the staircase, and stopped as she passed him.

"Excuse me, Ms. Jordan?" he asked politely.

Elena looked up.

"Yes?"

"My name is Tony, Antonio Farro, and I'm a friend of your granddaughter's."

Elena, her heart softening at the innocent politeness of the teen, smiled slightly and offered her hand.

"It's nice to meet you, Tony."

"It's nice to meet you too, ma'am," Tony replied as they shook. "I heard that Lorena was in the hospital and I was just wondering if she's okay."

Elena sighed.

"Well, she's holding on, and slowly getting better—so they say—but her breathing has been altered. The doctor says she'll have difficulties from now on."

Tony's face immediately fell, and he bit his lip.

"Oh," he replied quietly, then swallowed slowly.

A silence followed, and Elena wondered if she should tell him about the attempted suicide.

Before she could, though, Tony spoke up, "I guess things must be hard for you at home—if you need anything fixed or maybe food, my pop says I'm pretty handy at fixing things and my mom is a good cook—"

"Oh no, we're managing, Tony. Thank you very much for your offer, though."

"You're welcome."

Elena had begun to walk off upon seeing that the bus had arrived, when she stopped and turned around.

"Tony."

Tony looked up from where he was kicking at a rock, his hands stuffed shyly into his pockets.

"Yes, Ms. Jordan?"

"If you want to visit her, you can stop by in a couple of days—when she's a little more conscious, okay?"

Tony smiled.

"Okay."

Lorena glared at the large, red pill resting in the palm of her hand, then cast a pleading glance at the nurse holding a cup of water.

"Do I have to?" she finally asked in a dry tone.

"If you don't want to experience any more excruciating pain," replied the nurse with a shrug, "yes, you do."

Lorena sighed, popped the oversized pill into her mouth, and washed it down with the water provided. After downing it with slight difficulty, she slowly leaned her upper body back up against the pillows propped behind her, taking care not to cause her chest to hurt any more than it already was.

"That should help with the pain," the nurse said as she gathered up a half-empty tray of lunch sitting on a table near the bed and made her way to the door. "I'll see you in a few hours, Ms. Selenez."

Lorena watched her leave, then grabbed the remote to flick off the TV set. She was tired of watching the same shows over and over, and wanted to be released soon.

She began to carefully scratch at her collarbone, where the edge of the bandages reached (and caused her great irritation). She stopped when her lungs burned suddenly and grimaced when she felt a cough coming on.

"Oh God, no—" she stated in aggravation but was soon cut off as the coughing fit erupted and the torturous pain in her chest commenced.

When it finally ended, Lorena gripped the rail on the side of the bed as she tried to recover the air she had lost. After a few painful minutes, the burning gradually subsided and she closed her eyes, breathing slowly and carefully.

The silence of the room (occupied solely by the low "hum" of the oxygen machine she was hooked up to) caused her mind to wander, and soon enough she began to relax.

Lorena felt a slight sense of loneliness, despite the constant buzz of activity outside of her door, and wondered why none of her friends had come to visit her.

"I probably don't even have any anymore, not after leaving the gang I don't," she thought.

She was certain they hadn't shown up only because they were afraid. Afraid to see her, Lorena Selenez—notorious vice-chief of the most intimidating of female gangs—weak, bedridden, and unable to even scratch an itch without being sent into a fit of coughing.

Though she had been unconscious for most of the past few days, Lorena had still given thought to the experience that had ended her up in the hospital. It seemed as though it were only a dream, and she found herself feeling a slight sense of anxiety when she thought about it. She recalled the lack of control she felt over the situation, and the feeling that she wasn't alone when it happened—not that she hadn't yet acknowledged the fact that she saw figures surrounding her at the time, as her memory hadn't been altered, but rather that she was realizing someone truly was ordering her around . . .and she was obeying them.

Before Lorena's mind could dwell on her enigma, the impertinence of the door opening interrupted her thoughts.

"Ms. Selenez, there's someone here to see you," came the voice of an elderly nurse standing in the doorway.

Lorena opened her eyes and frowned.

"Who is it?"

"A young ma—"

"I don't want to see him," Lorena interrupted, thinking right away that it must have been Cobra.

The nurse stared at her, then shrugged.

"Are you sure? He brought flowers, candy and a teddy bear."

Lorena looked at her in disbelief.

"Cobra?" she questioned under her breath, then added aloud, "What's his name?"

Momentarily the nurse peeked her head outside of the room, obviously holding a discussion.

"He says his name is 'Tonio," she said when she returned.

Immediately a smile lit Lorena's face, and she quickly consented to his entering.

The nurse exited and in walked Tony, carrying a flower basket arrangement of pink roses and cream tulips in one arm and a white polar bear plushie holding a small box of chocolate candies in the other.

" 'Tonio, you didn't have to bring all of this," Lorena stated as he handed her the bear and flowers.

"Of course I did," Tony replied as he pulled a chair up to the bed. "It's an Italian tradition."

Lorena looked at him skeptically.

Tony scratched the back of his neck and looked thoughtful for a moment.

"We-ell . . ." he began slowly, "it's this Italian's tradition," he finished with a lopsided grin.

Lorena laughed and shook her head.

"You are so-o crazy," she said with a sigh, then took hold of his hand, "but sweet to come and see me. Thank you," she added sincerely with a smile.

"Any time," Tony returned the smile and squeezed her hand.

"And not to mention these beautiful flowers," Lorena stated before smelling them, "—they smell absolutely wonderful."

Tony grinned.

"I'm glad you like them. They're as fresh as they come in the city, and the best of the pick—straight from my aunt's florist shop."

Lorena smiled lightly as she caressed a rose petal with her finger.

"You'll have to thank her for me," she said quietly, then set the flowers aside on the table nearest her before directing her attention to the bear. "He's very cute—I'll let Nathan keep him when I get out of here."

"Sounds like a good idea to me," Tony replied with a smile as he watched her smooth the bear's soft fur.

"So," Lorena began as she shifted her position slightly, "how have things been at the shop—you and Candy haven't been butting heads without me around to break things up, have you?"

Tony chuckled.

"No, things are busy—as usual—Mr. Elliot had to buy a new cash register because Candy broke the old one. It was ready to go anyway, though."

Lorena laughed.

"I hope she didn't get into too much trouble."

"Not too much—just extra cleaning duties, and you and I both know how much she loves that," Tony stated sarcastically.

Lorena smirked.

"Don't we, though?"

There came a pause, which ended when Lorena began to cough.

"Are you alright?" Tony asked when she finished.

"Yeah," she replied with a wave of her hand, "I'm fine."

Tony frowned slightly.

"That must be rough . . ."

"What does?"

"Having that cough and all."

Lorena smiled lightly.

"Oh, it's not that bad," she half-lied. "There are worse things."

Tony sighed and shrugged.

Lorena studied him for a moment, wondering if he knew that it was a suicide attempt that had ended her up where she was.

"You're good at taking pain," Tony commented, then smiled, "much better than I am."

Lorena chuckled.

"It only really hurts when I cough, or maybe a little when I laugh."

"So basically, I shouldn't make you laugh, right?"

She smiled.

"No, because laughter can cure people—haven't you heard?"

Tony shook his head with a laugh.

"I guess I'm a little behind."

"It's okay, though. You're a good doctor—better than these crazy ones walkin' the halls."

"Hey, my brother-in-law's a doctor!" Tony stated with pretend hurt.

Lorena glared at him.

"Doctors are O.K., I guess . . . except for when they start actin' creepy."

Tony appeared incredulous.

"Usually people can't stand needles . . . does that mean—"

"No," Lorena defended herself, "That doesn't mean that I can't stand them. I always figured that being afraid of a little piece of metal no thicker than string is ridiculous."

"I guess that means I'm ridiculous."

"Not you, too?! 'Tonio, don't tell me you're afraid of needles!"

Tony pretended to look ashamed.

"I'm sorry, Lorena. The truth is out," he replied dramatically.

Lorena began to laugh, then cough, and Tony scanned the room for a water pitcher.

When he found one, he brought it over and filled her cup.

"Thank you," she stated as she accepted the cup from him and took a sip.

"You're welcome," Tony replied as he resumed his seat. "Didn't I tell you that I shouldn't make you laugh, Lorena?"

Lorena set the cup down and rolled her eyes.

"Please don't worry about it, 'Tonio," she said with a small smile as she twisted the chain on her locket.

Tony watched her do so, then wondrously asked, "What's inside of it?"

Lorena frowned.

"Inside of what?"

"Your locket—I've always wondered."

Lorena became aware of her habit and glanced down at the locket.

"Oh," she voiced with a smile, then began to unclasp it. "Take a look," she said as she handed it to him.

Tony carefully opened the small, silver heart-shaped ornament, and studied the two pictures inside.

"Who are they?" he asked after a moment.

"One is definitely of my umpteenth great-grandmother—so my mom and gram say. They told me only one of them is her, but I don't really believe them. I mean, they're both wearing what looks to me like the same locket, and they look alike."

Tony contemplated. "So which one would you say is definitely your umpteenth great-grandmother?" he asked as he held the locket out to her.

Lorena frowned as she looked at the pictures, then placed her finger on one when she had made up her mind.

"When I was little—before it became my own and when my mom let me look at it—I thought maybe it was the lighter one, and I used to pretend that she was a Southern belle—like that girl from *Gone With The Wind*—and mostly because I wanted to brag that I was a descendant of riches. But now that I'm older I'm wantin' to say it's the other one—because she's darker and most of my ancestors were either black or Native American, until my mom broke the tradition with my dad, who's Hispanic."

"Okay, but how would you explain the obvious likeness between the two? And you can't rule out the fact that they both seem to be wearing the same locket."

Lorena shrugged.

"I don't know, I mean, I know that it wasn't really uncommon for races to mix in some way or form back then. If that's the case, then maybe they're mother and daughter, or half-sisters. Who knows?"

"You've got a mystery on your hands, then," Tony stated with a smile as he closed the locket and handed it back to her.

Lorena chuckled as she put the jewelry back on.

"In a way."

The two continued to talk for a few minutes more, until Tony announced that he had to leave for work.

It was a dull, cloudy and unwelcoming afternoon when Lorena made her way home from a counseling session at the local teen crisis center. Her mother and grandmother had to work all day that day and couldn't go with her, thus she was forced to take the bus home and back by herself.

When the bus came to a halt at the closest stop to her home that she could afford, Lorena alighted and began to walk the rest of the way, passing various shops and markets, drug houses, bars and adult bookstores. Not long after stabbing herself, her own knife was found by a very upset Elena Jordan, and confiscated until recently—when she realized that the teen would need some means of protection for her walks home.

Lorena had long since become deaf to the blatant, demanding sounds of the streets, and had learned when to tune them out and when to sharpen her senses and listen.

As she walked along, she decided to think about parts of her earlier conversation with one of the counselors. Lorena had recently found the woman to be quite funny and even entertaining—when she wasn't getting too far into her business. Every now and then the counselor would ask the girl a question that sounded like that which you would hear on a soap opera, or in one of those corny youth group sessions Lorena's grandmother had forced her to attend back in the day. Despite the similarity between the two, Lorena didn't feel that the crisis center was based on Christianity, as God wasn't ever mentioned. Instead they encouraged things like believing in yourself, restoring self-esteem, and finding power from within to change your ways. All of these factors seemed equally as unrealistic as Christianity to the teen, yet she had to admit that at least Christianity gave you an actual reason to make all of the achievements they demanded and hoped from the kids—despite whether or not she actually believed that God cared for her and could see her.

It had been a week since she was released from the hospital, and Lorena had only seen Candy and Tony since the incident. She had a feeling the gang would find her soon enough, and state how they felt about her actions to turn in her membership. She wasn't afraid, though, and didn't let her mind dwell on them very much.

Without the gang, Lorena felt almost as though she could breathe a little easier, and think a little harder. She no longer had anyone (around her age, that is) giving her orders, nor would she have to give anyone else orders anymore—except for when Nathan became older, in the form of telling him not to go near something dangerous or run into the street—rather than the command to kill the last person to annoy the gang or rob the candy store.

Lorena had gone a few more blocks when she realized she was located on the outskirts of the CP turf. Feeling a slight sense of unease, she began to shiver from the light breeze in the air and pulled her leather jacket closer around herself. It was now officially dark outside, as the sun had set.

It had been barely a month since she had last set foot in the neighborhood where the gang met and hung around, and Lorena soon found herself clutching the knife in her pocket as her eyes scanned the premises.

She kept walking, advancing to a brisk pace in order to pass through as quickly as possible, and felt like a sore thumb with a target on its back all the while.

Lorena could almost sense the crouched figures, leaning against the balcony wall of the tiny projects lining the streets on either side. Their pistols were loaded, senses sharpened, and knives drawn. They were waiting for the order to make their move—referring to a plan carefully and meticulously devised, as she had so many times in her past. But now it was her turn to be the victim . . .

"I've gotta stop thinkin' like this. The quicker I get outta' this neighborhood, the better."

Lorena passed a small market and liquor store, one the CPs had robbed countless times in the past, and ignored the hoots and whistles coming from drunkards laying in the front door.

She didn't, however, ignore the distant gunshots reverberating throughout the tense air.

At night, the CP turf was always quiet during evenings when the girls were about to rumble (fight) or hold someone up. It was dead silent that night, and empty—meaning something big was scheduled to take place.

Lorena thought she caught a figure hiding behind a trash receptacle on the other side of the street, and considered breaking into a run. Her hand, now covered in perspiration, gripped the knife more tightly, and she attempted to calm herself by clearing her thoughts and focusing on getting out of the neighborhood.

A loud, booming bass sound vibrated the earth beneath Lorena's feet, surging up into her chest. She could hear cackling sounding behind her in the distance, along with shouting, glass breaking and a car engine.

The headlights of an old Mustang inched forward, and Lorena turned around to see two guys hanging out of its windows, holding beer bottles high in the air.

The car suddenly shot forward, rushing by and far ahead, its loud, buzzing engine and rumbling bass echoing throughout the silent neighborhood.

But soon, and much to Lorena's disappointment, the car quickly did a U-turn in an intersection and now approached from the opposite direction.

The girl cursed under her breath as she watched it park on the other side of the street, slightly ahead of her, and one of the guys alighted, walking confidently her way.

Lorena, knowing from past experience that it would be foolish to make a run for it, decided to remain where she was (with her knife ready), and waited for him to arrive.

Because he was wearing a black hoodie, she couldn't identify him, and held her thumb ready on the switch to release the blade of her knife.

When he was around five feet away, he pulled his hood off and Lorena's stomach turned.

"Hey, baby."

"Oh, God," Lorena spat under her breath as she felt herself freeze.

Cobra smiled at her awkwardly, and he neared to give her a hug and kiss.

Lorena swiftly stepped to the side, realizing immediately that he was drunk and high.

Cobra frowned and rubbed his glazed eyes.

"What's wrong? Where you at, Lorena?"

"What do you want?" Lorena asked coldly, disgusted with him. "Why don't you go back to your crew?"

Cobra blinked several times and stared at her for a moment.

"I missed you, baby. Did you miss me?"

"Of course I did," Lorena said with pretend affection, then shoved him back when he started towards her once more. "You know where you can go."

At that moment, hoots and whistles sounded from the car Cobra had exited.

"Hey Cobra, if she won't take you, tell her I'm always available!" one guy shouted.

"What you talkin' 'bout, Carlos?! That chick's mine!"

Cobra bent over, picked a rock up off of the ground and threw it rather stupidly in the direction of the car—missing it poorly by a good twenty feet.

"Stupid niggas!" he yelled with a curse as they laughed maniacally at him.

Lorena had started back down the sidewalk when Cobra grabbed her arm.

"Come wit' me to my place, 'Rena—"

"Get away from me!" Lorena stated in annoyance as she shook her arm free and kept walking.

"Hey, I told you I owned you, didn't I? You'll be back soon, Lorena, you got that!?" Cobra called after her.

Lorena shook her head in disgust as she made her way down the sidewalk.

"Did you hear me, 'Rena?"

Lorena stopped dead in her tracks when she heard a sound that caused her heart to stop beating. The click of a loaded pistol sounded from behind, and she swallowed, turning around slowly to face him.

Cobra's arm was outstretched and in his hand was a silver pistol, aimed directly at her.

"Don't shoot her, man! She don't do us any good dead!" cackled one of the onlookers in the car.

Lorena, having been in similar situations many times before, took a deep breath and stood up straight.

"Put the gun down, Cobra—you ain't gonna shoot me," she said quietly, but firmly.

Cobra's clouded, confused eyes held a hateful gleam as an eerie smile lit his face.

"Why don't you go, Lorena?"

"You're drunk—shut up," she replied with a smirk, walking slowly towards him.

Cobra rubbed his eyes with his other hand, still holding the gun poised and ready.

"That's right, but I can't lose you if I've got a gun. Guns can kill people, Lorena."

"But what good am I if I'm dead?" Lorena returned calmly with a shrug, now within ten feet of him.

His hand began to quake when she was directly in front of him.

Lorena slowly reached her hand up to the pistol, and gently pushed it down towards the ground, then with a false smile she wrapped an arm around his neck and kissed him on the mouth, her other hand still holding the gun down.

"Buenas noches," she said as she drew away, holding back the urge to wipe her mouth and spit.

Lorena, confident that her life was now safe from danger, began once again to walk away, ignoring the hooting sounding from the audience.

After going a few yards she heard the car engine start and zoom back down the street, and when she turned to look over her shoulder, she saw that the sidewalk was empty.

With a shiver and sigh of relief, she spat into a patch of dirt and continued home.

~ Chapter VII ~

"Two are better than one, because they have a good return for their work: if one falls down, his friend can help him up. But pity the man who falls and has no one to help him up!... Though one may be overpowered, two can defend themselves. A cord of three strands is not quickly broken."

Ecclesiastes 4:9-10 & 12
NIV

†

The next day was Saturday, and after eating a small breakfast and feeding Nathan, Lorena sat on the floor of her room, helping him construct a block tower.

Nathan seemed more than occupied and happy with the task of completing a lopsided tower no taller than six inches, but Lorena's mind was miles away.

Of course, no one knew of her previous encounter, and despite the fact that telling her family about it was the last thing she would do, she still felt a slight sense of fear about the way things were going at the present.

Returning to her old turf—the place where she used to spend so much time and where she fought so many fights—brought back memories. Lorena remembered her initiation night, and how hard it was for her to keep from bawling like a baby in front of all of those intimidating individuals each time they pelted her with a blow. She remembered the first person she shot, near the market and liquor store.

Lorena almost couldn't believe those days were gone, but just the same found that she didn't want them back. It was fun to be wild, free, and able to do anything she wanted with friends, but at the same time she didn't miss the commitment, time and energy it required from her—nor the great amount of stress it caused. She still couldn't even walk down the street without having to glance over her shoulder every minute—just to be sure her ex-friends weren't stalking her—waiting to have their revenge.

Lorena remembered the night they had lit a building afire to kill another girl who had left the gang. They succeeded, and the teen never could erase the victim's mother's face from her mind, nor the tears streaming down her cheeks as the police held her back from the burning building her daughter was imprisoned inside. The screams of a tortured mother echoed in Lorena's ears at night when she couldn't sleep, and she had never been especially proud of that particular incident.

But there was something else to consider now: the fact that she could easily be next. Lorena never thought she herself would be the one they were after.

The girl started when she realized just how much she was daydreaming and with a sigh returned to the present.

Nathan had crawled over towards her bed and looked as though he wanted to climb onto it.

Lorena smiled and scooped him up as she plopped onto the bed, lying on her back while holding him up in the air.

The baby giggled and flailed his arms happily.

"Mommy doesn't want you to learn how to fly yet, Natty," Lorena said quietly as she sat him down on her stomach.

Nathan replied in baby talk, then reached for her locket.

"Do you like Mommy's locket?"

He began to giggle again, drooling while he did so, and Lorena rose to a sitting position while she wiped his mouth with a towel slung over her shoulder.

"You are a messy boy," Lorena stated as she shook her head, then smiled. "But I'm not any better," she added when she noticed the pile of blocks sitting in the middle of the floor.

After putting them away, Lorena sat leaning up against the bed while holding Nathan in her arms.

"After all of that playin' you must be tired, Natty."

A few minutes passed as Nathan started to fall asleep, and Lorena soon began to hum a lullaby.

After she was sure the baby was sound asleep, she stopped humming and yawned, realizing just how tired she herself was.

Suddenly her breath caught as a wave of pain shot through her chest, and Lorena gritted her teeth.

Fortunately Nathan hadn't been disturbed, and she breathed a silent sigh of relief when the pain subsided.

At that moment, her mother appeared in the half-open doorway, stirring a bowl of potato salad.

"Telephone for you," Elsa said quietly, noting the sleeping child.

"Who is it?" Lorena whispered.

"They wouldn't say," she replied with a shrug, then walked off.

Once again, Lorena sighed and stood up slowly, carrying the baby over to his crib. After gently putting him down to nap, she crossed the hallway, telling Elsa she would take the call in Elena's room (the only other room with a phone).

"Hello?" Lorena said into the receiver, and her mother hung up the other phone.

"It's Anita, Lorena, remember me?" came a harsh, yet feminine voice from the opposite line.

Lorena frowned slightly.

"Of course I do. What do you want?" she asked shortly.

"The chief would like to speak with you."

"So put her on the line," Lorena returned impatiently.

She sensed Anita smirking.

"In person."

"When?"

"Tonight—Clancy's lot."

Lorena rolled her tongue along her teeth and contemplated her reply.

Clancy's lot was located in the heart of the CP turf, and it was the place where all major inside fights and/or initiations were held; it was where her own initiation was held.

From across the hall, Lorena heard Nathan begin to cough and cry, and she watched her mother hurry over to his crib to pick him up and console him.

Feeling a sense of wanting to put an end to her problems with the gang once and for all, she replied firmly, "Tell Marisol I'll be there."

It was foggy and humid when Lorena made her way down the familiar sidewalks of her former turf much later that night. She had snuck out about an hour after she was sure her mother, grandmother and son were sound asleep, stopping by Candy's place for her pistol after giving her a call of notification.

Candy had sounded slightly skeptical at the idea of letting Lorena borrow her gun at a time when her friend was seemingly unstable (what with the suicide attempt) but consented when she heard it was to be used for gang business only.

As Lorena strode confidently down the intimidating streets of the CP territory, loaded gun on her belt and knife in her pocket, she felt as though she could conquer the world.

It wasn't until she climbed the chain-link fence of the abandoned lot that she felt a slight sense of anxiety.

It was said that before the lot was used as the CP's main hangout arena, it was owned by a notorious gang from the forties—which had long since died out. Stories stated that over a hundred murders, rapes and stabbings had been committed on the grounds over the years.

Clancy's lot was squeezed between two run-down, brick buildings, in which most of the CP members resided. A basketball goal without a net, with a rusty backboard sat hanging lopsided on one building, and tall grass and weeds sprouted from the crumbling, blood-stained asphalt.

The hollow black windows of the surrounding buildings stared eerily down on the teen, and seemed to be silently urging her to leave.

Seeing that she was alone, Lorena whistled the CP signal of arrival, and waited for her former gang-mates to show up.

Only a few seconds later, figures appeared—some jumping down from balconies, others casually striding out from behind a trash can.

Lorena couldn't help but marvel at how well the CPs could camouflage themselves into their surroundings.

Soon enough, she was surrounded by at least thirty girls, ranging from ages thirteen to seventeen—each one dressed to match their rank, and in CP apparel of black and pink.

Anita stepped forward, and Lorena noticed by light of a dim streetlight overhead that her clothes reflected the rank of vice-chief.

Lorena found herself smirking.

"Buenas tardes, Selenez," Anita said quietly with a smile.

"I'm lovin' the threads, *chica*," Lorena replied as she returned the smile accordingly.

"Are ya'? That's good."

"Yeah—I always thought you were meant to be a flunky."

Anita snickered at Lorena's remark, then gently patted her cheek with the back of her hand, her brass knuckles ice-cold on Lorena's skin.

"Keep smilin,' rookie," she stated quietly with one final pat, then blew on the brass knuckles and polished them with the collar of Lorena's leather jacket. "You'll need the enthusiasm."

"Selenez, I see you decided not to chicken out on me," came a voice from outside of the circle, and the girls parted to let Marisol through.

"You know I couldn't miss this for the world, Marisa," Lorena replied.

Marisol, dressed in tight black capris, an intentionally-tattered-and-slashed black tank that exposed her muscular stomach, and a pink scarf wrapped around her neck—along with other jewelry and piercings—strode up beside Anita and folded her arms over her chest.

"I've heard you've been feelin' a little down lately. I'm very sorry to hear that," Marisol stated with sarcasm.

Anita and the rest of the girls snickered, and Lorena merely smiled.

"Not down enough to not be able to fight as well as I have in the past. You yourself ranked me as the best of these ladies."

Marisol smirked.

"That was before we chose a new vice-chief."

"That doesn't change me."

"But it does change the way we run things around here." Marisol rested her elbow on Anita's shoulder. "You of all people should know what we do to the old—what's that saying again, 'Nita?"

"Out with the old and in with the new," Anita sneered.

"That's absolutely right," Marisol said authoritatively as she looked Lorena in the eye. "And now it's time to see if there is one better than you on these streets besides me, Lorena."

"Tell me the game," Lorena stated as she removed her leather jacket and tossed it to the side, revealing a white tank with the word "fighter" written across the front.

"Knives," replied Marisol, "and hand me that gun."

"I keep the gun," Lorena said quickly.

"We're not using—"

"I keep the gun."

Marisol and Lorena held a brief staring match, which ended when Marisol finally shrugged and walked off.

As Anita removed her jacket, Marisol placed her hand on her shoulder.

"Kill her," she muttered while glaring in Lorena's direction.

Anita nodded with a menacing smile, then quickly drew her knife.

Lorena did the same, and the two crouched while circling and keeping a trained eye on each other.

"I hear you already stabbed yourself not long ago, Selenez. This fight should be an easy one," Anita stated with a snicker before lunging.

Lorena quickly dodged.

"You think I'm not in shape," she replied, then swiftly lunged herself, "but you're wrong."

Lorena's knife shaved skin off of Anita's arm, and the new vice-chief soon returned the favor, only on both of Lorena's arms.

"Quit talkin' and kill her, 'Nita," Paulina shouted from the circle, and the others agreed.

"*Calma chicas*, these things take time," Marisol consoled her group.

Anita and Lorena were continuing to circle, when pain suddenly gripped Lorena's chest and she drew in her breath while collapsing to the ground—her knife sliding out of her hand.

With a shout Anita had lunged, but Lorena quickly reached up and took hold of the weapon before it could puncture her chest.

Struggling with pain and the task of keeping the knife only two inches from her skin, Lorena swallowed as drops of perspiration slid down her forehead.

"I thought you said you were in shape," Anita commented through gritted teeth as she tried to push the blade towards her opponent.

"I *am* in shape," Lorena grunted, then with the last of the strength she possessed, pushed the knife and Anita off of her.

Moving in a split-second time frame, Lorena quickly grasped her own knife and resumed a fighting stance before Anita could lunge again.

She held her chest with her other hand as she tried to restore her breathing.

"You seem a little winded, there, Selenez. We're only minutes into the fight," Marisol stated with a laugh.

Lorena ignored her and struggled to regain her composure, but she was gasping for air to no avail. She knew that if she didn't recover she would be stabbed, but also knew that she was tired and weak.

The other girls continued to cheer for Anita, who was continuously lunging at the disadvantaged Lorena. She could only dodge for so long, and soon enough found herself on her hands and knees, laboring to breathe normally.

Anita stood over her, a smirk on her face and weapon ready.

"I almost feel sorry for you, Selenez," she stated after shaking her head in pity, then raised her knife.

Before Anita could use it, police sirens echoed throughout the air, and each face held a look of anxiety.

Anita looked to Marisol for instructions as Lorena lay panting on the ground.

"Stick her and let's go!" Marisol commanded, and the group dispersed like a pack of scared mice.

Anita did as she was told, swiftly poking Lorena's shoulder with the knife, just deep enough to cause her to bleed a great deal, then quickly joined the rest of the group.

When all had left, Lorena felt her chest throb, as she was still wounded, and placed her hand over the fresh stab wound in her right shoulder.

The sirens were closing in, and she knew the police station was the last place for her to be at that moment.

Lorena grabbed her knife, returned it to her pocket, then awkwardly got to her feet—retrieving her jacket as well. Motivated solely by the desire not to be arrested, she clumsily climbed the chain-link fence and made her way as best she could along the shadows, not particularly knowing where she was headed. Her mind was clouding and the world was slowly going black; consciousness betrayed her as darkness prevailed.

¡*"Marisa, hay alguien vinienda a la puerta!"* ("Marisa, there's someone coming to the door!")

¿*"Quien es?"* ("Who is it?")

"Es un chico—Cobra, yo creo. ¿Debo dejarlo entrar?" ("It's a guy—Cobra, I think. Should I let him in?")

¡*"Si, arriba!"* ("Yes, hurry!")

The pre-teen girl quickly scurried from Marisol's presence, and down a ladder leading to the lower level of the warehouse.

Marisol leaned back in her reclining chair and set her feet (dressed in heavy boots) on a crate in front of her.

After fleeing the lot, the CPs had hurried to their warehouse, which they used as a storage building for drugs, weapons, or simply as a hideout when the police were on patrol.

Marisol, Anita, Paulina and Isabella (the four highest-ranking officials of the gang) sat reclining in their chairs, discussing the previous rumble and when to schedule the next one, over glasses of champagne and cigarettes.

"If Cobra gets in on this we're never gonna kill her," stated Isabella heatedly, obviously eager to get Lorena out of the picture.

"That's right—why are we lettin' him mess things up?" added Paulina as she got up from her seat and began to pace the floor.

"If he starts to interfere I'll kill him—no matter how hot anyone thinks he is," Anita voiced confidently, then drank the last of her champagne.

"Ladies, just calm down," Marisol offered her two cents before breathing a puff of smoke and picking up the champagne bottle to refill Anita's glass. "I know for a fact that we can use Cobra to help make Selenez's life miserable," she added before pouring herself some more alcohol.

"But I don't want to make her life miserable—I want to kill her," replied Anita, and Paulina and Isabella snickered. "You know, let her blood be on the heads of my descendants and all that good stuff."

Marisol smirked.

"Don't worry, I'm getting to that. But sometimes it's much more fun to feed 'em rat poison."

Isabella frowned.

"I don't know, Marisa, I just hope you really can make this work."

"Me, too," quipped Paulina. "I'm fed up with this Lorena chick."

Anita sighed, then finished her second glass of champagne.

"I'm sure Marisa knows what she's talking about."

At that moment, steps could be heard on the iron ladder, and Cobra soon appeared, dressed in black jeans and a white wifebeater.

"There you are," Marisol stated with a smile when he reached the top. "I'm glad you decided to pay us a visit."

Cobra walked in and took a seat in a chair Isabella provided.

"Yeah, I heard you all were up to somethin' and I decided to see what was goin' down."

"Anita here just had her first rumble with our former vice-chief."

Cobra scowled as he accepted a glass of champagne from Paulina.

"How did that go?"

Anita snorted as she stood up and walked over to a large window.

"She was weak—it wasn't no real fight," she muttered before swiftly turning around. "I thought you said I was gonna get my game time in, Marisa."

Marisol glared at Anita and exhaled another puff of smoke.

"Don't worry about it—you will."

"Not if this fool can't even last through a knife duel—what kind of fighter do you think I am!?"

"An obedient one. Now shut up and practice some etiquette—we have guests, remember?"

Anita gritted her teeth and pounded her brass knuckles into her palm.

"You just make sure he doesn't get in my way, eh, Carvajal?" she spat in a tone barely above a whisper, then stalked out of the room, glowering hard at Cobra.

He grinned, then laughed.

"She's got a temper on her hands."

Marisol beckoned Isabella and Paulina over, handing one a nunchuck and the other a pair of brass knuckles.

"Make sure I don't see that attitude from her again," she ordered quietly, and the two nodded with a smirk before leaving to do as they were told.

"She does have a temper—but it's nothing we can't fix," Marisol replied to Cobra's remark when they were alone.

"Selenez was the same way—young and stupid."

"Still is, too," he stated as he propped his feet up on the crate Marisol used, folding his hands over his stomach.

The two stared at each other for a moment, then smiled when a silent understanding was made.

"So what do you plan on doin' with her?" asked Cobra as he picked up a cigarette from a nearby coffee table; Marisol lit it for him.

"The usual—mess around with 'em just to show 'em who's boss, then knock 'em off. Though I'm startin' to worry about 'Nita—she's liable to ruin my fun and get it over with now."

Cobra nodded understandingly.

"And if she does you'll be lookin' for yet another vice-chief."

"Exactly," Marisol replied as she squashed her cigarette into an ash tray and lit another one. "And you happen to play a crucial role in this particular case."

"Do I now?" Cobra asked.

"Of course. You're the devoted boyfriend that would never hurt her in any way, shape or form," Marisol answered with obvious sarcasm, and they both laughed. "I need you to do anything and everything that you think would tear Selenez down."

Cobra smiled lopsidedly.

"Sounds easy enough."

"But that's not all," she stated as she got up and walked over to a table by the window, where a suitcase was located. "You'll be rewarded for your actions with these," she added as she returned with the suitcase, opening it up on the coffee table to reveal stacks of hundred dollar bills.

Cobra scowled as he studied the briefcase's contents.

"If it's not enough I can easily get more. This is about two-thousand right here."

"Two?" Cobra repeated as he began to scratch his chin.

Marisol sulked when she noticed he hadn't yet showed his satisfaction.

"Will you need more?"

He shook his head.

"No, this is fine," he began slowly, rubbing the back of his neck, "—it's just that the boys have been a little bored lately, and I'm sure they wouldn't mind some CP company every now and then."

Marisol smiled and nodded knowingly.

"Ah, I see. I'm thinkin' I can arrange for that," she replied as she sat down and crossed one leg over the other. As a matter of fact I'm sure that I can." She pressed a button on a small table by her chair, and a few seconds later the same girl who had announced Cobra's arrival appeared at the top of the ladder.

¿"Si, Marisa?"

¿"Maria, se dices a las chicas de catorce a diecisiete anos que se preparan que recibir las ordenes de la mia para que visitar a las amigos de Cobra, comprendes?"

Maria nodded and quickly left.

"That went completely over my head—what'd you tell her?" Cobra asked, and Marisol laughed.

"I just said to tell the girls to be ready for orders to meet with your friends."

He smiled.

"Perfect—now I can carry out the plan," Cobra stated as he rose, setting his drink down and putting his cigarette out.

Marisol walked him to the ladder, and he stopped and turned suddenly.

"I can do 'anything and everything' I want to her?" he asked as he raised his eyebrows.

"Anything and everything," she confirmed with a smile, then slyly wrapped her arms around his neck. "Just don't get your priorities out of order, *sí?*" she added quietly as Cobra smiled and they closed in.

The two shared a passionate kiss, and when they drew away Cobra replied, "*Sí.*"

When Lorena awoke, she found herself in pitch darkness and laying on a very uncomfortable, spring mattress bed. She blinked several times, trying to get her bearings before a wave of pain shot through her shoulder and into her chest.

Lorena cried out, gritting her teeth as she gripped the sheets.

Tenderly, so as not to cause her any extra pain, she reached up to touch the wound on her shoulder. She was surprised to find that it was bandaged (though poorly, from what she could feel) and frowned when her memory returned.

The last thing she could remember was staggering down the sidewalk, trying to escape from the police.

"Am I in jail?"

After a few moments of lying in silence, Lorena's eyes began to adjust to the darkness of the room, and she was soon able to distinguish that she was probably in an apartment, judging by the size of the room. A solitary window in what she guessed to be the kitchen provided the only dim lighting, and Lorena had to squint to see her hands in front of her.

She soon realized that the right side of her shirt was soaked in blood, and wondered where she was and who had bandaged her up.

"It must have only been a few hours ago that I fought Anita—the blood is still fresh, and so is this pain. I need to get out of here, wherever I am."

Lorena had just made up her mind to feel her way for the door and try to make it home or at least to Candy's, but was arrested in her actions when the sound of a door opening filled the room.

A tall figure, wearing a ball cap and leather jacket stood silhouetted against a very dimly-lit hallway.

Before she could brace herself, fear gripped Lorena's entire body and she swallowed.

Instinctively, she reached for her knife, only to find that it was gone.

Cursing, she searched for her gun—only to find that it was gone as well.

The figure entered, the door closed and the entire room was clouded with darkness once again.

Lorena couldn't remember feeling more afraid in her life as she sat helplessly listening for footsteps, breathing—anything to give her a clue as to where her visitor was.

But the only sounds heard in the tense, dry air were the heartbeats of the two individuals—one quicker than the other's.

After a full minute of listening and antagonizing waiting, Lorena finally decided to make a mad dash for the door. She remembered where it was located when she saw the figure open it, and felt that she could find it if she hurried and used her other senses.

Her plan, however, was thwarted when she attempted to shoot out of the bed, only to find that her ankle was tied to the bedpost.

Out of frustration she loudly spat a curse, but it was when an ice-cold hand clamped around her neck that she screamed out of terror.

~ Chapter VIII ~

"Then we will no longer be infants, tossed back and forth by the waves, and blown here and there by every wind of teaching and by the cunning and craftiness of men in their deceitful scheming."

Ephesians 4:14
NIV

†

Elsa helped her daughter through the door of their apartment, slowly guiding her towards the couch to sit down.

The mother headed for the kitchen to prepare a small meal for Lorena to eat in order to be able to take the pain medicine the doctor prescribed.

Elsa watched Lorena sitting there, hands folded in her lap while staring into space with a hopeless expression on her face.

"Do you want some water to drink, 'Rena?" she asked gently, hoping she could get the teen to at least look at her.

Lorena merely shook her head slowly, continuing to stare into oblivion.

Elsa sighed, and had begun to put a can of beans on the stove when the telephone rang.

She quickly made her way to Elena's room to answer it, leaving Lorena sitting in her shocked state.

"Hello?" the girl heard her mother answer from the living room. "Yes, this is she . . .oh, hello Reverend McCullough, how are you?. . . that's good . . .yes, that's right . . .well, it seems like God is testing us right now . . .mm hmm . . .yes, we are . . .no, but we're making plans to… yes, it's either that or something to help things get better. . . no, she couldn't recognize him—it was dark . . .that's right . . .some friends had found her—" here Elsa dropped her voice slightly, "—in a trash receptacle," she stated with difficulty, and Lorena heard her mother sniffling. "Yes . . .we already have Nathan, I guess we're not exactly hoping for another, but if it should happen we'll trust God to help us along . . .yes, thank you so much . . .God bless you."

Elsa hung up the phone and returned to the living room, carrying a tissue in one hand, using it to dab at her eyes.

"I'm making one of your old favorites, 'Rena: baked beans and macaroni and cheese," she stated cheerily, heading back to the kitchen.

It was around seven o'clock the next evening, and Lorena's family had been occupied with visiting doctors, social workers, private investigators and counselors.

The night before, the teen had been raped by an individual she couldn't even see, beaten unconscious, and eventually thrown into a trash can not far from Clancy's lot. Elsa and Elena were awakened in the middle of the night when the baby began to cry, and when they found Lorena absent, called the police. After being told that the teen would have had to have been missing for twenty-four hours or more before they could file a missing person's report, Elsa called all of the friends whose numbers Lorena had on file in her belongings. After consulting Candy and finding out that Lorena had left to rumble with the gang, she received the location of the turf and planned on setting out to bring her back home. Mr. Elliot—Candy's father—quickly offered to do it himself, and after reluctantly allowing Elena to persuade her not to go, Elsa allowed him to search for her daughter instead. About an hour later, Lorena's family received a phone call from Mr. Elliot, saying that he had found Lorena near the lot Candy described—beaten up and unconscious.

The girl was rushed to the ER to be treated and soon released with bandages, ice and medications. Lorena was only allowed to rest for a few hours for the rest of the early morning, then soon carted off to meet with social workers, private investigators who agreed to look into finding the assailant, and lastly the family doctor.

The escapades took up the whole day, and all four members of the small family were weary from the decision-making and turn of events.

At the present, Nathan was with Elena as she discussed future plans for the teen with a social worker at the local crisis center Lorena attended, and Lorena and Elsa were at home, trying to wind down from the day's events.

After all of the food was put on and could cook on its own, Elsa sighed and slowly walked over to sit beside Lorena on the couch.

"I know you must be tired, Lorena—we all are, but you more than anyone," she said gently as she placed her hands over hers.

Lorena slid a hand out from under her mother's, reaching up slowly to her black eye, which was swelling and very painful to the touch. Her face was badly beaten, and she had a broken rib. Adding to this, her healing time on her original stab wound had been extended, and her breathing was suffering even more than before.

"Do I have to eat? I'm not hungry," she stated quietly, wheezing as she spoke.

Elsa closed her eyes momentarily and swallowed back the lump forming in her throat.

"Yes, Lorena, you do. You have to take your medicine, remember?"

A silence followed, and Lorena's quiet, yet uneven breathing filled the air.

"I don't want any medicine . . .I would . . .I would rather hurt," Lorena said in a tone barely above a whisper as she ran quivering fingers over her wounded eye, wincing silently as a solitary tear slid down her cheek, landing on her mother's hand.

Slowly, wearily, Elsa rose and walked off for Elena's room, tears rolling down her own cheeks.

At that moment, the front door opened, and Elena walked in, carrying a sleeping Nathan and a bag of groceries.

"I see your mother's making you some food to eat," she said conversationally as she set the bag down on the table. "Where is she?"

Lorena pointed in the direction of her grandmother's room.

Elena frowned when she heard the sniffling sounding from her room, then handed Nathan to Lorena and left to console her daughter.

Lorena sat holding her sleeping son, gently smoothing his fine, brown, curly hair with one hand as her mother cried over her circumstance.

Six months had passed since the great turn of events unfolding before Lorena's eyes, and come the middle of December she was six months pregnant. Her condition wavered between fair and poor, but she still managed to keep up with a growing Nathan when the holiday season came up.

Elena and Lorena's first Christmas with Elsa in five years would have been a happy one, had it not been for a proposal that would send the family into yet another dark season of their lives.

It was the end of an overall good day after Thanksgiving, perhaps one of the best days of the year (which were scarce) when Elena, Elsa, Lorena and Nathan spent the evening talking, over warm mugs of apple cider and hot cocoa (Nathan being supervised with his bottle of milk) in the living room, sharing pleasant memories of past Christmases—including those of when Lorena herself was little and even those of Elsa at a young age.

There was laughter, reminiscing, and quality time spent that evening, and even Lorena had to admit that her spirits were raised. But it was only when Elsa spoke up about her plans that Lorena's heart sank.

"As you two know, I've been glad to be home for so long, and this Thanksgiving has been the best one I've had in years." Elsa began slowly as she wrapped her hands around her mug, smiling over at her mother, who sat beaming with a sleepy Nathan in a chair across from her, and then Lorena, who sat contentedly on the floor, leaning up against the couch where her mother sat. "I know we've been hit with some storms recently, and lately I've been feeling a call . . .to help other people who are struggling—like we are. These people deal with similar problems, but to a worse degree if you can imagine it. They don't have much food, live without enough money to be housed and fed properly, and are subject to diseases spreading quickly in their homes. These people are in Africa, and I've been reading about missionary trips that ordinary people like me take over there every once in a while, and I've been considering joining them someday." Elsa paused for a moment. "The call has been coming louder . . .so loud that I know that I have to leave as soon as I can, and I think that will be once the baby is born."

As soon as her mother mentioned the "people" being in Africa, Lorena felt a strong sense of disappointment, stronger than what she had thought herself capable of feeling in the situation at hand. Her mother was leaving her, and soon, apparently. There was something about this realization that caused Lorena to feel a familiar feeling of loss as well, as she had experienced something similar before.

Elena, having received this information for the first time herself, cleared her throat awkwardly.

"Well . . .it's like they say—the Lord works in mysterious ways. Obviously this is your call and I trust that you're making a good decision, Elsa. But I have to admit that we'll miss you quite a bit. How long do you plan on staying?"

Elsa sighed.

"I'm not sure, I'm guessing six months to a year—as long as it takes."

"How will you pay for the trip?"

"I've been consulting local churches in the area, and several have donated more than enough money to fund it."

Elena mustered up a smile.

"Well, they'll be getting a good missionary. I'll be praying for you on this."

Elsa smiled.

"Thank you, Momma," she replied, then turned to Lorena, whom she noticed hadn't yet said a word. Before saying something, she looked to Elena, a question in her eyes.

The other woman shrugged her shoulders slightly, then spoke up, "What do you think about all of this, Lorena? You seem awfully quiet."

Lorena swallowed hard before replying, refusing to let anyone know that she was on the brink of tears.

"Um . . .I think I need to be excused," she stated shortly before setting her mug down on the coffee table and swiftly exiting the room, taking care not to make eye contact with anyone.

When the door to Lorena's room closed, Elsa released a heavy sigh.

"I'll go see what's—" she began as she started to Lorena's room, but was cut off by Elena.

"I'll handle this one," she said as she handed Nathan off to his grandmother. "I'm pretty sure I know what's wrong."

"Alright, good luck," Elsa replied quietly as she watched Elena head for her daughter's room.

When Lorena heard a knock on her door soon after plopping onto her bed to have a good muffled cry, she quickly sat up and wiped her eyes with the sleeve of her shirt.

"Come in," she called through the door.

The door opened and Elena appeared, closing it behind her before slowly walking over to the bed and taking a seat beside the teen.

"Are you okay?" she asked softly.

Lorena nodded a lie, leaning forward on her elbows while rubbing her arms.

"I'm fine, Gram."

Elena nodded, watching Lorena closely.

"You know," she began as she leaned up against the bedpost, "I can remember stories I heard of you when you were a little girl, no older than two or three, and you, your mother and Grandma Rosalina used to attend church on Sundays. After service the ladies would want to play with your cheeks or pick you up to give you a hug, but you would always run to your mother for refuge—even if your grandma was within closer running distance." Elena shook her head and smiled. "It seemed to me that you would do anything to be with her."

Lorena swallowed again as she tried to focus on a ball of lint on her comforter.

Elena sighed.

"I know that you and your mom haven't exactly hit things off in the past year and a half, but . . ." She paused as she frowned, "I know that you're hurting from a wound that never really seemed to heal, Lorena, and I can see quite clearly that it bothers you . . ."

Lorena sniffed and wiped a tear from her cheek, trying with everything in her to keep from sobbing.

"But you know what else I can see?" Elena asked slowly, "I can see that you really haven't changed at all, Lorena. That little girl exists in everyone, and she exists in you. You love your mother very much, and it hurts you to see her leave."

Lorena had finally begun to cry, holding her head in her hands as her shoulders trembled.

"Please," she whispered beseechingly as she cried into her grandmother's shoulder, "talk her out of it, Gram."

Elena sighed as she held Lorena's quivering body.

"I can't interfere with God's plan, Lorena," she began softly, "but someday you'll understand all of this . . . I pray that you will."

It was in the early hours of the rainy morning of February 17 that Lorena was awakened from a restless sleep by sharp contractions.

She was taken to the maternity ward, where some painful eight hours later, Celeste Vanessa Selenez entered the world. The labor was hard and draining, but Lorena survived without any complications. Celeste, meaning "heavenly," was a personal favorite of Lorena's which she had decided to name her daughter many years back, and "Vanessa" was thought of by Elsa, who felt that the child was carried and born during a growing segment of Lorena's life, therefore they gave her a middle name meaning "butterfly."

Though Lorena had never actually told her mother and grandmother, she felt almost certain that she knew who Celeste's father was. When the baby came out, her eyes were a dark green, which soon decided to lighten into more of a mellow jade—ultimately with a bit of a familiar electricity to them. Even though it could easily have been a mere coincidence, the many aspects pointing towards Cobra caused Lorena to be sure of the father's identity.

She refused, however, to tell anyone, as life with the gang following her every move persuaded her to keep what she felt she needed to keep a secret, secret.

About a month following Celeste's birth, Elsa packed up her bags and boarded a plane that would take her to Africa, where thousands of needy people awaited the arrival of missionaries sent to help them.

Without her mother around, things were harder for Lorena and her two children. Elena's boss had refused to allow two screaming babies in the office at one time, therefore Lorena was forced to get a job in order to be able to afford a sitter to watch Celeste. Nathan continued to stay with his great-grandmother and Lorena attended much-needed summer school.

Lorena's updated summer schedule consisted of waking up at four o'clock, feeding and dressing the babies (along with herself), gathering her books together, waiting for the sitter to arrive, driving a run-down charity car given her by a compassionate church member to school, sitting through several classes until three o'clock in the afternoon, heading for work at Tony's aunt's florist shop where she worked until about seven, returning home, bathing, feeding and changing the babies for bed, and lastly doing hours of homework and studying.

Lorena was especially grateful for the vehicle she now owned (despite the fact that it was falling apart), as she could drive through the CP neighborhood rather than walk on nights she found herself fifteen cents short of bus fare.

Even though things were just barely working for the family—food, diapers and other baby needs were in short supply, along with just enough money to get by—Elena still struggled to watch her granddaughter come home every night looking more and more drained each time. She realized that the money she herself made wasn't going towards the kids, but rather the bills and groceries, thus Lorena was supporting two children on a salary just barely above minimum wage. And just how she managed to juggle school with her already-busy life while keeping up a B minus average, Elena didn't know.

But it was one Sunday evening Mrs. Gianni (Tony's aunt) gave Lorena the day off that the girl returned from a trip to the market with the news that she had been offered yet another job.

"Gram, you won't believe what just happened to me at the market!" Lorena stated excitedly when she walked through the door of the apartment.

Elena smiled from where she was sitting sorting bills on the couch while keeping an eye on the two infants amusing themselves with toys on the floor.

"Let me guess—you bought some much-needed groceries?"

Lorena rolled her eyes at her grandmother's sarcasm.

"No, Gram—I was offered a job!"

Elena's smile faded, and she began to cloud up.

"Oh?"

"Yeah, and guess how much they'll pay," Lorena replied as she set the bag down on the table and walked over to greet Nathan and Celeste.

"How much and what exactly is the job?"

"Eight dollars an hour and working at the register—can you believe it, Gram? That means I'll be making close to sixty dollars a day—more than enough money to support the kids, and myself. You won't have to spend a dime on us, therefore you'll be able to be more flexible with yourself." Lorena placed a kiss on each baby's cheek. "Maybe you could even buy yourself a car."

"Lorena—"

"Or maybe if I save long enough, you could move out of here!"

"Lorena," Elena tried again, sighing as she watched Lorena beam with joy as she picked up the infants and spun them around. "Baby, have you even considered how much of a work load that would be? I mean, I'm glad that you've received this offer, but you've got to be reasonable here."

Lorena sighed.

"I have, Gram. I've got everything calculated, even down to the last second and dime of how my time and money will be spent. Now I know what you're thinking—that I should just let you stretch things a little and help me out so that I can get time in for school so I can have a career someday," Lorena stated knowingly as she set the giggling infants down and took a seat on the couch next to Elena. "But I'll still have time for school, as long as I move my work hours to the night shift—"

"The night shift?" Elena repeated in disbelief. "You're barely able to make it home without falling asleep at the wheel as it is, Lorena. How on earth do you plan on taking a night shift? And what about the florist shop?—they close at six."

"I've already discussed that with Mrs. Gianni, and she says that if I'm willing to stay after closing time for a few hours to make the flower arrangements I would usually be doing in the day and work full time over the weekend, she'll pay me the same amount of money as before."

Elena sighed, not completely assured.

"And what about sleep—not to mention the dangers of working in that market after dark. Do you realize how many times and just how often they've been robbed?"

Lorena laughed at her grandmother's over-protectiveness.

"Gram, c'mon, I think I can handle this. Besides, my friend Tony said himself that he would check on me every now and then," the teen reassured. "And if something goes wrong I'll simply remember to stop, drop and roll," she added with a laugh, then after giving Elena a quick hug, rose from the couch to put the groceries away.

"Well," Elena began as she shook her head and scooped Nathan and Celeste up into her lap, "we'll just have to see if your will outweighs your energy and human limits, Superwoman."

A week later, Lorena and Tony were walking down the sidewalk, headed to the baby-clothing store to buy Celeste a few items.

" 'Tonio," Lorena began cautiously as she pushed Celeste along in her stroller, "what if I were to tell you that I'm failing my history class?" she asked, then stopped to tuck the blanket around the baby when a breeze came along.

"I would tell you that I don't believe it."

Celeste began to protest being fixed up and started to whine.

" 'Lessie, if I don't get this blanket around you you'll freeze in this Chicago weather," Lorena stated with a sigh, then gasped when the contents of her unzipped purse spilled onto the ground.

"Let me help you," Tony said as he bent to assist her in retrieving the items.

"I've gotten to the point where I can't even remember to close my purse, 'Tonio."

"You're juggling too many things, Lorena," Tony replied as they finally returned the last item to the purse, and continued walking. "And what's with this failing history stuff?"

"Well, it's just as I said—I'm failing because that's the one subject I never have the time to complete the homework to."

"That's not good," Tony commented with a frown. "Especially if you want to keep your GPA up."

Lorena sighed.

"I know, and I do want to pull my B average up to an A—but that may require taking time off of work . . .or finding a tutor."

Tony appeared skeptical.

"Who did you have in mind?"

"Oh, just a guy . . .that I know from school," Lorena stated carelessly with a wave of her hand.

Tony grimaced slightly, his over-protective side taking control. "Who—do I know him?"

Lorena smiled inwardly, struggling to keep a straight face.

"Yeah, actually you do. He's kind of tall, with dark hair—extremely cute, sweet and kind—"

"Wait a minute—you describe him to be some kind of Prince Charming and you claim that I know him when I don't," Tony stated as he began to walk backwards, looking slightly frustrated, disturbed and altogether left out.

"Let me give you one more hint, 'Tonio: his aunt gave me a job at her florist shop."

"Hey, wait a minute—"

Immediately, Tony shook his head and began to blush slightly, stuffing his hands into his pockets as he turned around to walk forward.

Lorena was doubling over with laughter, and had to take a few moments to recover.

"It's not that funny, Lorena," Tony said quietly, trying without success to look hurt, but was already beginning to smile himself.

"You should have seen the look on your face when you thought I meant another guy—it was absolutely timeless!"

Tony rolled his eyes.

"You're never gonna let me live it down, eh, Selenez?"

Lorena finally managed to stop laughing, and held a straight face as she replied, "Yes, I will," she began slowly, "—but only because of the second look you had, the one after you found out that I meant you," she added as she began to laugh again.

"Lorena," Tony whined with a sigh. "I'm deeply hurt now."

Lorena cleared her throat as she regained her composure.

"I'm sorry," she replied with little sympathy, then chuckled when Tony began to smile again. "But seriously, I know for a fact that you're a whiz kid, and I need your help."

Tony cast a sideways glance in Lorena's direction, noting the pleading look on her face.

"Do you see this woman, Celeste, do not copy her actions—she's a con artist that puts you down before asking you for a favor."

Lorena pouted and playfully punched his arm.

"C'mon 'Tonio, you know you want to help me," she said with puppy-dog eyes.

Tony sighed.

"I might have agreed to a lot earlier if you hadn't decided to make me look bad . . .but, I guess I don't have any choice."

"I knew you would!" Lorena stated victoriously as she gave him a quick hug, then resumed pushing the stroller.

"Sure you did," Tony replied before yawning, then sighing as a light drizzle began to pour from the sky. "Now tell me again why we didn't take your car to the store, Lorena?"

"You're not afraid of rain, are you 'Tonio? It's called saving money. Besides, you need the exercise."

Tony looked stern.

"What do you mean I need the exercise—you're the one who needs it, Lorena."

"Lesson one: never tell a woman she's fat, or suffer the consequences."

Tony snickered.

"What consequences?"

Lorena shrugged.

"I haven't thought of any yet."

A few minutes later, they reached the store, and after buying the necessary items, stepped back outside into sunshine.

"That was a quick drizzle," Tony commented as he slung the plastic grocery bag over his shoulder.

Lorena sulked.

"I told you the rain wouldn't hur—"

"Hey, Selenez!" a voice called suddenly from behind, and the two turned around.

"Oh God," Lorena muttered as she watched Isabella and Paulina, standing near a light post a few yards away, beckoning her over. "The devil's minions themselves."

"How kind of them to drop by," Tony stated sarcastically.

"I know, right. I'll be back in a minute," Lorena replied as she walked over, leaving Tony standing with the stroller.

"Looks like you and church boy decided to hook up after all," said Paulina with a smirk when Lorena arrived, and Isabella snickered.

"What do you want?" Lorena asked shortly, ignoring the remark.

"Anita's ready for round two when you are," Isabella answered as she folded her arms over her chest.

"Well, you can tell Anita and her mistress that I'm through with all of that. I've got two kids, two jobs and zero time to be rumbling with some thick-headed, wanna-be banger, ain't never gonna grow up loser."

Paulina and Isabella shared a glance, then both sighed.

"Those are some harsh words for someone in as much hot water as you're in, Lorena," Paulina said as she raised her eyebrows.

"Yeah, well, tell Anita she'd be better off getting by on her own rather than hustlin' for Carvajal."

"Oh don't worry," Isabella replied with a menacing smile. "We will."

"She said what?!" Anita growled at the top of her lungs, then swiftly turned to punch a stack of crates piled halfway to the ceiling, bringing them crashing down to the floor.

"Calm down!" Marisol, equally as choleric as her naive adherent, shouted as she kicked a crate out of her way. "Yo, what are you all just standin' there for—get over here and clean this mess up!" she commanded a group of girls standing wide-eyed in the middle of the warehouse floor.

"Calm down? Calm down?! Did you hear what they said she called me?! She's gonna wish she'd never said that!!" Anita nearly shrieked, cursing as she pounded her fist into her hand and began to stalk off for the door.

"Hold up, Valdez!" Marisol said in frustration as she roughly grabbed Anita's arm.

"You're holdin' me back from gettin' my game time in and right now I'm so angry I could—"

Anita was cut short by a swift, blazing blow delivered to her chin by an exasperated Marisol.

"Did I not just tell you to calm down?!" Her cracking voice echoed throughout the silent warehouse as she stood menacingly over a muted Anita. "Or have you gone deaf? If I hear one more complaint outta' you, I swear you're gonna regret it!"

There came an awkward pause.

"You don't know how bad I wanna kill her . . ." Anita finally muttered as she wiped away the blood dripping from her lip and down her chin.

A tense silence followed as the Marisol let out a sigh, attempting to regain her composure.

"Yes, Anita, I do know. Why do you think I'm planning everything so carefully?" Marisol replied, lowering her tone to a more civilized level. "You'll have your moment soon enough." She chuckled slightly while helping Anita to her feet, exercising her incredible mood swing capability. "You know, Valdez, sometimes I think you take me for a complete idiot."

The summer of 1985 rolled by quickly, as life for Lorena continued to be at its busiest. She was making enough money to support herself and the children, her grades were holding up (thanks to Tony), and the gang had actually seemed to have altogether forgotten her, giving the teen a sense that her dictation to Paulina and Isabella had finally closed the chapter for good. Little did she know the fault in her thinking, as things were destined to change along the road ahead, but until then Lorena was kept busy enough to keep her mind off of her troubles outside of school, work, and home.

Despite the rush of her average day, Lorena found herself greatly fatigued when it reached its end. Elena, despite her gladness to see her granddaughter so exuberant about her future and positive outlook on the present, was at the same time worrying about the girl's health. Lorena was constantly running and had been adhering to her new lifestyle for almost five months nearly nonstop, and Elena worried more and more each day that the teen's exhaustion would soon catch up with her.

Come the middle of September, Elena received a letter from Elsa, stating that she would be coming home at the end of the month. Thus, as they had prepared for her release from prison, the small family anxiously awaited her return from Africa.

It was a Friday evening when Elsa's plane made its landing, and when she arrived at the apartment she was greeted by a warm welcoming party made up of Elena, Nathan and Celeste.

After hugging each relative and placing her bags to the side, Elsa inquired of Lorena's whereabouts and was slightly surprised to hear that she had to work late, but was on her way.

Elena had long since reported Lorena's recent employment to Elsa through letters, and had confessed about her fear for the teen.

"I have so much to tell you, Momma," Elsa stated excitedly as she headed to the couch, carrying Celeste in arms. "But first you can tell me what's with this new, busy life I've heard my child has been leading."

Elena sighed as she walked over and sat down, carrying Nathan as he awkwardly flipped through a coloring book.

"Well, it's just as I said in the letter: she's on her way to burning herself out, and you and I both know that this isn't helping her lung condition at all. I hear her coughing in the middle of the night—hacking coughs as though she had a bad cold, and it only makes me worry even more.

"When I ask her if she ever considers slowing down for a while—even if just for a short vacation—she immediately reassures me that she's doing fine and lapses into one of her 'things are going perfectly' speeches." Elena shook her head as she set Nathan down on the floor when he began to whine from being held. "I used to joke with her that she's almost seventeen years old and getting more driving experience than a working adult. But I believe one of the reasons she pushes herself so hard is because she absolutely refuses to accept any kind of financial aid from me. About a week ago she was even talking about paying the sitter extra to babysit both of the kids in order that I wouldn't have to keep Nathan at work."

Elsa frowned, deeply troubled by her mother's update. She well knew that Lorena had always been the rebellious type—as she herself had been growing up—but worried now that even though she was certain the girl had quit the gang, Lorena was investing all her energy into work and putting her health on the line.

"I don't know what to say," Elsa began slowly, "except that I hope I can at least help with the kids now and maybe try to talk some sense into her," she added quietly while smoothing Celeste's light-brown, honey-highlighted curls.

A long silence followed her reply and Elena let out another sigh.

"Well I'd probably better get these two to bed before you tell me all about your summer," she stated as she rose.

"Oh I'll do it, Momma," Elsa offered as she bent to pick Nathan up and headed for Lorena's room herself. "You look a little tired."

"If you say so," Elena replied with a shrug and smile, then walked to the kitchen. "I'm making coffee, do you want any?"

"I sure would," Elsa called before entering the bathroom and filling the tub with water for Nathan's bath, and Elena plugged the coffee machine into the wall.

At that moment, a knock came on the door and Elena frowned.

"I wonder who that could be, Lorena wouldn't knock. . ." she murmured as she set the bag of coffee down and went to answer it.

After looking through the peephole, she let out a gasp and quickly opened the door.

"Lorena, what's happened to you?!"

~ Chapter IX ~

"Even in laughter the heart may ache, and joy may end in grief."

Proverbs 14:13
NIV

†

Standing propped against the doorframe was a very-exhausted and bleeding Lorena. A trail of blood dripped from her lower lip, which was obviously cut, her breathing was heavy and uneven, and she held one arm wrapped tightly around her stomach.

"Oh my Lord, you're hurt!"

"Is she here yet?" Lorena asked quietly, gasping as she spoke.

"Yes, now come inside to lay down," Elena replied quickly as she reached out to help her inside of the apartment.

Elsa had just entered the living room to retrieve one of Nathan's toys when her eyes fell on the pair heading towards the couch.

"What's happened?!" she exclaimed as she took hold of Lorena's other arm and helped her to the couch. "Lorena, who did this to you?"

"I'm alright," Lorena stated with difficulty before lying down, which proved to be a painful process that made her cry out as she held her stomach.

"It's her stomach; she's wounded," Elena stated worriedly before covering her mouth with her hand.

After raising Lorena's shirt they found a large, discolored, bruised area on the right side of her ribcage, which Elsa soon found to be over a broken bone.

That night, the ER was paid what seemed to be an annual visit once again by Lorena and her family. She was examined and released with the diagnosis of a fractured rib and exhaustion, and instructed to rest for a few weeks before returning to her schedule.

When they arrived at the apartment, it was well past midnight and everyone was ready for a long period of peace and quiet.

Lorena was sent to bed and the cribs were moved to Elena's room in order that they wouldn't wake the invalid, and Elsa offered to sit up with her while Elena received some much needed sleep.

The apartment was finally quiet when Elsa entered Lorena's room with a glass of water in one hand.

"I thought you might like some water," she said as she handed Lorena the glass, then took a seat on the edge of the bed.

"Thanks," Lorena replied quietly as she accepted it and took a sip.

There came a short pause, until Elsa sighed.

"Getting out of a gang isn't easy, is it, Lorena?"

Lorena stared down into the glass of water before replying.

"They'll get tired of this someday," she answered with confidence in her tone, but not her heart.

"Obviously they refuse to rest until they've gotten you, though."

Lorena sighed as another silence filled the air.

"What did you do?" she asked suddenly.

"About my gang?"

Lorena nodded.

Elsa rubbed the back of her neck and focused on the base of a lamp resting on the bedside table.

"Nothing really; besides moving to the South Side. They used to do the same to me as they're doing to you."

Lorena frowned as she picked at a loose thread on her blanket.

"So how did you get yourself out?"

Elsa shrugged.

"I didn't," she replied quietly, looking Lorena in the eye, "God did."

Over the next month, Lorena was held to the doctor's orders to lie low (oftentimes against her will), and despite the fact that she usually found herself feeling useless, she took advantage of her break from work to study and spend time with her kids. Besides, she wasn't exactly lonely, as Tony would visit every other day—at first staying to chat, and when Lorena was more up to getting out, taking her and the kids to the park or to get a bite to eat.

Along with Tony, there was Candy, who would often call Lorena to chat or would join her and Tony when invited.

It was one Saturday afternoon that Lorena returned home from an outing with Tony to find the apartment quiet and seemingly empty, except for the murmur of her mother taking a call in Elena's room.

She casually walked over to the sofa, taking a seat after carelessly tossing her purse to the side. She decided she would retrieve it and return it to her room after she had taken a moment to sit for a while.

Lorena sighed as her mother continued with her phone conversation, then dragged her purse towards her with her foot. After opening it, she brought out two tickets to a Broadway musical which Tony had given her—originally intending for them to go together, until he found out that he had to work that particular night. Therefore, he had given the tickets to Lorena, suggesting that she might go with her mother instead. Having come from Tony—

one of her closest friends—Lorena didn't find the idea half bad at first, but after a little bit of thinking, she began to have some second thoughts. First of all, her mother would be shocked, to say the least, that out of the blue her rebellious, slightly wayward daughter would even stop to consider inviting her to a more than rare "girls' night out." Secondly, Lorena herself was shocked that she was thinking about making the move. It was risky, as the teen was used to watching herself get hurt whenever she reached out too far. However, it was also of great intrigue to her, and something of the sort that she had wanted to do for a long time (despite how much she tried to deny it). As much as Lorena was shocked to say it, she was finding life with her mother just a little bit easier than it had been in the past.

With a slightly self-confident smile, Lorena placed the tickets in the pocket of the jacket she was wearing, deciding to give it a shot after all.

At that moment, Elsa wrapped up her conversation and made her entrance into the living room, smiling when she found Lorena sitting on the couch.

"Did you two have fun?" she asked, making her way across the room to the kitchen.

"Yeah, we did," Lorena replied conversationally, crossing one leg over the other and resting her head on the back of the sofa. "We went to that new sandwich shop on 159th Street."

Elsa appeared inquisitive as she opened the refrigerator and retrieved a stalk of celery.

"Oh? How was it?"

Lorena shrugged as she picked at a loose thread on the seam of her capris.

"It was okay, I guess."

"You guess?" Elsa repeated questioningly as she began to slit the vegetable down the center.

Lorena chuckled slightly.

"If you like pickled onions, beets and hot sauce on your Swedish-meatball hoagie—it wasn't pretty, Mom."

"Well that sounds appetizing," Elsa replied with a laugh.

"Yeah, but Tony made up for it by treating me to some ice cream afterwards."

Elsa smiled.

"I'm glad you two are getting along. He's a nice boy."

Lorena smiled slightly.

"He is," she said quietly, then cleared her throat. "I'm guessing Gram's out with the kids. What magical place did they head to this time?"

"The park—the sun's starting to set so I'm sure they'll be back soon."

A pause followed, and Lorena found herself fiddling around with the two tickets in her pocket as her mother continued to chop the celery.

"Now might be a good time to ask . . ."

"Which do you prefer, 'Rena, mayonnaise or ranch salad dressing?" Elsa piped up before the teen could present her offer.

Lorena sat up and uncrossed her legs, sliding her hand as casually as possible from her pocket.

"Oh . . . um, ranch is fine for me."

Elsa smiled as she set the celery cuts onto two plates and spooned ranch dressing onto each.

"I thought so—anything else would make me seem like the cook running that creepy sandwich shop, eh?"

Lorena chuckled.

A few seconds later, Elsa had made her way over to the couch, bringing the two plates of vegetables along with her.

"This is for you," she stated as she handed Lorena one of the platters, then took a seat beside her.

"Thanks," Lorena replied as graciously as she could.

"Doctor's orders, you know. You need to be getting more vegetables, 'Rena."

"I guess so," Lorena stated slowly before dipping one of the stalks in the pool of dressing.

The two continued to eat in silence, until Elsa finished and arose to take her dish to the sink.

As she held the plate under running water, Lorena decided to attempt light conversation before resorting to presenting her idea.

"So who was that you were talking to earlier?" She asked the first question that came to mind, however immediately regretting choosing such an imposing one to begin their talk.

But surprisingly, Elsa looked glad to answer her inquiry, and smiled.

"Actually, I've been meaning to talk with you about just that."

"Really?"

"Really."

The woman turned the water off, halting her actions to stare at the wall in front of her for a few seconds, then abruptly set the plate in the sink before returning to the couch.

"Lorena," Elsa began, sitting slightly sideways on the couch, looking down at her folded hands.

Lorena popped another stalk into her mouth as she waited for her mother to continue.

"Lorena, how do you . . .how do you feel about Africa?" Elsa finally asked.

Lorena chewed her celery and swallowed, then placed her less-than-half-eaten plate onto the coffee table before her.

"Well, it's okay, I guess. I mean, most of my ancestors did come from there." She shrugged slightly while pushing the plate a little farther from the edge of the table. "I've never really thought about how I'm supposed to 'feel' about it."

Elsa nodded slowly.

"I was talking to the head of the family I was staying with in Soweto—Mr. Ayandho—"

"Ah, I remember him," Lorena cut in with a small chuckle as she picked up a stalk of celery. "Gram said you talked about his funny accent and strange house rules in your letters."

Elsa laughed shortly, then bit her lip.

" 'Rena, I don't want to . . .beat around the bush," she stated in a tone somewhat more serious than before. "You see I'm . . .I'm going back to Africa, Lorena," she stated quietly.

Immediately, Lorena ceased chewing and swallowed abruptly, her hand paused halfway between the plate and her mouth. She blinked, then slowly set the stalk of celery she had originally been holding back down onto the plate, resting her hands in her lap.

After noticing that the teen was at a loss for words, Elsa spoke up, "They needed more missionaries, and without being there I feel a sense of guilt . . . and fear even—for all of those people. If you could only see, 'Rena, how their faces light up when we get off the bu—"

"How long?" Lorena interrupted in a slightly hushed tone, her eyes holding a melancholy gleam as they focused on the coffee table's chipped, dull wooden surface.

Elsa swallowed as she looked down, uneasily rubbing the back of her neck.

"If there's anything I've learned, it's not to lie to you, Lorena," she began quietly, placing her hands over Lorena's. "I'm moving to Africa . . .for good."

At the sound of her mother's words, Lorena felt her heart skip in disbelief. It was only a few months earlier that her grandmother read comfortably after dinner a paragraph from one of Elsa's letters that she was coming home—for good. And now the tables had turned completely.

This time Lorena swallowed, and slid her hands out from under her mother's as the words began to sink in.

"I'm going to hope," she began slowly while trying to control the growing tremble in her voice, "a-and believe that for some strange reason you're kidding with me."

Elsa sighed and closed her eyes.

"Lorena, I've been considering this for a while—"

"Oh, really? I suppose now you're going to tell me that you prayed over this—received a 'word from the Lord,' and now you need to leave your daughter and grandkids so that you can carry out His orders!"

Elsa ran her fingers through her hair.

"Lorena, please—"

"The 'unseen force' strikes again—I might as well just roll over and die so that I can leave you two alone!"

"Lorena, would you just listen to me?"

"Not today, Momma," Lorena stated heatedly as tears rolled down her cheeks and she stood to her feet. "What makes you think that I'll support you on this decision? Did you expect me to come crawling to your feet—my hands full of money for those disgusting paupers that are stealing my own mother away from me—"

"Lorena!"

". . .gigantic crucifix slung around my neck," Lorena continued heatedly, her voice cracking and growing louder, "Holy Bible in hand, and a testimony that could knock everybody's godly socks off?!"

"Listen to me, Lorena!" Elsa nearly shouted as she herself shot to her feet. "I'm getting tired of this—so tired that I'm willing to do anything to change things! You aren't the only one that wants me around—"

"But I am the most important one!" Lorena countered angrily, beginning to shiver with disgust. "Or at least I should be—a-and am supposed to be! Somehow I'm second-banana to every freakin' thing that's important to you! And it's been that way ever since I was born! I may not be your ideal Bible-hugging, slang-deprived, abstinence-addicted, purity-loving daughter—but I'm still your daughter—despite whether or not you ever stopped to notice!" Here the teen collapsed to her knees, sobbing uncontrollably as she buried her face into her trembling hands.

"Dear God!" Elsa whispered prayerfully as tears fell from her eyes. She lowered herself to the floor and, once again, took Lorena's hands into her own. "You didn't let me finish, Lorena," she managed to say through her tears as she watched her daughter quiver with depression and cry over lack of understanding. "I want you to come with me—more than anything I want you to come with me. What else am I supposed to say? What else am I supposed to do? I've reached out to you for the past two years and even from prison as best I could."

Lorena lowered her face to the floor; her mother holding her hands to her forehead, beginning to whisper sentences as she herself continued to sob.

"I can't do any more, Lorena—but God can."

Suddenly, Lorena's sobs turned to gasps for air as she felt the strangest sensation she had experience in all of her life. Her mother's low, steady whisper almost seemed to be the cause for her hands to begin to tremble even more, and because of the manifest significance she realized that the situation possessed, Lorena didn't notice that her mother's words were of a language she had never heard before.

It was when a warm, flashing surge entered her hands and traveled throughout her whole body that Lorena felt herself jerk abruptly to the side. Immediately, she got to her feet, feeling the same urge to get as far away from her mother as possible as once before.

Before Elsa could even begin to stop her, Lorena had bolted out the door, the tickets slipping from her pocket and falling to the floor behind her.

Two years had passed since Elsa packed up and set off for Africa, leaving an even bigger emotional gap between herself and Lorena. Despite how hard Elena pleaded with the teen to go with her, Lorena held firmly to her decision to stay, and stay she did.

Her hands were more than full what with the two growing toddlers romping about the place, and at times she couldn't believe that soon enough Nathan (now three years old) would be attending preschool. Celeste wasn't too far behind, and Lorena enjoyed watching her develop her motor skills and learn new words.

Adding to this, Lorena had been accepted at a local community college, where she would begin classes in early September.

To darken things, however, was the gang. Every time Lorena ended up fighting to defend herself when walking home at times when her car was under repair, or whenever she had to hang the phone up on a threatening call, her mother's words echoed clearly in her mind. She did have to admit—leaving a gang wasn't easy.

It was on a calm, lazy mid-August afternoon that Lorena sat at the kitchen table, looking over her college schedule while supervising Celeste as she sat bouncing in her high chair, clumsily stuffing Cheerio bits into her mouth.

It was a little bit past one o'clock on a Sunday, and Elena was out with Nathan at the park.

"Wan' more, Mommy, wan' more!" the toddler exclaimed exuberantly after managing to get another "o" down.

Lorena sighed as she looked up from her schedule.

" 'Lessie, you've got plenty sitting on your plate. Finish those and I'll give you a little more."

Almost as though she hadn't even noticed them before, Celeste placed her pudgy little hand over the remaining cereal and grasped a few before obediently transporting them (most of them, at least) to her mouth.

A few seconds later, she began to sing a made-up tune about the cereal, her mouth full of food.

Once again, Lorena looked up.

"Don't sing with food in your mouth, sweetie, okay?"

Celeste ceased for a moment, then spoke up. "Why?" came the time-old question.

Lorena let out another sigh.

"Because it's dangerous," she replied matter-of-factly as she reached over to pluck a random, Cheerio escapee from her daughter's hair. "You might choke yourself."

Lorena had just gotten back to her schedule when the question came again.

"WhyYy?"

Before Lorena could reply, the telephone rang suddenly, and she got up to answer it.

"Hello?"

"What's up?" a familiar voice returned.

Lorena smiled.

" 'Tonio! Long time, no talk."

Tony chuckled.

"Yeah, life's been a little hectic for me, though."

"Really? Somehow I can't picture that accompanying a vacation in Italy."

Shortly after Lorena and Tony's graduation, Tony left for a summer vacation with his family—taking place in his hometown. They had been saving up for the trip for a few years, and decided on taking their graduating senior back to his roots as a sort of graduation present.

Though Lorena missed him greatly while he was away, she knew that he needed the break and hoped he was having a good time.

"It's possible—try having relatives surrounding your every move, pinching your cheeks while rattling off in Italian and constantly asking if you would care for any more meatballs."

Lorena laughed as she picked up the phone base and carried it to the table.

"Sounds like you've got your hands full."

She sensed him shrug from the other line.

"Yeah, but I'm always too busy missing you to care." Lorena smiled as she took the now empty bowl from Celeste and began to pour more Cheerios into it.

"I miss you too, 'Tonio," she replied quietly, then remembered something when her college schedule caught her eye. "I haven't talked to you in months—which college accepted you?"

"Oh—can you hang on just a sec,' Lorena?" Tony stated suddenly, and Lorena could pick up the sounds of voices talking in the background.

"Uh, sure," she quickly replied, placing the refilled bowl of Cheerios before a squealing Celeste.

After waiting for almost a minute, Lorena took a seat at the table, watching Celeste continue to devour her cereal while playing with the phone's cord.

It was almost a full five minutes later that Tony returned to the phone.

"Lorena?"

"Yeah?" she responded while sitting up slightly in her chair.

"Hey, I'm sorry I was gone for so long—my mom was introducing me to some random cousins I've never met before."

Lorena smiled lightly as she twisted her locket chain.

"Don't worry about it."

"I'll hope you'll be equally as forgiving when I tell you that I've gotta go now—my aunt's about to serve dinner and you know how Italians get about meals."

"Oh . . .oh, yeah sure. If you've gotta go, then you've gotta go," Lorena replied quickly, trying to hide the disappointment in her tone by covering it with a short laugh.

"I'm really sorry, Lorena—I promise I'll fill you in on everything when I get back at the end of the month," Tony's sincere voice stated.

"Yeah—that's fine. I'll let you go, then."

A very short pause followed, and Lorena wondered what was running through his mind.

"Okay, then. 'Bye," Tony finally said.

" 'Bye."

After hearing a click on the other line, Lorena bit her lip and slowly placed the phone back onto the receiver.

"At the end of the month . . ." she whispered to herself as she stared into space.

It was when the sound of dishes crashing to the floor met Lorena's ears that she was brought out of her trance.

"Uh-oh," Celeste stated before covering her mouth with her hand.

Lorena sighed as she bent to pick the bowl up, returned it to the table and began cleaning up the fallen Cheerios.

"You've probably had enough anyway, Ms. Cheerio."

A few weeks later, Tony arrived at Lorena's doorstep, asking Elena if she was around that he might take her out for a cappuccino. When she confirmed that she was, the two set off to chat about the past and future.

It was a Saturday evening, around seven o'clock, when Lorena sat talking with Tony over coffee at a local diner, enjoying her day off.

"So, you've gotta tell me—which college accepted you?" Lorena asked excitedly, having finally gotten the chance to ask him.

Tony smiled slightly, then bit his lip.

"Well," he began slowly, wrapping his hands around his mug, "remember how I told you I was applying for two places: University of Chicago and the University of Illinois?"

Lorena nodded with a smile.

"Well, there's a third one I didn't really tell you about...because I sent my application in a little late, and was already out of the country by the time I got the news."

Lorena shrugged carelessly.

"And?"

"Well, they accepted me..."

Lorena grinned brightly.

"So who is this mystery college?"

Tony ran his fingers through his hair before replying.

"Yale."

Lorena's smile began to fade, until she forced it to remain for her friend's sake.

"Not you too, 'Tonio?"

"Oh..." she stated quietly, picking at the side of the table. "I-I'm really...really proud of you, 'Tonio...that you made it to such a..." she paused and swallowed, "...such a prestigious school. Didn't I tell you that you were smart?"

Tony appeared serious as he reached out to take Lorena's hands in his.

"You know what, Lorena?"

"Yeah, 'Tonio?"

Tony shook his head, then smiled.

"If you aren't the best friend I've got, I don't know who is," he stated sincerely as he looked her in the eyes.

Lorena smiled lightly, looking away from him modestly.

"C'mon, 'Tonio—"

"No, seriously. Even my family wasn't too big on me going away and all . . ."

"Glad I could be of some help . . ." she stated as a lump formed in her throat. "I think I need to get some air," she added quickly as she stood up and walked briskly out the door.

Tony, alarmed by her actions, immediately followed.

When he stepped outside into the chilly, Chicago night air, he found Lorena standing with her forehead against the brick exterior of the building, sobbing silently.

"Lorena . . ." he said quietly with a worried frown as he gently placed his hand on her shoulder.

"I'm sorry," Lorena stated as she turned to face him slightly, "I-I know that I should be happy for you . . .a-and I am, but—" Here she was cut off as she began to cry harder.

Tony pulled her into a hug as she continued to cry, beginning to wonder if college was such a good idea after all.

"Everyone's leaving me, 'Tonio . . .a-and I just don't know what to do anymore."

"Are you sure you're okay now?" Tony asked Lorena cautiously as the two of them made their way down the hallway leading to her apartment.

Lorena smiled over at him reassuringly, straightening his jacket on her shoulders—which he had offered her earlier.

"Yeah, I'm fine now," she replied, "I guess I just panicked a little bit."

"I mean, maybe I'll only stay a few years, then transfer back—"

" 'Tonio," Lorena interrupted as they came to a stop at her door, "I'm happy for you—really I am. Please don't let me keep you from accomplishing your goals." She chuckled slightly. "Yale was practically made for you."

Tony smiled.

"As I said before—you're a great friend and I'm gonna miss you, Lorena."

Lorena looked down at her hands.

"Right back at ya,'" she replied quietly. "So, um, when do you leave?"

Tony sighed.

"Tomorrow afternoon."

Lorena nodded slowly, and a long, somewhat-uncomfortable silence filled the air.

The two of them stared down at the ground, Tony with his hands stuffed awkwardly into his pockets and Lorena hugging herself.

"So . . ." Tony finally spoke up, ". . . um, you know how I go to that church across the street from yours?"

Lorena looked up and nodded once again.

Tony bit his lip before continuing.

"Well, they've got this group thing that they do on Wednesday nights—"

"You mean Bible study?"

"Yeah . . .actually."

Lorena glared slightly.

"What about it?"

Tony cleared his throat.

"Uh, well, I was wondering if you would go. . . sometime, you know. They're really cool towards new people—"

" 'Tonio," Lorena cut in with a sigh, "I don't have good past experiences with churches . . ."

Another silence followed, and Tony ran his fingers through his hair.

"Why?" he asked suddenly.

Lorena shook her head slightly, looking away from his concerned stare.

"Some stuff happened . . .when I was younger—that's all."

Tony rubbed the back of his neck as Lorena's eyes did their familiar fade-away act, and he watched her seem to mentally re-visit her past.

"If you ever change your mind, here's a flyer telling the hours of the meetings," Tony stated as he handed Lorena an orange, folded piece of paper from his pocket.

Lorena looked at the paper, then slowly reached out her hand to accept it.

"Thanks," she said accordingly as she slid the paper into her jeans pocket.

"No problem," Tony replied quietly, then sighed. "I guess I'd better get going now."

Lorena nodded, then managed to put on a small smile.

"Yeah—you need to get some rest before your trip."

"Yeah . . ." Tony replied while returning her smile.

Lorena removed the jacket from her shoulders, handing it back to its owner.

"You might not wanna leave without this. Thanks for letting me borrow it."

Tony started to reach out to accept the black-and-blue football jacket, then pushed it back towards her.

"No, you keep it."

Lorena frowned slightly, then cast him a questioning glance.

"What?"

"Yeah, I want you to have it," Tony stated as he placed the jacket back around her shoulders.

Lorena smiled as she shook her head.

"Thanks, 'Tonio."

"Any time."

The two shared a glance for a few seconds, and Lorena finally reached out to bid him farewell with a hug.

"Don't get into too much trouble, okay?" she stated quietly before closing her eyes and blinking out a tear.

Tony smiled as they drew away.

"Of course not, you just keep yourself in line," he replied jokingly, then became serious as he raised his hand up to gently touch Lorena's face, catching the tear. "I'll keep in touch."

Lorena nodded as she swallowed, placing her hand over his.

Tony frowned slightly as they looked into each other's eyes, then sighed inwardly as he started to leave, Lorena's hand sliding slowly out of his.

Another tear slipped down her cheek as she watched him go, and she felt her heart ache.

She bit her lip and forced herself to turn to open the door.

She had barely placed her hand onto the knob when a voice sounded from down the hall, "Lorena?"

Lorena quickly turned around to see that Tony had paused, and was now facing her.

"Yes?" she replied.

Tony felt his breath catch inside him slightly as his tongue seemed to become paralyzed. His heart skipped a beat and he eventually looked away from Lorena's piercing stare.

"I, uh...I'll see you later," he finally managed to say, immediately becoming angry at himself for changing his words.

Lorena bit her lip, then smiled slightly with a nod.

With that, she opened the door of the apartment, and Tony continued down the hall.

~ Chapter X ~

"All day long my enemies taunt me; those who rail against me use my name as a curse."

Psalm 102:8
NIV

†

"Come see your Auntie Candy, Natty."

Nathan, looking slightly timid, hid his face in the ruffles of his mother's pants leg.

Lorena chuckled.

"Nathan, you're the last person I'd expect to be shy," she stated as she pried Nathan's arms from around her leg. "Go give Auntie Candy a hug."

Nathan obediently did as he was told, and Candy scooped him up into her arms.

"You're getting so big!"

It had been about a year since the beginning of college, and since Tony had left. Life continued for Lorena, and she was still juggling work—only now college was in the picture. Her schedule was packed, but now that the kids were a little older, life wasn't quite as busy as before. Tony had kept her posted on life at Yale, writing every month at first; yet eventually the letters decreased to once every other month. This didn't surprise Lorena, as she knew he was obviously very busy (as she herself was), yet she missed him more each day.

One late summer evening, Lorena received a call from none other than Candy—who had been away at college in California—bearing the news that she was passing through Chicago to see her family and friends before setting off for school in September.

Lorena now smiled as she watched Nathan begin to drop his shy and timid act by taking it upon himself to show Candy all of his new toys about the apartment.

"Celeste is around here somewhere," Lorena said as she set off for her room to retrieve Celeste.

As soon as she reached the hall, however, the toddler had made her way past Lorena and to Candy—demonstrating that she didn't need any warming up to become herself.

"Auntie Candy, Auntie Candy!" Celeste squealed as Candy turned to greet her with a hug as she lifted her up.

"Hey, 'Lessie! My goodness, you're growing up so fast!" Candy exclaimed, and Nathan tugged on her sleeve while pointing at one of his toy fire engines.

"She's crazy over your name, you know," Lorena said to Candy with a laugh as she watched the kids compete for her friend's attention.

Candy chuckled.

At that moment, Elena entered the room, and smiled when she saw their visitor.

"Candice—it's good to see you. How have you been?" Elena asked as Candy set Celeste down, then wrapped her in a hug.

"I'm alright, Ms. Jordan. It's good to see you too," she replied cheerfully.

"I'm glad to hear that," Elena said warmly, then sighed at the sight of the sea of toys covering the floor. "Why don't I take you two to the park while your mommy and Auntie Candy talk?"

At the word "park," Celeste's eyes lit up, but Nathan immediately looked disappointed.

"But I didn't get to show her my fire engine, Grammy," he complained.

Lorena chuckled as she shook her head.

"Nathan—" she started to scold, then changed her mind with a sigh as she bent over to try to clean up some of the toys.

"It's alright, Natty," Candy quipped. "I already saw it—it's a great fire engine, too."

"We can have fun at the park, can't we Natty?" Elena asked him gently as she helped Celeste put on her shoes.

Nathan finally shrugged as he went to put his Velcro sneakers on all by himself.

"Oh, alright."

Candy took a seat on the couch as Lorena knelt before Celeste, looking her in the eye.

"Be good for Grammy, alright? If she says you can't get on something, or that you can't eat something, listen to her, okay 'Lessie?"

When Celeste nodded, Lorena smiled and placed a kiss on her forehead, then moved on to Nathan, who had just finished putting on his shoes.

"Are you going to be a good little man for Mommy? You won't give Grammy any trouble, right?"

Nathan nodded as well, and after giving him a kiss, Lorena watched the trio head out the door.

"We'll be back in a few hours or so," Elena called over her shoulder.

"Have fun," Candy replied, then sighed after they had left. "Your kids are absolutely adorable, Lorena."

Lorena smiled as she went back to straightening the living room.

"Yeah, well, don't let those cute little smiles and big eyes fool you," she replied, a mischievous twinkle in her eye. "They're monsters in real life—and will wrap you around their pudgy little fingers."

Candy laughed.

"Monsters or not—they're very sweet, and I like sweets."

Lorena chuckled.

"Don't worry about cleaning that now, 'Rena—you're supposed to chill while I'm in town," Candy stated as she stretched out comfortably on the sofa.

Lorena sighed.

"I guess you're right," she said as she ceased cleaning and now moved to a comfy, oversized chair she had recently purchased. "It's a habit for me to go into mom mode, though."

A silence arose, and was broken when Lorena began to cough. When she finished, Candy frowned.

"That's what I forgot to ask you about—how are your lungs and everything? That cough's not still bugging you as much, is it?"

Lorena sighed again, rubbing her forehead as she closed her eyes.

"Sometimes it does—but it's all good."

Candy nodded.

"Well, at least you're not as bad as you were before. Speaking of which—what's CP been up to?"

Lorena groaned as she draped her legs over one arm of the chair, leaning her head back comfortably on the other.

"Ugh—don't even mention their name. They're still around," she said with a wave of her hand. "They've been letting off a bit for a while—probably so that the chief can efficiently think out some evil plan to have me killed," Lorena joked, shaking her head with a smirk.

Again, Candy appeared stern as she twirled a light-brown bang on one finger.

"You know, it's not really as light of a situation as you so often put it, 'Rena—not somethin' to joke about . . ." She hesitated. "Maybe you should go to someone about this."

Lorena opened her eyes and looked over at her friend.

"Who do you have in mind?"

Candy shrugged slightly.

"Oh, I don't know . . ." Her voice drifted off, almost a bit uncertainly.

Lorena shrugged carelessly, letting out a yawn as she dismissed the topic.

"Well, then," she replied conclusively.

Candy bit her lip, watching as her friend sat distantly staring into space.

"I was thinkin' the police . . . maybe," she finally voiced, deciding to be honest.

Lorena's eyes widened.

"The police?!" she exclaimed in disbelief, then laughed wryly. "Candy, if I went to the police about this I'd be shooting myself in the foot. Chaos would break loose and I can't afford that to happen."

Candy sighed.

"There you go again—why can't you just simply tell them that you're being threatened and—"

"Because if I do, Marisol would find out somehow, someway, and kill my family if not me."

Candy frowned, then closed her eyes.

"Why do gangs have to be so stupid? I can't believe I once tried to get into the CPs."

Lorena smirked.

"I was worse—I'm the one who actually got in—mostly because I hung around them when I was younger."

"Well, that's life, I guess."

Another silence followed, and Lorena massaged her temples as Candy drew imaginary circles on the ceiling with her index finger.

"Gotten any letters from Tony lately?" she asked out-of-the-blue.

Lorena sighed this time, then yawned.

"Last month I did. He's busy, you know."

"I know," Candy replied with a shrug. "I guess you must miss him a lot, eh?"

Lorena bit her lip as she picked at a seam on the chair.

"Yeah, I do."

"Did you two have a good time?" Elena asked Lorena later that night, after Candy had left and the kids had been put to bed.

Lorena smiled from where she sat with a calculus book open on the couch.

"Yeah, we did. I'm glad Candy's back for a while."

Elena smiled as she poured herself a cup of coffee.

"Good to hear that. How is she liking life away from home?"

"She says it's okay—but misses Chicago pretty often," Lorena replied. "Don't tell her I told you that, though, okay, Gram?" she added quickly.

Elena chuckled.

"I won't."

Lorena smiled, then returned to her book as Elena sat down at the kitchen table with her mug of coffee.

After pausing for a few minutes of silence, Elena spoke up, "I got another letter from your mom today. She says she's going to go meet with a tribal chief in a few days."

Any and all traces of a smile on Lorena's face immediately disappeared.

"Really," she replied dryly, then tried to focus on her math book.

Elena looked down at her hands, then back up at her granddaughter.

"She asks about you in each letter, Lorena."

The intensity in the air caused Lorena to have to swallow, and this time she didn't bother to reply.

Elena eventually sighed, then decided to make another attempt to melt the large wall of ice around the girl.

"How much longer are you going to go on like this, Lorena?"

"I don't want to talk about this anymore," she replied quietly, yet firmly.

Elena frowned worriedly as she watched her granddaughter hurt herself again.

"Lorena—"

"I'm gonna go brush my teeth and get ready for bed—I can finish studying tomorrow since it's Friday and I don't have any weekend classes," Lorena stated suddenly as she rose to her feet and exited the room, ending the discussion entirely.

"Mommy, did you like my drawings?" Nathan asked from the back seat of the car.

Lorena smiled before replying, bringing the car to a stop at a red light.

"I loved your drawings, Natty—they were incredible."

"Do you know how to paint, Mommy?" Celeste's tiny voice questioned curiously.

Lorena chuckled slightly.

"Not as well as you or your brother, I'm sure."

The small family had just gotten out of an art show held at Nathan's kindergarten, and Lorena was presently driving them home.

It was about half past six, and because the days were getting shorter, darkness was arriving quickly.

Lorena didn't waste any time in getting the '76 Cadillac down the slightly crowded, city streets—as she knew much better than to linger (especially at night).

As the stop light forced the car to remain still, Lorena noticed a group of girls standing on the street corner clad in tight, revealing outfits and heavy makeup. She watched them attempt to gain the attention of another group, this one composed of slightly older, teenage males.

Lorena felt a twinge of reminiscence in her heart when she noticed that the girls were no older than twelve or thirteen.

Eager to get home as soon as possible, she accelerated to the maximum speed permitted in the area when the light changed from red to green.

"I'm hungry, Mommy!" Nathan exclaimed suddenly, and Celeste chimed in agreement.

Lorena sighed, her eyes spontaneously scanning the premises.

"You can have a snack when we get home."

"Are we almost there?"

"Yes, Nathan—be patient."

The next red light Lorena came to was at an intersection where a strip club and bar were located.

Seeing no other cars around and drunks staggering out the door of the building, she immediately decided to proceed.

When she arrived at another intersection, Lorena frowned when she saw a police barricade blocking further passage, and an officer directing cars to a detour on the street perpendicular to that which she was on.

"You're kiddin' me," she muttered as she gradually came to a stop, realizing that the street which the officer was pointing to was one that ran through the heart of the CP turf.

"Ooh, look, look, Natty!" Celeste voiced delightedly while pointing out the window at the many police cars. "It's the police, it's the police!"

Seeing that she was the only car around, Lorena rolled down her window and called to the officer.

He walked over, then bent down to see through the window.

"Ma'am, we're gonna have to ask you to take the detour."

Lorena sighed.

"Do you know if I could possibly take another street off Halsted and then return to this one?"

The officer frowned.

"I don't think so, ma'am. We've got a hostage situation and several shootings over here—we've extended the barrier out a good distance for security reasons."

Lorena's heart sank.

"Oh."

"Where are you headed?"

"Cabrini-Green."

"Well, I advise that you stick with State Street, then, ma'am."

"I guess you're right—any other street besides this one would take me out of my way. Thanks for your help, officer."

"Any time."

Hoping fervently that she wouldn't encounter any trouble, Lorena turned the car onto State Street. Any other time, she would have taken the alternate route without as much unease, but with the kids in the car, she didn't feel as carefree.

"Mommy, what was the policeman talking about? What are hos-hos—" Celeste tripped over the word.

"He was just telling us a safer way to get home, 'Lessie," Lorena replied, wondering if she was right.

About a mile later, Lorena noticed that she had entered the territory, and instinctively pressed a little harder on the gas pedal. An upcoming green light soon turned yellow, then red, and because there weren't any other cars in sight, Lorena planned on running it.

Her plans were thwarted when another car turned onto the street in front of her, and stopped.

Lorena reluctantly did the same, then wondered if she should simply go around the other car and proceed. The thought remained in her mind until yet another car came up behind her, this one closing her in to cancel her actions.

With a sigh, Lorena impatiently waited on the light to change.

"Mommy?"

"Yes, Nathan?"

"Look what I can do—"

"Not right now, sweetie—Mommy's driving."

At that moment, the light finally turned green and they moved forward once again.

Lorena had continued on for about two more miles, passing the familiar high rises, projects, clubs and liquor stores as quickly as possible.

Her stomach tightened when the two other cars turned off and she became aware of the emptiness of the area.

"That could only mean one thing . . ."

About one-hundred feet ahead, Lorena noticed a solitary figure crossing the deserted street, dressed in a long, black hoodie and carrying a string of tin cans over one shoulder.

Planning on going around them, she reduced speed slightly as she approached.

However, when she was within twenty feet of the stranger, they stopped suddenly and before Lorena knew it, a bright, white light met her eyes and blinded her momentarily.

Feeling a sense of panic and not wanting to hit the individual, she swerved to the right, causing the tires to make a loud skidding cry before the front bumper made contact with a hard object—jerking the vehicle's passengers forward.

Lorena felt the wind leave her for a few seconds as soon as her chest hit the steering wheel.

Half of the car was on the sidewalk, the other in the street, and it had hit a light post.

As soon as she was able to speak, Lorena turned around and asked if everyone was okay.

Celeste was crying, and Nathan simply sat with a look of fear on his face.

While verbally consoling the kids, Lorena immediately attempted to start the engine back up upon recalling the figure and their desperate need to get out of that part of town.

After several attempts to get the car to start, Lorena jumped when there came a knock on her window.

As the children screamed and cried, she looked to see four individuals surrounding the car, one of whom had reached it and was now attempting to open her door.

Gritting her teeth in frustration, Lorena continued to try the engine, ignoring her menacing audience. But it was when the person closest to her withdrew a pistol from underneath her leather jacket that she gave up.

With an exasperated sigh, Lorena reluctantly let her window down after telling the kids to stay seated and consoling them as best she could.

"I see you're having a little car trouble, there, Selenez," Anita stated with a snicker as she continued to hold the pistol poised in Lorena's direction.

An echo of snickers sounded from the other three individuals—Paulina, Isabella and a new girl whom Lorena didn't recognize.

"Just tell me what you want and let us go, okay?" she asked quietly, trying to hide the anxiety in her voice.

"Of course," Anita replied carelessly, then cast a glance at the two wailing children in the backseat of the car. "Cute kids—I wouldn't want them to eavesdrop on our conversation."

Lorena sighed.

"Get outta' the car," Anita ordered firmly, and Lorena did as she was told.

"I'll be right back—I promise," she said gently to Nathan and Celeste before opening the door and exiting the car. "Cut to the chase—what do you want?" she asked once she had closed the door behind her.

"Well, to tell you the truth, I came for two reasons—"

"To wreck my car and gun me down?" Lorena asked wryly. "Not to mention terrorizing my kids." She clenched her fists in anger before lowering her voice. "If you lay one finger on them, I swear to God I'll—"

"Lorena, *calma, chica*," Anita interrupted slyly. "I didn't plan on doing any of that . . .that is, if you'll follow orders."

"Blackmail, eh?"

"That's right. As I was saying, I came for two reasons. One on behalf of Marisol, and the other on behalf of Cobra—that is, if you ain't too good to remember who they are—"

"Stop stalling and tell me what they want!" Lorena exclaimed as she rolled her eyes.

Anita narrowed her eyes slightly, obviously holding back the urge to use the weapon in her hand.

"Marisa wants you to show up at the warehouse tomorrow night—"

"I can't—I have a real job, unlike you."

"Oh yeah? Well if you wanna see those two babies make it to the first grade, I suggest you do as you're told."

The serious, acrid tone in Anita's voice caused Lorena's stomach to turn, and she had to swallow back angry, frustrated tears before replying, "If you want to kill somebody, let it be me—not them or anyone else in my family. This isn't even between you and them—it's not between you and me either. It's between Marisa and me."

"That's what you think, Selenez. The whole CP gang wants to watch you die a slow, terrible death—and if that means planning for years and years, murdering your little kids or your stupid momma too—"

"You know where you can go!!" Lorena shouted before lunging at Anita.

Anita was seconds away from firing the gun when Isabella and the new girl came forward to restrain their former vice-chief.

"Do you want me to kill you now, Selenez?! 'Cause I sure can!!"

While biting her tongue to keep from saying anything that could provoke Anita to carry out her threat, Lorena stared down the barrel of the gun, realizing that her kids were worth more than arguing her nemesis down.

As Anita's finger quivered around the trigger, Paulina spoke up, " 'Nita, it ain't worth getting Carvajal mad because you did things too soon. If you wanna let some heat off, stick to the plan—you know Selenez would do anything we say if her kids' lives were on the line."

After a long and intense glaring match between Anita and Lorena, the vice-chief finally let her hand relax as she held the pistol at her side.

"You think I don't wanna make you bleed, Lorena? You'd just better be glad I didn't use this on ya.'"

Lorena remained silent as the two flunkies held her firmly—making sure she wouldn't attempt another attack.

"But until that day comes when I can finally kill you—I'll make sure your life is a living torment," Anita stated harshly, returning the pistol back to her belt. "Cobra expects you to meet him at his place after you head over to the warehouse. If you don't want me to kill your kids, you'll be there. But if you're anything like Carvajal says your momma was, you'll not show up, so I can kill 'em."

Anita's last remark caused Lorena's fists to automatically tighten, and she cursed the days she used to treat others the exact same way.

But she continued to hold her tongue, and Anita smiled in satisfaction.

"Let her loose, *chicas*. We've got better things to do right now than chat with Selenez. Besides, I think she gets the picture."

Lorena replaced the phone onto the receiver with a sigh, then closed her eyes as she rubbed her temples.

It was the next morning, around six o'clock, and she had just gotten off the phone with Mrs. Gianni, reporting that she couldn't show up to work that day due to a made-up fever. Earlier she had called her school and the market with the same excuse, and though it would cost her money and the freedom from extra homework, she followed through nonetheless.

After the gang left, Lorena had the car towed, and it was currently in the repair shop. Because this cost her extra money, she knew that missing a day of work wasn't going to do her any good.

As she sat at the kitchen table, contemplating her appointment scheduled for that night, she rested her forehead in her hands with a heavy sigh. She was tired, and wasn't at all looking forward to dealing with the gang that day.

At that moment, Elena, Nathan and Celeste exited the bathroom from where the grandmother was helping them wash up for school, and the two giggling toddlers came running over to tell their mother goodbye.

"Tell Mommy 'bye, kids—you're almost late for the bus," Elena stated with a sigh as she donned a light sweater.

Lorena smiled faintly as first Nathan came up and gave her a hug; next came Celeste.

"You two be good at school today, okay?"

"Okay," they replied in unison, then accepted the backpacks Elena handed them.

"Mommy, why aren't you walking us to the bus today?" Celeste asked suddenly with curiosity.

"Because your mommy is tired," Elena spoke up, then after herding the kids to the door, turned to Lorena. "We need to talk when I get back, okay?"

"You'll be late for work . . ." Lorena replied with a slight frown.

"I'll make time."

Lorena nodded with a sigh.

"Sure, Gram," she replied dryly, not fancying the idea of sharing the escapades of the previous night (especially not with her grandmother). " 'Bye, Natty—'Lessie."

" 'Bye, Mommy!"

When Elena returned from seeing the kids to the school bus, she walked through the apartment door to see Lorena still at the table, only now her arms were folded over the tabletop with her cheek resting there as well—obviously asleep.

Elena closed the door quietly, but Lorena stirred nonetheless.

She yawned as she sat up and rubbed her eyes.

"How long was I out?" she asked as she looked around in confusion.

"One or two minutes—you look like you need more than that."

Lorena sighed as she got up to prepare some toast for herself.

"Which leads me to ask why you all got in so late last night and why the car isn't in the lot," Elena continued skillfully as she returned her sweater to the coat rack, then proceeded to take a seat in the oversized chair by the couch.

Lorena, her back turned to her grandmother, stopped buttering the toast and closed her eyes.

"I just had some car trouble, is all—"

"Or maybe this gang is beginning to take its toll on you. And yes, I do know about the gang, Lorena. I've known about them for a while, now."

"Oh well . . ."

"How did you find out?" Lorena asked as she returned the butter to the 'fridge.

"Well, your mother confirmed my suspicions—which have been around for a long time. But Lorena, why not just go to the authorities about it?"

Lorena sighed once again and turned around.

"Gram, you, of all people should know that that's not gonna help anything. Mom already told me about your previous experiences."

Elena remained silent for a moment, and Lorena continued preparing her toast before heading to the couch with it.

"I started some trend, didn't I?" Elena finally asked.

Lorena found herself chuckling slightly.

"Nobody's perfect—and at least I'm out of it."

Elena sighed this time.

"You may be out, but they certainly aren't through with you. You have to do something, 'Rena. What about the kids?"

Lorena set her plate onto the coffee table, staring thoughtfully into space, frowning.

"I'm not going to the police, Gram—that would only make things worse," she stated quietly, but firmly.

Elena leaned forward in her chair.

"What are you going to do, then?"

Lorena shook her head slowly, then bit her lip as she looked down at her hands.

"I'll think of something."

~ Chapter XI ~

"Hold on to instruction, do not let it go; guard it well, for it is your life. Do not set foot on the path of the wicked or walk in the way of evil men. Avoid it, do not travel on it; turn from it and go on your way. For they cannot sleep till they do evil; they are robbed of slumber till they make someone fall. They eat the bread of wickedness and drink the wine of violence. The path of the righteous is like the first gleam of dawn, shining ever brighter till the full light of day. But the way of the wicked is like deep darkness; they do not know what makes them stumble."

Proverbs 4:13-19
NIV

†

As the day slowly progressed, Lorena occupied herself with studying, realizing that answering to her professors with extra credit rather than none the next day would cut her a little more slack for skipping out.

Though as she sat attempting with little resolve to solve two pages of calculus problems, her mind couldn't help but dwell on her predicament. Despite her refusal to notify the authorities, a small part of Lorena known as her "will" was beginning to think otherwise. However she wasn't convinced that she would actually go through with seeking help, as too much past experience supported the fact that this action would most likely only make things worse.

With a heavy sigh, Lorena set her sharpened-to-a-bit pencil down in order to rub her sleep-deprived eyes. She was exhausted from having to sit up nearly half the night with a nightmare-inflicted Celeste (more than likely due to their far-from-friendly encounter with the gang on their way home), and wondered just how she planned on getting through the rest of the long day ahead.

The phone rang suddenly, jarring her edgy nerves.

Lorena reluctantly rose from the table and sauntered over to the couch, reaching over to pick up the receiver as she collapsed with a sigh.

"Hello?"

"Guess what?" came a familiar voice from the other end.

Lorena closed her eyes and leaned her head back on the arm of the sofa.

"What, Gram?"

"They just gave us the day off—they're replacing the flooring and remodeling."

Lorena frowned.

"And nobody told you this ahead of time?"

Elena chuckled.

"Nobody ever tells us anything ahead of time, Lorena."

"So what are you gonna do for the rest of the day?"

"Well, your Auntie Catt called me right before they let us off, saying she's in town and wants us to have a late lunch with her."

"Oh . . .how long is she here for?"

"Only until tomorrow night. She's just passing through to New York for that home-appliance convention—which she wants me to attend with her."

Lorena opened her eyes and sat up.

"Really? So are you gonna go?"

"I think it might be fun—but what about you and the kids?"

"Don't worry about us, Gram—go have fun. You need a vacation."

Elena sighed somewhat uncertainly.

"Well, the tickets are paid for . . ."

"So go ahead."

"I guess I will—just don't think that my taking a short leave gives you room to wear yourself out. If you need any help, Lorena, call the reverend's wife or one of the elders' families, alright?"

"Sure, Gram—stop worrying."

"So are you going to make it to lunch with us today?"

Lorena sighed this time, glancing at her watch to see that it was already two thirty.

"I'm sorry Gram, but I've got a lot of homework and all."

"Alright, Catt will understand—especially when she sees just how busy you've become these days."

"Lorena Selenez! Good Lord, child, you certainly are getting thin there, aren't you?"

"She certainly is—that's what leading such a busy life will do to you."

Lorena rolled her eyes slightly before reaching out to hug her great-aunt.

"You make me sound as though I'm anorexic, Gram," she called over to Elena, who was setting the mail on the kitchen table. "Hey, Auntie Catt."

It was around six o'clock that evening, and Elena had just walked through the door with her older sister and Lorena's great-aunt.

Catherine Jordan Lewis was a barely above middle-aged woman whom you could easily compare to an even more fun version of your average "cool" grandma. She was as up on youth society, slang and upcoming trends as the high school Homecoming Queen and could beat you any day at giving advice for confused youngsters (most likely due to the fact that she herself owned a successful advice column back in the day and succeeded at becoming Homecoming Queen several times in her prime). Looking like a slightly more laid-back version of her younger sister, only with complimentary silver hair, cut short to add class (in contrast to Elena's shoulder-length, mahogany locks), the only difference between Catt and Elena was their personalities—which weren't the same, yet complimented each other and worked together to make a very interesting friendship.

"Hey yourself, Ms. Busy-Body," Catt replied when she drew away, holding Lorena back slightly to look her over. "I don't know now, El'—I think she's got us beat."

"Leave her be, now, Catt," Elena scolded while shaking her head. "You know she's got us beat, though," she added slyly with a chuckle.

Lorena blushed slightly and smiled.

"You know we're just messin' around, 'Rena," Catt stated with a grin as she walked over to the couch and took a seat. "If we had figures like that we'd—"

"We'd what, Catt?" interrupted Elena with an inquisitive glance.

Catt shrugged.

"Well, we'd look better, now wouldn't we?"

Elena glared as Lorena laughed and headed to the kitchen.

"Coffee, Auntie Catt?" Lorena offered as she plugged in the coffeemaker.

"That would be wonderful, Lorena. Now where are those precious children of yours?"

"Out under the care of other people—so that my granddaughter can take a rest for a change," Elena quipped with a "look" at Lorena.

Catt frowned in confusion.

"Say what?"

Lorena did a slow burn and shook her head.

"She means they're out at friends' houses to spend the night."

"Hmm," Catt pondered aloud. "Aren't they a little young for that, 'Rena?"

"Lorena's too young to be burning herself out—so no, they're not," Elena spoke up as she continued to sort through the mail.

"Well, I remember when you told me not to let Elsa out of my sight for even a second longer than necessary, El.' How is she doing, by the way? Still going around speaking Swahili, gorging herself on grubs and meeting various tribes I suppose?"

"That's right—well, mostly," Elena replied.

"Well, I guess somebody's got to do it. Next time you drop her a line, tell her I said 'hey.' "

Lorena poured the coffee into a mug, and proceeded to take it to her aunt.

"Thank you, Lorena," Catt stated gratefully as she accepted it.

"No problem," Lorena replied, and was about to walk off when Catt touched her arm.

"I didn't know you still wore that locket, 'Rena. I guess I should have assumed you did, though. Let me have a look at it—it's been so long . . ."

Lorena did as she was told, unclasping the locket to hand it to her aunt.

"Your mother held to her word—both pictures are here and still intact," Catt murmured as she held the open locket in her hand and Lorena took a seat beside her on the sofa. "You remember how you, me, Pam and Angela used to argue over who would get it, El'? And how Momma eventually decided to give it to the first of us to have a girl?"

Elena chuckled from where she sat sipping from her own mug of coffee at the kitchen table.

"Do I remember? We argued over that more than we did over clothes and boys."

Catt smiled as she seemed to mentally return to her past as she studied the locket.

"Yeah . . .and then you beat us all to the punch with Elsa. I don't think that poor child ever was fully accepted by her female cousins because of it."

"She got along nonetheless," Elena stated with a slight shrug.

"So I suppose the next recipient is Celeste Vanessa Selenez. I'm guessing you're going to wait until she turns thirteen, right, Lorena?"

Lorena nodded.

"That's the plan."

Catt smiled in satisfaction as she closed the locket and returned it to its current owner.

"I'm glad you're choosing to carry on the tradition. You don't have to, you know. Your mother probably didn't tell you, but it was decided that each time the locket is handed down, its fate lies entirely in the hands of the owner." Catt sighed as she watched Lorena adorn the necklace. "It was a little idea thought up by its original owner—your ancestor. It's said that she thought it would be interesting to see—for as long as she lived, at least—if the tradition to pass it on when the recipient reaches thirteen would withstand time."

"I didn't know that, Auntie Catt. You never told me, Gram."

Elena sighed.

"There's not much we know about that 'original owner,' Lorena—except that she was a Southern belle from Alabama—"

"And whose name we don't even know," Catt finished matter-of-factly.

Lorena appeared confused.

"She must have had a daughter, though, to have been able to pass it down," she pondered.

"True, but it could have been a son, and his wife could have been the next recipient," Catt replied with a shrug.

"Or his daughter," Elena quipped.

"Which would cut off any blood relation to the original owner," Lorena added thoughtfully. "You know, I've always wondered if the two women in the pictures are related."

"You've got a point there," Catt suggested as she set her mug down on the coffee table. "Anything is possible."

"And they do look quite a bit alike," Elena stated as she rose to place her mug in the sink.

"That would suggest a mixed relationship on the part of the Southern belle."

Catt nodded slowly and contemplated.

"You could be right, Lorena. The younger girl does look a little darker."

"And if the pictures were taken at two different times my theory would be supported," Lorena said slowly as she ran her fingers through her hair.

"Not to mention the fact that they both seem to be wearing the original locket," added Elena.

Catt nodded once again.

"Suggesting that the darker one would most likely be the first recipient."

A silence followed, and the relatives sat quietly contemplating the "family mystery" on their hands.

"Didn't you two want to catch that seven o'clock showing tonight?" Lorena spoke up suddenly while looking at her watch.

"You're absolutely right," Catt exclaimed as she rose to her feet. "How did you let me forget, El'?"

Elena rolled her eyes and chuckled as she quickly wiped her hands off on a towel and made her way for the coat rack.

"You let yourself forget, Catt. We'll be back later on tonight—"

"Much later—we old gals can have a good time too," Catt added as she affectionately patted Lorena's chin and headed for the door with her purse in hand.

Elena held the door open for her sister, and Lorena handed her her purse.

"Thank you," she said as she accepted it and adorned her coat. "Don't study too hard, now. Take some time to relax sometime, 'Rena."

"Don't worry about me, Gram—now go before Auntie Catt leaves without you," Lorena replied with a chuckle.

"C'mon El'—it's almost seven already!" Catt called from down the hall.

Elena sighed.

"I'll be back before you're too sleepy to say goodbye to us before our flight."

"Alright."

After giving Lorena a quick hug and kiss, Elena finally hurried after Catt.

Lorena stood in the doorway, watching them go, with a small smile on her face.

"Have fun!"

Making her way up the rusted, old, iron ladder leading to the second floor of the warehouse, Lorena tried her best to ignore the growing butterflies in her stomach.

It was only a matter of seconds before she would find out just what it was that Marisol wanted. Her mind and heart were racing; all she could do was hope she would get out of the building alive.

"Lorena Selenez—it's been a long time," Marisol greeted when her guest reached the top rung and climbed onto the platform.

Lorena took a moment to take in her surroundings, absorbing the bitter reminiscence of being in that building once again. The wooden floor still held its same rustic, knotted appearance—with ancient nails sticking up randomly about the place—and the idle, long metal pipes continued to extend from one wall to another along the ceiling.

Standing directly before her, in front of an old and large, smoky window was Marisol, blending in so well with the hard surroundings that one might have thought she could disappear.

She stood with her feet slightly apart in an almost-demanding stance—her tough arms folded across her chest to radiate sovereignty. A very slight, almost permanent smirk-like smile sat curled across her lips, which rested on a face that—had it not been for the effects of time and substance abuse—seemed frozen in the fancies, whims and pitiful dreams of an abject youth. Her eyes were stone-cold and red at the same time—due to lack of heart and health, respectively. Despite the wear and tear of heroine, cigarettes and stress of the street hustle, they held a youthful glint—which seemed more in favor of staying on her toes than possessing a "girl-next-door" aura. Lastly, her shoulder-length hair was dyed a deep black, hanging loosely in her scarred and drawn face.

At that particular moment, Lorena believed her to be the very personification of power, intimidation and deity.

"It has," Lorena replied shortly.

Before another word was exchanged, Marisol took a few steps forward and sat down in her leather, swivel chair.

"It almost seems like only yesterday we were planning the rest of our lives in this run-down, dirty building," she finally stated thoughtfully as she propped her feet up on a nearby crate.

Lorena smirked.

"Yesterday, Marisa. Things have changed—whether or not you've learned to deal with that."

Marisol's eyes narrowed slightly as the air tensed, and she eventually let out a sigh when the minute-long staring match subsided.

"Have a seat—"

"I'm fine."

"Okay then—cigarette?"

"No."

"Whatever you say—"

"Why don't you just tell me why I was dragged all the way out here?"

Marisol chuckled lightly, lighting a cigarette from a box on the coffee table.

"You always did like to get down to business, didn't you, Selenez?"

"What can I say?" Lorena shrugged, crossing her arms over her chest. "You've been having your flunkies terrorize me and my family for long enough—shouldn't I be allowed to have my chance to end this by now?"

Marisol scowled, then glanced up at her former friend with a smirk.

"Oh, don't worry—you'll have your chance to 'end this' soon enough. But in order to do so, you'll need to work a little bit."

Lorena frowned.

"What do you mean?"

"You haven't forgotten how we run things around here, Lorena, have you?" Marisol asked as she frowned and exhaled a small puff of smoke, holding the cigarette skillfully between two fingers. "If a member quits without the chief's approval, it's solely up to that member to accomplish all of their incomplete jobs and account for all overdue finances in full before the set deadline of two weeks following their resignation."

At the words "overdue finances," Lorena felt her stomach turn. She swallowed before replying, "I must have forgotten that rule."

Marisol frowned, rubbing her palms together.

"But in this case I'm willing to give you your time back—that is, if you're willing to cooperate . . . if you don't—well, simply remember what you and I used to do with our members who skipped out . . . and their families."

A long silence followed, and Lorena contemplated her choices. She could either stress over making what was sure to be a large sum of money in a short time, or answer to the CPs.

"How much time and money?" she asked quietly, as her mouth went dry.

Marisol removed the cigarette from her mouth and looked Lorena in the eye.

"Three grand, one week—no more time, no less money."

With a sick heart and troubled mind, Lorena closed her eyes and let out a sigh.

"Done."

Walking down the dark, mostly vacant sidewalk that night—on her way home from the warehouse—Lorena decided to forsake her instructions to head to Cobra's place, as he was the last person she wanted to associate with at the present. It was hard enough for her to accept the idea of working for the CPs again, and she certainly didn't want to add to her troubles by getting involved with her abusive ex-boyfriend.

Without her car to aid her, Lorena kept her pace brisk, hugging herself slightly to shield her body from the chilly Chicago, late-summer-night breeze.

The homeless and drunk few sat or lay in alleyways or against buildings, paying no particular mind to the young lady making her way down the pavement.

If she kept up her speed it would be less than a half an hour later that she would return home to her kids and relieve the sitter whom she was barely able to pay.

While passing countless bars and strip clubs, Lorena became aware of a pair of oncoming, rushing footsteps from behind. During one of her routine glances over her shoulder, she was surprised and disturbed to find none other than Cobra himself, jogging towards her.

"Oh God . . ." she muttered in frustration as she turned back around and gritted her teeth.

"Lorena, wait!" he called, but she ignored him—quickening her already swift pace.

"Hold up, 'Rena!" Cobra stated when he finally reached her side, grabbing her arm.

"Get away from me!" Lorena returned firmly, roughly shaking her arm free and continuing down the sidewalk.

"Lorena, can we please talk?" Cobra pleaded, now walking backwards and in front of her.

Lorena, being absolutely fed up, glared daggers at him.

"What do you think?!"

"C'mon, Lorena, please—"

"Go away!"

Cobra, obviously not planning on giving up any time soon, stopped dead in his tracks, blocking any further continuation on Lorena's part.

"I'm not letting you go until you agree to talk."

Feeling anger burning inside of her, Lorena literally bit her tongue to keep from getting herself overheated by giving him the cuss-out session of the millennium.

"Cobra," she began quietly, yet heatedly, for the sake of sparing her sickly lungs the beating of a shouting match, "I do not want to be bothered with you right now, so if you would move outta' my way we can both get on with our lives."

"Not until you hear me out, Lorena. You may be stubborn but I ain't any different. We're more alike than you think."

"Don't make me sick—" Lorena began disgustedly as she attempted to brush by him.

"If you'd just listen to me you wouldn't get sick," Cobra replied firmly as he stepped in front of her and placed his hands on her shoulders.

"What do you care about me?" Lorena returned angrily, feeling tears springing up into her eyes.

Wanting more than anything for him not to see her crying, she cursed herself for being weak, but was unable to conceal her pain.

Within seconds, Lorena had burst into tears, sobbing hopelessly into her hands as the mishaps of the past four years began to catch up with her.

"Lorena, look at me . . .please," Cobra said in a highly-out-of-character, soft tone as he removed her hands from her face, placed his own hands on her tear-stained cheeks and looked into her eyes. "Will you hear me out?"

With much difficulty, Lorena somehow managed to get a hold of herself, beginning to realize that it was futile to not let him have his way.

After taking several deep breaths, she pulled away from him, running her hands through her hair with a sigh as she took a few steps to reach the nearest light post.

"You want me to . . .you want me to hear you out," Lorena began slowly and quietly, resting her forehead on her arm, which she held wrapped around the post. "You want me to . . .hear. . . you. . .out?" she repeated confusedly, and Cobra let out a sigh. "What about me?" she asked slowly as she turned to face him, looking him in the eye. "I was . . .I was beaten, humiliated . . .betrayed . . ." Here she paused as her voice caught slightly, and she blinked a few tears out before continuing, ". . . raped, beaten again . . . a-and finally tossed into a dumpster as if I was trash." Lorena swallowed, leaning her head back on the light post as she placed her hands on her forehead and closed her eyes. "And you want me to hear you out?"

Cobra focused on the ground as he stuffed his hands into his pockets.

"Lorena—"

"No, Cobra—I don't have much . . ." she cut in as she opened her eyes, looking at him once again, ". . .I-I'm not the most popular around these parts anymore—I don't have a group of people standing behind me, I don't even have many people I can call my true friends anymore, and I've been abandoned and betrayed a lot of times . . .by a lot of people. But you know what? I'm still here. . . and I've got people counting on me to stay here—whether you ever noticed or not, I didn't abort my son, or my daughter. Because if I did, I would be just like you—and no matter how much you think we're alike." She paused to shake her head. "We're not. We may both be aimless minorities in this world—this-this God forsaken place—but we're not one and the same. And as for my kids—whether I'm layin' dead in a gutter or fighting for my life until I'm too old to remember this place—they're gonna soar, accomplishing every dream, every aspiration you and I could only dream up. They're gonna be able to touch what we can't touch—open doors that we can't even approach . . .because I'm not gonna stop them. And that's why we're not the same."

Cobra finally looked up to meet her piercing stare.

Lorena swallowed and shook her head, wiping a few stray tears away.

"Now you tell me what makes you think I want to hear you out, and then maybe we'll all be free," she stated in conclusion, then finally set off down the sidewalk once again.

"Maybe I've changed . . ." Lorena heard him call after her, but she merely shook her head, wiping the last teardrop from her eye.

The next morning, Lorena awoke to her alarm clock, which was set to go off at five o'clock.

After slowly rolling out of bed, she remembered that she had to somehow come up with $3,000 in six days. Realizing the only half-rational way to do so was to skip school, she called the college with a made-up story about her grandfather passing away and having to leave for Europe to attend the funeral. This seemed to convince them enough to let her off the hook, therefore at least one of her obstacles was out of the way.

That morning, Elena and Catt's plane was scheduled to leave at seven o'clock. Therefore after freshening up and donning a bathrobe, Lorena stepped into the living room to find Elena reading the newspaper over a light breakfast, her luggage sitting at the door.

"Morning, Gram," Lorena greeted, making her way over to the kitchen.

"Lorena," Elena stated in slight confusion as she looked up, "what are you doing up so early? When I got in last night I found you conked out over a pile of books in your room. What time did you fall asleep?"

Lorena scowled as she began to prepare herself a cup of coffee.

"I don't know, Gram—three or four—"

"Three or four?!" Elena exclaimed, then lowered her voice (the kids were still sleeping). "You must have only gotten two hours of sleep, child."

Lorena shrugged, turning the coffeemaker on.

"That's a record high for the past few days," she replied with a smirk.

Elena frowned deeply as she watched her granddaughter begin to pour water into the machine with trembling hands.

"Lorena, I know you don't like me to worry about you, but what else am I supposed to do? You really are burnt out—I used to say that you were on your way, but now I see that you're already there, baby," Elena stated softly, her tone laced with concern.

"I know. But I don't really have a choice," Lorena said quietly with a slight wry laugh.

Elena sighed heavily, shaking her head.

"I can't do this—I'm calling your aunt to tell her I'm not going," she announced as she rose and headed for the phone.

Lorena frowned and quickly walked over to place the phone back on the receiver.

"No, you don't have to do that, Gram. I'm alright—really. I'm only living like this to keep you all safe."

Elena sighed once again.

"Lorena," she began slowly, looking her in the eye, "if you only know what it's like to hear you say that. I'm about to go to the police—you can't carry this weight much longer."

Lorena swallowed as she took a much needed seat on the couch, resting her head in her hands while rubbing her burning eyes.

"I can try," she replied quietly.

A long silence followed, and Elena eventually sat down beside her granddaughter.

"There is such a thing as simply not being able to do something by yourself, Lorena."

Lorena took a slow, deep breath.

"But I'm the only one who can fix this. I-I'm trying to make things normal."

"That's all well and good," Elena replied understandingly, "but just don't let this turn into punishing yourself," she added softly as she smoothed Lorena's hair.

At that moment, the coffee pot began to boil over, and Lorena quickly rose to turn off the machine.

After Catt arrived to take Elena to the airport and goodbyes were exchanged, Lorena made her way back up the staircase to the apartment, and after walking through the door, stood in the middle of the living room for a few seconds, thinking.

The small home was suddenly very silent, and empty—as Elena had suggested that the kids be dropped off to the Barnum family (longtime friends of Elena's and fellow church members) to stay until she returned, in order that Lorena might not have to worry about paying the sitter extra money. Lorena reluctantly allowed the plan to be carried out, and now stood wondering what to do next.

She couldn't remember ever feeling so exhausted in all of her life, and suddenly was forced to sit down in a kitchen chair when the world began to spin.

Slowly massaging her temples, Lorena realized that she was reaching the end of her rope. A few seconds later, after looking up, she noticed that she was seeing things that weren't actually there before her eyes. Black circles would flash every now and then, and she closed her eyes and rubbed them when the images became more persistent.

"How am I gonna get this money?" she voiced aloud with a groan. After sitting a few minutes more, Lorena finally rose to get dressed, and set out for the market to begin her twelve-hour-long work day.

During lunch, as Lorena sat in the tiny break room of the market, munching on a peanut-butter-and-jelly sandwich, a fellow employee came forward, carrying an envelope in one hand.

"This came for you today, Lorena," the girl stated as she handed it to her.

Lorena, puzzled, accepted it.

"Thanks, Jen. Who's it from?" she asked when she saw that there wasn't a return address.

"A guy—one of the NGBs, I think," Jen replied with a shrug.

Lorena raised an eyebrow in curiosity.

"Black—muscular, with blue eyes?"

Jen nodded.

"He dropped by when you went out for your lunch—said to give you that as soon as possible."

"Really?" Lorena inquired quietly as she studied the envelope. "Thanks."

"No prob,'" Jen replied, then left the room.

When Lorena was alone, she set the envelope to the side, planning on trashing it as soon as she finished her sandwich. When she did finish, however, her curiosity began to overtake her anger, and she soon found herself opening it.

Squinting slightly in the dim lighting of the room, she was surprised to find a check inside—addressed to her—and was barely able to make out a three, followed by three zeros, in the space for the amount.

"Three grand . . ." she murmured in disbelief as she held the check in her hands.

Lorena couldn't believe that she was holding a check for the exact amount of money needed to pay the CPs back—no need to work, lose more sleep than she already lost daily, no more stressing…or, at least, that's the first thing that went through her mind. Next came the realization that it was Cobra who had given her the money. Cobra, a guy in whom she would trust on the day that pigs decided to fly.

Seeing that something was obviously amiss, she returned the sizeable check to its envelope with a frown, making up her mind to deal with it after she got off from work.

After being turned away by a highly-sympathetic Mrs. Gianni and instructed to go home to get some much needed rest, Lorena returned home at around six o'clock that evening.

When she walked through the door, the first thing she did was toss her purse to the side, and after that staggered over to the couch to collapse onto it. She had just trekked from the florist shop to the apartment (a two-mile trip)—not to mention gotten through the day standing on her feet for the majority of it.

Lorena felt as though she could fall asleep right at that moment, and was well on her way to doing so, when there came a sudden knock on the door.

At first she pretended as though she didn't hear it, then groaned and somehow managed to get herself off the sofa and to the door.

After looking through the peephole, Lorena was shocked to see Cobra standing on the other side of the door, holding a bouquet of roses.

"Oh God, no . . ." she muttered, then with a sigh, called through the door, "Nobody's home!"

"Lorena, can we please talk?" Cobra replied.

Lorena, in a huff, turned to lean against the door. She was feeling an oncoming headache, and didn't want it to get any worse.

"No—we can't talk. Go away."

"Please, Lorena . . ."

She closed her eyes, wondering how her life could have ever gotten as bad as it currently was. While analyzing her circumstance, she recalled the check, and realized that she did want to know just why he had supposedly given her all of that money.

Once again, her curiosity outweighed her issues, and after taking a full two minutes to consider whether or not she had actually lost her mind, she opened the door—half expecting him to be long gone by then.

But Cobra remained there, only now standing at the railing overlooking the parking lot, his back to the door.

"You wanted to talk to me?" Lorena asked dryly, and he swiftly turned around.

"If that's alright with you," he replied slowly.

Lorena gave him a look as if to say "nothing's alright with me anymore," and rather reluctantly stepped aside for him to enter.

After walking inside, Cobra handed Lorena the roses.

"These are for you."

Casting an unimpressed glance at them, she reached out to take them.

"My birthday's not 'til January."

Cobra shrugged slightly.

"It ain't no crime givin' away roses on a day other than somebody's birthday."

Lorena studied him for a moment, then set the roses on the kitchen table—first clearing away a few school papers and bills.

She could feel his eyes on her the whole time, and wanted their meeting to end as soon as possible.

When she turned to face him, she stood with an expectant look on her face, crossing her arms over her chest.

"So I guess you got that check today . . ." he began slowly.

When Lorena didn't reply, he bit his lip and looked down at the floor.

"I heard about your situation. It's to help you out, you know."

"I don't take money for pity."

"It ain't for that—"

"I don't take money to make amends, either."

Cobra, impatient, nodded.

"You ain't changed at all, Lorena."

"Who has?" she quickly returned, her tone far from kind.

He merely shrugged.

After giving him one more stone-cold glare, Lorena brushed past him to a table by the door, where she had set the check.

"How about you give up whatever revival you're planning and take this back?" she asked coldly as she held the envelope out to him.

His eyes burned into hers; he didn't look at the check.

"Lorena, I ain't takin' it back," Cobra stated firmly.

Clenching her jaw at his stubbornness, Lorena took a deep breath to control her growing anger.

"Just take it, okay?"

But Cobra merely shook his head.

"I don't take back money I give to help make amends," he replied meaningfully, looking her in the eye.

Lorena swallowed back the angry lump forming in her throat, and after tossing the check to the side, wearily made her way for the couch.

Cobra watched her sit down, placing her head in her hands—while sighing heavily.

"Is it alright if I sit?" he asked slowly.

Lorena didn't reply, and Cobra walked over, awkwardly taking a seat next to her.

They remained as they were for a long, silent five minutes, until Lorena finally spoke up, "Why are you torturing me? My life is already a living torment, so you might as well just quit."

Cobra picked at a seam on the sofa, taking a deep breath as he did so.

"Maybe I'm sorry."

"Maybe I'm crazy."

Yet another silence.

"Maybe I'm in love with you," Cobra stated quietly, and with a sincerity that caused every emotion Lorena hated to love feeling for him burn with a passion.

For the first time since she had sat down, she opened her eyes, though kept her head in her hands.

"I am crazy," she muttered hopelessly, wanting to kill herself for allowing her ears to tingle and heart to skip at his words.

"I guess that means I am, too," Cobra replied thoughtfully.

Realizing that she would disintegrate were she to remain near him for another second, Lorena swiftly got to her feet, originally intending to head for the kitchen for some water, but only making it as far as to a kitchen chair.

Gripping the back of the chair while leaning on it slightly, Lorena noticed that she was slowly transforming; part of her wanted him to leave for eternity and another to stay forever. And adding to this, she felt the bittersweet fear she had of him at the young age of fifteen slowly, but surely, returning—and she truly wondered if she really was losing her mind.

"This can't be happening to me . . . I'm stronger than this . . . I am stronger than this!!"

Her mind was slowly drifting . . . making its way back to a place she didn't want to return to, yet wanted to at the same time.

"What's wrong with me?!"

Somehow her obvious exhaustion wasn't aiding matters, and she began to rub her eyes once again.

Cobra, with impeccable timing, spoke up suddenly, "If I were to have changed, Lorena, would you love me?" he asked quietly, standing up and gradually making his way toward her.

Lorena swallowed as hard as she could, but a tear fell nonetheless. The pressure was immensely suffocating, and she suddenly felt as though she couldn't breathe. She felt as though she were fighting without weapons—battling an invincible opponent to no avail whatsoever.

Cobra stopped, having now reached her side.

She could feel his eyes locked onto her, but didn't dare turn to meet them for fear that it would kill her on the spot.

"If you were to fall, would you need me?" he continued softly, and Lorena closed her eyes as she felt the oh-so-familiar sense of defeat. "Or do you already love me. . . already need me?" He finished in a whisper, slowly reaching to gently place his hand on her face, turning it to meet his.

Lorena finally looked into his lightning-blue eyes, and froze—becoming paralyzed like a deer caught in headlights.

For a split second that seemed to last an hour, she felt the whole world stand still, her heart stop beating, and heard pure silence mix with the only audible sounds: their breathing.

When her heart did beat again, she was reunited with her fifteen-year-old self, and returned to the place she hated to consider loving.

~ Chapter XII ~

"When you are assembled in the name of our Lord Jesus and I am with you in spirit, and the power of our Lord Jesus is present, hand this man over to Satan, so that the sinful nature may be destroyed and his spirit saved on the day of the Lord."

I Corinthians 5:4-5
NIV

†

"Is this the building?"

"Yeah."

"A'ight—I'll let you out here. I'll be in once I find a place to park."

Lorena nodded, stepped out of the passenger seat of the brand new Cadillac, and watched Cobra drive off in search of a parking space.

It was about a week after the two had their "talk," and since then they had picked up what they had put off when they broke up. Lorena had forgiven a remorseful and seemingly-transformed Cobra, and life was moving on in what looked to be a good (or at least "better") direction for her. Her car was currently being repaired, groceries and bills—and even some tuition—paid for, and all courtesy of Cobra.

While her car was in the shop, he had been driving her around to work and school—wherever she needed to go—and that particular Friday afternoon, Lorena was urged by her grandmother to see a doctor when she began complaining of not feeling well. Thus, Cobra took up the cab service once again, and drove her to the doctor's office.

When Lorena stepped into the waiting room, she couldn't help but feel a slight sense of nervousness. She had been vomiting often, hadn't been sleeping well, and was fainting every now and then. Lorena knew these were good reasons to see a doctor, but still felt a little uneasy.

After signing in at the front desk, she took a seat in the virtually-empty waiting room. A minute passed, and she finally decided to flip through a magazine. When this became a task, she set it down and stared at the floor.

A few long minutes later, the entrance door opened and in walked Cobra. Lorena felt somewhat relieved to see a familiar face, and attempted to smile when he sat down beside her.

"Hey, how are you holdin' up?" he asked after placing a quick kiss on her cheek.

"Enough to get by . . .I guess."

Cobra smiled, then took her hand in his.

"Relax, you're Lorena Selenez—what's a visit with the doctor to you?"

Lorena chuckled, and less than a few seconds later a side door opened and a nurse stood looking down at a clipboard.

"Lorena Selenez," the woman stated, and Lorena swallowed and stood up.

"Good luck," Cobra whispered, and Lorena managed to smile back at him before letting her hand slide out of his as she followed the nurse through the doorway.

Several tests and three hours later, Lorena sat riding home with the news that she was pregnant . . . again.

When Cobra pulled the car into a space in the high-rise parking lot, he let out a sigh.

"So how are you feelin' now—are those meds kickin' in yet?" he asked after turning the engine off.

Lorena massaged her temple and yawned.

"I'm feelin' a little better. I guess I'm mostly worried . . . three kids, you know?"

"Yeah," Cobra replied slowly, running his thumb along his key ring. "I'll be helpin' out, though. You're gonna work tomorrow, right?"

Lorena nodded.

"Well, how 'bout I take the kids out to the zoo or somethin'—relieve you and your grandma?"

Lorena bit her lip thoughtfully. This was the first time since they had gotten back together that Cobra had volunteered to watch the kids. Pushing away her second thoughts, Lorena shrugged.

"If you can keep up with two energetic toddlers—be my guest," she replied with a smile.

Cobra grinned.

"A'ight then—lemme walk you to your door."

After climbing the steps and reaching the correct floor, Cobra walked Lorena to the door, his arm wrapped around her shoulders as she leaned against him with hers around his waist.

"You tired?" he asked when she let out another yawn.

Lorena smirked.

"I could fall over."

They stopped when they reached her door, and Lorena leaned up against it with a sigh.

"Well, wait until after you've eaten somethin'—you're gettin' as thin as a twig," Cobra stated with a smile. "By the way, is your grandma still makin' that big Sunday dinner?"

Lorena grinned slightly.

"You know it. Lemme guess—you wanna come?"

Cobra shrugged and pretended to look undecided.

"Maybe."

Lorena laughed, then shook her head.

"She won't mind."

"That's good," he replied, and the two stood smiling into each other's eyes for a moment. "I've gotta run—I'll be here to pick you up at around six—"

"Five thirty—please," Lorena corrected. "I wanted to get some extra time in tomorrow."

Cobra looked inquisitive.

"Always wantin' that extra mile, eh?" he questioned, then chuckled. "I'll see you tomorrow."

She smiled, and the two shared a kiss before Cobra headed off down the hall, and Lorena entered the apartment.

For nearly a year and a half, life was smooth sailing for Lorena, and her relationship with Cobra remained intact. During this time, on the eleventh day of June, 1989, the baby was born—this time another girl. Before that day arrived, Lorena knew the baby's gender, however, she didn't know her name, and spent long hours each day flipping through baby-name books—trying to get an idea of what to name her. Once, while browsing through the "E" section, Lorena stumbled upon her mother's name and meaning. Apparently "Elsa" was a variation of "Elizabeth," and could be translated into "consecrated to God"—a meaning that more than seemed to suit her mother, in Lorena's eyes.

When the name books, friends, and even television couldn't give Lorena any name good enough for what she planned to be her last child, she simply let time pass by—deciding to perhaps name her after she was born.

This was exactly what Lorena did, as when the child was born, her skin color immediately suggested a name pertaining to honey or toffee—but mostly caramel. Thus the name stuck, and Caramelle Sade Selenez was born. Her middle name translated into "light" in Finnish—an idea given Lorena when she saw that the baby's eyes turned out to be a most interesting shade of light blue—the lightest she had ever seen, thus they almost seemed glassy or mirror-like. The doctors explained that they would most likely change to a more common shade as time progressed, but even though Caramelle's skin (which was very light at first) darkened to a bronzed milky chocolate, her eyes remained the same.

One Monday night, in the early days of autumn, Lorena was about to begin studying after putting the kids to sleep (including the baby), when she felt thirsty and decided to head to the kitchen for a drink of water.

Walking past through the living room, she noticed her grandmother seated on the couch, her reading glasses adorned as she sorted through a large pile of bills on the coffee table.

"How's it coming?" Lorena inquired as she opened a cabinet to find a glass.

Elena sighed and rubbed her forehead.

"Good enough," she replied with a light smile. "They're all asleep?"

Lorena smirked as she held the glass under the faucet.

"Let's just say they're almost there. I think today's trip to the theater with their dad got them so excited that they'll be a while."

Elena shook her head and chuckled.

"It'll catch up with them soon enough."

At that moment, the baby could be heard crying from Lorena's room, and Nathan appeared in the hallway, rubbing his eyes.

"Mommy, she's crying again," he stated wearily before yawning.

Lorena sighed, and set her glass down on the counter.

"Alright Natty—go on back to sleep. I'll get her," she replied as she made her way across the room.

"I'll heat up her bottle," Elena offered as she rose.

"Thanks, Gram."

After gingerly picking her up from her crib, Lorena returned to the living room with a crying Caramelle.

While waiting for the bottle to heat, she took a seat in the oversized chair with a sigh, attempting to console the child. When the bottle was finally readied, Lorena began to feed Caramelle, who after several minutes eventually fell asleep.

Elena looked up from her paperwork with a smile when she saw Lorena's success.

"You're getting good, there, Lorena."

She chuckled.

"Shouldn't I already be good? What about the other two?"

Elena laughed lightly.

"There's always more to learn."

Lorena rolled her eyes and shook her head with a smile.

A moment of silence followed, which was soon broken by Elena being in a coughing fit.

When she finished, Lorena frowned.

"You okay, Gram?"

Elena cleared her throat and waved her hand before getting up for a glass of water.

"Of course I am—you're starting to sound like me."

Lorena smiled at her grandmother's sense of humor, then sighed contentedly as she looked down at the sleeping child in her arms. Every now and then, Caramelle's tiny fingers would twitch, and her chest rose and fell as she breathed silently. Lorena smoothed her soft, chestnut hair—taking care not to wake her.

"I forgot to tell you—a call came from Connecticut today," Elena stated when she returned to the couch.

Lorena pondered the statement. She hadn't heard from Tony in a good four months, and wondered how he was doing.

"Oh?"

"Yeah—it was Tony, and he just said he was calling to see how you were doing, and explain why he hadn't contacted you in so long."

"Really . . ." Lorena replied thoughtfully, hoping things were going well for him.

"So how did that math test go today?" Elena questioned, changing subject as she glanced over several bills.

Lorena leaned her head back in the chair, closing her eyes.

"Okay, I guess. I just wish I understood the subject better, you know?"

Elena nodded as she punched a few calculations into a nearby calculator.

"You'll make it."

"I sure hope so . . ." Lorena replied quietly, her mind beginning to wander as she felt sleep calling her name.

She was on the brink of reaching full unconsciousness when a voice sounded from her room, "Mommy! I had a bad dream!"

Opening her eyes with a slight start, Lorena was about to get up when Elena gestured for her to remain seated.

"I'll take care of it—you've got enough on your hands with that newborn."

Lorena smiled gratefully as Elena left the room.

"Thanks Gram," she said softly, then closed her eyes once again.

Less than fifteen minutes later, Elena returned to find Lorena sound asleep in the chair—looking as peaceful as the child in her arms.

She smiled, and quietly went back to her work.

A few days later, driving home from a long day at work and school on a cloudy autumn evening, Lorena yielded to a string of emergency vehicles, paying them no particular mind when she continued on. Minutes later, she pulled into the Cabrini-Green lot and was slightly surprised to see that the ambulances were parked outside of the building.

Immediately thinking there was a mishap with gang members or any other urban disturbance, she parked the car and alighted with a sigh.

Children on bicycles crowded around the ambulance, playing and laughing, and Lorena slowly made her way up the many flights of stairs to the top floor—keeping her eyes peeled for anything out of the ordinary . . . just in case.

When she reached the top floor and exited the stairwell into the hall leading to her door, she noticed a great commotion, involving neighbors standing in their doorways, or bunched in the hall—each with their eyes glued on the other end.

With a deep frown and elevated heart rate, Lorena pushed through, quickening her pace when she realized that the trouble was near her own apartment . . . possibly even *at* her own apartment.

Not stopping to think to ask someone what was wrong, she continued forward, soon enough suddenly noticing that she wasn't having to push through anymore—the people were creating a path for her, their eyes filled with fear and even sympathy as they stared at her.

Beginning to feel sick to her stomach, Lorena was finally close enough to see that the paramedics were, in fact, in her apartment.

A teenage girl who attended Elena's church stood near the door, holding Caramelle in her arms while Nathan and a crying Celeste hugged her leg.

Lorena's first instinct was to go to her kids, but after realizing that her grandmother wasn't anywhere in sight, she bolted for the open door, where paramedics blocked the entrance.

"Let me through—please, let me through!!" Lorena cried as she let her purse fall to the ground, trying desperately to get inside.

"Ma'am, I'm sorry, but you can't go inside—" a young EMS began to say as he held Lorena back.

"You don't understand—my grandmother's in there!" she interrupted in a panic.

The paramedic frowned slightly, then turned and called to the rest inside, "Her granddaughter's at the door here—can we let her in?"

At the same time, a tall and slim middle-aged woman exited the apartment, and paused when she saw Lorena.

"Lorena, you're here!" she exclaimed.

"Tell me what's going on, Mrs. McCullough!" Lorena cried when she recognized the woman to be the reverend's wife.

Mrs. McCullough took Lorena's face in her hands, a look of sympathy and concern on her face.

"It's your grandmother—she collapsed earlier today, and a neighbor arrived shortly after to call the paramedics. We don't know what's wrong right now—I was on my way over in the first place when I saw all the commotion."

The news hit Lorena like a slap on the face, and she swallowed as her heart stopped beating.

"Let me-let me go see her . . ." she began as she felt a sense of panic.

"Lorena, they're doing their job right now—just wait a moment—"

"No, let me go see her—I need to see her!!" Lorena protested, tears rolling down her cheeks as she attempted to get inside, but was held back once again.

The whole night was spent in the emergency room, with Lorena at her grandmother's bedside as she went through various tests and received treatment for what they diagnosed as slight "exhaustion." The next day, the woman was released, and instructed to take it easy for a while.

As for Elena, she insisted that she felt alright—and was merely a little tired. But one of the traits Lorena inherited from her grandmother was being responsible, and she saw to it as best she could that the doctor's orders were heeded.

A few days later, after most of the trouble subsided, Lorena's normal routine continued, and she continued on with her busy schedule.

Around two weeks after the incident, Lorena left a psychology class held in the evening at school to climb into her car for the drive home. While on the way, her mind drifted to the past train of events, and the way her life was unfolding before her. She still worried about her grandmother often, and despite the many times she had tried to persuade her to retire, the woman held firm in her decision to stay in the work field for at least ten more years. Oftentimes Lorena would wonder what events the next day held, and even though Marisol and the rest of the gang seemed to be satisfied with the cash she had given them about a year back, she found herself worrying that things weren't actually getting better. Somehow she felt as though the gang would always have a hold on her, and it was merely something with which she was forced to live.

When Lorena walked through the door of the apartment, she found the home empty and a note lying on the kitchen table. It read:

Lorena,

I took the kids out for a family game night at the church (wish you could come). I won't keep them out too long—expect us back at around eight.

P.S. Help yourself to some hot dogs that I bought at the market today—goodness knows you need the extra weight!

Love,
Gram

Lorena smiled lightly when she finished reading the note, then after placing her backpack in her room, began to prepare herself a hotdog.

Halfway through her light meal, the phone rang suddenly, and as she plopped onto the couch, she reached over to answer it.

"Hello?" she said after swallowing her food.

"Olà, signõrita."

Lorena sat up from her reclining position and smiled.

" 'Tonio! What's happenin'?"

Tony chuckled at her enthusiasm from the other line.

"Nothin' much—how are you?"

"I'm fine. I haven't talked to you in—what's it been—two years!"

"I know—I'm sorry I haven't written in so long. I've been so busy lately that I've barely had time to keep in touch with my family."

Lorena shook her head and grinned.

"Well, you can't rush a soon-to-be attorney. So you're not mad at me?"

Lorena laughed aloud.

"Of course I'm not mad at you 'Tonio—I'm just so glad to hear you right now . . . it's been forever."

"Yeah, it has."

"So fill me in—how's Yale treating you these days?"

Tony smiled.

"Well, they're definitely not the type to go easy on a guy—I've got so much work that relaxation is becoming a forgotten concept."

Lorena smirked.

"I feel ya'—college can do that."

"It sure can," he replied with a short laugh. "Other than that, things are going well."

"I'm sure you've met all kinds of new people—made new friends. Tell me, what's the dirt on the Yale crowd?"

Tony chuckled.

"Well, they certainly know how to use their money—a lot of the kids have parents that own yachts, and some even own yacht clubs! But they're cool—it's a big change from the city life, though."

"I can imagine."

"But, uh, I actually have made some good friends," he continued slowly. "After a lot of hard work, I became vice-president of the Student Council—most of the people in it are pretty cool."

Lorena smiled, picturing Tony as a vice-president quite easily.

"Congrats—that's no easy slot to advance to."

"Thanks, and it sure isn't. But the job is okay—I get to make decisions that impact the way some things are run, and it's good experience."

"That's really cool, 'Tonio," Lorena stated sincerely as she stretched out on the sofa. "So tell me about some of your friends—the ones closest to you."

"Well, there's the treasurer of the Student Council, Cynthia—whom I think you would get a kick out of. She reminds me a lot of you—a natural born leader."

Lorena chuckled.

"Then there's Aaron—the president. He pretty much helped me get into the whole council thing. And, um, Michelle—the secretary...whom I've been dating for about a year and a half now."

Lorena slowly set her hot dog down, this bit of news coming as a slight surprise to her ears.

"Oh," she replied with a small smile, "that's cool—so what's she like?"

Tony sighed lightly.

"Well, she's just pretty much your average girl. Her dad is chief of campus security, and her mom is a professor."

Lorena nodded.

"That's, um . . .interesting. So what are her plans for the future?"

There came a slight pause before Tony answered, and she wondered if he was hesitating.

"Um, things are a little cloudy for both of us right now. You see, Lorena, we're, uh, we're engaged."

Upon hearing Tony's last statement, Lorena felt a chill run down her spine, and her stomach turned. Suddenly having lost her appetite, she set her plate on the coffee table and swallowed.

"Oh," she responded in as normal a tone as she could manage, then bit her lip as she began to twist her necklace chain. "That's. . . great, 'Tonio. I'm, uh . . .really happy for you."

From the other line, Lorena thought she sensed him being able to read the uneasiness in her voice.

"Thanks, Lorena," he replied slowly. "She's a . . .nice girl, you know—the kind that you taught me to look for."

Lorena found herself struggling to keep her emotions calm, and realized that she was gripping her locket.

Somehow there was something far from rewarding in being told that she had helped her friend find a potential wife.

"I guess you didn't find her before . . ." she whispered.

"I'm sorry—what did you say?" Tony questioned as a sudden wave of static hit the lines.

Lorena couldn't believe that she had just stated her emotions aloud, but was glad to know that Tony obviously didn't hear her.

"Oh, nothing, I was just um . . ." She let out an inward sigh as she rose to a sitting position, " . . .thanking you . . .uh, you know, for, um . . .befriending me way back when," she stated in a slow and awkward rush of attempting to voice her feelings. "You know, I mean . . . I'm not really the greatest person on the planet," she finished, closing her eyes when she finally felt the tear falling down her cheek.

"But you are one of my favorites—and it's no problem, Lorena. Thank you for befriending me."

A remnant of a smile made its way onto Lorena's face, but soon disappeared altogether.

"It wasn't hard to do," she replied quietly and sincerely.

A short silence followed, and Tony finally broke it with a sigh.

"Well, um, I really need to go now—I've got work to do and I have to catch a late dinner with Michelle's paren—uh, some. . . people. But I'm sorry I couldn't hear more about you—I'll call again soon."

"It's fine, 'Tonio," Lorena replied as she placed her head in one hand. "I'll let you go, then."

"Okay, 'bye."

" 'Bye."

After hearing the click on the other line, Lorena slowly set the phone back onto its base, suddenly feeling numb. Her emotions seemed to be behind a good bit, and she wondered if she was only dreaming. But it was when the sudden overwhelmingly-deafening silence of the room filled her soul that her feelings caught up, crashing into her already cracked heart and altogether shattering it.

Lorena sobbed silently into her hands, feeling as though the world was slowly suffocating her; draining her life and artificial hope with a power she could no longer match nor fight. And what is a warrior without a weapon? A mere forgotten dream; fading in the boisterous winds of each passing trial.

Monday arrived cloudy, dull, and dreary, filling the sky with endless folds of gray blankets—ready to drench the earth with its rains while holding the sun captive behind its screen of darkness.

Setting out for school after the kids were bussed off and the sitter arrived to watch Caramelle, Lorena felt as though the weather couldn't match her feelings any better. Sleep the night before was non-existent, and she found herself running solely on caffeine; though she wasn't even sure as to why she was still running.

That night, she originally had planned an evening out with Cobra, but she soon called him to cancel, stating simply that she wasn't feeling well. It wasn't until after her conversation with Tony that Lorena realized the true reason as to why she was dating Cobra—she was using him as a sort of medicine, an antidote, something to numb the pain life was inflicting upon her. Every time he told her he loved her she felt as though she were the luckiest girl on the planet; but every time she recalled her past with him she felt like the trash inside of the garbage receptacle she was dumped into by the same "loving" guy.

Lorena was teetering on the edge of a cliff—every day she wondered why she had survived the attack she made against herself years back. Elena viewed it as a "miracle from the Lord," but Lorena couldn't see herself serving anyone who would allow her life to crumble before their eyes when they had the power to make things perfect—or at least better. She was to the point now where she was praying—in her own way, constantly questioning God; blaming Him for letting her rot.

The day progressed, though on a sour note. On the way out of the classroom in which her psychology classes were held, Lorena was stopped by the teacher and asked if she would see the student counselor on duty (she always marveled at Mr. Beacher's ability to almost read his students' minds—but then, he was a psychologist).

Not particularly caring where her mental status stood, Lorena took the professor's recommendation as exactly what it was: a recommendation; something she could either follow, or disregard. Therefore she chose to disregard it, and went on with her day.

After school came work—at the florist that particular day—and though Mrs. Gianni was constantly casting her worried glances, Lorena let the walls of ice surrounding her pile up even higher.

When she finally got off the job that night, she drove her car through the various neighborhoods home—functioning solely on "autopilot." Walking up those horrific flights of stairs, Lorena realized that she didn't want to help the kids get ready for bed, tuck them in, nor put up with a screaming four-month-old for half the night.

Finally, she reached the apartment door, and after unlocking it, opened it and walked inside.

The living room was lighted, and the smell of roast beef lingered in the air. Sitting on the floor by the couch, arguing over a toy truck were Nathan and Celeste.

With a heavy sigh, Lorena set her backpack and purse down by the door, deciding to get some water before going into her room to see Caramelle.

"MOomMy! He took my toy and won't give it back!!" Celeste shrieked as tears streamed down her cheeks.

"I did not—it's my toy, not yours!" Nathan shouted back at her, and Lorena's already-pounding headache upgraded to a migraine.

"You two don't even greet me anymore, now?" Lorena exclaimed in irate disbelief. After nearly slamming the cabinet door, she stated over her shoulder, "Both of you aren't getting any more trips to the park, zoo, or theater if you don't stop fighting. Do you understand me?"

Not very accustomed to hearing their mother quite so angry with them, Nathan and Celeste immediately grew quiet.

"Yes ma'am," they replied in unison.

Lorena held her glass under the faucet, and after finding no water coming out when she turned the knob, she sighed again, slamming the glass onto the counter in frustration.

¡"No puedo que creerlo! If I go another day worrying over these bills—where's Grammy?" Lorena asked in vexation as she made her way across the living room.

"In her room," Nathan answered quietly.

When Lorena reached the hallway, she was upset to hear the baby beginning to cry and scream from inside her room, and did a slow burn—not exactly feeling like dealing with her at the moment.

"Gram, did you pay the water bill today?" Lorena called through Elena's closed door after knocking.

No response.

Lorena sighed again.

"Gram, are you awake?" she pressed.

Silence met her inquiry, and with a frown in frustration and confusion, she slowly opened the door, only to see that the room was seemingly empty.

"Gram?"

This time, a very slight sound could be heard coming from the other side of the bed—an incoherent whisper, almost.

Lorena walked around the four-post bed, and felt her heart skip several beats when she found her grandmother lying on the floor by the bed, her face drawn and pale.

"Oh God! Gram—what's wrong?!" Lorena exclaimed as she immediately dropped to her knees at her side.

"Lor . . .e-ena . . ." Elena stated with much difficulty, her tone just barely above a whisper.

"Gram—what's happened to you?" Lorena questioned in a panic as she took hold of her grandmother's trembling hand.

"I-it's ti . . .me . . .f-for m-e to . . ." the woman struggled to voice, but her words were disconnected and slurred—sounding as though speaking had become a task for her.

Lorena's thoughts seemed to be colliding, and she couldn't think of anything else to do but hold onto her hand.

"I'm here—I-I'm right here, Gram. I-I-I'll call for an ambulance, and you'll be alright," she stated with a quivering voice as her eyes overflowed with tears. "Just don't leave me . . .please—oh God, don't leave me . . ."

Knowing that she had to call the paramedics, Lorena rose suddenly and dove for the phone on the nightstand to dial 911—cursing her fingers for not being able to dial any faster.

"911—what is the emergency?" came an operator's voice on the line.

"My grandmother—she's-she's having a heart attack, a-a stroke maybe! Please send help—we're at Cabrini-Green, apartment 10b-"

"Alright ma'am—try to stay calm. I'm sending an ambulance over immediately, okay?"

But Lorena didn't reply; Elena was beginning to draw her breaths in suddenly, as though she were having trouble receiving air.

Dropping the phone, Lorena was at her side in an instant.

"They're on their way, Gram—just hold on, you'll be alright," she tried to reassure her, holding her hand once again.

Elena's eyes roamed over the room, eventually landing on Lorena, and they immediately filled with tears.

"Do . . .n't . . .gi-gi..ve i-n to . . ." she made an attempt to put a sentence together, and Lorena swallowed hard.

"I'm right here—you'll be alright," she continued to say reassuringly; thinking that if she held onto her hand tightly enough she could keep her alive.

Rather jerkily, Elena rose her free hand up to Lorena's tear-stained face, touching it as a tear rolled down her own.

"Th-the . . .sn . . .ake . . .I . . .lo-o . . .ve . . .y-yo . . .u s-so . . .m-u ...ch . . .d-do..n't gi . . .ve . . .up."

Lorena felt her grandmother's hand go limp, and watched in pure shock as her glazed eyes slowly closed for the very last time; her head falling to the side as the life left her body.

~ Chapter XIII ~

"Comfort, comfort my people, says your God. Speak tenderly to Jerusalem, and proclaim to her that her hard service has been completed, that her sin has been paid for, that she has received from the LORD'S *hand double for all her sins."*

Isaiah 40:1-2
NIV

†

"Who can find a good person—a truly good person that you can talk to, want to be around, and love as your own self? Who can find a human being who would cut off their right arm in order to give you what is best for you? Tell me who can find a person who would sacrifice their time, money, and dreams in order that you may experience life to its fullest? If you could find this rare type of person on this earth, that person would mostly likely be our dear sister. For you can ask anyone who knew her and they would tell you that she was a true gift from the Lord. And I believe that she would not want us to remember her in sadness, but rather with a glad heart.

"Our sister is no longer in a realm where there is pain, sickness, bills, doctor appointments or even tears. Now she has joined those that have gone before us in glory, and is praising the King of Glory. God was on the pages of Sister Jordan's life, and we will always remember her in gladness until that day when we may see her again. May God bless each and every one of you, and to the family—you are in my prayers, and I believe that the whole church can stand with me and truthfully say that we are here for you."

"Our Father which art in heaven, Hallowed be thy name. Thy kingdom come. Thy will be done in earth, as it is in heaven. Give us this day our daily bread. And forgive us our debts, as we forgive our debtors. And lead us not into temptation, but deliver us from evil: For thine is the kingdom, and the power, and the glory, forever. Amen."

(Matthew 6: 9-13) KJV

Standing under an umbrella provided by Catt, holding a sleeping Caramelle in one arm and the other wrapped around Nathan and Celeste's shoulders, Lorena let another teardrop fall as the reverend came forward to hand her a rose from the arrangement atop her grandmother's casket.

Handing Caramelle off to Cobra, who stood to her right, Lorena silently accepted the rose and waited for the pallbearers to lower the casket into the ground. Nearby sobs echoed from a thin woman dressed in a black dress—five years over thirty—carrying her own umbrella as her aunts Pam and Angela each wrapped an arm around her trembling shoulders.

Lorena watched out of the corner of her eye as her mother was handed a rose by the reverend—next came her great-aunts and uncles.

The world around her seemed to be a false reality, though, and had it not been for the tormenting pain burning in her soul—granting the situation life—Lorena would have persuaded herself into believing it to be so.

"Are you alright?" Cobra whispered over to her, but she barely heard him and didn't reply.

With her eyes remaining to be riveted on the casket, Lorena left Nathan and Celeste's sides to step into the line that would file past the casket.

Feeling sick with grief, she waited at the end of the line for her other relatives to abandon their roses.

Finally, it came her turn, and Lorena stood staring over the lowered casket, inside which her sleeping grandmother, ultimate guardian and genuine best friend lay. Tears cascaded down her numb cheeks, but she refused to collapse under the pain. She was taught to fight her opponents, and wouldn't let her grandmother's last view of her be that of a weak pile of emotion. Swallowing back the unremitting, immensely tight lump in her throat, Lorena let the rose fall onto the casket, closing her eyes and tearing bitterly as life whipped her broken heart.

She didn't know how long she stood there, but it was when a familiar presence reached her side that she found herself crying into Elsa's shoulder—soon pulling away, though, to wipe hopelessly at her eyes and follow the rest of the funeral procession out of the cemetery.

The next few days (along with those before them) passed over a shock-inflicted Lorena, whose will to even get out of bed in the morning was virtually gone. Catt stayed with her for two full weeks—watching over the kids and taking care of the house, and when she left, Lorena was alone.

During the time that Catt stayed, Elsa (who was staying at a local hotel) visited the apartment several times, but each time Lorena would lock herself in her room—refusing to even look at her.

Before leaving, Catt informed Lorena that her mother had recently married a wealthy businessman whom she had met when she moved to Africa, and was living happily in South Africa—jump starting a ministry. This news came as no surprise to the hopeless Lorena, and only gave her more reason to believe that the world was slowly coming to a bitter end.

After the outpouring showers of sympathy through phone calls, cards, flowers, meals and gift certificates, life gradually returned to its normal state.

It took a full four weeks for Lorena to recover enough from her grief to be able to resume her schedule, and though she managed to stay alive for her children's sake, the pain and burdens she daily carried weighed more heavily seemingly each passing moment.

Close to two months following Elena's death, Lorena plodded through the snow-covered sidewalk to a lot where she had parked her car. The temperature was well below freezing, and with a shiver she pulled her heavy winter coat closer around herself. She had just wrapped up a tutoring session with a college freshman in her psychology class, and was hurrying home from the student's apartment to pay the sitter and prepare the kids some dinner.

The relentless, bone-chilling Chicago gusts soared through the dry, wintry air—carrying the snowflakes safely to the ground.

Lorena adjusted the scarf around her neck, and sighed as she neared a building she was forced to pass: Tony's church. Every Wednesday night, she walked by the building from the lot where she parked her car, and each time she would remember Tony's invitation for her to visit.

Now Lorena paused when she reached the building, feeling winded suddenly and slightly exhausted from the long walk in the cold and snow. She took a moment to lean up against the iron railing of the building's outer staircase, attempting to catch her breath. As she did so, the door opened, and a small family walked out—the mother carrying a little child in her arms while the father held the hands of two toddlers.

After casting Lorena a courteous smile, the parents continued down the sidewalk, laughing and chatting about that night's activities.

The large, oak doors of the old church building remained open for several seconds—obviously too heavy to swing closed with much speed.

Lorena felt a warm rush of air float from the inside of the building to the sidewalk, and could smell the sweet fragrance of apple cider.

After lapsing into a coughing fit, she sighed and closed her eyes. She didn't know how much more of life she could take, and suddenly felt the full load of the exhaustion she had been carrying for years. But when she found herself considering entering the church building—even if just to momentarily escape the harsh weather—she quickly set off down the sidewalk, wondering what had gotten into her.

Several months went by, and the end of June ushered in an unusually hot and humid summer pattern for the city of Chicago. Because she was already slaving to retain possession of the apartment, Lorena was unable to afford air conditioning. Adding to this, her car seemed to be slowly drooping towards a state of simply not being able to go two inches down the road anymore. Bill collectors rang her number seemingly every hour, the mailbox overflowed with tuition bills, and twice the young homemaker had to pawn belongings in order to keep her children fed.

Besides the material problems in existence, there also stood the social issues—those concerning Tony, and how Lorena hadn't heard from him since their revealing conversation at the end of the previous year; but what concerned her most was Cobra. A few weeks after her grandmother's death, she had told her boyfriend that it was time to call it quits. Lorena explained that she was tired, stressed beyond words, and tied up with so many financial dilemmas that she had no other choice but to keep her focus solely on work and school.

She had relayed her decision to him in the form of a message on his answering machine, and grew increasingly pensive and slightly anxious when he never returned her call. Weeks turned to months, and without any word from or sight of Cobra, Lorena became very concerned—wondering if she had set herself up for more trouble from him. Cobra was the most powerful member of his gang, and she well knew that being put in a situation where one is in a rocky relationship with a chief was unsafe, but still hoped that he had simply moved on. Something, though, was constantly telling her that her first hunch was the correct one.

The intimidating teenager made her way down the vacant, dark alleyway, not the least bit disquieted by the hovering shadows or distant gunshots in the air. With a restless sigh, she straightened her red, leather jacket, rolling the sleeves up slightly to reveal unsightly battle and drilling scars. A light passing breeze caused her to shiver, and she reached up to adjust a black bandana tied around her head and over one particularly sensitive eye, shielding it from the wind. In her pocket was her favorite knife, on her belt a solid gold pistol, and wrapped around her waist a 5-pound chain. Her lean frame wouldn't suggest one that could carry such a heavy weapon, but from long years of training she had become more than used to the extra weight.

At nineteen years of age she held the respect of every man, woman, boy and girl she had overthrown in the palm of her hand (or the barrel of her gun), and each day breathed by the fact that she was one of the most powerful beings on the streets. Her stone-cold eyes had seen countless individuals fall at the mercy of her hands, witnessed an infinite number of murders, watched in infatuated delight as the blood of the innocent cascaded down her assault weapons, and each instance with a sinister, unquenchable sense of desire for omnipotence.

There was something about her that caused others to feel a great amount of fear when she passed—something wicked; demonic. It was as if an evil being existed inside of an otherwise simply-unfortunate teen who had fallen for an infamous lie; feeding off of each murder, fight, or increase in power. It controlled her, and the more she gave in to its desires, the stronger it became.

With much ease, the gang banger climbed over a chain-link fence, landing gracefully on the other side, where a vast, run-down lot was located. The air held a tense quality, and one could almost smell the hunger for action, adrenaline; anything that would add life to a virtually-boring night.

Standing in the middle of the lot, she waited, stuffing her hands into her pockets while looking up at the clouded sky.

Seconds later, another individual made his way over the fence, walking up behind her.

"What took you so long?" she asked without turning.

"Bull," he replied shortly, rubbing his light blue eyes before slowly pacing between two weeds in the asphalt.

"Did you talk to her today?" the girl asked, plucking at a leather band around her wrist.

"Did I talk to who?" he returned, in slight annoyance.

"Who do you think?—Selenez."

He smirked suddenly, then laughed.

"No way—I got her thinkin' I done fell off the planet."

She laughed shortly, pulling the end of her chain taut several times.

"Just like we planned. I could murder her right now if I wanted to."

He cast her a quizzical glance.

"Do you want to?" he asked sarcastically.

Before replying, she spotted a large weed on the ground and swiftly chopped it in half with the weapon—displaying her skill clearly, and answering his question.

At that moment, more individuals mounted the fence—Hispanic teenage girls and black teenage guys coming from all directions.

Eventually, a young woman clad in a heavy, black leather jacket and pink bandanas wrapped around her forehead and arms pushed her way through the crowd.

"You're late," the younger girl called as the other made her way to the center of what was now a circle of youths.

"*Lo siento*, 'Nita—you're early," she replied shortly, then smiled when the guy came forward, wrapping her in a tight embrace. "*Buenas noches*, Cobra."

"I don't care who's late or who's early—I just wanna know why we've been dragged out here!" a guy called from the outskirts of the group.

"Yeah, Marisa,—what's the deal?" another added—this time a girl—and the others chimed in agreement.

Marisol sighed in annoyance, and Anita glared at the group.

"Keep your shirts on! How am I s'posed to talk over all of you?"

Cobra rolled his eyes at the crowd, then whistled through his fingers.

"Yo, listen up!" he shouted, and immediately the youths became silent. "We've got somethin' real important to discuss here, so shut up!" With that, Cobra gestured for Marisol to speak.

"Alright, you all know the CP's current long-term goal: to wipe Selenez out. Well, it turns out we're nearin' the homestretch, here. We can pick her off soon—"

Before Marisol could finish, the crowd began to whistle and cheer, but Anita folded her arms over her chest, clearing her throat meaningfully while casting an expectant glance at Marisol.

Menacingly, Marisol continued, "I mean, you can help wipe her out—the actual job has been left up to Anita. But right now we can approach this in one of two ways: either we take the time to keep making Selenez's life just a little bit more tormented and set a date to kill her, or we can go ahead and do it."

When the crowd started to discuss the situation amongst themselves, this time Marisol cast Anita an expectant look.

With a sigh of boredom, Anita stepped forward.

"All in favor of killin' Selenez now, say 'ay,' " she called, and a little under half of the group agreed.

With a sideways glance at Cobra and Marisol, she continued, "All who oppose and wanna set a date . . ."

This time, more than half of the group opposed the first option, and the final decision was made.

Marisol shrugged, and Anita gritted her teeth at the thought of more waiting.

"There's nothing wrong with a little more torture, Anita. Now relay the rest of the plan," Marisol ordered, then turned to Cobra, wrapping her arms around his neck as he wrapped his around her waist. "This will require some extra help from you and the boys," she stated quietly with a twinkle in her eye.

He smiled understandingly as Anita began to explain the plan to the group.

"Anything you ask."

"Hurry up kids—you're gonna be late for the bus!" Lorena called over Nathan and Celeste's giggling as she passed by the open bathroom, where they were brushing their teeth.

In her arms was a sleepy Caramelle, whom she soon handed off to the sitter, Tanya, (a girl around nineteen or so), who stood waiting in the living room.

"Okay, the baby's medicine's in the 'fridge, so if her cough comes back, you can give her a dose," Lorena stated as she began to write out the directions for taking the medicine, then stopped when she remembered something. "I'll be right back," she said as she set off down the hall—and kept walking, to the other side—where Celeste and Caramelle's new room was located (thanks to Cobra, who had long since paid the landlord off to make an agreement to use part of the next apartment over as an additional room for Lorena—as when Caramelle was born, there would soon be a shortage of rooms for the small family). After grabbing a soft, polar bear plushie from out of Caramelle's crib, Lorena returned to the living room and handed it to Tanya.

"I just bought this the other day—she seems to like it and it usually keeps her from crying for too long. If there's any trouble with her cough, just gimme a call."

Tanya smiled slightly at Lorena's determination to cover everything.

"Alright, Lorena. I'll manage—you're gonna be late for class if you don't leave."

Lorena sighed.

"I know, but I've gotta walk them to the bus," she replied as she bit her lip and headed for the bathroom once again, but stopped when the two kids came running out—racing to the front door to put their shoes on.

Once they had done so and had their backpacks adorned, Lorena kissed Caramelle goodbye, wished Tanya luck, and finally left with Nathan and Celeste for the parking lot.

Hours of school and a long shift at the market later, Lorena found herself struggling to keep her eyes open at the wheel as she put up with the noontime heat while driving from the market to the florist. The air seemed to be oppressing her, causing her to feel sleepy and even more exhausted than she already was.

Without a cloud in the sky, the bright sun glared off of the mirrors and windshields of other cars, and Lorena had to squint in order to get down the road without a collision.

Turning on a nearly-fried radio, she learned that the temperature was nearly ninety-four degrees, yet felt more like ninety-eight. Adding to this, the humidity was ninety-five percent.

". . . this is not a good day to be outside, folks. Any picnic plans, bird watching, sightseeing—whatever—is not a good idea today. Take it from me, the weather guy—stay inside as much as possible…"

Lorena slowly brought the car to a stop at a red light, then rubbed the sweat from her eyelids. Without air conditioning in her car, she had to keep the windows down, but without air circulation, she felt as though she could pass out.

With a swallow, she reached over into the passenger seat for a paper fan she had created in a desperate attempt for relief, only to find that it had slid out of the chair and onto the floor (out of her reach).

As soon as she had made up her mind to take her eyes off the light to stretch for the fan, it finally turned green, and she was forced to do without.

About a mile later, however, Lorena realized that her mind was beginning to wander, and she considered pulling over.

With a heavy sigh, she parked the car in front of an old magic shop along a strip mall, and opened her door while swinging her legs over the side of the driver's seat.

Placing her sweaty face in the palms of her hands, Lorena sat for a few minutes, absorbing each breeze a passing car provided. Her hair clung to her forehead and neck, and because she couldn't find anything with which to tie it up, she was forced to suffer.

Realizing that if she remained in a relaxed position any longer she would pass out for sure, Lorena reluctantly returned to the inside of the car, and closed the door.

She attempted to start the engine, only to hear an exhausted grunt escape, followed by a putter that slowly wound down to a hissing noise. Suddenly feeling gripped by panic, she waited a full five seconds before trying again. This time the car gagged, sputtered, and eventually died out in one pitiful wheeze that seemed to say "I am dead."

After cursing and slamming her fists on the steering wheel, Lorena swiftly alighted the car and stalked to the hood to take a look at the engine. However, when she placed her hands onto the metal hood, she immediately removed them with a shout. The entire surface of the car felt like a blazing-hot stove top, and Lorena spat curses as she reached into the back seat for an old jacket to use as a potholder.

With the aid of her jacket, she was able to lift the hood, but was choked by a sudden gust of black smoke which billowed from the defeated engine.

Taking a moment to clear her lungs by coughing and fanning at the cloud of pollution, Lorena realized that her car was done for, and even if she could fix it she didn't feel like doing so.

With a swift kick at the nearest tire (which immediately began to sag after attack) and a rattle of curses and disapproval in Spanish, Lorena paced back and forth on the sidewalk, wondering just what to do next. She was flat broke, without even a penny on her, therefore couldn't make a phone call. Also, she had to be at work in fifteen minutes, and by foot the trip to the florist would take at least forty-five (not to mention the fact that being outside on a day like that particular one was close to suicide).

Seeing that she didn't have any other choice but to walk to work and apologize to Mrs. Gianni for being late, Lorena sighed heavily, slung her purse over one shoulder, her six-pound backpack over the other, slid the two one-pound, loose textbooks that couldn't fit into her already stuffed backpack under one arm, and began her long trek to the florist.

She had only gone a half block when she realized just how futile of an attempt she was making, but didn't know what else to do. Without money she couldn't make any phone calls, and without both money and/or a car she couldn't get anywhere any other way but by foot.

Swallowing back the dryness in her throat, Lorena began hallucinating black-and-blue splotches lining the sidewalk, and blinked several times to clear her mind. Feeling suddenly heavy, as though she could melt into the ground, she realized that the world was slowly fading. The sounds of the few cars on the street, along with passing airplanes or a barking dog, soon began to muffle until they disappeared altogether. Lorena could only hear silence as her body began to go numb.

When she barely had a third of her vision left in both eyes, she felt her knees buckle as a heavy object collided with the back of her head—aiding her sudden physical disadvantage in causing her to blackout.

Rain drummed gently on the window, providing tranquil lullabies for those sleeping in . . .a light breeze soared gracefully from the lake to the land on a pleasant day at the beach . . .water, and how much Lorena thirsted for a cool, refreshing glass of it.

Her mind was devoid of thoughts, and she felt herself in a sitting position in a comfortable, cool leather seat. It was soothing, though it didn't feel like enough to just sit and let her muscles relax; Lorena wanted her limbs to melt through the seat and to the ground.

A light rumble and the low "hum" of what seemed to be an engine met her ears, but she didn't bother to question her surroundings. All she wanted to do was rest.

Suddenly the seat shifted to the left slightly, causing her head to be pulled to the right, and she felt as though her brain was going to explode from the amount of pressure and pain this movement initiated.

She now felt her eyes burn as waves of intense pain surged from one particular spot on the back of her head to her neck, back, forehead and eyes.

Lorena tried to raise her arms up to cradle her throbbing head, but was thwarted when she found that her arms were held to her sides by a belt of some sort.

She groaned when the pain worsened, but wanted to scream when the chair lurched forward, bringing her limp head back to the headrest with a painful thud.

Lorena heard the low rumble stop, the rain end—along with the light breeze—and slowly attempted opening her eyes.

"Wake up, Selenez," a familiar voice sounded from far away, but when it repeated it seemed to be closer.

Lorena eventually opened her eyes, which only ached even more at the sight of a whirlpool of various shades of dark blue. The picture eventually cleared, and after blinking several times, she found herself to be in a car.

A familiar scent suddenly met her nose, and she knew exactly who the other passenger was.

"Cobra," she murmured, carefully turning to look at him.

His eyes were cold and dark; his face devoid of any signs of sympathy or even slight regard. Immediately Lorena knew all suspicions she had of him starting more trouble were confirmed.

It was then that she became afraid.

"What am I doing in his car? Where was I earlier today? What did I do today? Why aren't I at work right now . . .it's dark, so I need to be on the job . . ."

"What's happened to me?" she asked as she awkwardly unfastened her seatbelt, freeing her arms and rubbing her eyes. "Where are we?"

"I followed you from the market up until you broke down. Then I hit you over the head with the back of a gun. Right now we're in Harvey."

At the word "Harvey," Lorena felt her pulse deaden as her heart stopped beating.

"Harvey," she repeated in a hushed whisper.

"I'm in the heart of the NGB territory!?"

Being in the same car with an extremely dangerous ex-boyfriend whom she had kicked to the curb (whom she knew had significant anger-management problems), who happened to be the chief of a powerful gang, being in that powerful gang's neighborhood and with a physical handicap couldn't possibly be a good thing for Lorena at that moment. In fact, she was certain that she was going to die that very night.

Feeling her tongue tie, she swallowed hard, wondering desperately what to do.

"Why are we here?" she asked slowly, and in a tone barely above a whisper as she looked around to see that they were in a dark alley.

"Get outta' the car and you'll see," Cobra replied in a harsh tone and with a glare that could kill.

Cobra got out first (taking his keys with him), and in a split-second decision Lorena scanned the car for anything that could be used as a weapon. Suddenly remembering the fact that she always kept a spare key to the apartment in her pocket, she felt to make sure it was still there as she exited the vehicle. Feeling that it was, she quickly removed her hand from her side as Cobra walked around to close the door for her—looking her square in the eye.

"Now will you tell me why we're here?" Lorena asked as normally as possibly, trying hard to keep the disgust out of her tone.

"Walk," Cobra commanded shortly, the gun in his right hand pointed directly at her.

She glared at him before doing as she was told, walking forward down the alley until she reached a dead end composed of a solid brick wall.

"Now, what?"

"Turn with your back against the wall."

Lorena obeyed, keeping her eyes trained on both him and the gun. She had been in a situation such as this one countless times in the past, and knew that the best thing to do was maintain her composure.

"I'm guessin' you got my message," she began slowly, buying for time to formulate a plan. "Why didn't you call me back?" she asked conversationally—pretending to ignore the gun.

At that, Cobra suddenly began to smirk, then he laughed.

"I hope you didn't actually think I was really stickin' around to support you 'cause I loved you. I only look out for number one, honey dip, nobody else."

This time Lorena smirked.

"Why am I not surprised?"

Cobra became serious.

"Not even them little mongrels could make me crawl back."

His words seared through Lorena's heart, and she felt as though she could kill him.

Biting her tongue, she restrained herself—realizing that she would only get herself killed in trying to make a move so soon.

"Then what *did* make you come back—and why did you do it?"

Cobra smiled again, running his tongue along his teeth.

"Wouldn't you like to know?"

At that moment, a black Cadillac drove up the end of the alley, parking beside Cobra's car. Soon enough, two more NGB members joined Cobra—his vice-chief and stagecoach (or the third member in command).

Viper, the vice-chief, was a tall black guy around twenty years old, and despite his thin frame, was infamous for his skill at the use of weapons. R.J., the stagecoach, was of medium height, with his head shaved and face covered in scars. He was slightly more intimidating upon first glance than Viper—what with his many battle scars, tattoos, and husky build. Both were dressed in tattered denim vests with the letters "NGB" sewn onto the backs and black bandanas.

"What up, Cobra? I heard you were plannin' a little rumble for the night," Viper stated as he patted Cobra's shoulder.

"Yeah—Viper and me decided we'd come see what was goin' down—maybe witness us the downfall of Lorena Selenez, the ex-vice-chief of the *Chiquitas Poderosas*," R.J. quipped, slowly walking towards Lorena. "I guess you ain't feelin' so *poderosa* right now, eh *chiquita*?" he asked quietly with a smirk, caressing her chin with his hand.

Before he knew it, Lorena had swiftly gripped his hand and twisted his wrist.

As R.J. cursed and yelled in pain, Lorena caught the sound of Cobra's gun clicking.

"My gun don't like you messin' with my crew, 'Rena," Cobra stated matter-of-factly, and while glaring hard at him, Lorena let go of R.J.'s hand.

"Stupid chick broke my wrist!" R.J. shouted as he held his hand and grimaced.

Viper laughed.

"Shut up, R.J.—she couldn't break a twig."

"Try that again and you'll get a hole put in ya' head, Lorena," Cobra said with a smirk.

"Yo, let me show her how to mess with me, a'ight Cobra?" R.J. requested as he glowered maliciously at Lorena.

"Knock yourself out—or Lorena," Cobra replied with a shrug as he put his gun away, and Viper laughed again.

Lorena and Cobra held a glaring match before R.J. finally shoved her.

"What you got, Selenez, eh? What you got?" R.J. taunted as he patted his chest. "C'mon, hit me—I'll let ya' have one hit."

"She's scared of ya,' man," Viper stated as he leaned against the exterior of one of the surrounding buildings.

Lorena kept her eyes riveted on R.J., and he shoved her again, this time causing her to step back a few feet to keep her balance—however, she retained her composure, looking him hard in the eye.

"Is Lorena Selenez—once one of the best fighters on the street—scared of me?" R.J. questioned Lorena as he got up in her face, sticking his lower lip out in mock sympathy.

Lorena finally made her move when he took the time to blink.

In a heartbeat, she had swiftly gotten him into a reverse hold, with his wrists held firmly against his back with one hand while the other held his neck in an elbow lock. After kneeing him in the back, R.J. broke the hold, immediately assuming a fighting stance.

"So you wanna play now, eh, Selenez?"

"Who said I was playin'?" Lorena returned coldly, assuming her own stance.

Before they knew it, the two fighters were head-to-head, battling it out for their lives. Lorena would lunge, and R.J. would dodge, or R.J. would throw a punch, which Lorena would block. But eventually, one would get the better of the other, and soon the score seemed to be even.

Lorena stood panting, trying to ignore the throbbing in her head, while R.J. held his now-bruised side, breathing hard as well.

"I hear she's got emphysema or somethin,' man—she won't last long," Viper quipped with a laugh.

"Shut up, man—can't you see I'm busy?!" R.J. returned as he stared Lorena down, anger bubbling inside him at the mere thought of being beaten by her.

The two circled several times, keeping their eyes locked. Eventually, R.J. faked a punch, which Lorena fell for, and was soon victim to his backup punch, which landed on her cheek and caused her to do a complete 360.

Rubbing her jaw, she took advantage of his next attack (a lunge) by quickly stepping to one side and sticking her leg out to trip him. This worked, and when he began to fall forward, Lorena grabbed his arm and threw him into the brick wall as hard as she could.

R.J.'s cry of agony filled the streets, and the alley grew silent as Lorena stood watching him slide to the ground, wiping the blood from her lip in conclusion.

But the battle was far from over; immediately after R.J.'s body went limp, Viper's seemingly-permanent smirk vanished and he had rushed toward Lorena with his knife withdrawn when Cobra swiftly knocked him off his feet, shooting forward himself.

"She's mine," he muttered angrily as he roughly grabbed Lorena's arm.

Lorena, being taken slightly off guard, was unable to block the flurry of punches and kicks that proceeded to come into contact with her.

Eventually, she was on the ground, leaning against the wall while trying to regain her composure. But Cobra was determined, and allowed her no time for recovery as he kicked her in the stomach, then the chest (as he well knew of her lung problems).

Upon impact, Lorena felt her breath leave her and heard a slight crack. Something wasn't right with her airway—it was as if she had lost her wind but couldn't seem to get it back. Her chest ached and burned as she tried to gasp for air to no avail.

Cobra stood towering over her, looking on in pure delight as she struggled to complete a task as simple as breathing.

"How 'bout you try that one on for size, Selenez?" Cobra asked menacingly as he clamped his hand around her neck, turning her face up to look at him.

Lorena suddenly felt the air returning to her, but only in small amounts, and continued to gasp and wheeze.

Cobra shook his head and smirked.

"You asked me why I came back, right? Well I'll tell you why—this is all a setup for the day we decide to kill ya.' See, if you don't die from lack of air or collapsed lung right now—we'll get ya' anyhow. Who is 'we' you ask? 'We' is Marisol, me, Anita, the NGBs and the CPs—all of your old friends, Lorena. We hate you and wanna see you layin' dead in the gutter—as you put it so eloquently before. So there's all the information you wanted." Before releasing her throat and walking off, Cobra gave Lorena one final blow to her jaw, sending her a foot over and out of consciousness.

With that said and done, he rounded up his crew and left.

~ Chapter XIV ~

"Meanwhile, Saul was still breathing out murderous threats against the Lord's disciples. He went to the high priest and asked him for letters to the synagogues in Damascus, so that if he found any there who belonged to the Way, whether men or women, he might take them as prisoners to Jerusalem. As he neared Damascus on his journey, suddenly a light from heaven flashed around him. He fell to the ground and heard a voice say to him, 'Saul, Saul, why do you persecute me?'
'Who are you, Lord?' Saul asked.
'I am Jesus, whom you are persecuting,' He replied. 'Now get up and go into the city, and you will be told what you must do.'"

Acts 9:1-6
NIV

†

Lorena sat quietly thinking in the oversized chair in her apartment, staring out the window beside the front door. She had just taken another dose of painkillers for her chest and head, and was trying to get some rest. The kids were both at school, and Caramelle was staying with the Barnum's for the afternoon.

It was Wednesday, the day after her encounter with the NGBs. The night before, a police officer chanced to come across Lorena's unconscious figure and called for an ambulance. She was rushed to the emergency room and when she awoke was informed that she had a fractured sternum and minor concussion. She was instructed to lie low—doing as little activity as possible. According to Lorena's request to leave—despite the doctor's disapproval—she was sent home the next morning (as she knew staying in the hospital for days of healing was something she couldn't afford in more ways than one). She was already going to be faced with the bills from simply visiting the ER.

Lorena winced suddenly as she shifted position—her chest was hurting badly, despite the painkillers and fracture dressings.

She worried about the future, and what she was going to do without a car. The bus seemed to be the only alternative, even though she could barely afford food and clothing.

Cobra's revelations about himself and the gangs were fresh on her mind, and she knew that she shouldn't be surprised at the fact that Marisol had been behind virtually everything. It was just hard for Lorena to stop and remember that things weren't always this way; there was a time when she and Marisol were best friends. But now she hated Lorena for leaving the gang—betraying her. As angry as she was at her old friend, Lorena realized that she never could make herself hate her—they had been through too much in the past. Marisol was always able to relate to Lorena's family problems, and the two were even brought up in the same orphanage when Lorena's grandmother on her father's side passed away. As much as the circumstances told Lorena to hate her former friend, she couldn't—but rather dwelled in the pain it caused her to face reality. It wasn't easy for her to be hated by everyone she used to trust—it hurt quite a bit. But then, there was a time when *she* used to hurt other people for fun, and Lorena constantly found herself asking if this was some sort of punishment for her past wrongs.

Sitting in the silence of the room, without her grandmother's warm smile, children's innocent laugh, or even her mother's crazy, yet somehow always correct advice, Lorena realized that she was daring herself to talk to the other Being . . .the One who watched her every move.

Before she could summon up the courage to do so, however, the painful image of her grandmother struggling to tell her she loved her before she died—the tears in her eyes and quiver in her voice—filled Lorena's heart and she couldn't bring herself to talk to someone whom she thought to be her best friend's murderer.

About a week later, Lorena was back into the swing of things—studying and working from sun up to sun down. Her chest was still healing, and she had to make a few appointments with the doctor concerning her concussion; nonetheless, she kept running.

One Saturday afternoon, while the kids and the baby were off with the Barnums and Lorena was sorting through a pile of mail composed predominantly of bills, she came across one letter in particular, in a blue envelope with a return address from South Africa.

Immediately Lorena knew who it was from, and with a sigh, set the envelope aside—searching for an expected doctor bill for one of Nathan's appointments. As she did so, however, her eyes would occasionally glance over at the blue envelope, and she realized that she was wondering what was inside. Pausing her sorting to stare at the envelope, Lorena, troubled, began to wonder if something was wrong. Had her mother been involved in some freak accident—attacked by wild natives?

Lorena shook her head and took a seat on the couch with several bills and a calculator, chiding herself for allowing herself to worry so much.

Besides, if there was something wrong, she would simply call... wouldn't she?

With a deep sigh, Lorena returned to her work, knowing she had a lot to get done before picking up the kids.

Several hours later, after walking to the Barnum's and picking up Nathan, Celeste, and Caramelle, Lorena prepared them a light snack and helped them get ready for bed.

While tucking Celeste in that night, Lorena was faced with a random question.

"Mommy?" Celeste asked as Lorena picked a few stray toys up off of the floor, returning them to their box.

"Yes, sweetie?" Lorena replied as she sat on the edge of the bed, tucking the covers around the child.

"Do you have a mommy?" she asked suddenly, her eyes void of anything but innocence and simple curiosity.

Lorena blinked, slightly taken off guard by the inquiry.

"Um, yeah, 'Lessie," she began slowly, "I do. You probably don't remember her, though."

Celeste shook her head, picking at the ears of her favorite stuffed rabbit, then pausing as her eyes lit up at a sudden thought.

"Do you look like her, Mommy?" she questioned hopefully. "I look like you..."

Lorena smiled lightly, and nodded a little.

"Yeah, I guess I do."

"My teacher says that kids look like their mommies and daddies."

"Well, she's about right."

There came a short pause as Celeste played with a silver bangle around Lorena's wrist.

"Where is your mommy?"

Lorena cleared her throat, watching Celeste become engrossed in her bracelet.

"In another country—she helps people there."

Celeste cocked her head to the side slightly.

"What does she help them do?"

Lorena sighed, looking up at the ceiling.

"Well, she helps them . . .get food and clothes. Sometimes, I suppose, she teaches them to read and write."

Celeste looked up.

"Does that mean she's a teacher?" she asked excitedly.

Lorena smiled at Celeste's exuberance.

"I guess so, 'Lessie," she replied as she played with her daughter's curly hair.

"Oh . . .when is she coming back?"

Lorena's smile gradually faded, and she stared at the clock on the bedside table as she slowly released one of Celeste's curls.

"She's probably not going to come back, Celeste," Lorena said quietly.

"Oh . . ." Celeste replied, her eyes full of disappointment as she squeezed her rabbit.

"But anyway," Lorena spoke up, "you need to go to sleep, young lady, and I need to make sure your brother isn't reading comic books instead of his school reading."

"Okay," Celeste stated reluctantly as she settled into her covers. "Goodnight, Mommy."

Lorena placed a kiss on Celeste's forehead as she gave her a hug.

"Goodnight, 'Lessie."

Lorena reached over to turn the bedside lamp out, and after checking the crib to see that Caramelle was sound asleep, left the room—closing the door slightly behind her.

While heading to the living room, she passed Nathan's room, where he was sitting up in bed, his nose stuck in a "Ramona" book.

"Mommy?" he said as Lorena walked in, closing the doors to his closet—which were open.

"Yes, Nathan?"

"Why do I have to read a girly book?"

Lorena shook her head and smiled, then composed herself before turning around and making her way towards the bed.

"Because your teacher told you to—and who said it's a girly book?" she asked while taking a seat.

Nathan shrugged.

"It's all about girls, Mom."

Lorena chuckled, ruffling his hair.

"It's just one book, Natty—I think you'll be okay," she replied as she played with an hourglass on the bedside table.

"But I don't wanna know about girl stuff," Nathan stated as he scrunched his nose.

Lorena merely looked at him and smiled.

"Someday it may come in handy to know a thing or two about girls, Natty—but right now you can go to sleep."

"Do I have to?"

Lorena frowned slightly as she rose.

"I thought you didn't like that book . . ."

"Well, yeah, but it's still funny."

Lorena shook her head once again and sighed.

"Alright, ten more minutes—that means when the big hand reaches this point, it's time for lights out, okay?" Lorena asked while pointing to the clock on the table.

Nathan nodded.

"Okay."

Lorena smiled.

"Goodnight, Natty," she said before kissing him on the forehead.

"G'night, Mommy," he replied as Lorena headed for the door, closing it mostly as she headed to the living room.

After fetching a glass of water, she sat down at the table to study her psychology textbook.

A half hour passed with smooth sailing, and after getting up to routinely check the kids' rooms, Lorena found that they were sound asleep and returned to her work.

She was taking notes from the text when she paused for a moment to rest her eyes. Glancing about the room, she soon focused on a blue envelope resting on the coffee table. It almost seemed to be begging for her to open it.

Lorena rolled her tongue along her teeth as she thoughtfully stared off into space.

Realizing that if she didn't simply quench her curiosity she would only continue to wonder and stray from her studying, Lorena set her pencil down and rose from the table.

When she reached the coffee table, she bent down to pick up the envelope, collapsing comfortably onto the couch as she proceeded to break the seal.

Inside was a two-page letter and a photograph.

Lorena first examined the photo, setting the letter aside. It was a small portrait of her mother, standing with her arm around a tall, handsome African man with kind eyes and a perfect smile. Her mother was clad in a mauve blazer which complimented her skin tone, and the other was dressed in a sharp, pinstriped suit with a silver, satin tie.

Lorena couldn't remember ever seeing her mother look so successful and well-polished. Not that she wasn't already before, but she looked different—happier, almost. Her face seemed fuller, suggesting that perhaps getting married had aided her in gaining a little more weight.

Lorena proceeded to study the man—assuming that she was looking at her mother's husband. He was good looking, but also truly did look polite, kind and intelligent.

With a sigh, Lorena turned the picture over to see that it was taken recently—within the past few months.

After putting it to the side, she now turned to the letter, and unfolded the first page to see her mother's neat, elegant cursive handwriting.

Placing her feet up on the coffee table, Lorena began to read . . .

Dear Lorena,

This has to be one of the most awkward letters I will ever write, but hopefully I've accomplished a great feat by even getting as far as you reading this . . .if you decide to. If you don't, then this is being written to no one, therefore I hope you'll read this all the way through.

First of all, I haven't written home in ages—as you well know—and the reason why isn't exactly a good one. We aren't the best of friends, and after your grandmother's death I didn't really know how to approach you (when I tried to see you after the funeral, you wouldn't even look at me, remember? So I waited, writing all kinds of drafts of the letter you're hopefully holding right now. This had to be perfect, something that you wouldn't throw to the side, but read just to hear me out; if for anything at all.

So here I am, in Africa, fulfilling my passion to aid the impoverished and disease stricken. Through the ministry I've started, I meet hundreds of girls every day. It's called "Lorena's Freedom" and I'll soon tell you why I named it after you. (I hope the name is alright with you, because I've already printed the title on t-shirts, business cards, signs, etc.) We're in the process of building a large house for abused girls from all around the continent, and another one for those who are diseased. It's my dream to someday have the ministry reach every country in Africa.

This ministry is named after you because you (whether you know it or not) gave me the idea to start it. At the time, I didn't know that it would take me all the way to Africa, but God works in mysterious ways.

I think about you all the time, and if you don't mind I am praying for you as well. Even if you do, I'll do it anyway.

Every day I look into the eyes of lonely girls, hungering for freedom from their troubles, I see you, Lorena. I see your will in the girl who can't even attend our nightly prayer gatherings because of an abusive uncle who won't let her return home without $10.00 to present to him. She has to work all day and doesn't have time for a prayer gathering, simply so that she can stay alive in order to barely feed her two young sons. Or I'll see your courage in the girl who has to worry about being assaulted while getting water from a nearby well each time that she does so, but goes nonetheless. But mostly I see your hunger in the eyes of the children who search for food from day to day, only to get by on a cup of rice a day.

And someday I would like to see your freedom in the eyes of the girl who finds what she seeks, that you may share in her joy.

This is how you inspired the name . . . the ministry.

I'm married now, as you know, to a local attorney who is trying to introduce God into the legal system where we live. It's not an easy task, but if somebody doesn't take a stand, who will? His name, "Imani," means "faith," and he lives it out well. He's the nicest man I've ever met, and I love him. We met on that first trip to South Africa I took years back. A year later, we crossed paths again; this time in a market place, and as we are both Christians, we decided that it wasn't a coincidence (as nothing in life is). Therefore we began to see each other, and eventually we married—about a year ago. I recently found out that I'm pregnant. The baby's due around April of next year.

My job isn't hard, but I wish you were here to witness the miracles I see all of the time. I wanted you to come with me, Lorena, because I knew that in Chicago there are lots of individuals held captive, and they play it off as if everything is fine. But it's different here—these people hunger so much for fulfillment that they don't hide it. Their humility has taught me so much over the past few years, and I wish you could be around people who are real, Lorena.

There's something I didn't tell you about the gang I was involved in. You see, my gang was the Serpent Debs (or Serpent Debutantes), and we were the female version of the Serpents, a male black-and-Hispanic gang on the West Side. One thing you don't know about the Chiquitas Poderosas is that Marisol Carvajal didn't establish it—as she has most likely been telling you for years. Chiquitas Poderosas is the product of treason and dissension amongst the Serpent Debs. When I joined the Serpent Debs, it consisted solely of blacks and Hispanics. Things were going smoothly until one of the black members killed another Hispanic member by accident in a rumble. A rumor quickly spread, stating that it wasn't an accident, but murder in an attempt to divide the gang. There was lots of bloodshed, and I was given a choice on whether to stay in the black part of the gang and agree to help kill off all of the Hispanics, or I could leave and be murdered—along with your grandmother and you. Therefore I agreed to stay, and it was on a night filled with bloody rumbling that I was shot in the leg and unable to walk when police sirens sounded. Everyone took off—it was suddenly each person for themselves, and I was left in the middle of the battlefield with death around me and only a few other girls who were actually breathing. One of the few girls still alive was a younger girl in the gang—a rookie who still had a lot to learn. She was put sort of 'under my care,' if you will. That night during the rumble, Adrienne Jones, Marisol Carvajal's half-sister as well as the chief of the black side of the gang, shot one of the Hispanics in the leg, wounding her badly. We all thought she was dead, and when we heard the sirens coming, Adrienne panicked and quickly shoved the gun into the new girl's hands. Before we could run off, the police arrived, but not before I quickly snatched the gun from the rookie—I saw what Adrienne did and knew it wasn't right. I would take the blame instead—besides, she was my friend and I was responsible for her. Our gang had its problems alright, but we did teach to look out for our younger members. But Adrienne was, of course, angry at me for what I did, but mostly because I of a promise I had made to lead the black gang on if she were to die in action. As stagecoach I was next in line, because the vice-president had been shot dead that night. Four other girls were arrested with Adrienne and I, and she swore she would pay me back for letting the new girl off the hook. My sentence was lighter than hers, though, because the girl I supposedly "shot" didn't die *after all. However, Adrienne's still serving her thirty years, and I don't know what ever happened to the rookie I bailed for.*

Because I couldn't keep my promise to establish the new gang, and all the other blacks were either killed or too afraid to rise up, it was never born. However, the other half had better luck. "Niñas Fuertes" was established soon after the rumble, and when an older brother of Marisol's in the Serpents became displeased with the leadership, he set it up so that when she turned thirteen she would inherit the chiefhood. When she did, the name was changed to "Chiquitas Poderosas," issuing in a more youth-based feel for the next generation.

The reason Marisol didn't tell you about any of this is that she herself didn't even know until shortly after you were elected vice-chief—when she received word from Adrienne that you were my daughter, and that she was to avenge her by killing me or you. That's why you noticed such a sudden change in Marisol, and she was most likely threatened by other former black Serpent Debs when she turned on you.

That's why they're after you now, Lorena.

I'm sure you're wondering why I haven't told you about any of this. The reason is that I didn't have the full story until recently, when I decided to do some research while I was in town for your grandmother's funeral. I didn't know that Marisol and Adrienne were related until then, therefore I'm telling you now to let you know that the only thing that caused Marisol to turn on you was pressure she received from Adrienne. Adding to this, when you told Marisol that you wanted to leave the CPs, she probably felt threatened—thinking maybe you were turning on her the same way I supposedly "turned" on her sister. There's not really anything you can do, Lorena, except perhaps move (another reason why I wanted to take you with me to Africa).

As a side note, soon after the Debs broke up, the Serpents became angry and did the same. As a result, the blacks defeated the Hispanics, and the NGBs were formed. Your father, Ricardo Selenez, was a Serpent, by the way, and he and I met through our gangs. He wound up in jail because of a rumble, and as you know is still serving his sentence. Just to let you know, he wasn't abusive (towards me, at least) and when you were an infant he would provide for you as much as he could. I'm sure he loved you very much, and it was just unfortunate that he chose the path of a gang banger.

Every day my bad decisions echo in my soul, and I wish that I had never made the choices that I did. Once you told me that you weren't a blessing, but I don't believe that to be so. In fact, you are a blessing, and I pray that someday you'll understand that. There's something called "providence" that many believe to be only a secular thing, but in reality providence is simply God's plan. Lorena, I want to tell you that you are in God's plan—in His plan for me as well. Sometimes I wish I could kill whatever force that causes you to think that you aren't worth anything, but over time I have begun to realize that I myself can't do that. I guess it's a part of letting go, though surprisingly, it's not easy for me to do.

You weren't a mistake, Lorena, and I will never think of you as one. I just pray that you can forgive me for the mistakes I've made. You have so much potential, and I pray each day that you'll realize this. I know I've messed up, and hurt you, but I love you very much and I hope that you know that.

You've probably trashed this letter by now, and most likely haven't even gotten past the second paragraph (maybe even the second sentence). Maybe you'll forgive me someday, but if you don't, I'll still be here nonetheless—waiting to offer any help if you need me. If you only knew how badly I want to hear from you . . .

P.S. Clipped to the back of this letter is a check. It's all of the money left over in my American savings account, and though I hadn't planned on giving it to you until much later, I changed my mind. I've been saving since my first job in high school, and when the mission trips came along I had to use a good amount of it to get to and from Africa. There was some money left over, and I have long since made up my mind to give it to you. I'm sure you could use it, and God has blessed me with more resources since I married Imani—therefore I won't miss it. I hope it will help you, and I'm sorry it isn't instead a better life for you. If life were easy enough that I could solve your problems with the snap of my fingers, Lorena, I would.

Sincerely,

Elsa

Lorena felt the back of the paper to sure enough find a check. Its value caused her to gasp, and she immediately clamped a hand over her mouth.

"Twenty thousand dollars?!"

Lorena slowly set the letter and check down onto the coffee table, running her fingers through her hair. She couldn't believe that she had twenty grand in her possession. If she put the money into savings, she wouldn't have to worry about bills as much as she had in the past...and it was all thanks to...her mother. Elsa, the being whom Lorena had hated, been "okay" with, hated again, and now... what? For the first time in her life, Lorena didn't even know what to feel. She didn't know what to think of her mother.

Leaning back in the chair, Lorena stared into oblivion, thinking long and hard. Several minutes passed before she inadvertently reached over to pick up the letter, and began to re-read a few particular sentences.

"You weren't a mistake, Lorena, and I will never think of you as one. I just pray that you can forgive me for the mistakes I made . . . Maybe you'll forgive me someday, but if you don't, I'll still be here nonetheless—waiting to offer any help if you need me . . ."

After reading over the sentences for the third time, Lorena soon realized that tears were streaming down her cheeks. She let the letter glide to the floor as she hugged her knees to her chest and sobbed into her elbows, feeling more confused and alone than ever before.

She was hurting even more from the truth behind the CPs, memories from her lonesome childhood which now haunted her adulthood, her inability to trust her mother, but more than anything else, herself.

A month passed since Lorena had received her mother's letter, and soon enough, another one came. This time, Elsa further explained the ministry and life in Africa. Over time, this became a weekly ritual, and Lorena would look forward to reading about what her mother had done one week or how things were going with work. Eventually, Lorena would envision herself there with them, and each time she read an exciting letter, felt as though she actually was. Even though she knew in her heart that she was slowly forgiving her, Lorena didn't reply to her letters, and this was mostly because she didn't know what to say—as she wasn't completely sure about much of anything. Lorena did know that she really did miss her, and was beginning to admit that to herself—rather than wade in a pool of denial.

Little did she know, however, that this new habit would aid her in more ways than one.

It was a chilly, autumn Wednesday evening when Lorena made her way to the bus stop from another tutoring session with the fellow student whom she tutored. Leaves rustled over the sidewalk, and the gusty air grew somewhat restless as the evening progressed.

It had been almost a year since Elena's death, and Lorena was coping with things one day at a time. The letters still arrived from Africa, and Lorena still hadn't replied to any of them.

About a block ahead was the church she had passed almost every month for a year. Once or twice she had actually come to a complete stop outside of the door, contemplating whether or not to enter, but each time she had only resumed walking.

Lorena now stuffed her numbing hands into her jacket pockets as she passed by the old, stone building, breathing a sigh as she focused her eyes on the ground. Her thoughts, however, were on the church.

Across the next intersection was Elena's old church, and the familiar bus stop in front of it. Lorena couldn't believe that it was almost seven years earlier that she and Tony had their first conversation at that very spot. She felt as though she had known him her whole life, and missed him. The memory of him, though, seemed to be that of a dream—as if she had only made him up in her mind. Somehow not seeing or hearing from a person caused Lorena to regard them as a mere dream—even though she knew in her heart that this was not so.

After crossing the street, Lorena was glad to see a bus already driving up to the stop.

When it came to a halt, she gathered the appropriate amount of change in her hand and climbed aboard. Once she had placed the money into the box, she searched for a seat.

Lorena had barely sat down when a loud "crack" sounded from the front of the vehicle. Each passenger jumped, including Lorena, and the bus driver asked everyone to calm down. The driver then proceeded to get up from his seat and exit the bus, obviously going to check the engine.

About two minutes later, he returned, explaining that the engine had given out and he would have to call for a repairman.

The passengers voiced their disapproval, and Lorena frowned as she rose to get off the bus—wondering just how she was going to get home.

After getting her money back, she alighted into the cool, night air, and decided to call home to inform Tanya that she was going to be late.

Finding a pay phone nearby, Lorena placed the call, and after thanking Tanya for not charging her overtime, she hung up.

While standing on the sidewalk, she made up her mind to wait for the backup bus to arrive—which the bus driver had promised would come.

Five minutes passed, and Lorena hopped lightly from one foot to the other to keep warm. Every now and then, she would cast a casual glance over at Tony's church—where people were beginning to file through the door. Another five minutes passed, and eventually a full forty-five minutes elapsed without any signs of a spare bus. The first bus had long since been towed off, and Lorena found herself standing alone on the dark sidewalk.

With a heavy sigh, she decided to give the bus fifteen more minutes before she would set off for the next stop—even though she knew it was at least seven blocks away.

Glancing down at her watch, she realized that if the bus didn't show up soon, she wouldn't get home until around eight o'clock, as it was about seven o'clock at the present.

Lorena was reassured by the fact that Tanya had also mentioned dropping the kids off at the Barnums' if Lorena didn't get back before seven thirty—when the sitter had to get home.

Seeing that if she continued to stand near her old church (where Bible study was about to start), Lorena would undoubtedly be recognized and spoken to (something she wished to avoid), she crossed the street and stood at the opposite corner—the one near the other church.

Being closer to the building, she could faintly hear soothing music from inside, and the mass choir singing along gracefully. She had to admit—they did sound good.

After standing outside in the chilly night air for such a long time, Lorena began to shiver, hugging herself while standing against the wind.

Her mind dwelled on the inside of the church, the gentle music, and how warm it must be compared to the sidewalk.

Lorena frowned slightly, turning to look at the tall building. She had always thought that it looked terribly intimidating, what with its majestic steeple and rustic bell. But at that moment, being in her current state of desperation for warmth and rest, she didn't find that it looked quite as bad as it so often did—but rather almost inviting.

"Maybe if I just stand in the lobby for a few minutes—just long enough to warm up . . ."

Realizing that if she didn't receive warmth soon she would freeze, Lorena began walking up the stone staircase leading to the giant oak doors, one by one. With numb hands, she pushed them open, and stepped into a large, dark lobby. The only lighting came from a doorway leading to a small prayer room on her left, another one of the many rooms whose doors stood ajar, and lastly the sanctuary.

Lorena gazed up at the tall, cathedral ceiling as she found a seat on a bench nearby, marveling at the beauty of the structure. It had a very French château feel, with its stone walls, fresh plants, and iron railings.

Beginning to warm up slightly, she directed her attention to the sanctuary, and focused on the music, which she could now hear clearly. From what she could tell, the sanctuary was humongous, with a towering ceiling, many pews, and wide floor space towards the grand pulpit. A gigantic, golden cross hung on a wall behind the choir, and the walls were composed of a warm, rich cherry wood.

The congregation was mostly white, with the exception of a few blacks, and Lorena suddenly felt extremely out of place.

However, there was something highly intriguing about the sanctuary, and for some reason she felt like being in there.

Feeling a sudden wave of edginess, Lorena twisted her necklace chain and tapped her foot on the stone floor. She knew what she was considering, and was aware that she was probably losing her mind for wanting to do so.

But somehow, she just had to see . . .

Within seconds, Lorena was on her feet, making her way uncertainly into the sanctuary. She had expected the whole congregation to gasp, turn, and stare, but they instead continued to sing along with the choir—some standing with their heads bowed, others with their hands held high.

Looking hastily for a seat as far in the back as she could find, Lorena scanned the area. While doing so, a young, teenage boy, wearing a suit and a kind smile on his face, stepped forward.

"May I help you find a seat, ma'am?" he asked politely, and she nodded.

Much to Lorena's surprise, he began to lead her up the center aisle—as though he knew of a seat towards the front.

She stood her ground, feeling petrified, and when the boy turned around to find that he hadn't been followed, Lorena gestured that she was fine, then proceeded to take a seat in the very back.

Sitting in the middle of the pew, Lorena began to study her surroundings. Everyone was on their feet, locked into worship, and she was the only person in her pew—except for another girl, whom she noticed when she looked to her right. The teen sat with her arms crossed over her chest, a look of rebellion on her face, and Lorena guessed that she had been dragged into coming by, perhaps, a parent.

Lorena listened to the song, acknowledging how nice the tune really was. But soon, the music faded, the choir softened, and the keyboard dominated as a voice came over the sound system. She couldn't see over the mass of standing individuals, but perceived the voice to be that of a male—possibly the head pastor.

Lorena settled into her seat as he spoke.

"This wasn't planned, as you all know. Tonight we were supposed to have our guest speaker, Dr. Mitchell, come and share a word. He was detained, however, and couldn't show up, therefore I just asked God to take over, and He has. Just now I was listening to the music, deep in prayer and worship, and I felt God telling me something. He said that there are people who are here with us tonight—people who are lost. Four young people—one lost a father, the other one a job. Another has been consistently considering suicide, and yet another is running from God. I want to talk to you—each of you. God wants to comfort you—your father is in a better place. God wants to adopt you—you don't have to take those pills. God wants to give you a new life—you don't have to be afraid. And God wants you to stop running—He loves you even though you feel as though the whole world has abandoned you . . ."

Lorena began to feel chilly again, and hugged herself.

". . .There's a girl here with us tonight—she's been running for such a long time. She's been scarred, tormented, betrayed . . .I'm here to tell you that God loves you, He never stopped loving you. You don't have to dwell in the same place anymore—none of you do. None of us know how much longer we have to live—the Bible says that man is like a mist, vanishing from the earth someday. But I want to tell you that you can spend eternity with God, the Father. Jesus Christ—the Son of God—came to earth to die for you, that you might spend eternity with Him. He did it so that you wouldn't have to run anymore, wouldn't have to think about suicide anymore—wouldn't have to worry about family or a job. Jesus loves you and wants you to let him in today. Ask him into your heart—let Him in, let Him change you. If you want to accept a new life, if you're tired of running and worrying, if you want to be set free, then I ask you to come to the front of this house of worship. Come now—let His everlasting love surround you. In the name of Jesus

Christ I bind the enemy and his demons against these young people now and forevermore!"

At that particular moment, Lorena suddenly felt a rush of warmth surge throughout her entire body, and she drew in her breath.

All throughout the building people were crying, shouting, or speaking in strange languages. Lorena felt her head swim and gripped the edge of the pew in front of her.

"You come now who wants to see your father again! You come now who wants faith! You come now who wants to live for God! And you come now who wants to be freed of the demon that has tormented you for years! Come now!"

Lorena could barely comprehend the pastor's words, but soon found that she was trembling uncontrollably. She had to get to the altar—she had to get to . . .God.

Feeling as though electricity flowed throughout her body, Lorena pried her hands from the pew and rose to her feet. She was in the center aisle before she knew it, and slowly making her way to the front—suddenly blind to the mass of people stretching their hands out toward her, speaking in tongues over her and praying for her. Instead of seeing what should have been the altar and choir, she saw a tremendous sight that blew her mind. Before Lorena's tearful eyes was a vast, bountiful valley filled with lilies, tulips, and seemingly every flower known to man. A large, sparkling lake sat adjacent to the valley, and a green, wondrous mountain stood over the lake. An orchard filled with cherry blossoms was at the edge of the lake, and a flowing waterfall cascaded down the mountain.

Sensing God in the paradise, Lorena felt an uncontrollable urge to be there, and she made up her mind to run to it. However, when she picked her foot up off of the ground, she tripped suddenly—falling forward—and looked up into the face of the most hideous creature she had ever laid eyes on. It was a gremlin, seemingly merged with a human, with brilliant, red eyes that burned with hatred. Atop its scaly head was a large, black-and-red snake—the same one she had seen shortly before stabbing herself.

Feeling gripped by fear, Lorena began to scream.

All of a sudden, she threw herself toward the ground—as if something inside her was controlling her and trying desperately not to be pulled out. It held on tight, and Lorena went into violent convulsions as she felt a hand on her forehead. She had one thought in her mind, and one fervent prayer in her heart.

"Jesus, save me!!"

A final shock of some sort rushed from the hand to Lorena's body, and then a vacuum-like force seemed to pull the being controlling her out of her body.

When she opened her eyes again, a sky-blue ball of light hovered protectively over her, and she felt an incredible sense of peace. She blinked, and she was looking up at a circle of people who stood with outstretched hands, speaking in tongues with their heads bowed.

Tears streamed down Lorena's cheeks and she realized she was laughing and crying at the same time—praising God in a foreign language along with the others. Jesus had redeemed her once and for all, and she knew it was true.

~ Chapter XV ~

"There are three things that are too amazing for me, four that I do not understand: the way of an eagle in the sky, the way of a snake on a rock, the way of a ship on the high seas, and the way of a man with a maiden."

Proverbs 30:18-19
NIV

†

Three years had passed since the night Lorena finally entered the church, and ever since she had been gradually changing—learning more and more about the God she now served. Immediately upon becoming saved, she had started attending the church (Tony's church) with the kids, and had gone through the process of becoming a member. After speaking with senior pastor on the night of the prayer revival, Lorena explained everything she had seen and felt (including the demon)—going all the way back to the incident with the knife when she was a teenager, including her grandmother's final warning about a snake—and he told her that it was likely that it was the same demon each time. However, she was also reassured that the demon could no longer possess her due to her salvation, but it was possible for it to discourage her. Thus, Lorena kept alert—keeping her senses peeled for anything out of the ordinary. For a long time, though, nothing seemed to show up.

By the time she had gotten saved and freed from the demon, Lorena no longer felt any contempt towards her mother, and over time slowly began to forgive even the gang . . .and yes, eventually Marisol.

Occasionally, a hate letter would arrive, or she would be followed by hooded strangers when walking to the bus stop at night, but other than that, Lorena hadn't really been harmed by the gang since her last encounter with Cobra and his officials.

Before the kids went to bed, they began to say their prayers, and later told their mother that it was something they had always heard that other kids did, and had long since wanted to do so themselves.

As for communication between Lorena and her mother, it remained one-sided, as the letters had been constant for almost four years. Each month Elsa would write her daughter, lightly explaining what she had done with the ministry that particular month, or new ideas she had, and tried to write each letter to make Lorena feel as though she was there with her—and she had succeeded in doing so. One letter announced the arrival of Elsa's baby—a son, whom they named "Elijah."

After getting saved, Lorena began to understand more of the things her mother talked about, and she gained an interest in the ministry. Over time, she began to understand the meaning of "Lorena's Freedom," as she was currently living it out from day to day.

Though she hadn't ever replied to the letters, Lorena did want to tell her mother all that she was experiencing through church and her new lifestyle, but each time she set her mind to doing so, backed down out of guilt from the way she used to act and feel. She had become so used to reading the stories, looking at pictures of her mother and the girls—so accustomed to her unfailing letters—that Lorena didn't know what writing back would do. Would Elsa open the letter? Would she even glance at it? Lorena knew that her mother would close each letter with a statement of wanting to see her or at least hear from her again. Maybe Elsa only wanted a mute daughter, rather than a headstrong, rebellious one. But that was the old Lorena . . .

One quiet Saturday evening, as the kids played in their rooms, Lorena sat munching on a bowl of popcorn while watching an old, small TV set she had recently purchased. The news was on, and she was waiting for the weather report—as she had planned a day at the park with the kids after church the next day.

". . .in other news, there have been numerous suicide bombings in cities of South Africa, ranging from car bombings to buildings. No particular terrorist group has yet been identified, but CIA officials are on the case . . ."

Lorena felt her body go numb as images of shattered office buildings, houses and communities flashed onto the screen.

Was there any chance that the Lorena's Freedom headquarters had been hit . . .Elsa, Imani and little Elijah?

Lorena slowly set the bowl on the coffee table, tuning out as the weather report finally arrived. What should she do—try to find the number for the headquarters and call long distance? Wait and see if another letter arrived?

With a hard swallow, Lorena rose and began to pace the floor, wondering what to do.

Suddenly, the phone rang, and she quickly answered it.

"Hello?" she demanded in a rushed tone, thinking it was someone from Africa.

"What's up?"

Lorena sighed in disappointment, slowly taking a seat on the couch.

"Oh, it's just you."

"Thanks for the welcoming committee, Lorena," Candy replied with a laugh, then became serious when silence met her ears. "Hey, is something wrong? You sounded kinda' edgy."

Candy and Lorena had been calling each other long distance every now and then, as Candy had recently married and settled down in California. She was also getting into the swing of church, thanks to Lorena's example.

Lorena sighed.

"Did you watch the news today?"

She sensed Candy shrugging from the other line.

"No, not really. Matt and I were busy all day painting the guest room—why?"

"Well," Lorena began slowly, feeling her voice begin to tremble, "there were suicide bombings in South Africa today . . ."

"What parts? Is your mom okay?" Candy immediately asked, beginning to sound anxious.

Lorena bit her lip, picking at a seam on her jeans.

"Um . . .I don't really know."

"Is there any way you can find out about her city—any number you can try?"

"I have no idea. I don't know what to do," Lorena replied quietly, swallowing back the lump forming in her throat.

Candy sighed from the other line, and a pause followed.

"Gosh, Lorena, I'm really sorry I can't be of any help. How about I call you back tomorrow—so you can keep the line open if you need to?"

"Uh, yeah—that's fine," Lorena said as she ran her fingers through her hair. "I'll talk to you later."

"Hang in there."

Lorena smiled lightly, but more so nervously.

"I will—'bye."

" 'Bye."

After hanging up the phone, Lorena sighed, looking down at her hands. She was soon brought back to reality when a voice sounded from the hallway entrance.

"Mom?" Nathan asked carefully, seeing that Lorena was having a "quiet moment."

She looked up and put on a small smile for the sake of holding herself together.

"Hey, Nat. What do you need?" she asked as she picked up her bowl and took it to the kitchen.

"Celeste and Caramelle wanted some more animal crackers, and I told them I didn't know if it was okay with you, so I'd ask for them."

"They can have some more—as long as they don't spill them all over the place or start throwing them at each as they did last time," Lorena replied with a short laugh at the recollection of the two sisters pelting each other with animal crackers.

Nathan chuckled, then hurried off for his room to spread the good news.

Lorena didn't get much sleep that night, and eventually began to do some Bible-study homework and psychology assignments when staring up at the ceiling grew old.

After church the next morning, as promised, she took the kids to the park for a few hours, and the day passed as a relatively good one. However, South Africa weighed heavy on Lorena's mind.

Deciding to wait and see if another letter arrived, Lorena got through the next few days as best she could. Candy would call a little more often than usual, talking and joking with her friend to try to ease her mind some.

During one of their conversations, Candy bore some interesting information . . .

"So guess what happened today," Candy stated, and Lorena sighed as she washed that night's dishes, balancing the new cordless phone on one shoulder as she did so.

"Matt finally sold that old garden gnome he's had since childhood?"

Candy laughed in response.

"I wish—the old thing's gonna leave when pigs fly. But seriously, guess."

Lorena rolled her eyes and smiled.

"Candy, I can't possibly guess—just tell me."

"Okay, okay. You know how I sent Tony a letter a few months back, asking how he was doing?"

Lorena nodded as she stepped around Caramelle, who had recently joined her in washing the dishes—the toddler now climbing up on a chair to reach the countertops.

"Yeah—no, no sweetie, don't put those in there," she rebuked Caramelle when she began to place the clean silverware back into the dirty water.

"I thought they're s'posed to go in there, Mommy," Caramelle said with a frown.

"Well, they aren't, okay?"

"What?" Candy voiced confusedly.

Lorena sighed again.

"I was just telling Caramelle not to put the clean silverware in the dirty water—continue."

"Oh, okay," Candy replied. "So anyway, I wrote him this letter and about two weeks ago—when the mail came in—I saw that he had replied. When I read the letter, he explained how he's been crazy busy what with law school and everything—but guess what."

"What?"

"He's going to graduate top of his class!"

Lorena brightened.

"Wow—I'm guessing he's excited about that," she replied sincerely.

"Yeah, he is. He apologized for not keeping in touch with any of us, but also added that he's been busy with some other stuff as well—it turns out he's not gonna marry that other chick, and as a result her dad got all upset with him. He said it was something about she wasn't his type after all and she had cheated on him or somethin'—so he kicked her to the curb. Is that not insane?"

As soon as Candy mentioned Tony not getting married after all, Lorena had completely tuned out the rest of her ramble, staring off into space as she set down the dish she was holding.

"Uh, hello-o? Anybody there? Don't tell me you've gone and drowned in the dishwater, 'Rena," Candy said with a laugh.

"Yeah, I-I'm here," Lorena replied quietly.

"You sure don't sound like it—what's wrong?"

"Nothing's wrong—who said something was wrong?" Lorena asked, realizing that she suddenly felt lighter than she did when the conversation started.

Candy was silent for a few moments, obviously thinking.

"Hey, Lorena?"

"Uh-huh?" she replied, trying to keep the approaching smile at the thought of Tony not getting married from forming on her face."

"Um . . . I know this is probably a touchy subject for you," Candy began very slowly, ". . .but, uh, is there any chance that back when I used to joke around about you having a thing for Tony, I was. . . actually completely right?"

After managing to compose herself, Lorena cleared her throat awkwardly.

"Candy, uh—"

" 'Cause, I mean," Candy interrupted in a rush of words, "if-if you really did like him and probably were upset when he ran off with that Michelle chick, and now that you know what you know, what I know, then what does this mea—"

"Candy, listen, I need to go," Lorena cut in, sensing it not being the best time to have that discussion.

"C'mon, Lorena, I've gotta know—'cause if you've been holding all of this in for years, then you're probably wondering if Tony—"

"Candy—focus! I need to run, for real. I'll call you later."

Candy sighed.

"Alright—Godspeed."

"Later."

After clicking off, Lorena proceeded to finish washing the dishes, then got the kids ready for bed.

"Ma'am, spell the address, please."

"Well, that's the problem—I don't know how to spell it. You see, I heard it once at a church meeting, and you know how those young reverends can get—they'll talk so fast that a woman of my age can barely understand them . . ."

Lorena sighed while leaning over to place her elbow on the countertop, resting her cheek in her hand while balancing the phone on her shoulder.

"Perhaps you could flip through your church directory-"

"That's just the problem, though," the old woman persisted, "my church doesn't have one yet. It's new, and filled with new people. I told you those youngun's don't know anything about running a decent, respectable church . . ."

It was drawing near the end of a long, busy Friday afternoon at the florist, and Lorena was coming towards the end of her patience with an elderly woman she had been trying to take an order from for the past ten minutes.

She picked up a nearby glass of water, taking a sip before loosing her hair from a ponytail holder and running her fingers through it.

Several days had passed since her conversation with Candy, and she often found herself thinking about the questions her friend asked. Another thing on Lorena's mind were the bombings in South Africa—she still hadn't received word from her mother.

". . .and they're just as rude—and loud! Have you ever attended one of those churches where the reverends are just especially loud?"

Lorena closed her eyes, feeling the load of the day beginning to take its toll on her as she smiled out of what she was certain to be the commencement of hysteria.

"No, Mrs. Bridge, I haven't. But maybe you could enlighten me by attempting—I-I mean telling —me that address once more. The sooner you do, the sooner both of us can move on and enjoy the rest of our day."

"Well, you see, that's just the proble—"

"I'm aware, Mrs. Bridge. But there's no way to solve a problem without first taking steps. How about you tell me the address once again?"

"Well, I believe it was 115 Byrd Lane, in Chicago."

Lorena sighed in relief and quickly jotted the address down onto a form.

"Alright then, Mrs. Bridge. Now, the roses should arrive at the funeral parlor by—"

"Or was it *116 Byrd Court*, in Chicago?"

Lorena rolled her eyes and immediately crumpled the form, tossing it to the side as she blew a stray strand of hair out of her face.

A tall, elegant yet artistic, middle-aged Italian woman passed by the counter, carrying a large vase filled with tulips, carnations and roses—noticing the expression of disbelief on Lorena's face.

"Who is that?" Mrs. Gianni asked quietly with a frown while setting the flowers on display in the storefront window.

Lorena sighed before placing one hand over the mouthpiece.

"Some strange old woman," she replied in sheer bewilderment as the elderly woman continued to jabber. "I'm sure she's senile."

Mrs. Gianni nodded understandingly, then chuckled slightly.

"Good old Mrs. Bridge—I'll take it from here, Lorena."

Lorena willingly handed the phone over to her boss, then slid out from behind the counter to arrange a few more bouquets before quitting time.

A few minutes later, the front doorbell sounded, and Lorena heard Mrs. Gianni hang the phone up to tend to the customer.

Lorena stood with her back to the entrance of the storage room, arranging a bouquet of roses in a vase.

She had just begun to add baby's breath to the arrangement when a voice sounded behind her, "Excuse me, miss—I would like to purchase a bouquet of roses for a Lorena Selenez."

Lorena, confused, swiftly spun around.

A handsome young man stood tall in the doorway, his friendly smile lighting up his tanned face while exposing youthful dimples. A few loose strands of his dark hair fell carelessly over piercing, raven eyes filled with a confident glow, and his distinguished brow added an almost "finishing" touch to his adorable, yet mature, countenance. A casually dignified, navy-blue, mock turtleneck with rolled up sleeves complimented his built, athletic figure, and he sported sharp, black slacks over black dress shoes to complete the look.

" 'Tonio . . ."

Later that evening, Tony and Lorena chatted lightly over dinner at a local café, and took their time in catching up with each other's lives . . .

"So I guess you're wondering what's up with Michelle and I . . ."

"I already know—Candy told me a few days back. She's keeping pretty close tabs on you."

Tony nodded, raising an eyebrow in curiosity.

"Is she?" he asked quizzically, then chuckled. "I guess I should have known she'd tell you."

Lorena smiled lightly, picking around at her fettuccini alfredo dish.

"She just cares about you—in her own 'Candy' way. She doesn't want you to get hurt and all," she replied with a slight shrug. "So how are you taking it?"

Tony sighed mildly, then dabbed at his mouth with his napkin.

"I'm alright—I was sorta' expecting it, you know?"

Lorena frowned as she looked up at him, shaking her head slowly.

"I didn't know things were rocky."

Tony smiled wryly, focusing his gaze on the tabletop.

"Yeah, she was a little unsure. I think that even if we were meant to be, we still rushed a little. We didn't really know each other well enough."

Mindlessly touching a scar on her collarbone, Lorena nodded understandingly.

"I know what you mean," she stated quietly.

A brief silence followed, until Tony spoke up, "So what does Lorena see herself doing in the future? How's that psychology degree coming?"

Lorena sighed.

"It's not easy. But if I try hard enough I'll graduate with the GPA I wanted."

"And what's that?"

Lorena shook her head with a sigh.

"Don't laugh—4.0."

Tony smiled.

"The incredible Lorena Selenez. That's what you've got, isn't it?"

She nodded slowly.

"Yeah, for the past semester," she replied lightly. "Thank God," Lorena added before taking a drink of her soft drink.

Tony looked up suddenly from his meal at her last words, a question in his mind. Lorena was eating in silence, not particularly aware of his staring.

"And your plans after school?" he asked, deciding to move on.

She paused for a moment, setting her fork down while looking thoughtfully off in the distance.

"You know, it's really strange. It's like I'm not worried about my future, and I'm okay with things right now—not that I'm kicking back or anything, but it's just that I . . ." Her voice faded momentarily as she bit her lip, trying to formulate her thoughts. "I don't really . . . know what I want to do. Psychology's cool and all, but . . . as crazy as this may sound, I've just had a feeling lately—a feeling like somethin's coming, or about to happen. I don't know what it is, though . . ."

Tony was perturbed as he watched Lorena twist her necklace chain while zoning out again.

She finally laughed lightheartedly, returning to her food.

"I guess I'm just talking like any other person about to graduate," Lorena voiced carelessly with a smile at Tony.

He returned the smile, though somewhat nervously, then after scratching the back of his neck, turned conversation to local news.

". . . so after the caterers completely screwed up the main course, the cake was dropped on the way to the church."

"You're kidding me."

Lorena shook her head.

"Nope."

Tony gazed at her in disbelief.

"Wow, that's . . ."

"Crazy?" she offered with a smile.

He laughed.

"Yeah."

The two friends had just finished dinner, and were now strolling down the old, familiar hallway to Lorena's apartment. She had just finished telling Tony all about Candy's wedding earlier that year, and how it had flopped. However, the bride and groom fortunately had a good sense of humor and were able to laugh at the turn of events.

"They say it's gonna snow this week," Tony stated as he stuffed his hands into the pockets of his leather jacket.

"Yeah," Lorena replied quietly, her mind soaring off to Africa at the mere mention of the opposite extreme to its climate.

Noticing the distant gleam and sudden disquieted look on her face, Tony frowned.

"Is everything okay, Lorena? You've seemed kinda' distracted."

Immediately, Lorena adorned one of her apologetically wry smiles.

"Am I? I'm sorry—"

"No, no—nothing to apologize about. I just wondered if something was wrong."

Lorena let out a heavy sigh, rubbing the back of her neck as she walked over to the railing of the balcony overlooking the parking lot.

"Yeah, I'm . . ." she started to say that she was "okay," but thought against it when the realization occurred that she wasn't.

Tony remained silent, watching her fold her arms over the metal railing.

"It's um . . . my mom . . ."

Tony frowned again, walking up beside her.

"Is she okay? I'm sorry I'm not up on things—she's still in Africa, right?"

"Yeah, she . . ." Lorena sighed once more, then took a deep breath as she rubbed her forehead. "I don't really know, 'Tonio."

She changed her reply, trying hard to keep from crying. "She was sending me letters for a while—you know, just updating me on how things were going—and she did this for about four years . . .until now. There were suicide bombings in her country and. . ." She paused as her voice caught in her throat, and a few tears fell.

Tony looked down, giving her a moment to finish.

"I haven't replied to any of the letters, and there's so much I haven't told her . . .you know?"

"I'm sorry, Lorena—I don't know what to say . . .I mean, you haven't gotten any calls or anything?"

She shook her head, beginning to get a hold of herself.

"Nothing," she stated before taking a deep breath while looking down at her hands. "I guess I just need to keep on waiting."

Tony nodded understandingly.

"You can do it," he said sincerely as he took her hand in his.

Lorena smiled as she squeezed his hand, then wiped at her eyes. "Thanks, 'Tonio."

After he returned the smile, the two continued down the hall. When they reached the door, Tony sighed.

"Keep me posted. If you need anything, you know where to find me."

"I would appreciate your prayers."

Tony nodded.

"I'll do that."

Lorena smiled gratefully, then began to open the door.

"So will I. Goodnight."

Tony smiled.

"Goodnight."

With that, Lorena left and Tony made his way back down the hall. Seconds later, he stopped dead in his tracks, something suddenly occurring to him.

With a wide grin, he turned around to look behind him, then continued forward—his question finally answered.

"Thank you, God."

~ Chapter XVI ~

"Love is patient, love is kind. It does not envy, it does not boast, it is not proud. It is not rude, it is not self-seeking, it is not easily angered, it keeps no record of wrongs. Love does not delight in evil but rejoices with the truth. It always protects, always trusts, always hopes, always perseveres. Love never fails."

I Corinthians 13:4-8
NIV

†

The holiday season ushered in bitter temperatures for the lakeside metropolis, and its sidewalks were soon crowded with shoppers and merchants. Snowflakes floated gracefully from a sky of navy-violet abyss, or hastily traveled wherever the raging winds directed. Despite the fickle weather, the warmth of the holidays soothed last-minute-present-buying stress, and a sense of peace filled the air.

When Lorena had the time, Tony would take her and the kids on trips to Chicago's many Christmas venues, such as FAO Schwarz, River Oaks Mall, or Lorena's personal favorite, the Marshall Field's flagship store (a towering department store which held a tall Christmas tree on display).

A few days before Christmas, a pregnant Candy and her husband, Matt, arrived in town, surprising Lorena and Tony. With two of her close friends (and one of her new ones) to celebrate the holiday, Lorena felt a great sense of joy. Though every now and then she couldn't help but allow her mind to travel to Africa.

Christmas Eve arrived more quickly than anyone expected, and Lorena and Candy (along with the help of Celeste and Caramelle) found themselves preparing a large dinner for the evening, while Tony, his younger brother Angelo, Matt and Nathan conducted what was supposed to be a secret gift-wrapping session in Nathan's room.

"How many eggs does the recipe call for again, 'Rena?" Candy asked as she reached across Celeste's head to the 'fridge.

"Um . . .four, I think," Lorena replied as she glanced over at a cookbook from where she was helping Caramelle place marshmallows atop a sweet-potato casserole (by holding her up to where she could reach the counter). "Make sure you get the edges, 'Mella."

"I know, Mommy," Caramelle replied as though she had everything under control, and Lorena and Candy shared a smile.

"Four eggs, eh?" Candy questioned as she raised her eyebrows. "This is gonna be *some* pumpkin pie. Who put us up to making both sweet potato and pumpkin dishes anyhow?"

Lorena smirked.

"Your husband, remember?"

Candy frowned, then shook her head with a laugh.

"Oh, yeah."

"Mom, I can't get the skin off this onion—and my eyes are startin' to hurt," Celeste stated with a sigh as she set the onion down and rubbed her eyes.

"Your eyes are hurting because the skin *is* off, 'Less," Lorena replied as she shook her head.

"Oh," Celeste replied, looking highly confused all of a sudden.

"Lemme give you a hand with that, 'Lessie," Candy offered as she took up the duty of peeling the onions needed for the green beans.

"I wanna go see what they're up to in there—can I please go?" Celeste pleaded.

Lorena sighed, setting Caramelle back on the ground when the toddler had finished decorating the casserole.

"Alright—just knock before you go in. You don't want to see any presents that may be for you, right?"

"Of course not," Celeste replied as she glared and hurried off.

"Me too, Mommy?" Caramelle asked with wide eyes.

Lorena smiled, gently tugging one of her little pigtails.

"I guess so."

After the kids had left (and were summoned into "the wrapping room"), Candy shook her head again with a smile.

"They're too adorable—and I know I say it a thousand times, but it's true."

Lorena chuckled, stirring a pot of green beans.

"Try living with 'em—doing their laundry and cooking their food."

Candy laughed, beginning to dice the onions.

"Every time I notice how big they're getting I feel old ... wait a minute." She paused for a moment. "I *am* old."

Lorena laughed.

"That makes two of us, I guess."

At that moment, the doorbell rang, and they both looked up.

"That must be Mr. and Mrs. G.—I'll get it," Lorena voiced, referring to Mrs. Gianni and her husband.

When she reached the door, she checked the peephole to see four UPS men on the doorstep, two of them each holding a pallet piled high with three large boxes, and the other two with three more boxes that sat on the ground—these much larger than the others, standing about a yard off the ground.

Bewildered, Lorena opened the door.

"May I help you?"

"Is this the residence of a 'Lorena Selenez?' " asked one of the men.

Lorena, still gaping at the sizeable boxes, took a moment to reply, "You're speaking to her."

"Would you sign here, please, Ms. Selenez?" he asked, holding a clipboard forward and a pen.

Staring in disbelief, Lorena signed her name where indicated.

"Are you sure these are for me? Who are they from?"

"Goodness gracious, Lorena!" Candy, who had just joined her friend at the door, exclaimed while munching on a cookie. "I didn't know you were expecting any large packages."

"Me either," she replied, stepping aside so that the delivery men could enter.

"They're from a long way away, ma'am—read the return address," one of them answered her question as his co-workers brought each box into the living room.

Frowning in deep confusion, Lorena scanned a label on one of the larger boxes, and gasped when the words "Soweto, South Africa" caught her eye.

At that moment, Tony, Matt and the other gift wrappers entered the room, each one asking what was going on.

Feeling speechless, Lorena swallowed.

"Look, Mommy, there's a letter!" Caramelle piped up suddenly when after setting the last box down, one of the men brought a letter out of a satchel—handing it to Lorena.

She accepted it with trembling hands, realizing that this was the letter she had been awaiting for nearly four long months.

"Open it, Mom!" Celeste stated excitedly as she peered over her mother's arm to see the letter.

"Why don't we let your mom read it in private, okay? We can go decorate those cookies and cupcakes." Tony spoke up persuasively as he led Celeste, Caramelle and Nathan off to the kitchen. Matt and Angelo soon followed.

"Merry Christmas," the delivery men stated politely as they left, and Candy closed the door behind them.

"I'm gonna go read this," Lorena said quietly as she started to her room for some privacy.

Candy smiled as she gave her friend a warm hug, then squeezed her hand in reassurance.

"Take your time."

Lorena returned the smile, then headed off.

When she stepped inside her quiet room, she made her way to the bed after closing the door. Once she had taken a seat, she opened the envelope to see her mother's graceful script, and felt her spirits lift as she began to read . . .

Dear Lorena,

Merry Christmas! I hope you're having a good holiday season.

I know you must want an explanation for why I haven't written in so long, therefore I'm going to give you one.

You may have seen on the news the trouble we've been having in Soweto. None of the bombers hit us, but our neighbors did get injured. Part of the Lorena's Freedom headquarters was hit—the Eastern wing—but fortunately the damage isn't too great that we can't pay for it. God will make a way.

The reason I haven't written you is that Imani suggested that we lay low for a little while, in case more trouble arises. The terrorists behind this have caused a lot of people (including friends of ours) to decide against sending anything out of the country for security purposes. But now that most of the danger has passed, I've sent you this letter—along with a few gifts. Don't open them until Christmas morning! I remember how when you were a little girl you would always ask me if you could open your presents before Christmas, but I'd always tell you no so that your surprise wouldn't be ruined.

Unfortunately, this letter can't be as long as I hoped it to be, as I'm in the middle of a big Christmas program and gift operation for the girls right now—and it's taking up most of my time. We're going to hopefully get 500 gift-boxes for the girls, and host a party for them and their friends. Imani and I are hoping this will brighten their day a little.

As for your gifts—when you open them, don't worry about the money we spent on them, you and the kids are more than worth it. Please tell them that I love them and wish them a Merry Christmas. Sometimes I'll picture what they must look like in my mind—trying to get an idea. Little "Natty" must be nearly ten years old by now. It's amazing how time flies by. And you, Lorena, I miss you so much—as you've found that I say in each letter. Please write back, if I could just hear one aspect of your life—one story about how things are going for you. Every day I pray that they are going well.

I love you,

- Elsa

Feeling overjoyed at the realization that her mother was alive and well, Lorena let a few tears fall, sighing as she set the letter to the side. She knew that she owed her mother at least one letter—let her know that she wanted things to be "okay" between them. But as she reached over to her desk for a pen and paper, she felt the familiar fear returning. How much longer would she be held back by her past?

Lorena decided with a sigh that she would simply wait... until after Christmas—when life slowed down.

Heading back into the living room, where everyone sat socializing by the decorated tree, she announced that all was well. After hugs were exchanged and the celebration began, the friends and family sat down to dinner (and were soon joined by Mrs. Gianni and her husband), then stayed up chatting over cider and cookies.

The following morning carried a gentle snowfall to compliment the holiday, and after much pleading from the kids, Lorena helped them open the presents from their grandmother. It turned out that Elsa had gotten each child a brand new bicycle (Caramelle's with training wheels), dolls, tea sets, action figures and African instruments such as whistles and drums. When Lorena opened her presents, she was surprised to find beautiful African jewelry sets, a much-needed iron, and a new cordless phone to replace the testy one she already owned.

After gifts were opened, Candy, Matt and Tony arrived to share dinner with the family, and that Christmas progressed as a peaceful one.

Over the course of the next year, Lorena and Tony graduated—Tony at the top of his class and Lorena with the GPA she had hoped for—and the two began seeing each other more often; almost unofficially declaring themselves an item. The letters from Africa persisted, and as one might expect, Lorena didn't, in fact, reply as she had determined to do so after the holiday season.

Months passed, and life traveled forward for the small family. Around autumn of 1994, Lorena was employed at a local publishing company, and her job was to help edit pieces by offering her psychological input (thanks to her psychology major). Her pay increased greatly, and she soon found herself considering renting a new apartment. She knew that things were getting tight in their tiny Cabrini-Green home, as Nathan and Celeste were growing up and often could be found fighting over the bathroom. Caramelle wasn't far behind, and Lorena knew that someday they would need more space.

"Mom, Nathan won't come outta' the bathroom—and I need to get to my hair stuff so you can style it!" called Celeste through Lorena's door one hectic Monday morning.

Lorena sighed, trying to quickly apply her mascara in front of her dresser mirror.

"How long has he been in?" she replied.

"I dunno,' an hour maybe! Please make him come out!"

"I haven't been in here for an hour—you're just being dumb 'cause you wanna look good for Andy!" Nathan's annoyed voice could be heard calling from the bathroom.

"I am not being dumb—you are! I don't need an hour to get ready!"

"That's right—'cause you need two hours!"

Beginning to get fed up with the arguing, Lorena finally emerged from her room.

"That's enough!" she exclaimed, adjusting her earring. "Nathan, you've got one more minute, and when you go in there, Celeste, just get your hair stuff and come right out. Your sister still needs to brush her teeth and wash up," she concluded as she brushed by Celeste to the living room, and on to the kitchen for some coffee.

At that moment, Caramelle came galloping up to her, a worried look on her face.

"Mommy, I gotta go real bad!" she stated, tugging on Lorena's blazer sleeve.

Again, Lorena sighed, turning on the coffee machine.

"Be patient, sweetie—they're almost done," she reassured her, shaking her head as she quickly poured the coffee beans into a filter. "One of these days we're gonna have more space."

At the sound of the doorbell ringing suddenly, Lorena jumped—spilling the beans all over the floor.

"Get that for me, please, 'Less!" she called as she bent over to clean up the mess, and Celeste sighed her reluctance as she headed to the door.

After pushing a stool up to it, stepping up to see through the peephole, Celeste squealed in delight, " 'Tonio's here!!"

Caramelle immediately echoed, running to the door where Celeste was opening it.

"Nathan, I think a minute has passed, don't you?" Lorena called over her shoulder as Tony picked up the giggling girls, spinning them around.

"Guess where my field trip's gonna be, 'Tonio!" Celeste stated excitedly.

"How come you get to tell 'Tonio where your field trip's gonna be but I don't?" Caramelle complained (her school field trip was scheduled for that afternoon as well).

Celeste scowled. "I think the Museum of Science and Industry is much cooler than a dumb old zoo."

"Why don't you both tell me? I think the zoo *and* the museum are cool," Tony offered when Caramelle began to pout, heading over to the couch with Caramelle in his arms and Celeste at his side.

"Hey, 'Tonio," Lorena finally greeted when she finished cleaning the floor, then made her way to the bathroom. "Nathan, you've been in there for—"

Before she could finish her sentence, the door opened, and out walked Nathan, dressed and ready to leave.

"Okay, okay. I'm out," he replied before joining the girls with Tony.

Lorena sighed, then upon seeing that Celeste was too engrossed in telling Tony about her upcoming field trip, retrieved the hair products herself.

"'Mella, you've gotta go wash up. You can tell 'Tonio about your trip later."

Caramelle frowned her disapproval, then finally headed off for the bathroom.

Meanwhile, Celeste continued her ramble, ". . .so anyway, my friend Andy—"

"She means her boyfriend—"

"Nathan," Lorena warned, taking a seat on the couch beside Tony while Celeste sat on the floor as her mother styled her hair.

"Sorry," Nathan apologized with a sigh as he picked at his leather watch band.

Tony listened politely to Celeste's incredible account of what the trip would include, until Lorena finished her hair and announced that it was time to head outside for the bus.

After rounding the kids up, Lorena (with the help of a very-cooperative Tony) escorted them to the parking lot, and after watching them board the bus, headed for her own (recently purchased and used) car.

"Now you see what I mean when I say that I need to move."

Tony chuckled as he held the door open for her and she slid in to the driver seat.

"It's hectic, but it's a home," he replied with a smile.

Lorena shook her head and smiled lightly.

"I guess you're right. I'll see you at around five."

"Alright—they'll be at the school, right?"

Lorena nodded, answering his question concerning where to pick up the kids.

"Right. Later."

"See ya,'" Tony replied, squeezing her hand before she drove off.

A few days later, Lorena was flipping through a magazine one evening, trying to wind down from a long work day, when the telephone rang suddenly.

"Hello?" she asked after reaching over to the coffee table for the phone.

"Ms. Selenez?" a female voice replied.

"Speaking."

"Hello, this is Amy Wexler—Nathan's teacher. How are you?"

Lorena frowned slightly at the realization of her caller's identity. Was something wrong?

"Hi, Mrs. Wexler. I'm fine, thanks—and you?"

"I'm alright. I'm sure you're wondering about the reason for my call. You know more so than I that Nathan is a very bright student, and a cooperative child—but lately he's been acting a little . . . how should I say . . . unlike himself."

Perplexed, Lorena ran her fingers through her loose hair.

"How so?"

A pause sounded from the other line, and eventually a sigh.

"Well, he's been hanging around a particularly unruly bunch of boys in class, and occasionally I'll see him with large groups of older boys, up to four years older than him—fourteen- and fifteen-year-olds—when I'm walking to my car after school. Now, I don't mean to alarm you, but I feel that he's not giving his all to his work—as he used to. He hasn't done anything wrong, but he seems distracted, and it's not like Nathan to be this way—usually your son is very dedicated and even interested in his work."

Lorena sighed this time, knowing the chances of Nathan slipping away from school due to friends were high.

"Have you questioned him about this at all?"

"I've only asked him to focus more and try harder, Ms. Selenez. I'm sorry I can't give you any more information on those older boys. Perhaps you could find out through him."

"You've done all that you can, Mrs. Wexler. I'll definitely talk to him," Lorena replied as she set her magazine down on the coffee table, and watched as Celeste entered the room, heading to the kitchen for a snack. "Thank you so much for your concern."

"You're welcome, Ms. Selenez. I wish you and your family the best."

After clicking off, Lorena set the phone down with another heavy sigh, rubbing her temples as she rested her elbows on her knees.

"I know you told me to think hard on my math, Mom, but it's just too hard for even thinking hard to work. Can you help me, please?" Celeste pleaded while rummaging through a bag of Cracker Jacks for the prize.

"In a minute, 'Less—is your brother doing his homework?" Lorena replied while rising from her seat and making her way to the hallway.

"He should be—is this milk any good?"

"Check the date—I can't do everything for you, 'Lessie," Lorena called over her shoulder, opening Nathan's slightly-ajar door to find him lying on his side on the bed.

"Nat, I'd like to have a—" she began to say, but stopped short when she noticed that he was sound asleep—a pencil in his left hand and his right resting on an open history book.

"Have a word with you," she finished barely above a whisper, walking over to remove the pencil from his hand, and take the history book off the bed.

After placing the covers over him, she reached over to turn the lamp off, kissing him on the forehead before walking to the door; silently praying his youth wouldn't mimic her own.

It was only the next day that Lorena found herself driving home from the kids' school with a black-eyed Nathan in the passenger seat—the latter fresh from a rumble with another classmate. Upon her request, Tony had taken the girls out to the park so that Lorena could speak privately with her son.

The drive home was a long, tense, silent one. Lorena directed the vehicle down the road—deep in thought and stress—while Nathan sat huddled against the window, staring out with a melancholy expression on his bruised face.

When they reached the apartment, he went ahead of his mother, his backpack slung over one shoulder. Waiting for her to unlock the door, he sighed, and when she did so, he quickly entered.

Lorena set her purse down on a table by the door, rubbing her weary eyes as she made her way for the refrigerator.

"Go ahead and wait in your room—I'll be there in a minute."

Nathan didn't reply, but simply ambled sluggishly off to his room—as though he didn't have to be told to do so.

After grabbing a slab of steak from the 'fridge, Lorena stepped inside his room to find him sitting on his bed, tossing a baseball back and forth between his hands.

"This will help your eye," she stated as she placed the meat over his injured eye, taking a seat beside him on the bed.

She gave him a moment to recover from the sting, remaining silent for a few minutes.

"Why is everybody mad at me for the fight? I didn't start it," Nathan said quietly, breaking the silence before Lorena could.

"That's only part of what this is about—and I'm not mad at you," she replied slowly.

He looked down at the floor, holding the meat up to his face with one hand.

"But you're still gonna punish me."

Lorena rubbed the back of her neck, twisting her locket chain as she did so.

"Tell me what makes you want to be like those boys."

Nathan shrugged slightly.

"People like them—"

"People are afraid of them," she corrected firmly, then paused, "And they're afraid of the people they hurt," she added in a quieter tone. "Nathan, you can't believe everything you see and hear—every time they steal something, hurt somebody, or take drugs, they're putting on a mask. It covers themselves, and when you wear a mask, people can't see the real you. That makes you temporarily feel in control of things that you're afraid of. Do you see what I'm saying?"

Nathan slowly lowered the meat from his eye, staring straight ahead with a frown of slight confusion on his face.

"I don't know . . .I guess so," he replied softly.

Lorena sighed deeply as she felt the weight of the situation falling on her.

"Nathan, the only reason I'm drilling you on this is because I really, really don't want you to have a childhood like mine. I'm grounding you for a week, but I don't want you to see it as something to go through and move on from when it's over without learning anything."

Nathan began to pick at a seam on his jeans, looking far from enlightened by the conversation.

"Nathan, look at me."

Obediently, he turned to look at her, his bruised and swelling eye causing her heart to ache.

"Nat," Lorena began slowly, placing her hand on his knee, "someday you're going to understand why I'm telling you not to believe certain things. It may seem as though I'm just being a mom, but there's more to it than that. Do you remember when you and 'Tonio went fishing last spring? How you used worms for bait? You put the worms on the hook to get the fish to bite it, and this means that they must like worms, right?"

Nathan nodded.

"Well, that's exactly what these people are doing to anyone who looks like they're going somewhere—anyone who's strong, and can think for themselves. But you've gotta resist the bait, Nat—you're much bigger than some gangsters with nothing better to do than hurt people for their own good. And right now you need to be acting bigger than that." Lorena sighed. "You've got to act like what you are: a leader. Someday I'm not going to be around to help you, and even though that's not easy for me to say, it's true. You've got to set a good example for your sisters—they're watching you, and though you may argue sometimes, they're counting on you more than you think . . . *I'm* counting on you more than you think. You are Nathan Antonio Selenez—God's own. Alright?" Show other people who you are; not some lost kid without a future.

Nathan bit his lip thoughtfully as he looked down at his hands, then back up at Lorena.

"Okay, Mom."

Lorena smiled, wrapping him in a hug.

"You know I love you."

Nathan finally smiled.

"Yeah—I love you too."

"Alright. Why don't you get to your homework, Mr. Wiz' Kid?" Lorena stated while rising and affectionately ruffling his curly, chestnut hair.

"Okay."

Making her way to the door, she stopped in the doorway—watching him begin to retrieve his books from his backpack. She closed the door slightly with one last sigh, then headed off for the kitchen to prepare dinner.

Spring of 1995 arrived stormy and cloudy, but on sunny days the air held a crisp, clean quality. It was a quiet, average Saturday evening when Lorena sat alone in the apartment, as the kids were out with friends. She didn't have anything in particular to do, and had it not been for the fact that he had an engagement with the president of the law firm where he worked, she and Tony would have gone out.

After surfing the TV for something to watch to no avail, Lorena finally flicked the set off and headed mindlessly for her room.

Another letter from Elsa had arrived earlier that morning, and Lorena had read it through when it came. She knew that nearly five years had passed, and she still hadn't replied to any of them. Her fear of change remained, yet she still wanted to take the chance...

Collapsing onto her bed with a sigh, she stared up at the ceiling until she grew tired of this particular activity, and then unconsciously directed her eyes to her bedside table, where four framed pictures sat. One was of her and the kids, taken about a year back—at the park. Another was of Elena when she was a teenager, on the day of her high school graduation. Yet another was a portrait of the kids—each one dressed up and smiling beautifully for the camera—even the coy Caramelle. Lastly, she found herself staring at a picture of herself and her mother—taken when she was about three or four. Lorena barely remembered posing for the picture, and how the dress she had to wear made her arms itch. Her mother looked as beautiful as always—her comforting smile lighting the image as she held a grinning Lorena in her lap. Lorena realized that she was smiling right back at the two individuals, but her smile soon faded when she remembered the wall of fear (built by her own self) separating them. Feeling as though she might cry at the thought of not being brave enough to write back, Lorena sat up, rubbing her eyes.

"Please help me, God."

A few minutes passed, and during this time she let her mind travel over her life—beginning with her first memories, up to the present.

Suddenly, something incredible took place.

Lorena opened her eyes, looking around the room. A voice had pierced the air . . .or her thoughts . . . It distinctly said one thing, "Reply." It was clear, and almost seemed to come as a comforting command.

Feeling warmth rushing over her, Lorena hugged herself, engrossed in thought.

"You've spoken, Lord. I'll do it."

Somehow sensing that her actions had something to do with her feeling that an event was soon to take place—something big was going to happen in her life—Lorena reached over to her desk for a piece of paper and a pencil. After several rough drafts, she finally came up with a winner:

Dear Mom,

Yes, it's me—your estranged daughter of nearly five years, but what most likely seems like a millennium. If there's anything I need to start out with, it's an apology—for the way I've acted. You did hurt me, but more so I hurt myself by building a wall of ice between us that towered to the sky—which in turn I used to hurt you. Maybe I should start at the only place I know how to: the beginning.

When I was a little girl, I remember you as being a nice, comforting, warm being that I could relate to as a sort of tower of support. Because you weren't around twenty-four-seven—as Grandma Rosalina took care of me—I had to deal with some of the other kids' jokes that you weren't really my mom. It made me wish that you were there all of the time . . . But when you could, if I found myself with a cut, you were there, when I had a nightmare, you were there, and when I was sad, you were there. But I'll never forget the day I woke up to find that you weren't there—for real this time. I understood that I wouldn't be able to see you for five years, but I was angry . . .at you. I was mad because I felt as though you had done something wrong and gotten into jail in order to get away from me. Somehow this added to low self-worth I felt for myself from how my dad seemingly wouldn't care about me enough that he would continue being a gang banger. But isn't that funny? I became what I hated—a person who puts so called "friends" above their family.

Well anyway, the more I began to blame you for my hurt feelings, the tougher I became. Around when I was thirteen, my friends told me about different drugs which were supposed to make you high and numb, but not hurt you (obviously these being lies). I didn't believe them, and because I had heard bad things about drugs, I didn't do them—but only tried them a little here and there for a short period. But when a friend told me how she would cut herself when she was sad or feeling hatred towards either herself or other people, I decided to give it a try. As to why I thought cutting myself was healthier than drugs, I don't know. Maybe I thought a skin wound wasn't as bad as a wound to the brain. Either way, I became slightly addicted, and stopped when I joined the gang—when they forced me to.

Without the cutting, I didn't know how to hurt myself, but I suspect that I must have been subconsciously aware of the bad effects the gang had on me. I guess my point is that my cold behavior was due to my own way of venting my pain—the thought of you, my dad, or anyone else (to me at the time) not caring about me made me feel as though I was obligated to almost do the same—not care about myself—in order to almost . . .get you to love me again. I thought that because there was obviously something wrong with me—something that caused people who were supposed to love me not love me—if I was able to play your game, I would be able to win your love somehow. But I guess I went too far when I let the hate for myself direct to both you and I. When I noticed that you were already reaching out to me, I decided that if I did the same I would get hurt again, therefore I gave up completely.

When you told Gram and I that you were saved, I felt as though God had stolen you from me when you had just gotten back into my life. When you announced your decision to leave for Africa, I felt robbed once again. I can even remember using my desire to be as different from you as possible to keep from putting the kids up for adoption when they were born. I had made up my mind that I couldn't abandon them the way I felt you abandoned me.

About four years ago, I finally came to the light, and got saved—for real. I'm a breathing, walking testimony of God's grace, and I thank Him for your prayers . . . for Gram's. I know now what she meant when she would tell me that everything happened for a reason, and why you named your ministry "Lorena's Freedom."

I know that this will surprise you and probably won't help the situation, but I forgave you a long time ago. I'm sorry for the things I've done, said and felt, and I wish I hadn't ever decided to be the way I was. I don't honestly know what you'll think when you read that I've been comfortably reading all of your letters (yes, I've read them all faithfully)—remaining silent for so long—while you've been tortured by guilt and the worry that maybe I've trashed them all. Not to mention whether or not I even care. But if the things you've said are true (which I now believe to be so), I'm sure you'll forgive me as well.

I just want to close in saying thank you for not giving up on me. A lot of people have walked away—I went from a popular girl with tons of supposed friends to one with a handful of true ones. But I'm being sincere in saying that you're the strongest one of them all. God has blessed me by giving me you as my mom. I love you, Momma.

Sincerely,

Lorena

~ Chapter XVII ~

"Then Jesus said to His disciples, 'If anyone would come after me, he must deny himself and take up his cross and follow me. For whoever wants to save his life will lose it, but whoever loses his life for me will find it.'"

Matthew 16:24 & 25
NIV

☦

Lorena sent her letter, and during the time that she waited impatiently for a reply, she received a phone call from the last person she had thought she would speak to: Anita Valdez. The call was far from social, and it turned out that Marisol wanted to speak with her in person . . .again. When she was told that it was an obligation, Lorena followed orders, and soon found herself driving through the CP neighborhood towards her former friend's apartment.

After alighting from her car, she locked the doors and warily scanned the premises—hoping trouble wasn't lurking around any corners.

Making her way down the familiar-yet-forgotten, muggy, dim hallway to Marisol's apartment, Lorena began to wonder what she wanted this time.

When she was halfway to the end of the hall, quick footsteps echoed from behind, and she turned to see two young children racing over—a boy and a girl that looked alike enough to be twins. The boy was around Caramelle's age, with a warm, medium-brown complexion, dark, semi-curly hair, and milky-brown eyes. The girl was about the same age, with her long, raven, wavy hair flowing after her, and her large, ebony eyes dancing with laughter and mystery all at once.

They were squirting each other with little water guns, and seemed as though they got along very well.

Lorena watched as they approached, and couldn't help but sense a familiar aspect about them both when they got closer. What could it have been, though?

She had just knocked on the door of Marisol's apartment when the children reached her side. The door opened, and a much older-looking, weary—yet somehow-still-intimidating—Marisol stood in the doorway.

Her cold eyes fell on Lorena, and before saying anything to her, she quickly ordered the two children in Spanish:

"Go back outside and play—I've got company over!"

They both voiced their reluctance in the same tongue, and eventually skulked off down the hall.

Lorena watched them go, fully comprehending the words exchanged.

"I thought you'd be abortion all the way, Marisa," she finally said after they'd left.

Marisol met her with an icy stare, then stepped aside for her to enter.

"You'd be surprised to know who the father is," she replied evenly as she closed the door behind her and Lorena took a seat on one of the beds. The only difference in the apartment was its living conditions, and the run-down toys scattering the floor.

"I don't really wanna know."

"Your old friend Cobra," Marisol stated sarcastically.

Lorena smirked before replying, "Good for you—and no, I'm not surprised."

Marisol ran her tongue along her teeth before kicking a few broken toy trucks out of the way as she headed to the window.

"I want you to know that I'm getting as tired of you as I can get, Selenez."

"Why?" Lorena returned swiftly, watching her ex-friend cross her arms over her chest.

When Marisol didn't reply, Lorena took a deep breath.

"Is it Adrienne, Marisa? Huh? You want me dead because my mom ruined your sister's gang plans?"

"You don't know anything about my family," she replied heatedly, yet quietly.

"That doesn't sound like much of a reason to hate your best friend, Marisa."

Marisol quickly turned around, her glare burning into Lorena's eyes.

"Who are you to tell me whether my reasons are good or bad, Lorena? Who are you to tell me anything?"

"A friend—and probably the only real one you've got left," Lorena returned evenly. "At least that's what I'd like to be again—I'm willing, Marisa, but are you?"

"Shut up, Selenez! You betrayed me—why should I trust you?!"

"When did I betray you? You need to forget whatever lies your sister's been telling you, Marisa! She's only using you the same way you tried to use me!"

"I said shut up, Selenez! As soon as I'm ready you're gonna regret every bad decision you and your mother made! Now get outta' here!"

Lorena nodded, standing up slowly with a sigh.

"I know you want it to be that way—I know that. But as I told you back before I even knew what I was saying—it doesn't haven't to be like this. You don't have to stay this way."

"Get outta' here!"

"If you wanna run from God the same way I did, Marisol, then do it. Just don't let it hurt anyone in my family anymore!"

"I said get outta' here!!"

Lorena finally made her way for the door, but stopped when she reached it. Turning around, she saw her friend standing with a sick look on her face—as though she was acting against her will.

But it was something else that caused Lorena to draw in her breath.

A solid sheet of darkness covered the window behind her old friend, with a pair of piercing, red eyes glowing in its midst. When Lorena focused her attention back on Marisol, she noticed that she had regained her composure, and almost seemed calm and collected again—only now even more wickedly intimidating.

"Your time is coming sooner than you think, Selenez," she said in a voice that sounded much unlike her own, and the evil in her tone could have melted ice with its black fire.

"If it's the Lord Jesus' will," Lorena replied confidently, and Marisol suddenly returned to her state of panic at seemingly the mere mention of His name.

Because she felt God telling her to leave that room as soon as possible, Lorena swallowed and opened the door, hurrying into the hallway. She had done so at the precise moment; as almost as soon as she closed the door behind her, a spray of bullets shot through the door and hit the wall across from it—each one missing Lorena by a hair.

Hurrying down the hall, she quickly left the building and climbed into her car to drive home.

A few days had passed since her encounter with Marisol, and Lorena was keeping her eyes peeled and ears open. She knew that Marisol was finally serious in her threat, and realized that the "something" she had been sensing for so long just might be a final showdown with the gang. Knowing she could easily be wrong, she often shrugged off her jitters as she had been doing for the past eleven years, and moved on as best she could.

It was a rainy, Thursday afternoon when Lorena found a letter from Africa in her mailbox upon returning home from work and school with the kids.

After putting the kids to bed that night, Lorena finally found peace and quiet as she closed herself into her room to read the letter. Opening the envelope, she unfolded the paper to read:

Dear Lorena,

I couldn't help but get on my knees and thank God as soon as I got your letter! If you only knew how glad I am that you wrote back—that you've forgiven me, that you're saved! I'm so overjoyed that I can't even write a long letter for a change!

I wish I could see you again—or at least hear your voice . . .

Please write me back again. I'd love to hear from you.

Love,

　　Elsa

Feeling that there was no better time than that moment to do what she had needed to do for a long time, Lorena quickly whipped out a blank sheet of paper, a pen, and began to write:

Dear Mom,

If you can, I would love to have you over to visit. We have so much catching up to do, and the kids haven't seen you in ages—Celeste and Caramelle don't even remember you.

A lot of things have changed for me. I graduated with my psychology degree, and I'm currently working with a publishing company as an advisor/editor. I help make psychological changes to pieces sent in, and I work with a few other senior editors. I like my work, the pay is a huge blessing, and it's interesting to see the different ideas sent to our floor. One of the recent pieces was a story about missionaries, and I think of you whenever I work on it. Yet another was a biography of a former Blood—and as you might have guessed, I think about the gang when I'm working on it.

I'm sure you're wondering how things are going with the CPs, and I wish I could give you some positive feedback . . . but I can't. I was so stupid not to listen to you when you told me how they weren't good for me to be around. Sometimes I'll wake up in the middle of the night from a nightmare, and I'll panic as I look around frantically—expecting to see the gang there. Life is scary right now, but better still—now that I know Christ. I do have trouble forgiving myself for what I've gotten us into, but God is helping me through that.

I remember actually feeling afraid when you first told Gram and I that you were saved—you didn't even have to say it for me to see that something was different about you. I think the gang has gotten that way with me—they see the difference, and it scares them...but I just wish that it could chase them away. I suppose life can't be that easy, though.

Sitting here writing this letter in my room, I feel tired, and somewhat lonesome. The kids are all asleep—it took me a while to settle them down from attending one of Nathan's football games. He's one of the best players, you know. Sometimes he'll say or do something that makes me stop and realize that he's growing up. It's hard to believe that only ten years ago he was a tiny, helpless infant. Celeste and Caramelle are sprouting up as well—they have their arguing moments, but I'm sure they'll grow out of it eventually. The kids stand up for each other, and I'm really proud of them.

My friend Tony and I are sort of/ kind of dating right now—I've liked him for a while now, and we told each other our true feelings some months back. He really does love God, and is strong in his faith. I like to think of you, Gram, and Tony as lighthouses in my life that guided me—as each of you refused to give up on me while I was struggling. Your examples were so strong—thank you again, Momma.

I'm not really sure what the future holds for me—I'll have to watch and wait like the rest of us. I'm praying for your ministry, and have been doing so as much as possible. I love what you're doing for those girls, and as you said in your first letter—I did need to see 'real' people.

I want to see you again so badly. Please come—it's been so long...too long.

Love,

Lorena

With a light sigh, Lorena set her pen down, biting her lip as she folded the letter and placed it inside of an envelope. After writing the appropriate addresses on it, she sealed it and set it to the side—planning to mail it the following day.

Before pulling the covers over herself to get some sleep, Lorena reached over to her bedside table for her Bible. Engrossed in thought, she flipped through the pages for a certain Scripture discussed over Bible study the night before. When she found it, she paused to read:

"Dear friends, do not be surprised at the painful trial you are suffering, as though something strange were happening to you. But rejoice that you may participate in the sufferings of Christ, so that you may be overjoyed when his glory is revealed. If you are insulted because of the name of Christ, you are blessed, for the Spirit of glory and of God rests on you. If you suffer, it should not be as a murderer or thief or any other kind of criminal, or even as a meddler. However, if you suffer as a Christian, do not be ashamed, but praise God that you bear that name."

(I Peter 4:12-16) NIV

Rubbing the back of her neck with a sigh, Lorena scanned a few verses ahead, until she found another Scripture:

"Be self-controlled and alert. Your enemy the devil prowls around like a roaring lion looking for someone to devour. Resist him, standing firm in the

faith, because you know that your brothers throughout the world are undergoing the same kind of sufferings."

(I Peter 5:8-10)NIV

Closing the Book slowly, Lorena lay on her back, staring up at the ceiling once more. The more she read about the hard parts to being a Christian, the more she wondered if she was strong enough.

"I can do all things through Christ who strengthens me. . ."

(Philippians 4:13) NKJV
she whispered thoughtfully, quoting the first verse she had memorized years back.

Turning onto her side and pulling the covers over her to go to sleep, a thud met her ears, and she realized that her Bible had fallen to the floor. Sitting up and swinging her legs over the edge, Lorena got up to retrieve the Book. When she knelt down to pick it up, she saw that it was open to the book of Esther—a book about an orphan girl who became a queen, and later risked her life upon God's calling to save her people, the Jews.

She was just about to close it, when a few particular verses caught her eye . . .

" 'For if you remain silent at this time, relief and deliverance for the Jews will arise from another place, but you and your father's family will perish. And who knows but that you have come to royal position for such a time as this?'. . . Then Esther sent this reply to Mordecai: 'Go, gather together all the Jews who are in Susa, and fast for me. Do not eat or drink for three days, night or day. I

and my maids will fast as you do. When this is done, I will go to the king, even though it is against the law. And if I perish, I perish.'"

(Esther 4:14-16)NIV

"Blessed is the man who perseveres under trial, because when he has stood the test, he will receive the crown of life that God has promised to those who love Him."

(James 1:12)NIV

Beginning to feel fear creeping inside of her heart, Lorena sighed and closed her eyes—wondering why God was showing her that she could do something she felt was impossible: live without fear.

"I can't do this anymore, God . . .I'm scared . . ."

Silent tears falling down her cheeks, Lorena placed her face in her hands, sobbing softly.

When she looked up, she sighed heavily and began to turn randomly through the Book—desperately searching for some source of comfort. A few moments later, she found herself in the gospel of Matthew, and read:

"During the fourth watch of the night Jesus went out to them, walking on the lake. When the disciples saw Him walking on the lake, they were terrified. 'It's a ghost,' they said, and cried out in fear. But Jesus immediately said to them: 'Take courage! It is I. Don't be afraid.'

'Lord, if it's you,' Peter replied, 'tell me to come to you on the water.'
'Come,' He said.

Then Peter got down out of the boat, walked on the water and came toward Jesus. But when he saw the wind, he was afraid and, beginning to sink, cried out, 'Lord, save me!'

Immediately Jesus reached out His hand and caught him. 'You of little faith,' He said, 'why did you doubt?'"

(Matthew 14:25-31)NIV

Suddenly feeling a great sense of peace rushing over her, Lorena allowed a few more tears to fall—these more so from joy than distress. She wasn't completely sure what was going to happen in the near future, but suspected that God didn't want her to be afraid. And somehow, the thought of Jesus loving her so much that He would walk with her even when she doubted was more than enough to comfort her pain.

Elsa's reply arrived about a week after Lorena sent her last letter—announcing that she would set off for America in two weeks.

"C'mon kids—your grandmother's plane has already landed!" Lorena called over her shoulder as she straightened her pinstripe blazer while hurrying down the hall to the living room.

"Mommy, 'Lessie hasn't done my hair yet!" Caramelle complained from her room, where Celeste was finishing up her own hair in front of a mirror.

"Hold your horses, 'Mella," Celeste replied with a sigh.

"She can do it on the way—let's go," Lorena stated as she shook her head and made sure that her keys were in her purse. "Natha—"

"Here I am, Mom," he cut in, standing ready behind Lorena at the door—his jacket adorned and shoes on.

Lorena sighed.

"Okay, I was just making sure you were ready."

Celeste and Caramelle finally left their room, and the small family climbed into the car to set off for O'Hare Airport. Soon they stood searching for Elsa's face amongst a sea of people near the first gate.

"Do you see her, 'Lessie?" Caramelle asked as Lorena continued to scan the crowd.

Celeste shrugged.

"I don't remember what she looks like."

"Mom showed us a picture of her last night, 'Less," Nathan replied in slight annoyance, then suddenly pointed to his right. "Isn't that her, Mom?"

Lorena frowned as she looked to where he was pointing. "Where?"

"Oh, I see her now—standing by those benches. She's pretty!" Celeste stated in excitement as she stepped around her brother to get a better view.

Lorena finally spotted her, and a smile lit her face.

A barely-middle-aged woman stood searching the bunch of faces around her, her luggage at her side. She was dressed in a maroon, sleeveless blouse and stylish, black slacks. Her long, wavy mahogany hair was down and parted down the middle—giving her a youthful look.

"Where? I don't see anybody," Caramelle whined.

Elsa grinned when she found her family amongst the crowd, and hurried over. Lorena was the first person she hugged, and they both shed a few joyous tears. The kids looked on smilingly, taking an immediate liking to their grandmother.

"Oh my goodness, 'Rena, you're an adult!" Elsa exclaimed as she held her back to look at her—speaking as though Lorena had grown up right then and there on the spot.

"You don't look a day older, Mom," she replied with a light laugh.

Elsa smiled brightly, wiping a few tears from her eyes as she now turned to the kids.

"I don't believe it!" she voiced in surprise when her eyes fell on Nathan. "Natty? You're practically grown up!" she decided as she wrapped him in a warm hug, and he blushed slightly.

Lorena smiled.

"Not quite, Mom."

Elsa returned the smile.

"I know, I know."

Lorena patted Nathan's shoulders as Elsa moved on to Celeste.

"Don't tell me this is little 'Lessie, 'Rena . . ."

Lorena shrugged with a smile.

"Exact likeness to your mother, Celeste—I thought for a second there I was looking at Lorena at your age," she stated as she gave her a hug. "You're ten now, right?"

Celeste nodded.

"Ten-and-a-half."

"She has to get it down to the last second," Lorena explained with a chuckle, and Elsa laughed while nodding knowingly.

"And who is this pretty little girl?" she questioned as she bent down to smile at Caramelle (who had taken hold of her sister's arm).

" 'Mella—quit bein' shy," Celeste stated as she shook her head.

"She's precious, Lorena," Elsa said over her shoulder. "And you look a lot like your Mommy, too," she commented to Caramelle as she hugged her. "All of you do, as a matter of fact," Elsa added with a chuckle.

A few moments later, after all greetings were exchanged, the family dined at the famous, downtown Frango Café in Marshall Field's. During this time, Elsa got a chance to catch up on things with both Lorena and the kids, and in turn she shared some of her experiences in Africa with a fascinated Nathan, Celeste and Caramelle.

A few hours later, they arrived at the apartment, where the traditional Sunday dinner was already cooking for later.

Because Elsa had skillfully planned her stay to take place during spring break, Lorena received time off from work to spend with her mother.

One evening, while the kids were out with Tony, Lorena and Elsa sat flipping through old photo albums in the living room.

"This one's from Auntie Pam's wedding—look at how small you were, 'Rena."

Lorena looked at the photo Elsa held, and smiled. It was of Elsa and a toddler Lorena at one of Elena's younger sister's weddings.

"Oh, I remember that—but mostly only eating the cake at the reception."

Elsa chuckled.

"I do remember that cake being especially good."

Lorena smiled, sifting through a stack of pictures of herself when she was a child.

"Hey, Mom?"

"Hmm?"

"I don't think you've ever described your wedding."

Elsa knitted her brow slightly.

"You're absolutely right—I haven't, have I?" She shook her head with a smile. "It wasn't your average wedding—Imani and I were wed in a tent, to tell you the truth."

Lorena's eyes widened.

"Really?"

Elsa nodded and Lorena smiled.

"That sounds like fun, actually."

"Yeah, it was different. The ceremony was held in a tiny village near Soweto."

"Whose idea was this?"

"Mine."

Lorena laughed lightly.

"I thought so."

A moment of silence followed, and the two scanned over pictures in contentment.

"You know what I have to ask you, now, 'Rena . . ." Elsa spoke up slowly.

Lorena frowned in confusion.

"Um . . .not really."

Elsa did her best to keep from smiling, but failed. Soon enough it rubbed off onto Lorena, and she did the same.

"What is it?"

Elsa shrugged, focusing on the pictures in her hand.

"Well, you know I've noticed things getting a little...serious with you and Tony . . ."

Immediately Lorena began to blush, shaking her head.

"Ugh, I shoulda' seen it coming," she said with a smile.

"So . . .?"

"There's nothing to tell . . ." Lorena replied as she got up for a cup of water.

Elsa stared at her incredulously.

". . .yet," Lorena finished with her back turned, and could sense her mother smiling.

"Do you feel like he's the one?"

Lorena sighed and shrugged.

"I don't know . . ." she stated slowly, then stopped pouring her water suddenly as she turned around. "If I were in charge of things..."

"Yes?"

Lorena smiled.

"Yeah—he's definitely the one."

Elsa grinned.

"I knew it!"

Lorena shook her head with a sigh as she made her way back over to the couch.

"But it's not my call . . .I mean, I don't know how Tony feels . . ."

"But you did tell me that he said he likes you."

"Like, Mom—that's the key word here."

Elsa shook her head.

"If this young man showed signs of liking you eleven years ago, was reluctant to attend a prestigious university in a state other than yours, dropped another girl while he was away from you—"

"Mom, c'mon," Lorena complained as she blushed again, "he didn't drop her because of me."

"—because he couldn't be with anyone else," Elsa continued, "and now he's your boyfriend. Now why don't tell me how you think that Tony doesn't feel the same way about you?"

Lorena shook her head and smiled with a sigh—leaning back in the sofa with her feet propped up on the coffee table.

"I don't know . . . Tony's such a great guy—how could I actually get a happily ever after with him?"

Elsa gave her a scowl.

"That's the same thing I said with Imani, Lorena—and where are we now?"

Lorena shrugged.

"Happily ever after . . ." Elsa chimed quietly, and Lorena sighed again.

At that moment, the phone rang, and Lorena reached over to answer it.

"Hello?"

"Be ready to meet us at Clancy's lot on Friday night—next week."

Lorena frowned slightly, immediately recognizing Anita's serious tone.

"What time?" she asked, regaining her composure slightly—trying to stay calm to keep her mother from worrying.

"Whenever you're able—just be there . . . or else."

A click followed, and Lorena swallowed as she hung up the phone.

"Who was that?" Elsa asked as she sorted through a pile of photos on the coffee table—leaning forward for better access.

Lorena paused before replying, "Um . . .it was uh . . ."

"The gang?" Elsa quipped.

Lorena grimaced.

"How did you know?"

Elsa looked at her.

"A hunch, I guess. They're still giving you trouble?"

Lorena nodded, looking down at her hands as she set the phone back on the table.

"I guess I'm starting to get a little worried . . ." she began quietly. "You know, lately they've been sounding kinda' . . .serious. Or at least more so than usual."

"Lorena, my offer is still standing. I'll fund the trip even—the kids could experience a different culture and . . ." Elsa stopped short, seeing the worry on her daughter's face as she looked away.

"No, Mom . . . it's fine. I don't mean to turn you down the way I did before—it's not like that at all . . .it's just . . ." Lorena paused as she frowned. "I don't wanna feel like I have to run—as crazy as that sounds. Somehow I feel like I'm supposed to be . . . here."

Elsa nodded slowly, then sighed.

"Either way, it'll work out," she said reassuringly as she placed her hand over Lorena's. "You know where to find me if you need anything."

Lorena put on a small smile, and Elsa gave her a warm hug.

The next day, Lorena and Elsa headed to a jewelry store, with the intention of finding someone who could split the locket in half for a fair price. Lorena had received permission from a somewhat-confused-but-overall-interested Elsa to do so, and explained that by doing so she could give the locket to both Celeste and Caramelle. It would require placing new backs on the hearts, an extra chain and an extra clasp, and each girl would get one of the pictures. According to age, Lorena had decided that Celeste's locket would carry the older individual's picture, and Caramelle's the younger.

The jeweler was able to carry out Lorena's wishes, and he charged a decent price. A few days later, she presented the lockets to the girls early—as the tradition wasn't even mandatory.

Over the course of the week, the once-estranged mother and daughter caught up on the present, reminisced about the past, and basically made up for missed time.

But eventually the time came for Elsa to pack up her bags and leave for home, and after driving to the airport, they bid their goodbyes.

Elsa had first hugged and kissed the kids—who went on to wait in a supervised children's waiting area—and Lorena walked her to the first gate.

"Well, I guess this it," Elsa stated with a sigh, pausing to set some of her bags down, while Lorena carried the others.

"Yeah," she replied as she set her load down.

"I'll stay in touch," Elsa said with a smile.

Lorena chuckled lightly.

"Me, too."

They shared a slightly teary hug, and when they drew away, Lorena wiped at her eyes with a sigh.

"Send me more pictures of Imani and Elijah—and I'll send ones of the kids when I can."

Elsa smiled.

"I will—and I'll be glad to get pictures of the kids to show off to my friends. Half the time they don't believe me when I say I'm a proud grandmother of three."

Lorena smiled and shook her head.

"Let me guess: you look much too young."

Elsa laughed, and then took Lorena's hands in hers.

"Promise me you'll come and visit sometime."

Lorena sighed, and then squeezed her hands reassuringly.

"I will—"

"And let me fund the trip—I believe your grandmother had a nickname for you, 'Superwoman,' " Elsa cut in, becoming serious. "I don't want to get any news of you burning yourself out anymore, okay?"

Lorena nodded.

"Sure, Mom," she replied sincerely.

Elsa sighed again, looking Lorena in the eye.

"You mean too much to me for me to stand by and watch anything like that happen—I worry about you a lot, 'Rena."

Lorena, saddened, looked down at the ground.

"Things are gonna be alright, Mom."

Seeing that Elsa didn't look completely convinced, Lorena added,

" *Blessed is the man who perseveres under trial, because when he has stood the test, he will receive the crown of life that God has promised to those who love Him*' (James 1:12) NIV," she stated boldly. "I'm in good hands."

Elsa smiled brightly, wiping her eyes.

"You're going to make me cry again, 'Rena—I'm very proud of you," she said as she gave Lorena another hug.

At that moment, the loudspeaker reminded the two of Elsa's scheduled flight, and Lorena spoke up, "You'd better get going—they're checking the bags."

Elsa sighed, picking her bags up once again.

"You're right," she replied, then squeezed Lorena's hand. "I'll write soon enough—I love you."

Lorena smiled.

"I love you too, Mom."

Elsa returned the smile, slowly releasing her daughter's hand.

As she walked off for the baggage check gate, she turned around—looking over her shoulder for one last glimpse.

~ Chapter XVIII ~

"Then Jesus said to His disciples, 'If anyone would come after me, he must deny himself and take up his cross and follow me. For whoever wants to save his life will lose it, but whoever loses his life for me will find it.'"

Matthew 16:24 & 25
NIV

†

"Momma, I hate my hair!" Celeste announced decidedly one stormy Friday morning—standing in front of her mother's dresser mirror with her hair sticking out in every direction.

It was less than a week after Elsa's departure, and Lorena and the kids were getting back into the busy lifestyle as spring break faded off in the distance. Because her company had given her an extended vacation, Candy had set off for Chicago to visit Lorena (including helping out with the kids), and arrived Thursday evening.

Lorena sighed from where she stood gazing out the window while fastening on her hoop earrings.

Because Candy was staying in the girl's room, Lorena shared her room with Celeste and Caramelle, and let's just say that sharing a room with two growing girls wasn't always easy.

"What are you talking about, 'Less?" she asked as she walked over, twisting Celeste's almond-and-naturally-honey-highlighted curls around her fingers.

"Look at me! It's horrible—I can't go to school like this!" she exclaimed hopelessly, a tear falling down her cheek.

Lorena, beginning to grow used to Celeste's reaching the pre-teen phase of rollercoaster emotions, allowed her heart to soften as she took the comb from the girl's hands.

"Shh, you're gonna wake Auntie Candy. Now c'mon—your hair is beautiful, Celeste. I know people who'd do anything for hair like yours," she reassured her as she began detangling her hair.

"Yeah, right."

"I was the same way—but people always told me my hair was nice. Sometimes you've gotta just accept things instead of making up your own ideas."

Celeste sighed, blowing a curly strand from her forehead as she crossed her arms over her chest.

"Maybe I'll dye my hair purple someday—maybe I'll shave it off," she muttered as Lorena skillfully regained control of the thick locks, a few more tears falling.

Lorena couldn't help but smile, knowing that someday the girl would appreciate things rather than complain.

" 'Lessie, stop worrying," she replied as she finished tying her hair into a ponytail. "You're gorgeous and have nothing to worry about," she added as she wrapped her arms around her shoulders consolingly, and then set the comb back on the dresser.

"You're supposed to say that—not everyone else thinks that way!" Celeste called after Lorena as she left to check on Nathan.

"Hey, Mom," he stated from his desk when he saw her standing in the doorway.

"Good morning," Lorena replied, walking in to open the blinds on the window. "You're already ready?"

He nodded as he placed his books in his backpack.

"Yup—what's wrong with Celeste?"

"She's just having some trouble getting ready."

"Oh. 'Melle's in the bathroom—she said she's almost done."

"Okay, Celeste already did her hair, so when she's out we can leave—hey, your planet model is coming along well," Lorena stated as she examined Nathan's science project, which sat on the windowsill.

"Yeah, I guess so," he replied, zipping his backpack closed. "Hey, Mom?"

"Uh-huh?"

"You know how I walk 'Less and 'Melle from the bus stop here?"

"Yeah."

"Well, sometimes the other kids like to make fun of 'Mella's eyes—you know, how they're bright and stuff—or how she gets shy and all."

Lorena frowned, turning around.

"Oh?"

Nathan shrugged, picking at a hole in the knee of his jeans.

"Well yeah, I mean, 'Less and I got that all the time when we were her age. Some of the other kids are just dumb like that. I guess I just wanted to let you know why sometimes 'Mella's sad—and Celeste too; she's trying to get some Tommy kid to like her and all."

Lorena nodded slowly, rubbing the back of her neck with a sigh.

"Well...I'll talk to Caramelle about it later," she replied, frowning slightly. "Thanks for letting me know, Nat."

"No problem, Mom."

Lorena cast him a light smile before exiting the room, and headed to the kitchen for some coffee.

Throughout the morning and well into the afternoon, the weather worsened as the clouds poured rain persistently for hours. The distant, low rumbling of thunder or a flash of lightning would occur every now and then, and the wet streets caused commuters to build up traffic jams.

When Lorena finally returned home from work, she first headed to the kitchen with a weary sigh. She was hungry, thirsty, but mostly tired. She was having trouble getting an approval on her latest piece, and was finding it difficult to work with several co-workers who had their eyes on her position. Instead of going to work to make money, Lorena oftentimes felt as though she was working to compete with others.

Pouring herself some apple juice, she could hear Candy and the kids in one of the other rooms.

"Hey, Mom, can we please go to the mall with Auntie Candy?" Celeste asked as she, Nathan, and Candy came walking into the living room.

Lorena sighed as she returned the apple juice to the 'fridge.

"C'mon, 'Rena. It's a rainy day—let 'em out for a little bit. You might wanna consider coming with us," Candy persuaded, and Nathan nodded.

Lorena smiled and shook her head, taking a sip of her apple juice.

"No, I'm fine—I've gotta look over this piece some more tonight. You kids can go ahead, though."

Celeste clapped her hands together in delight, giving Lorena a quick hug before rushing off to put her raincoat on.

"Thank you, thank you, thank you!" she squealed, overjoyed at the thought of a trip to the mall.

Lorena chuckled, and Candy grinned.

"I'll have them back before it gets too late. Are you sure you don't wanna come?"

Lorena nodded.

"Yeah, but thanks Candy."

"No problem—Caramelle, let's go!"

When the girl didn't emerge from her room, Nathan spoke up, "Um, I don't think she wants to go. She had a hard time at school today."

"Oh that's right," Candy added, uncomfortably. "I meant to tell you about that, 'Rena—she looked pretty sad when I picked them up from the stop."

Lorena frowned, setting her glass down as she headed for her room with a sigh.

Inside sat Caramelle, sitting Indian style on the bed, holding her favorite stuffed polar bear, "Frosty," in her arms.

" 'Mella, you wanna go to the mall with Auntie Candy and your brother and sister?" she asked quietly, noting the down expression on her face.

Caramelle shook her head, picking at Frosty's ear.

Lorena nodded, then turned to call over her shoulder.

"You guys go ahead—I'll see you later."

Nathan and Celeste shared a look, and Candy bit her lip.

"Okay, see ya,'" she replied as she opened the door.

"See ya'!" Nathan and Celeste added in unison, and they walked out the door.

When they had gone, Lorena slowly walked over to the bed, taking a seat sideways while leaning on her elbow as she watched Caramelle distantly pick at the stuffed animal.

"How did school go?" she asked after a few seconds.

Caramelle shrugged.

"Do you wanna talk about something?" Lorena questioned gently, and this time the girl shook her head again.

Lorena bit her lip with a sigh, rubbing the back of her neck.

"It must have been when I was about . . .mmm, let's see, seven years old—about your age—that I knew two girls from school that used to pick on people. No one really knew why, but that was just what they'd do. And every day for about two years they would follow my friends and I to the bus stop while calling us names—making fun of us and all. And you know how Mommy has a small Hispanic accent?"

Caramelle nodded.

"Well, that's what they would find about me to make fun of. But you know what? It wasn't until fifth grade that I realized that there were a lot of other kids who talked like me. And my friends soon found that other kids had funny habits, strange accents, or hair that's curly or straight. But what we didn't know was that all of these things were what made us beautiful."

"But I don't think that your accent sounds bad, Mommy," Caramelle finally spoke up, and Lorena smiled.

"I know," she replied as she gently tugged on one of her light-brown pigtails. "And that's because you're used to it. But when people see or hear something that they aren't used to, they sometimes like to make jokes about it—to help them feel better. But that doesn't mean that the something is bad, but just different from what they're used to. Do you see what I'm saying, 'Mella?"

Caramelle cocked her head to the side, wiping a tear away as it fell down her cheek.

"That's not fair . . ."

Lorena sighed as she got up to sit behind the girl, wrapping her arms around her.

"I know it's not. But you have to try to not let it bother you, because you know how beautiful you are and how wrong they are. And soon you'll understand it all, and even what made them say those things."

A silence followed, occupied solely by the rain drumming on the window, or a calm rumble of thunder.

"Mommy?"

"Mm-hmm?"

"When will I understand?"

Lorena sighed again, leaning her head back on the headboard as she smoothed her daughter's hair with her hand.

"When God wants you to, baby."

Caramelle sighed this time, resting her head on Lorena's shoulder as she focused out the rainy window, where outside the sky drenched the earth from purple-azure clouds. The last hints of daylight were slowly fading, and it seemed as though a long, wet night was ahead.

A few moments later, Lorena noted that the girl had fallen asleep, and upon contemplating whether to get up, decided not to—as she might wake her.

Before she knew it, her mind began to wander, and she herself soon fell asleep.

What seemed like only seconds later, the sound of the telephone ringing woke Lorena up, and she gazed around in confusion. They were still sitting on the bed, only now the scene outside the window was that of darkness, and the rain persisted.

Reaching over to grab the phone off of her bedside table, Lorena quickly answered it, so that Caramelle wouldn't be awakened.

"Hello?" she stated quietly, slowly and carefully sliding off of the bed as she let Caramelle's head hit the pillows.

"Selenez, you've got an hour to be at Clancy's lot," Anita replied from the other line, her voice holding nothing but seriousness.

Lorena wondered as she pulled the covers over Caramelle, then left the room.

"What happened to the Friday of next week and letting me get there whenever I'm ready?"

"Marisa and I don't trust you, if you haven't already noticed. Be there—you know the consequences."

With that, there came a click, and with a sigh Lorena hung up.

Standing in the middle of the living room, trying to get her thoughts together, she started when the door opened suddenly and Candy and the kids entered—their arms full of shopping bags.

"We weren't gone too long, were we?" Candy asked as she closed the door behind them, and Nathan and Celeste removed their shoes and coats.

"Uh, no—of course not," Lorena replied quickly, running her fingers through her hair.

"Oh my gosh, Mom, you won't believe what Nathan and I got!" Celeste exclaimed as she rummaged through the pile of bags, trying to find something.

"It's just some toys from FAO—she's all excited about getting another troll doll," Nathan added with a sigh as he joined in the search.

"That's great, guys," Lorena responded distantly, biting her lip as she stared off into space.

"Hey, Lorena, you okay?" Candy questioned when she noted her friend's distracted expression.

Immediately, Lorena smiled reassuringly.

"Yeah, yeah, I'm fine."

"Tell Mom what the lady said, 'Less," Nathan spoke up.

"Oh, guess what, Mom?" Celeste stated suddenly, jumping up from where she sat near the bags. "You were right earlier—a lady at a hairstyling stand told me that she thought my hair was really cute. Thanks for styling it, Mom!" she stated exuberantly as she gave Lorena a hug.

"That's right—I thought for a minute there she was going to hire Celeste as a part-time model for her agency," Candy added with a chuckle as she removed her own raincoat.

Lorena smiled.

"Now didn't I tell you? You're welcome," she replied as she hugged back, and Celeste returned to the task of finding her toy.

"Did you talk to Caramelle?" Candy asked as she began balling the empty bags up to throw them away.

Lorena nodded.

"Yeah, she's asleep. I think she's getting over it."

Candy sighed in relief.

"That's good."

Lorena agreed, then headed off for her room to fetch some comfortable clothes to put on. While she did so, Caramelle began to stir, causing Frosty to fall to the floor.

When she had settled sleepily back into the covers, Lorena walked over, retrieved the fallen stuffed animal and returned it to the girl. She placed a kiss on her forehead, then went to close her dresser drawers.

At that moment, Celeste entered the room.

"Hey, Mom," she greeted, then lowered her voice when she saw Caramelle sleeping. "You look kinda' tired—want me to cook dinner?"

Lorena hung her clothes over one arm, then walked over to place her hands on Celeste's shoulders.

"I'll tell you what—you and Auntie Candy can get started. I'm gonna run out for a few errands really quick," she replied. "And when I get back, you'd better have the best dinner on the planet waiting," she added jokingly with a smile.

Celeste chuckled.

"Nada problema."

Before walking off, Lorena caressed her cheek with her hand, saying, "I'm glad you didn't let stuff get to you for too long—keep that up."

Celeste nodded with a smile.

"Me too—I will."

Lorena returned the smile, then headed for the bathroom to change. On the way, she passed Nathan's room, where he was sitting at his desk over a book.

"Hey," Lorena said as she leaned in the doorway.

Nathan looked up, then smiled.

"Hey, Mom."

"Candy and Celeste are gonna be busy cleaning up the kitchen after dinner tonight—I'm gonna go run a few errands. Could you help Caramelle with her reading for me before she goes to bed?"

He nodded.

"Sure."

Lorena smiled.

"Thank you."

"No problem."

After changing into some jeans and a sweatshirt, Lorena made her way to the living room; in the kitchen Candy and Celeste were already starting up dinner.

"See you guys later," Lorena stated with her hand on the doorknob.

"Later, Mom," Celeste replied with a smile.

"Don't be out too late," Candy added, and Lorena walked out the door.

Walking down the cold, dark and damp streets of the CP neighborhood from where she parked her car, Lorena couldn't help but feel uneasy. She knew that the gang wasn't pleased with her, and were undoubtedly planning something big. She just didn't know if she would get out of this battle alive.

Climbing somewhat rustily over the chain-link fence, she caught a glimpse of her welcome party standing in the middle of the lot, waiting for her.

"*Buenas tardes, Selenez,*" Anita greeted as she stepped forward, Marisol not far behind—her arms crossed over her chest. "I've been waiting for this night for a long, long time."

After dinner was prepared and eaten, the dishes came next. But upon seeing that there wasn't any detergent left, Candy wondered how they would clean them.

"Mom usually borrows stuff from Mrs. Barnum down the hall when she's out," Nathan suggested from where he was finishing his desert of vanilla ice cream at the kitchen table.

Celeste nodded as she took Caramelle's plate from her and placed it in the sink.

"Yeah, Mrs. Barnum's just a few doors down," she added.

Candy frowned slightly, thinking things over.

"Are you sure your mom does this all the time? I don't wanna impose—"

"You won't be bothering her—just tell her who you are," Celeste replied with a shrug.

Candy sighed, uncertainly.

"Well, if you think you'll be alright for a minute—"

"We will—you'll only be right down the hall, Auntie Candy," Nathan reassured her.

Candy finally relented, and headed for the door.

"Okay—but don't open the door for anyone. Act like you aren't at home, and if you hear a special knock—" she knocked on the doorframe three times, "—then open it, because it's me."

"Okay, Auntie Candy—we know. Mom is like this all the time," Celeste replied.

"Alright, I'll be back in a minute," Candy replied, then finally left.

"Lock the door, 'Less," Nathan said as he got up from his seat.

Celeste scowled.

"C'mon, Nat, she's only gonna be right down the hall."

"Lock the door," Nathan repeated firmly, and Celeste reluctantly did as she was told.

"I'm sleepy," Caramelle commented as she headed to the couch, looking as though she planned on taking another nap right then and there.

"You're always sleepy, 'Mella," Celeste stated with a sigh as she began rinsing the dishes off.

"I can't help it."

"C'mon Caramelle—let's go do your reading," Nathan said as he took hold of the girl's hand and led her to Lorena's room to read.

They were only halfway down the short hallway when there came a sudden knock on the door.

Stopping in his tracks, Nathan turned around—instructing Caramelle to go on in the room.

While making her way to the door, Celeste was arrested when Nathan grabbed her arm.

"What are you doing?"

"Checking to see if it's Auntie Candy," she replied as she brushed his arm off.

"But she said not to open it if it's not the special knock." Celeste glared impatiently.

"C'mon, Nat, you didn't actually expect her to do that—they only do that kind of thing on TV."

" 'Less, why did you think—"

Before he could finish his sentence, he was cut off by the sound of the doorknob rattling wildly. Whoever was at the door was trying to break the lock.

Her eyes widening, Celeste swallowed before stating in a whisper, "What do we do?"

Quickly placing his finger on his mouth as he grabbed her arm again, Nathan led her to their mother's room.

"Stay here, and keep 'Mella quiet," he instructed firmly, and Celeste nodded cooperatively.

Before heading to the living room, Nathan quickly ran into his room for his large, metal baseball bat. When Nathan returned to the living room, the knob's lock had been broken, and the door stood ajar with only the chain keeping it closed. Within seconds it broke, and a figure dressed in black from his head to his feet walked in. A gun sat in his right hand, and Nathan froze.

"Candy, wait up!" Tony called, and she turned around.

"Hey, Tony, what brings you here? Wait, lemme guess—Lorena Selenez?"

Tony smiled, blushing slightly.

Candy had just emerged from the Barnum's apartment, and was making her way down the hall back to Lorena's. She had been held up by polite questions from the kind, mid-elderly couple—who had taken an immediate liking to her.

"I had to come—I was napping for a little bit, and I had a dream and everything happened so fast that I—"

"Whoa, wait a minute—slow down. Start from the beginning."

Tony sighed, trying to catch his breath.

"I ran all the way up the stairs—'cause I had a dream that, well... it was a nightmare, and basically tomorrow's never guaranteed, a- and because I love Lorena, I want to marry her."

Candy's jaw dropped to the ground, and a mile-wide smile lit her face.

"You're kidding! You've gotta be kidding!"

Tony grinned, amused by her reaction.

"I mean, oh my gosh! I've been waiting for you to say that forever—Lorena's been waiting on you to say that forever!"

"I don't even have a ring, but that's okay. I hope she's not asleep—no, she can't be, she almost never sleeps," Tony stated as he made his way down the hall, Candy at his heels.

"Wait a minute, she's not home right now—she went to go run some errands."

Tony stopped, biting his lip.

"Oh . . .I guess I'll just have to wait, then."

"Which shouldn't be too hard—since you've waited all this time," Candy added with a laugh.

Tony chuckled as they continued down the hall.

"The kids will be blown away," Candy stated as she knocked three times on the door.

Tony looked worried.

"You think so?"

Candy looked relieved.

"They love you, Tony. Of course they will."

When after fifteen seconds, the door didn't open—nor did any sounds come from inside the apartment—Candy knocked again, this time calling through the door, "Kids, it's me—Auntie Candy!"

No reply.

With a frown at Tony, she tried the knob to find it unlocked.

"I should have told them to lock i—"

"Wait," Tony interrupted in a hushed whisper, slowly opening the door and stepping inside.

The kitchen chairs sat overturned, along with the table, and there was a hole in the TV screen.

Candy gasped when her eyes fell on the wrecked apartment.

"Nathan . . .Celeste . . .Caramelle!!"

Surrounding Lorena in a circle were not only the CPs, but the NGBs as well. Each member held an expression on their face that could kill, and she couldn't have felt any less appreciated at that moment.

"I'm actually surprised you showed up, Selenez," Marisol stated with a wicked smirk. "I've heard that you're not much of a fighter anymore—but it won't matter now. We plan on having a little fun with you before 'Nita finishes you off."

"Why, Marisa? What's happened to you? I had nothing to do with the temporary fall of the CPs—"

"No, but you had everything to do with our new problems!" Marisol returned heatedly, her eyes flashing madly as she tightened a leather strap around her fist.

"That's why you want to end our friendship . . .and kill me?" Lorena questioned quietly and disbelievingly. "Marisa, c'mon, we've been through more than that. I trusted you! That day back in high school that I came to you when I was sick—I could've gone to so many other people, I even chose you over my own family. That's how tight we were . . . a-and if you're gonna just stand by and watch me die I'll know for sure that we never were friends in the first place. Or at least you didn't see me as your friend . . .but I saw you as mine . . .and that hurts. But I guess that's what you wanted—me to hurt . . .really badly," she concluded with all seriousness as she looked her in the eye.

Marisol returned the stare, and for an instant Lorena thought she could see a slight waver . . .a twinge of regret. But before she could search any further, Anita stepped forward, lashing her chain out to the side.

"That's enough of this, Selenez," she stated, allowing the chain to get a piece of Lorena's jaw—knocking her to the ground. "What do you all say we get this show on the road?"

The audience agreed, and one by one, ten members—five NGBs and five CPs—stepped forward, and began beating Lorena by hand.

Marisol stood watching for a moment, and as Lorena cried out, she looked away, grimacing while wrestling with her feelings.

"See, Selenez? I'm letting you die in style!" Anita stated with a laugh, "If you haven't already noticed, you're going down the same way you rose up as a CP member. You've gotta give me credit for that."

After one long minute of battle, Anita ordered them to halt, then rolled up the sleeves of her red jacket.

"Alright now—lemme have some."

Lorena was lying on the ground, holding her bruised side as blood dripped from her lip. Fighting ten individuals back wasn't easy, nor possible for her. Seeing that Anita could call out the whole legion of gang bangers on her, she knew that she was going to die one way or another.

"Get up," Anita muttered hatefully as she watched Lorena suffer.

Grinning wickedly to her peers, she lashed her chain onto Lorena's leg, and she cried out in pain.

"I said get up!!"

Taking a moment to recover from what she was sure was a broken leg, Lorena slowly came to her feet—refusing to go down without a chance to defend herself to the best of her ability.

Anita smirked, holding her hands up in the air.

"C'mon, Selenez. I'll let you have two free hits at me."

Holding her side while struggling to stand, Lorena watched Anita carefully, then felt her stomach turn when she saw the solid gold pistol on her belt.

Anita frowned mockingly, looking worried suddenly.

"What's wrong? Scared of this?" she asked as she held up her gun, then cackled as she returned it to her belt. "Don't worry—that's for later. But this is for now!"

Anita had lunged at the wounded Lorena, tackling her to the ground. After giving her what Lorena was sure was the beating of her life, she rose, wiping the blood from her hands on her jacket.

"That was simple—I can't believe this. Paulina, Isabella, hold her to the fence!" Anita ordered, and when they didn't step forward, she glared over her shoulder. "I said hold her!!"

Both Paulina and Isabella stood with uneasy looks on their faces, as well as a few other members of each gang. They seemed almost afraid of Anita's sudden demonic addiction to power. Ever since she was a young teenager they had revered her, and were genuinely afraid of what she could do when her mind was made up.

"Maybe Selenez might've been . . ." Isabella began slowly, visibly trembling from head to toe at Anita's ice cold glare.

"Might've been what?" Anita questioned in a quiet tone laced with hatred—almost daring her to finish her sentence.

"Maybe she doesn't deserve all of this—you've been acting ridiculous for years, Anita—we all have!" Paulina voiced confidently, throwing her leather CP identification band to the ground.

"Maybe you need to die!" Anita shouted no sooner than the words had left her mouth, firing a shot from her gun—hitting Paulina dead in the chest.

Cries of disbelief reverberated throughout the large crowd, and several members from each gang stepped forward to attack Anita.

"You've seen what I can do against crowds! I suggest you all calm down!!" Anita exclaimed as half of the group stood behind her and around her, protecting her from the others.

"You killed her . . ." a voice sounded from her left, where a young black guy in his twenties sat weeping over Paulina's fallen figure as Isabella and a few others closest to her sobbed uncontrollably. Those standing in the crowd knew the guy to be her boyfriend, and shared uneasy looks. "You killed her!!" he screamed as he quickly withdrew his own gun to fire at Anita, but was too late.

His lifeless figure fell to the ground, only feet away from Paulina's.

A dead silence echoed throughout the crowd, and each person against Anita stood dumbfounded by her actions.

"Who's next?" she called out, scanning the crowd in delight.

"Who gave you permission to kill one of my top members!?" Marisol asked suddenly, stepping forward from where she had been watching the scenes in surprise. "Did I give you permission, 'Nita, huh?"

"Do you need to shut up, Marisa, huh?" Anita returned, throwing a punch at Marisol, which she immediately grabbed hold of.

"I didn't hire you to rise up against me—nor take care of my business!" Marisol spat as she crushed Anita's hand.

Cursing in Spanish, Anita swiftly broke free before violently kicking her in the jaw—sending her reeling.

"You've been watching me do so for the past ten years, idiot!" Anita stated with a laugh, and her minions snickered. "You're just soft like the rest of 'em—now where was I . . ."

A few members of Anita's new posse obediently stepped forward to hold the shocked Lorena to the chain-link fence. Anita was about to withdraw her pistol to finish her off, when a voice sounded from the group, "Cobra's here!"

Everyone looked to where Cobra was ushering in three young children to the lot, a gun at his side to keep them from running off. Pushing through the crowd, he noticed the two bodies on the outskirts, and raised his eyebrows.

"What happened here?"

When the children saw Lorena struggling to keep alive against the chain-link fence, two began to cry as one attempted to run to her side.

"Where are you off to, little boy?" Anita asked as she roughly grabbed Nathan's sleeve, dragging him to her side.

Finally seeing from two bruised eyes her children at gunpoint and in mortal danger, Lorena instinctively pulled away from the individuals holding her—trying desperately to break free.

"No!!!" she shouted at the top of her lungs, trying to no avail to get to them.

"Leave my mom alone!" Nathan cried, struggling against Anita's death grip.

"Shut up!" she stated in annoyance, slapping him across the face as he fell back in a daze.

"Leave my son alone, Anita!!!!" Lorena shrieked, unable to break the hold while feeling as though she could strangle her enemy.

"Natty!!" Celeste screamed, sobbing in disbelief as Caramelle did the same while clutching her side.

Grinning in satisfaction, Anita sighed as she paced the ground.

"You realize that all of this is your own fault, Selenez. I mean, you could have stayed with the gang, cooperated, and spared your children some terror . . . and if I decide, their lives."

Lorena's jaw dropped in horror and she shook her head in complete shock.

"No . . . no—kill me, then—please, Anita, kill me!!! Oh Lord, they didn't do anything . . . they didn't do anything . . ." Lorena begged as she sobbed and let her head fall.

"Hold up, 'Nita, you ain't really killin' 'em, are ya'?" Cobra asked, seeming as though he was trying to keep the worry out of his tone. "I thought we were just usin' 'em as bait for Lorena."

"So did I," stated Marisol, walking over with her jaw clenched. "You're gettin' a little too caught up in yourself, 'Nita."

Anita smirked at Marisol, roughly grabbing both Celeste and Caramelle by the arms.

"You're just gettin' soft 'cause you've got a few mongrels at home yourself."

"You're gettin' on my last nerve, 'Nita!" Marisol shouted as she prepared to throw a punch at Anita, but was arrested by the sound of over ten guns clicking behind her.

"See, I've got people to back me up, Marisa. Apparently, yours are too scared to move on your behalf."

Punching her fist into her hand angrily, Marisol glared daggers at Anita.

"I'll see you in h***, Anita!!"

Anita smirked again.

"Won't we all?"

Being completely helpless, Marisol, Cobra and Lorena looked on as Anita ordered several members of her group to hold the kids a few feet away from where Lorena still struggled at the fence.

"Please, Anita, take me instead!!" Lorena continued to beg to no avail, and Anita sighed.

"Here comes the fun part. If there's one thing I owe you, Marisa, it's for teaching me to have a little bit of fun with my victims," she stated in delight as she withdrew a whip from her belt, and Lorena felt her heart cease beating.

"Oh God...no...NO!!!"

Biting his lip as he looked from the guns poised at both he and Marisol to Lorena's tortured, agonized expression, Cobra eventually shouted, "Viper, where you at, man!?"

Viper stepped forward, but unfortunately from Anita's half of the group. Folding his arms over his chest, he smirked at Cobra.

"What—you gonna go out for some wild chick!?" Cobra exclaimed in disbelief.

R.J. did the same, and Cobra gritted his teeth.

"Let's see how hard we can get Selenez to beg," Anita pondered with a smirk.

Nathan had placed himself in front of his sisters, who continued to cry in terror. Seeing him as her first target, Anita let the whip go forward.

Crying out in pain, Nathan grabbed his bleeding arm.

Lorena's cries filled the air, and she prayed as she had never prayed before that she could reach him.

Casting a sideways glance at her, Anita grinned and moved on to Celeste.

After whipping the girl, she began to laugh maniacally, absorbing power from the combination of the children and Lorena's screams.

Before Anita could go off into a fury of lashing, the people holding Lorena watched a miracle occur. Seemingly out of nowhere, her skin began to burn like fire, and they immediately let go upon getting singed.

Shooting forward, Lorena tackled the unsuspecting Anita.

Before she could get any kind of punch in, however, R.J. had pulled her off of his new boss, pinning her arms behind her back.

"You're gonna pay for that, Selenez!!!" Anita screamed, grabbing her pistol from her belt.

She first directed it at Lorena, looking as though she might shoot several times, but smiled suddenly, turning the gun over to the kids.

Saying the only thing she could say as a prayer, Lorena shouted, "**JESUS!!!!**"

At the instant Anita had pulled the trigger, three individuals appeared standing in front of the children. They were dressed in solid white, and had glowing faces, which portrayed peace to Lorena and the kids but death to the others.

Upon hearing Lorena shout that Name, Anita had suddenly thrown herself onto the ground in a convulsion—many others including Marisol doing the same.

Shocked at the images before him, R.J. let go of Lorena, and she was joined by another heavenly being—this one standing at her side with his hand on her shoulder.

"It's time, Lorena," he said softly and comfortingly as the rest of the world around them stood as though frozen in time.

The three angels protecting the children began singing the hymn, "We Shall Overcome," and with a loving smile at each child, disappeared.

Nodding as though she understood his message, Lorena looked away from her angel to where the kids were looking around in confusion. All of the angels were gone, but she felt as though Jesus Christ Himself were standing at her side.

Recovering from her seizure, Anita gritted her teeth in hatred as she picked her gun up from where it had fallen. With one final shout, she fired three more shots at the children once again, but this time Lorena had jumped in their path—receiving all three.

Gasps filled the tense night air, and the kids screamed.

Feeling something inside of her ache, Marisol quickly ordered Cobra, "Grab your kids and get outta' here!"

Cobra frowned, staring at her strangely. There suddenly was something very different about Marisol, and he wondered what had taken place.

"What?"

"Just go!"

For some reason deciding not to argue, Cobra quickly ran over to where Nathan, Celeste and Caramelle were sobbing by the wounded Lorena, and commanded them to come with him.

Wanting to do anything but that, they remained where they were, and Cobra swiftly scooped Celeste up—grabbing Nathan's arm as well. Not having enough hands for Caramelle, he hurried off—exiting the lot.

Before anyone knew it, sirens echoed throughout the damp, night air, and each face held a look of fear.

"Let's go! Our work here is done," Anita ordered, and everyone quickly fanned out in all directions—leaving the lot empty except for the fallen individuals.

She was about to walk off herself, when she heard quiet crying coming from near Lorena's half-unconscious figure, and turned to see Caramelle weeping by her dying mother.

Laughing to herself, she caught the girl's eye, and smiled when she saw her cowering in fear before her. A black-and-red snake sat at Anita's feet, and after seeing that her work was completed, she smirked and hurried toward the chain-link fence to leave.

Marisol, who had been hiding behind a nearby trash receptacle, stepped out suddenly, and with a quick, meaningful glance between her and the wounded Lorena, she hurried off after Anita, a gun in her hand.

Struggling to speak, Lorena turned to the frightened Caramelle.

"Don't be afraid," she said comfortingly, leaning up against the fence in a sitting position, then looked over at the demon. "In the name of Jesus Christ, I rebuke you!"

Immediately, the snake slithered off and disappeared, singed by Lorena's words.

Caramelle continued to cry, shocked and gripped by fear.

Holding her stomach with one arm, Lorena reached out to draw the girl to her side.

"It's alright, 'Mella," she stated, then winced. She knew that she was going to die very soon, and worried for her daughter and other children—whom she had watched get whisked away.

"Listen to me, Caramelle," she said with difficulty, holding her away some. "There's power in that Name—Jesus Christ. Don't be afraid; we're going to be okay," she said reassuringly as she placed her hand on her teary cheek.

"I don't want you to die, Mommy!" Caramelle cried, unable to get a hold of herself.

Lorena felt a tear falling down her cheek, and slowly lowered herself to lie down.

"You'll be alright—I will too . . ." she whispered, feeling her strength leaving. "I love you . . .'Mella…" Lorena finished, her voice barely at a whisper, and she finally closed her eyes.

The saga continues in
"Caramelle: Metamorphosis"

About the Author

"I consider that our present sufferings are not worth comparing with the glory that will be revealed in us."
Romans 8:18 NIV

My youngest child, my daughter Stephanie Renée Bell, was on the earth for approximately 654,969,000 seconds, i.e. 20 years, 280 days and 16 hours. At the age of 10 years, she prayed a prayer to accept Jesus Christ into her heart as her Lord and Savior. Total immersion baptism during her teens was her public profession of faith. As a Christian, I ***know*** that she went to Heaven on March 25, 2010.

"Jesus said to her: I am the resurrection and the life. He who believes in me will live, even though he dies; and whoever lives and believes in me will never die."
John 11:25-26 NIV

"It's all about Jesus." In November of 2009, during a lucid interval in a hospital room, Stephanie was urgently writing on her blanket with her right index finger. When we gave her a pen and paper to decipher what she was writing, she repeatedly scrawled that sentence, superimposing it on one spot on the paper. That was one of the final sentences and the underlying message of her prolific writing career.

In April of 2008, I was reduced for several weeks to sitting in a chair, leaning back; the only position that afforded me relief from continuous, excruciating abdominal pain. This was due to a large liver cyst pressing on my stomach. My appointment with a surgeon specializing in liver disease was weeks away. Surgery was finally scheduled for May of 2008. Stephanie spent the night in a chair in my hospital room the night after my surgery. As time went by I was recovering and requiring less narcotic painkillers. Stephanie had just completed her 1st year at a local community college where she had an "A" average, earning induction into Phi Theta Kappa International Honor Society of the Two-Year College. On June 1, 2008 Stephanie told me that since her May 17, 2008 birthday she had experienced severe headaches. I took her to the local hospital Emergency Room where an MRI revealed a brain mass. She was transferred to Vanderbilt Medical Center in Nashville, Tennessee, where most of the mass was removed and discovered to be a malignant brain tumor, glioblastoma multiforme. Stephanie told us that the night before surgery angels came to her in a dream, telling her to do what they said and be very still and they would protect her, not allowing her to awaken during surgery; this had been her fear. The procedure was done June 2, 2008, 1 year to the day after she gave her Middle Tennessee Home Education Association High School Graduation speech.

In July of 2008 my husband William, myself, Stephanie and our 2 sons Sean and Brandon embarked upon the first of numerous over 1100 mile-round road trips Duke University Medical Center in North Carolina where Stephanie enrolled in a clinical trial that was to be administered by them in conjunction with the local medical center, where all of the radiation treatment and most of the intravenous chemotherapy would be given. She also took oral chemotherapy at home. Before heading for home after the first trip to Duke, we went to the coast since Stephanie had never before seen the ocean. We ended up on Carolina Beach on the 4th of July. During a later trip we were sideswiped on Interstate 40 in Knoxville, on the way to an appointment; the window next to my seat shattered; my shoulder was injured; no one else was injured and there was body damage to our vehicle; we continued on to Duke.

Stephanie was unable to attend school during the Fall, 2008 and Winter, 2009 semesters. However, as MRIs and PET scan began to show no evidence of tumor, Stephanie enrolled for the Fall, 2009 semester at the only local university where Speech Language Pathology (her chosen major) classes were offered at the undergraduate level. She joined the National Student Speech Language and Hearing Association and maintained an "A" average in her coursework and attended classes even when MRIs started to show recurrent tumor and her left arm began to just hang at her side and flail around. She continued to attend until she began to literally stumble and fall.

During that November, 2009 hospitalization she became bedridden. She was discharged to home where we cared for her between ambulance rides, ER visits, further admissions at 3 different hospitals. William and I spent every day and night in her hospital rooms, including the critical care units; Brandon spent most days and nights there. Low blood counts, platelet counts and aggressive tumor growth caused doctors to stop further chemotherapy. Among her requests, I read to her the book of Luke and other Scriptures; her brother Brandon read to her from the book of Ezekiel and other Scriptures. Her brother Sean and many others also read the Bible to her. Our family, church pastors and members as well as other friends held prayer vigils and worship sessions at home and at the various hospitals. The Lord held us up during those times as He does now. Our Strong Tower Bible Church family provided a tremendous level of support. We played nearly continuous music in her hospital rooms. As far as we could tell, God in His infinite mercy spared her from agonizing pain throughout, because after she recovered from the surgery she denied any pain whenever we or her doctors would ask.

On a breakthrough, wonderful day, at Vanderbilt, Stephanie was alert, talking and able to swallow. She began to ask for all kinds of foods. I fed her for hours on end while she ate ravenously. The next day I fed her breakfast but by lunchtime, she was unable to swallow or talk. In the final throes of the disease, her brother Sean asked her how she was doing. She replied, "Good." She was semi-comatose and during her final admission at the local hospital she lapsed into a coma, eventually going to heaven on March 25, 2010. Her faith never wavered.

Stephanie attended a private school until the middle of 1st grade; I homeschooled her through high school, except for 2nd grade, during which she attended another private school. She earned many badges as a Girl Scout and was in the National American Miss Pageant. For many years she was a camper and eventual counselor at a Christian camp promoting unity of all people through Christ.

God supplied Stephanie with multiple gifts. An accomplished classically-trained pianist, she also was a guitarist, music composer (copyrighted instrumentals and lyrics, including Christian rap deliberately written in the vernacular of youth, particularly urban youth, for whom she felt a particular burden), artist and dancer.

Some of her music included her pseudonyms "NiteLyte" and "AjiaJade". A petite basketball player with great skills, she played for over 10 seasons in a local community league. She took ballet classes at age 5, stopping because she said it made her neck hurt. When she was older, she attended a church Vacation Bible School and was practicing for a group dance that was to be done during the final day, portraying dancers around the throne of Jesus, but injured her ankle and was unable to be in the final group dance. When we told the nurse at the walk-in clinic the circumstances of the injury, she gave us a card bearing the name of a Christian dance studio. Stephanie subsequently took Christian hip-hop dance classes at that studio, which was owned by that nurse and, along with her brother Brandon, she ministered through dance at local churches, parks, a shopping mall and at the Rescue Mission. Although another injury, a tear of the left knee medial patellar retinaculum in August, 2006 (while doing an exercise routine at home) culminated in open knee surgery and ended her dancing here on earth, she continued to serve as a member and longtime President of the 212 Dance Team of our church where she attended since 1999, becoming a member in 2007. She also served on the church Student Youth Council.

It is, of course, her gift of writing that brings me to this foreword. I have spent much time just trying to find all of her writings and probably still have not found them all. Some were handwritten, others in her computers. Looking back through her home school notebooks I found poetry in spiral notebooks on bound sheets interspersed with bound Chemistry, Biology and Math homework and tests that I had graded. I don't recall seeing this poetry as I was grading the work. She completed 3 novels and started many others. I was aware of the 3 completed novels but only found the poetry and lyrics to her more than 40 songs after she went to Heaven. She also wrote several installments of "fan fiction" as well as many unfinished stories. In her blogs she speaks of her "secret life" of writing.

The fact that many of her *handwritten* works included the date and time of day (of course, the computer writings automatically do) caused me to arrange them chronologically. For those whose date could not be ascertained, I inserted them where the subject seemed to fit with the writings around it. The dates as well as time of day, in my estimation, lend to the poignancy and urgency of her writings, in light of the length of her life on earth. Apparently, oftentimes, she wrote well into the night. As I found more of them, I realized that this compilation was actually autobiographical as well. Her works reflect the degree to which she felt ostracized, especially as a result of the way people, adults and students alike, reacted to her as a home schooled student. As many of the writings were heartbreakingly difficult to read, I procrastinated in collecting them and typing the handwritten ones; not to mention my cataloguing the recordings of her keyboard renditions of her instrumental music compositions and my typing of handwritten song lyrics. Reading her works, however, also provided me with inspiration and comfort, due to the Gospel that she proclaimed. For me, this has been a humbling, incredible journey.

Stephanie touched the lives of many people, including her family, through her ministry of dance, as a camper and camp counselor, and in many other ways. I accepted Jesus Christ as my Lord and Savior after seeing my children on fire for Christ. Stephanie's faith sustained her, supplying strength and courage through a ravaging illness. She walked well in her purpose, which was to glorify God, always acknowledging that her gifts came from Him. She is now perpetually worshipping the Lord, dancing at the foot of the throne of Jesus without limitations. Like the numerous unfinished stories that she wrote, the story of her eternal life will never end.

Stephanie was a gift to us and I thank God for the honor and privilege of being her mother. I'm sure that I did not convey this to her as I should have. These pages are, by far, the most difficult yet joyous that I have ever had to write, their completion facilitated by the guidance of the Holy Spirit. This writing does not encompass everything that I could say about her. Since her transition to Heaven, the Lord has been holding me up more than I could ever imagine; I am much better than I thought I would be. We more than miss her but we grieve with hope, knowing that we will see her again when we, too, get to Heaven.

In her autobiography containing the poem "Abandoned," she writes: "Why am I writing poems that no ear will ever hear?" I could not let that happen.

To God be the Glory,

Denise Bell, M.D.

Made in the USA
Middletown, DE
12 May 2019